He kissed her long and hard before he began to tease her lips with his tongue, begging for entrance to her mouth. To her amazement, she felt herself part her lips ever so slightly, to allow him the opening he sought. His tongue probed and played games with hers and she tentatively copied his actions.

It was Devan that broke the embrace and pulled away. "I'm sorry, Julie. You're very vulnerable. I've taken advantage of you. Like I said, I almost didn't come tonight. When I saw you and realized who you were, I knew I wanted you. It's wrong. I know it is. We're friends, but—"

"Are you telling me the truth or just what you think I want to hear?"

"It's the truth."

"Maybe I want a one-night stand. Maybe I just need to be special to someone for a little while. Whatever it is, I wouldn't blame you if you left right now. I really don't know what's come over me, but I want you to stay with me tonight."

"Do you mean it?"

"Yes. Just for tonight, I need to be loved. Please stay. I'll give you the garage door opener so you can get your car off the street. There's room for two cars in there."

"Look Julie, if you want to call this off—"

She put her finger to his lips to silence him. "I don't think so."

When Devan went out to the car, she wondered if she did know what she was doing. He'd become a stranger. The boy she knew thirty years ago was all grown up. Maybe this would be best, just good healthy sex between old friends. Could it be so wrong? Wasn't that what the kids did, what their society had come to? Who would ever know, other than herself and Devan? They were no longer in high school. She certainly wouldn't be the topic of tomorrow's locker room discussion. They were grown people, consenting adults. Certainly Devan must have strayed more than once.

Wings

A Precious Jewel

by

Sherry Derr-Wille

A Wings ePress, Inc.

Romantic Suspense Novel

Wings ePress, Inc.

Edited by: Leslie Hodges
Copy Edited by: Kathryn Lively
Senior Editor: Lorraine Stephens
Executive Editor: Lorraine Stephens
Cover Artist: Christine Poe

Wings ePress Books
http://www.wings-press.com

Copyright © 2004 by Sherry Derr-Wille
ISBN 1-59088-770-0

Published In the United States Of America

July 2004

Wings ePress Inc.
403 Wallace Court
Richmond, KY 40475

Dedication

To my birthday twin, Trish,

and all of the girls I graduated with

from high school.

I couldn't have better friends or fans!!!!

One

Julie looked into the mirror hanging over the sofa. Her naturally dark hair seemed to have more gray than it had just a year ago, but the new style her kids insisted she adopt seemed very flattering. Behind the slightly tinted lenses of her oversized glasses, her ice blue eyes still looked saddened. Of course, her light skin tone did look paler than usual, but all things considered, she didn't look bad for a woman of almost forty-eight.

Over the years people always said, "You're such a pretty girl, if you lost some weight, you'd be beautiful."

"Am I beautiful?" she asked the reflection in the mirror.

"I look different, perhaps, but not beautiful," she assured herself aloud. "Beautiful is for twenty-year-old models. I'll settle for attractive."

Still pondering the reflection, she decided, if by some miracle Steve were to come back to her today, he wouldn't even recognize her. At the thought of Steve, unbidden tears sprang to her eyes. One year ago today had been their last day together. The mourning period should have ended by now. She should no longer get weepy at the thought of Steve, but she did.

Turning from the mirror, she watched her neighbor, Meg Preston, playing in the snow with her grandchildren. It seemed strange how grandchildren changed your life. Meg had never built snowmen with her own children, but the new addition to the Prestons' front lawn even sported Meg's old ski jacket and knit hat. The scene only made Julie feel more lonely and depressed.

Turning from the window, she sank into a chair and stared blankly into the fire blazing in the fireplace. Almost automatically she relived last New Year's Eve.

She and Steve, like everyone else on the cul-de-sac, had moved into their dream home over twenty-five years earlier. They were all young couples, just getting a start in life. It didn't take long for the New Year's Eve tradition to begin. Since everyone seemed to be struggling with house payments and growing families, no one could afford the gala New Year's Eve parties advertised in the paper. At first, everyone brought a dish to pass and met in a different home each year with someone else hiring a babysitter to oversee a slumber party for the kids. One by one, the children grew too old for a sitter and the couples became more affluent. The party became an opportunity for the wives to show off their culinary talents.

Last year she and Steve were to host the annual party. With Steve's help, she prepared succulent prime rib, baked potatoes, and a new salad that would be the envy of everyone at the party. They had just finished putting the final touches on the hors d'oeuvres when the guests began arriving.

The party had been a mixture of good conversation, soft music, and an assortment of games, including charades and a few hands of euchre. By midnight, the conversation turned to memories of the soon to end old year and expectations for the unknown of the future.

Like a well-orchestrated concert, they rang in the New Year with a bang. With the neighborhood on the edge of town, the men always planned for this night throughout the year. Over the Fourth of July, they took a trip out of state for the fireworks Steve kept stored in the basement for this special celebration.

They had read in the previous week's edition of the *Ledger* that the fire whistle would sound and signal the stroke of midnight. While it still blew, the first skyrocket whistled into the air, exploding with a burst of color. Each skyrocket brought oohs and ahs from those who watched, along with an occasional shriek of delight for the more spectacular displays.

Silently Julie counted the number of skyrockets. Steve planted twenty in the snow and he wanted her to make certain none were missed. After number nineteen took off, she felt a chill.

Several moments passed and she wondered if something could be wrong. *No,* she thought, *Steve must be having a problem finding number twenty.* One minute passed, then two, and as the third minute began, a feeling of dread overtook her.

"Steve!" she could still hear herself calling. "Steve, is something wrong?" Her answer had been silence, her reaction panic.

Involuntarily reliving the moment, she could feel the cold metal of the flashlight in her hand, as well as the horror of seeing Steve lying face down in the snow.

George Martin, the only doctor in the neighborhood took over immediately. "Steve's dead," he announced after taking a few minutes to do an examination and trying to pump breath back into Steve's lifeless body.

Someone helped her into the house. Someone else told her they would take care of everything. For hours the nightmare continued. George gave her some kind of medication, which only caused her to remain in a dreamlike state, feeling no emotions. People came and went: the coroner, the undertaker, and her friends. They all assured her everything would be all right, everything would be normal, but she knew nothing would ever be the same again. Her husband, her friend, her companion of almost thirty years, no longer existed and she would be forever alone.

The next few days were a blur. A massive heart attack had taken Steve instantly. Someone called the kids. Someone else met them at the airport and brought them home to Minter.

Jill and her husband, Karl, had been the first to arrive, flying in from Denver early on New Year's morning. They'd been home less than two hours when Lance's red Volkswagen pulled into the driveway. His exhaustion, after the long drive from the Michigan ski resort, was painfully evident.

Mark's trip from California took much longer. Stationed in San Diego, the Red Cross worked diligently to arrange a flight, but it had taken until New Year's evening to find a vacant seat.

The visitation, with its unending line of mourners, and the funeral, with its mournful parade of cars, passed her as though she was in a daze.

When everyone left and she found herself at last alone, it hit her. Every day, she forced herself to get out of bed, to go to work and to smile for her friends and laugh at their jokes. Every night, she escaped into her shell of depression and desperation. Every corner of the house reminded her of Steve. Unable to throw anything out, his clothes remained in the closet, his razor and shaving cream in the medicine cabinet.

It took months for her to be able to sleep in their bedroom. Night after night, she tossed and turned on the couch until, usually well past midnight, she would collapse into exhausted sleep. By five, she would find herself wide-awake.

Meals, too, became a thing of the past. Breakfast began to consist of several cups of coffee laced with cream. Lunch became a salad from the cafeteria, eaten hastily at her desk. She found dinnertime to be the hardest. Sometimes, she would grab a sandwich on the way home, but more often than not, she fixed a TV dinner in the microwave.

It hadn't taken long for the word to get out, for the barrage of unmarried men to find out how lonely she felt. One by one, Steve's former friends began setting her up with dates, even asked her out personally. She didn't have to look far for male companionship, whether she wanted it or not. Sometimes, it would be one date, sometimes more, but it always ended the same way, with the insistence they go to bed together. She hadn't felt ready, hadn't wanted that kind of a relationship.

Sometimes when she sat in the living room alone, she could hear Steve's voice mocking her, as though from the grave he could monitor her thoughts. *::You miss it, don't you Julie? Isn't it a shame you'll never find love again, never find another man like me. Face it honey, any man can have sex with you, but no other man can love you, not the way you look.::*

By summer, when Lance returned from college, he had been shocked by not only her appearance, but also of her lack of enthusiasm. Although she hadn't heard his worried conversations with Jill and Mark, she'd learned of their content.

Lance breathed life into the quiet house and urged her to momentarily forget her loss.

Together, they went to the Dells, House on the Rock, Great America, and several Brewers games. They ate picnics sitting in the car during rainstorms and attended every parade and festival in the area.

By the end of August, when Lance began his senior year at college, she'd convinced him the worst had passed and she would be fine. With his departure, she tried desperately to maintain the level of activity she enjoyed when she did things with him, but to no avail. It became easier to slip back into the routine of work and home she'd maintained throughout the winter, than to join the singles scene. She had no desire to go to the bars, nor did she feel the need to join one of the dating clubs, which seemed to spring up almost everywhere anymore.

By Christmas, she finally began sleeping at regular hours and found herself looking forward to the holidays. The kids would all be home and her year of mourning would end. She took great pains in selecting and decorating the perfect tree, in buying and wrapping the perfect gifts.

Over the past year, Mark had been transferred to Honolulu and worked in an office at Pearl Harbor. Once inexpensive phone calls to California were replaced by expensive calls to the South Pacific, which they limited to one a month in each direction. She'd missed talking to her oldest son and looked forward to his return for the holidays.

One by one the kids came home, and once again there seemed to be new life breathed into the house. At their insistence, she sought out a counselor and started going to sessions. While she and Jill shopped and visited the beauty shop, the boys disposed of their father's belongings.

Now, with the kids gone, with the old year drawing to a close, she felt she had become comfortable with her widowhood. After three meetings with the counselor, she found herself able to put the past behind her. Dale Bentz came highly recommended, and she enjoyed their sessions. She began to put words to the feelings that plagued her, even her frustration at hearing Steve's voice, which seemed to come to her unbidden. For the first time in a year, she looked forward to tomorrow. She didn't fool herself. Three sessions by no means meant she could call herself whole.

The ringing of the phone made her jump. "Hello," she said.

"Julie, it's Meg. Are you coming to the party tonight?"

Meg's question met with silence while Julie pondered her answer. Her first instinct told her to decline the invitation, stay in the warmth of her home; if it were any night but tonight, maybe she would feel differently.

The voice of her counselor overpowered her instincts. "Before you can heal, Julie, you must take the first step. Don't hide from relationships. You can't keep your emotions bottled up forever. You're a young woman. Don't put yourself in the grave with your husband."

"Julie, did you hear me?" Meg asked. "Are you coming to the party?"

"I'm sorry, Meg. I was having a tug of war with myself. If I know you, you've already arranged a dinner companion for me. I should say no, but it's time to start living again. I'll be over at seven."

"Oh, Julie, I'm so happy to hear you say those words. You'll see, you won't regret coming tonight."

~ * ~

Devan Yates wondered how he ever allowed Jim Preston to talk him into coming to a New Year's Eve party, especially a neighborhood party. Other than Jim, he would know no one there.

Certainly Jim would have set him up with some lonely widow or love starved divorcee. How he hated that. Every time he got transferred to a different town, his new friends would set him up with their lonely acquaintances in the hopes of cheering him up.

What made Minter different from the other places he'd lived was it had been his hometown. He'd grown up and gone to school here, his parents lived here until they died in a car accident, twenty-five years ago. If he felt terribly lonely, he could look up old friends. He knew Minter had become a growing community, but someday he was bound to run into someone who remembered him.

In the six weeks he'd been in town, he took only time enough to drive past the old high school and visit his parents' graves. He could have looked up old friends, but there would be no point.

After almost thirty years, he doubted if anyone would actually remember the boy voted most likely to succeed from his graduating class.

This summer would mark the thirtieth anniversary of his high school graduation. He wondered if there would be a reunion or if his small class would let the anniversary pass without fanfare. He couldn't remember ever receiving an invitation to a reunion in the past. Of course, he'd moved repeatedly over the last twenty-six years, and with his parents gone, no one would have known how to reach him. Maybe he would attend this reunion, if there were still enough classmates around Minter to warrant such a commemoration.

Before leaving the apartment, he checked his reflection in the mirror. No one would guess him to be fast approaching forty-eight. True, he'd recently noticed some gray at his temples, but it only enhanced his features.

Ever since his divorce from Missy became final, he'd been considered an eligible bachelor, set up at every opportunity. Tonight, he knew, would be no different. Jim would most certainly have arranged for him to enjoy the company of a woman. Would she expect him to take her to bed? Would she be an exciting challenge or an obnoxious bore?

The thoughts of things to come were overshadowed by those of the past. When he prepared to go out socially for the first time in a new town, his thoughts turned to Missy. They'd been married for five years when his first promotion happened. At that time, they were living in Dallas. From there they moved to a small town in Oklahoma, a town whose name he couldn't remember. His next promotion sent them to Albuquerque.

He could still hear Missy's tirade when he told her they were again being transferred. "I can't understand why that company of yours thinks it can run our lives. They think they can take us from town to town, move us like chess pieces. If you were any kind of a man at all, Devan, you would stand up to them, tell them you don't want to move every few years."

"Did it ever occur to you I could say no, Missy? I don't mind moving, achieving the promotions, making good money," he'd countered.

"Then you're a bigger fool than I thought you were. If you move, this time you'll do it alone. I'm quite content here. If you want to move, go right ahead. What is the name of that little town they're moving you to?"

"That little town happens to be Seattle," he shouted back.

"Well, I hope you're happy there without me and the boys."

"Don't do this to us, Missy," he remembered pleading. "Come with me to Seattle and I promise you won't have to move again. I can't stand being so far away from the kids, but this time I'm committed. I've already accepted the position."

In the end, he moved alone. He missed the boys, but realized how unhappy his life with Missy had become. Within six months, she joined him, but there had been no reconciliation. In the agreement for his portion of the divorce settlement, he bought her a small house not far from his apartment. All the while the boys were growing up, he enjoyed a close relationship with them.

Almost eight years passed before he again moved. With his oldest son, Todd, in college and his youngest son, Brandon, nearing his high school graduation, he felt comfortable leaving Seattle for Missoula.

Now he'd come full circle and returned home, if he could still call Minter home. The apartment complex where he rented an apartment seemed sterile in its newness. In the past few weeks, he'd begun looking for a house to buy. Jim suggested he look for a place like his, on a cul-de-sac, in one of the new neighborhoods, which were sprouting up all around the city.

He grabbed his leather jacket and put it on over his Aaron sweater and Levi's. Before he could leave, the phone rang. He waited until the machine picked up and listened to see who called.

This is Devan Yates. I'm currently unavailable. Please leave a message, he heard himself say. He almost laughed at how sterile the words sounded. At least they matched his apartment.

Missy's voice came across the line, the sound of it still annoying him. "I just wanted to wish you a Happy New Year, Devan. Julian and I, I told you about Julian, didn't I? We're going out to a lovely restaurant. He has time for New Year's Eve, dear. I'll be thinking of you when we ring in the New Year." She punctuated her statement with a high-pitched laugh. Missy's laugh, like her voice, irritated him. Of course, when they met in college they were carried away by overactive hormones and he'd thought it cute. Lust had been mistaken for love and not stood the test of time.

He closed the door, still pondering love. He would never understand the concept. How could he? Where would he find it? He hated the bar scene, hated the drunks and the girls high on pot.

He did enjoy sex, but in this day and age, you had to be so damn careful, it didn't seem worth the effort. Most of the girls he met had enjoyed so many partners, he found himself almost afraid to take them to bed even with protection.

When Devan pulled up in front of Jim and Meg's house, he wondered if he was too early. Seeing a couple walking up to the door, he remembered this would be a neighborhood party.

Once the couple entered the house, he switched off the ignition. Before he got out of the car, he saw an attractive woman leave the house next door and hurry up the sidewalk. He wondered if she would be his companion for the evening. He'd endured worse, much worse.

He waited until she entered the house before he got out of the car. Meg Preston met him at the door. He recognized her from the picture Jim kept on his desk. "You must be Mr. Yates," she said, extending her hand. "Jim's told me so much about you, I feel I know you already."

Before he could say anything, Jim appeared behind her. "I thought you must have gotten lost. Come on in and meet everyone."

Devan followed Jim into the warm living room. Several couples were already engaged in conversations. On the far side of the room, he saw the attractive woman talking with a couple by the fireplace.

"Devan, this is George and Shirley Martin. He's the best doctor Minter has to offer."

Devan shook George's hand and acknowledged Shirley before moving on to the next couple.

"Craig and Paula Walker, I'd like you to meet Devan Yates, he's new in town. Don't let Craig sucker you into a game of golf. He's the pro at the club."

Inwardly Devan laughed. Minter certainly had grown. When he'd lived here, the only golf you could play had been in Greg Marsh's cow pasture, shooting balls into gopher holes.

He exchanged pleasantries with those he met although he couldn't take his eyes from the lone woman who captivated his imagination.

When almost everyone had been introduced, he took Jim aside. "So, who is the woman by the fireplace?"

"Her name is Julie. We thought—" Jim began.

"Look Jim," Devan interrupted, "we agreed if I came tonight, you wouldn't try and set me up."

"It's not what you think. Julie's not looking for a man, if that's what you're getting at. She lost her husband a year ago tonight. She's part of the neighborhood. We certainly aren't setting anyone up, we just wanted to make the party even, give you each an interesting dinner companion."

Devan again looked at the woman. For some unexplained reason, he thought he might know her, but dismissed the idea. If she'd been a former acquaintance, he certainly didn't recognize her. Before he could dwell on his thoughts any longer, Jim guided him over to the woman, who now, seemed engrossed in conversation with Meg.

"Devan Yates," he said, "This is our neighbor, Julie Weston."

Her name brought instant recognition. "Julie Morgan Weston?" he asked, breaking into a smile as he clasped her hand. "You're the last person I thought I'd run into tonight."

Julie began to smile as well. "How long have you been in town, Yates? I thought you'd dropped off the face of the earth."

He enjoyed hearing her call him by the name she'd used when they were younger and two of The Four Musketeers. "Six weeks. I took a transfer when Missoula got too boring. I thought I might try coming home."

"I don't think you'll find Minter to be a hot bed of excitement," she teased.

"What is this?" Meg asked. "Do the two of you know each other already?"

"Already?" Devan exclaimed. "I've known Julie forever. We went to high school together. We were coconspirators in the great Minter Panty Raid."

Devan's words made Julie laugh out loud and drew attention from the other guests.

"Panty raid?" Paula Walker asked, appearing at Julie's side. "Shy, retiring, little Julie involved in a panty raid? I don't believe it."

"Shy?" Devan questioned. "Since when were you ever shy, Julie?" He held her hand tighter and watched as she shrugged her shoulders.

"Just grew up, I guess."

"I don't care about that," Paula said. "I want to hear about this panty raid."

"It wasn't that big of a deal," Julie replied.

"Not a big deal!" Devan echoed. "It happened at the end of our senior year and a group of us decided to do something no one in this town would easily forget. Julie and Sandy Sullivan swiped Miss Flynn's panties, while she took a shower. She was the girls' gym teacher. After the girls got our trophy, Jerry Gaines and I ran them up the flagpole."

"And you didn't get caught?" Paula questioned.

"No, thank goodness," Julie said with a sigh. "Devan and I were National Honor Society, Sandy was a cheerleader, and Jerry was captain of the baseball team. If word had gotten out who did it, the principal, Mr. Andrews, could have kept us from graduating."

Devan enjoyed the almost forgotten memory of the past, although he could sense Julie's uneasiness.

At last they were seated for dinner and he could engage Julie in more quiet conversation. "Jim mentioned your husband. Since the last name is Weston, it must have worked out between you and Steve. I wouldn't have given that relationship a snowball's chance, if you know what I mean. I know you said you loved him, but he always seemed so much more... what's the word I want to use? I know he was more reserved than we were. I am sorry about his passing. I didn't know."

"Thank you, Devan. There was no way you could have known. I always knew you guys thought I made a terrible mistake marrying so young, but somehow we stayed together. It wasn't always easy, but I guess we made it. I just had to learn to be a little more reserved and accept the demands his job made on our personal lives."

"So what have you been doing with your life?"

He watched as Julie pondered her answer. "When the kids were finally all in school, I took a business course at the college. After I received my degree, I got a job in the personnel department at LisPro. Now I head the department. I guess you might say my job preserved my sanity this past year."

"I can understand what you're saying. You mentioned kids, how many?"

"Three. Mark's the oldest, he's twenty-eight and stationed in Honolulu with the Navy. Jill is twenty-five. She got married just before Steve died and is going to make me a grandma in June. Lance is the baby. He'll be graduating from Gustavous Adolphus College in Minnesota this May. How about you? Wife? Kids?"

"Ex-wife and two boys. My ex stayed in Seattle. My oldest, Todd, is twenty-three. He graduated from MIT last year and is working for a large company in Philadelphia. Brandon is twenty-one. He'll be starting his senior year at the Air Force Academy next fall."

~ * ~

After dinner, Julie joined the women in the kitchen. "Are you still mad at me?" Meg inquired.

"I couldn't be mad at you. To be truthful, I expected you to set me up. I just didn't expect it to be with Devan."

"Were you two, well, you know, a thing in high school?" Paula asked.

"Good grief, no. Steve and I dated all through high school. Devan and I were just good friends."

"Some friend," Meg commented. "Was he a hunk back then?"

"Hunk?" Julie questioned. "I never thought much about it. Devan was Devan. He lived around the corner from my parents. We were buddies. I certainly couldn't have been called anyone's dream girl in school. Let's face it, I've always been on the hefty side, always one of the guys."

The evening passed with the usual conversation, the usual games. At the stroke of midnight, Julie felt herself encircled within Devan's arms. "Happy New Year," he whispered just before he kissed her.

In the next few minutes, several other men kissed her, but the security of Devan's arms, the warmth of his kiss, lingered in her mind. Could it be her imagination or had she felt a tingle of excitement she hadn't felt in so long?

With midnight past and the party ended, Devan and Julie decided to leave.

"May I walk you home?" he asked when they stepped into the cold snow filled January air.

"I'd like that. I dread going into the house alone at night. I think it's the hardest part of being a widow."

They walked the short distance between the two houses and Devan took Julie's keys to open the door.

"If you'd like to build up the fire, I'll make us a pot of coffee," Julie said.

She hung up her coat on the hall tree and went into the kitchen. It seemed comfortable to have a man in the house. The ringing of the phone startled her.

"Happy New Year, Mom," Jill's cheery voice came over the receiver. "Where have you been? I've been calling for over an hour."

"I went to Meg and Jim's party."

"Did you have a good time?"

"I have to admit, I did. How about you? Did you and Karl go out?"

"We're at the party now, but I want to hear about your party. Did they have a man for you?"

"Jill! What a thing to ask. If you must know, they arranged for a dinner companion for me."

"Was he a hunk? Did you let him kiss you?"

13

Julie wondered why everyone was so concerned about Devan being a hunk. To her, he was just Devan, an old friend from high school, someone comfortable to be with and nothing else. "To everyone's surprise, including mine, he turned out to be an old friend from high school. He just brought me home and I'm making coffee."

Jill laughed out loud. "Then I won't keep you. I'm just glad you met someone nice."

Jill's words, 'someone nice,' rang in Julie's ears while she wiped out her crystal mugs. Devan certainly could be called nice, nice and comfortable, unlike the other 'dates' she'd endured.

"Do you take your coffee black or with cream and sugar?" she called to Devan.

"Black," he said, joining her in the kitchen. "You shouldn't fuss."

"Please, Devan, let me fuss, I enjoy it. I hope you like flavored coffee. I only drink hazelnut when I'm at home."

Before she could pour the coffee, the phone again rang. "That has to be Lance," she said, before picking up the receiver. On the other end of the line sounds of a party full of young blood and life blared.

"Happy New Year, Mom," Lance shouted above the din. "I'm sorry to be calling so late, but we just got in from a midnight ski run."

"It's okay, honey. I just got home myself. I went to the party next door. It sounds like everyone is having a good time there."

"We sure are, Mom. I just wanted to talk to you. Are you all right?"

"I'm fine. You get back to your party. Love you lots."

"Your kids?" Devan asked, once she hung up the phone.

"Yes, they do worry about me. I guess I've given them cause this past year."

She finished pouring the coffee and handed Devan the first cup, adding cream to hers before leading the way to the living room.

"You're lucky," he said. "My boys won't call me, they'll just wait for the old man to call on his dime."

Julie sat down on the couch and Devan seated himself next to her. "I almost didn't go to that party tonight," he commented.

"It's strange to hear you say such a thing. I felt the same way myself. I knew Meg would be setting me up. I'm glad I didn't go with my first instinct. I had a good time tonight."

"I did, too. I'd forgotten how nice it was to be with you. I've always been comfortable around you."

Comfortable. Julie contemplated the word she'd thought of earlier when she was talking to Jill. Devan made her feel comfortable as well. Talking to him reminded her of old tennis shoes, a comfortable change from the tight pinch of her daily routine. At the same time, she felt a sense of excitement, of adventure, just sitting next to him and remembering their friendship.

"What about you?" he asked, holding her hand a little tighter. "Has it been terribly hard?"

Julie pondered her answer. Of course, it had been hard. Steve was her husband, her companion, for almost thirty years. In the blink of an eye he disappeared from her life, leaving her alone.

She eased her hand from Devan's, put her mug on the coffee table, and went to the patio door. In one movement, she drew open the heavy drapes and switched on the patio light. For a moment, she stood watching the snow accumulating in the back yard. To her surprise, she no longer saw a replay of last New Year's Eve, only the heavy snowfall.

"Hard, very hard," she finally said, "but I'm learning to live with it. Steve's gone and he's not coming back. I've accepted it. Now it's only me."

"And you'll make it alone?"

"I have so far. It gets easier every day."

"I suppose it does."

His voice sounded close behind her. When she felt his hands on her shoulders, she shuddered involuntarily. For one moment, she thought about life, about the man behind her.

Devan wasn't Steve. She didn't want him to be Steve. The reflection in the window only acted to confirm her thoughts. She turned to him, her eyes filled, not with tears for Steve, but for herself.

"You must think me terrible, but you don't know how good it feels to have you in this house tonight, to have you touch me, to think you might care. I know we're just buddies, good friends..."

Before she could say more, he pulled her into his arms and kissed her tenderly. With the kiss, her floodgates of emotions opened. She needed this. She wanted it. Did it make her evil? She hoped not, it felt too good to be wrong.

He kissed her long and hard before he began to tease her lips with his tongue, begging for entrance to her mouth. To her amazement, she felt herself part her lips ever so slightly, to allow him the opening he sought. His tongue probed and played games with hers and she tentatively copied his actions.

It was Devan that broke the embrace and pulled away. "I'm sorry, Julie. You're very vulnerable. I've taken advantage of you. Like I said, I almost didn't come tonight. When I saw you and realized who you were, I knew I wanted you. It's wrong. I know it is. We're friends, but—"

"Are you telling me the truth or just what you think I want to hear?"

"It's the truth."

"Maybe I want a one-night stand. Maybe I just need to be special to someone for a little while. Whatever it is, I wouldn't blame you if you left right now. I really don't know what's come over me, but I want you to stay with me tonight."

"Do you mean it?"

"Yes. Just for tonight, I need to be loved. Please stay. I'll give you the garage door opener so you can get your car off the street. There's room for two cars in there."

"Look Julie, if you want to call this off—"

She put her finger to his lips to silence him. "I don't think so."

When Devan went out to the car, she wondered if she did know what she was doing. He'd become a stranger. The boy she knew thirty years ago was all grown up. Maybe this would be best, just good healthy sex between old friends. Could it be so wrong? Wasn't that what the kids did, what their society had come to? Who would ever know, other than herself and Devan? They were no longer in high school. She certainly wouldn't be the topic of tomorrow's locker room discussion. They were grown people, consenting adults. Certainly Devan must have strayed more than once.

"I guess it's a good thing I got the car off the street when I did," he said, interrupting her thoughts. "It's really coming down. I don't think I would have made it home."

She glanced again at the patio doors. The snow didn't look menacing in the backyard.

"There's a good six inches out there," he continued. "The roads are getting treacherous." With the words, he studied her face, as though trying to read her expression. "You don't have to go through with this, you know."

"I know, but I want to. It's probably the best medicine I could get. Maybe I'm lucky you were at the party tonight."

He put his finger under her chin and lifted it to look into her eyes. "I know I'm lucky to have met you. The gods must be smiling on me."

"You always were a smooth talker, always knew the right words to say, but I don't care. For tonight, nothing matters but you and me."

Again he took her in his arms and kissed her, before she pulled away. "Let me close down the house. I'd rather not get carried away on the living room floor."

Julie turned off the lights and heard him laugh. She too saw the humor in her statement. She'd become so set in her ways spontaneity seemed to come with great difficulty. Yet she had been the one who asked him to stay.

In the bedroom, Julie switched on the lamp on the bedside table. She thought momentarily of how lonely the room had felt until she redecorated it to her tastes. The definitely feminine furnishings reflected her personality.

While she pulled back the comforter, Devan turned down the lamp and closed the blinds. When he finished, Devan undid the buttons on her blouse slowly, until at last he exposed her bra enclosed breasts. She inhaled deeply as he slipped the silky fabric of the blouse from her shoulders, allowing it to fall to the floor.

Julie closed her eyes, feeling his finger trace circles across the exposed portion of her full breasts. Almost unaware of what was happening, she felt her bra slide to the floor to join her discarded blouse.

A year ago, I would have been embarrassed to stand like this, even in front of Steve. Why is it so different tonight, with Devan?

She allowed him to enjoy the sight and feel of her breasts, while she opened his shirt and ran her hands over his chest with its thick mat of hair. Slowly, she moved her hands downward, tracing the line of hair, which ran from his navel to the promised delights hidden just beyond her view. When his pants and her skirt had been removed, she wasn't sure, but the realization of his masculine attributes excited her more than she felt possible.

Before Julie knew it, Devan swept her into his arms and lowered her to the bed. He took just a moment to take the necessary precautions and she marveled at how even this excited her. He lay down beside her, and she felt his roving hands touching her, exciting her. Without hesitation, she reached for him, stroking his sheathed organ, touching the sack containing the two hard balls, making him moan with pleasure.

At last, he entered her and she matched him stroke for stroke with wild abandonment. She neared climax several times only to have him slow his movements to prolong her pleasure.

As though adhering to a script, he manipulated her to a final climax, which drove everything from her mind, except the oneness they shared.

"I never thought it could be like this," she whispered. "I feel alive for the first time in a year. Thank you."

Without saying a word, he took her in his arms and kissed her. "You need to be loved, Julie, loved and made love to, often. I should be thanking you."

With the coming of morning, Julie turned over and found she no longer slept in Devan's arms. Opening her eyes, she became painfully aware of his absence.

What have I done? How could I allow myself to act in such a way? Why did I initiate a shameless relationship on the anniversary of

Steve's death? Flashes of last night entered her mind. Sex with Steve had become automatic, a Friday night tradition. Foreplay had ceased years earlier, although it never had been extremely passionate in the past. What she experienced with Devan was unlike anything she had ever known before.

"You're awake," Devan's deep voice invaded her thoughts.

"I thought you left," she said, pulling the sheet up to her shoulders, surprised by her modesty after last night.

"Hardly. Did you honestly think I'd go without a word?"

"I didn't know. I'm not sure how these things are handled."

"These things?"

"You know, one night stands. What does one do in the morning, shake hands or just disappear?"

"Believe me, Julie, this wasn't a one night stand and it certainly wasn't anything to be ashamed of. We've known each other forever. We're both lonely. We only seized the moment. If it makes you feel better, I was attracted to you before I even realized who you were. I even thought about getting better acquainted, perhaps seeing you after the party. Last night held a special meaning for me. I hope it did for you. I want to see you again and again. Not just to make love to you, but to get reacquainted. Now, if you'll follow me, breakfast is served."

"Breakfast?" she questioned. "You made breakfast?"

"Of course."

She swung her legs over the side of the bed, pulling the sheet around her like a security blanket. To her surprise, he only smiled at her shyness and left the room while she slipped into her new red velvet robe and matching slippers.

Two

Julie pulled into her parking space at work. She always found going back to work after a holiday difficult, and today proved to be no exception.

Seeing the maintenance crew still at work annoyed her further. She made a mental note to talk to Tom Randall, the plant manager, about her concerns. She could see no reason why they couldn't come in an hour early on days like these. More than likely, they had arrived at six with the rest of the crew, and now at seven they were merely moving the snow into piles around the assembled cars. She knew the parking lot would become a treacherous no man's land of hard packed ice and snow, which would last for the remainder of the winter.

After picking her way toward the building, Julie felt relieved to be inside, out of the cold. As usual, she went to the cafeteria for her cup of coffee. From the kitchen, she could hear the sounds of the staff getting ready for the first shift coffee break. She helped herself to a coffee mug and filled it with the strong, dark brew from the fifty-cup urn, then dropped two quarters into the dish that sat next to the pot.

With coffee and brief case firmly in hand, she made her way to her second floor office. Everything remained dark and when she switched on the light, she found herself greeted by the Christmas decorations which reminded her of the holiday just past. Today her secretary, Roxie, would take them down. For now she could enjoy them and remember the delights of New Year's Eve.

Once she seated herself at her desk, she switched on her answering machine to see who called in sick for work today. She enjoyed the family atmosphere of the plant, of knowing everyone well enough to call them by their first names and recognize their voices on the tape.

"Morning, Julie," the first voice said. "Ted Arneson here. I won't be in today. My mom passed away last night. The visitation is tomorrow night and the funeral will be held the day after. I'll be back to work next Monday."

Send flowers to the funeral home and attend visitation, she jotted next to Ted's name. She'd known Amelia Arneson all her life and now her passing seemed a blessing. The cancer she'd fought so valiantly ravaged her body until death was a welcome guest.

"Hi, Julie," a woman's voice said. The voice seemed to falter and Julie knew the woman had been crying. "This is Carol Warring, Joe won't be in today. He was in an accident yesterday. He lost control in the snow. They have him in the hospital and they're keeping him for observation for a couple of days. I'll keep you posted."

Joe Warrin—Send flowers to the hospital, she noted.

"Hi, Julie, sorry to do this to you. I'm down with the flu. In case you can't recognize my voice in my weakened state, this is Chuck Schultz. Can't keep a thing in my stomach. Pam's calling the doctor to get me an excuse. I hope I'm back there tomorrow. This stuff is the shits in more ways than one."

Julie laughed at Chuck's statement. He always tried to find something funny, no matter what the situation.

She listened as the messages rambled on and on until the list of absentees numbered ten. She checked each name against her master list, to see which department heads to notify. When Roxie came in, she would call the proper people, send flowers to those she had noted, and do the necessary paperwork.

By eight, Julie heard a commotion in the outer office. "Hi, Julie," Roxie said, entering Julie's office. "How was your holiday?"

"It was good," she replied, smiling at the memory of her night with Devan. "How was yours?"

"Great!" Roxie said, holding out her hand to display a glittering diamond.

"So, he finally popped the question. I didn't think he'd ever come around. When is the wedding?"

"Not for a year and a half yet. He needs to finish school and he won't be done until a year from this June. It will give us plenty of time to save for the kind of wedding I want."

A sigh of relief escaped Julie's lips. "Then I don't have to start looking for your replacement right away."

Roxie laughed. "Not hardly, someone has to keep working so we can afford the rent on our apartment."

Julie handed Roxie the list of absentees, knowing she would have everything under control within the hour. "When you have time, check my schedule, Rox. If it's fairly light, make appointments for me with Mr. Randall and Jerry Gaines, then bring in the file of current résumés."

"Are we hiring again?"

"Yes. They're starting a new product line and we're to look for another engineer as well as two technicians, four for the line and three for maintenance. I want to see what we have in the files before I run an ad in the paper."

Roxie took Julie's notes and left the office while Julie started organizing her thoughts for the day.

When Roxie returned with the résumé file, Julie had already started her first pot of coffee. "I made an appointment with Jerry for ten-thirty and one with Mr. Randall for eleven," Roxie announced.

"Good. Give me a call at ten-fifteen so I can be ready for Jerry."

Julie began leafing through the résumés, but she couldn't focus on them. The upcoming meeting with Jerry crowded her thoughts, robbing the concentration from her mind.

She'd known Jerry ever since grade school, and this morning's confrontation bothered her. They were friends, good friends, even though Jerry could drive her crazy on occasion. She knew reprimanding him wouldn't be easy.

In high school, Jerry's reputation as a ladies man came easily, but marriage seemed to have settled him down. Julie had noticed the change about four years ago when the rumors began, and recently she'd begun to receive complaints from his co-workers as well as the married secretaries. She'd tried to ignore the stories, but now she knew she could no longer continue to overlook such behavior just because Jerry was her friend.

The intercom on her phone buzzed, startling her. "Yes, Rox."

"There's a delivery man here from Minter Floral."

"Who'd be sending me flowers? I guess it doesn't matter. Send him in."

For a moment Julie's heart seemed to stop. Had this been a year ago, she would have expected the florist to arrive. Steve always sent her flowers the day after a holiday as a welcome back to work gift.

The dozen roses of assorted shades were beautifully arranged. "Looks like you have a secret admirer, Mrs. Weston," the young man said, as she dug into her purse for the tip.

"Could be," she replied.

When he left the office she opened the card and read it.

> *Thank You For Everything... Especially For*
> *Being You*
>
> *Devan.*

Could this be payment for services rendered? As soon as the thought entered her head, she dismissed it. Devan was being considerate and she too suspicious.

"It's ten-fifteen," Roxie announced, when she entered the office. "Aren't those roses beautiful? You must have had a good holiday for someone to send you such an unusual arrangement."

Julie nodded, wondering if Roxie would read the same meaning as she into the attached note.

Jerry arrived at exactly ten-thirty. "Well, Julie, what can I do for you?" he asked, trying as usual, to put her on the defensive.

"Sit down, Jerry. We need to talk," she said, in an attempt to keep their meeting on a business basis.

Before he took the seat across from her, he moved closer to the desk, seemingly enjoying the beauty of the delicate blossoms in the arrangement, then took the card from its holder.

"Devan?" he questioned. "As in Devan Yates? Is he back in town?"

"I didn't ask you here to discuss Devan," she said, annoyance sounding in her voice.

"Yes, ma'am," he replied, giving her a mock salute before seating himself in the chair opposite her and putting his feet on her desk.

"Don't be flip with me, Jerry. What I have to say is serious. Now take your feet off my desk and listen to me."

Jerry swung his feet to the floor. "What's come over you, Julie? Can't you take a joke anymore?"

"Your actions have come over me, and I can see nothing funny about them. Rumor has it you're coming on to everything in a skirt. This has to stop, that's all there is to it. Everyone's talking about you. To be honest, I've even had some complaints from your intended conquests. One of these days they might do more than complain to me. In this day and age, someone could easily file a sexual harassment suit, and then where would we be?"

"Get off it, Julie," Jerry said, getting to his feet. He put his hands on her desk and with his face close to hers, he continued. "Everyone does it and for God's sake, who am I hurting when the girl says yes?"

"You're hurting yourself, Karen, the girl, her family... even this company. I can't have it. Everyone does it? Hardly Jerry, Steve and I were married for almost thirty years and..."

"And what?" Jerry interrupted. "Steve never strayed? Get real, Julie. I know better than that."

"What are you saying?" Julie asked, as she came around to the front of the desk to stand face to face with Jerry.

"Come on, you have to know. Everyone else does. Steve had been having an affair for years. I ought to know; it was with my wife, with Karen. Do you think I started fooling around for no reason? I decided what was good for the goose was good for the gander. If Karen could have her fun with Steve, why shouldn't I do the same with whomever seemed willing? Grow up, Julie. Steve wasn't as pure as the driven snow. No one is, unless you fit into the little goody two shoes role."

Jerry's voice droned on, but Julie ceased listening. Her mind wandered to the last months, the last years of Steve's life. *Had there been warning signs? Had she sensed trouble?*

Certainly their lovemaking had cooled, but it never excited her as Devan's did. Of course, after almost thirty years, what could she expect? Their sex life, like their daily routine, became predictable, almost boring. *Could Jerry be right?* He couldn't be telling her the truth. Steve wouldn't have an affair, and if he did, she felt certain it wouldn't be with Karen, not with someone she considered to be her friend.

She felt her head begin to spin, and Jerry's words spun in tandem. The world started closing in on her. Above Jerry's voice, she could hear Steve and Karen laughing at her. "Poor, naive Julie, she has no idea what's going on," Steve's voice sounded in her head.

When she came to, she lay on the floor, her head pillowed on something soft, perhaps someone's coat. Opening her eyes, she looked into the worried face of the company nurse.

Glancing around, she made eye contact with Tom Randall. To her surprise, he knelt at her side, holding her hand in his.

"Are you all right?" he questioned.

"What happened?" she managed to ask.

"You fainted. I'd just arrived for our appointment when Jerry came out of the office. He said you'd been talking and just collapsed."

The mention of Jerry's name brought back his hurting words. Steve and Karen had been having an affair, sneaking around, laughing at her. Had Jerry told Tom what they were talking about? *No,* she thought, *Jerry would never disclose the reason for my collapse.*

She tried to get up, but Tom's hand on her shoulder forced her back. "We've called the paramedics, Julie. I think they should take you to the hospital and have you checked over."

"Hospital! I have too much to do to be going to the hospital," she protested.

"There's no use in fighting about this. The decision has been made, and you'll abide by it," Tom informed her.

Before she could say more, two young men, dressed in the uniform of the local fire department, entered the office.

"Hi," the first man said, kneeling beside her. "My name is Bob. Can you tell me yours?"

"Of course I can," Julie replied sarcastically. "It's Julie Weston."

"That's good, Mrs. Weston. It is Mrs. Weston, isn't it?"

"It's Ms.," she corrected him, remembering more of Jerry's words. She wondered what the people around her were thinking. Judging by Tom's expression, she decided they must be concerned to hear her so easily relinquish the title of Mrs. she had so fiercely clung to this past year.

"Can you tell me what the date is?" the young man continued.

"Of course I can. It's Monday—no it's Wednesday."

"Do you know the date?" he repeated.

"January... ah... second."

"What year is this?"

"This is ridiculous. It's 2000... no, it's 2001."

"Who is the President?"

"What does that have to do with anything? This game of twenty questions is getting old pretty fast," she quipped, hoping her tone denoted her annoyance with the entire situation.

"Please, Ms. Weston, just answer my questions. Who is the President?"

"The way the election went it's hard to tell. If you must know, it's Bush, the young one, George W., not his father."

"Can you tell me the name of your doctor?"

"Sure, why not? Maybe he can make you understand how utterly ridiculous this is. He's George, George Martin."

The young man turned his attention away from Julie and spoke directly to Tom. "May I use your phone, sir?"

Julie wanted to scream that it wasn't Tom's phone, but hers, and she certainly didn't want him to use it, but the other man had slipped a thermometer under her tongue and attached a blood pressure cuff to her upper arm. Instead, she listened to the one-sided conversation going on at her desk.

"We have a patient here, Dr. Martin, a patient of yours, a Ms. Weston. She collapsed... yes, I agree... she seems to be a bit disoriented."

"I am not disoriented," she pleaded once the thermometer had been removed from her mouth.

"Calm yourself, Julie," Tom said.

Before she could continue, the man on the phone continued, "Yes, we're bringing her in right away. You will be able to meet us at the hospital, won't you?"

"Calm myself!" Julie exclaimed, once the man hung up the phone. "Everyone here wants to take me away and you want me to calm myself. Tell them what happened, Jerry. You know there is nothing wrong with me. I fainted for God's sake."

"I can't tell them that, Julie. I'm worried about you myself. You were so pale. You passed out for no good reason. We only want what's best for you."

"What is this, a conspiracy?" she shouted. "Jerry, Tom, someone tell them this is a mistake, a terrible mistake."

"If you don't calm down, Ms. Weston, we'll be forced to sedate you. You don't want that, do you?" the paramedic who'd introduced himself as Bob asked.

Julie shook her head. "What other choice do I have? I certainly don't want to be sedated."

Tom held her hand a bit tighter. "This time you're going to play by my rules. I've been worried about you for a long time now. I want some answers. I want to know why you've lost so much weight, why your color is so poor, and why it's taken you so long to put the past behind you. I'm sorry it has to be this way, but that's life."

Julie closed her eyes and turned away from Tom's voice. His concerns galled her and yet, at the same time, he made sense. She felt her control slipping away as tears spilled from her eyes and ran down her cheeks. The last thing she ever wanted was to lose control.

She opened her eyes as they lifted her from the floor to the gurney and through her tears noticed the flowers on her desk. Would anyone guess the meaning behind the words on the card? She closed her eyes again as her tears began flowing faster. Who would care what Devan's words meant? Men, suddenly, were all the same. They said the things you wanted to hear until they decided to hurt you, then made no move to reverse the hurt. Steve had betrayed her trust, Jerry her friendship—how would Devan betray her?

George met her in the emergency room. "I didn't think I'd be seeing you again so soon, Julie. What happened?"

27

"I don't know. I was having a discussion with one of the men at the plant and I got dizzy."

"What were you discussing?"

"It doesn't matter, George. Just do what you have to do and get me back to work."

"It does matter, Julie. Now, who were you having this discussion with and what did he say to upset you?"

"It was Jerry Gaines. Is that what you want to know? I can't see where it makes any difference who I was talking to."

George's expression became one of concern. "What did he tell you?"

"I don't know why it should concern you," she lied.

"I think you do. I can see it in your eyes. He told you about Steve, didn't he?"

"You knew? I can't believe you never told me."

"I wanted to protect you, to persuade Steve to think about what he was doing to you."

"Apparently my dear husband didn't feel the same way, did he?" Julie could hear the hurt and anger in her voice.

"No, he didn't. Everyone tried to reason with him, but he thought he wasn't hurting you, since you didn't know. After the fact, well, it didn't seem to matter anymore. Now, I'm going to admit you to the hospital for a few days."

"Admit me! Admit me? You can't be serious."

"I'm very serious. I've been trying to get you into my office for a physical for the better part of a year and you've been avoiding me like the plague. This time I want you to do as I say. After I saw you at Jim and Meg's party, I told Shirley either you would slow down or I would slow you down. I guess your body took the first step."

Julie sighed. "I don't believe this is happening to me. I'm perfectly fine. Why waste your time and my money?"

"Perfectly fine? Hardly! You're not eating right or sleeping well, I can tell that much without any tests. Anemia, exhaustion, they're only the symptoms on the surface. Underneath, I'm looking at some vitals that are off the wall and I haven't done any blood work yet."

"Steve's death devastated me, you know that. I've been in mourning. Isn't that a joke? I've been in mourning for a man who didn't love me, who didn't care. What's wrong with me, George? Why did Steve need to have an affair? Wasn't I good enough for him? You were his best friend. What did he tell you about me?"

"Don't do this to yourself, Julie," George said. "Whatever you want to blame this on is your decision, but mourning and depression are only excuses. What Steve was or what he did, doesn't matter now. Steve is dead. Bury the past with him. You're the one I'm concerned about, and I won't allow you to continue to abuse yourself."

Julie knew George's concern was genuine. The look on his face, the tone of his voice confirmed it. She wanted to give in and allow him to care for her, but her anger threatened to override her better judgment.

"All right, you win. Put me in the hospital, run your silly little tests. I'll do whatever you want, but I'll never forgive Steve for what he did to me."

Three

Once settled in, Julie began a battery of tests. When at last she returned from X-ray, she found her room filled with flowers. She could only guess who sent them. The events of the day, coupled with the stress of the last year, left her drained. An aide helped her into bed and gratefully she relaxed for the first time all day. Surprisingly, she fell into a fitful sleep. Dreams of Steve and Jerry and Devan invaded her subconscious, to confuse her further.

When she awoke, she got out of bed to see who sent the flowers. The first arrangement she checked came from Devan. As she read the card, she realized the last person she wanted caring about her was Devan Yates. He was a man, and men only wanted one thing. How could she have given in to him so easily? Had it been an affair, a one-night stand, or a fling? Why had it seemed so right two days ago and so wrong today? Devan tried to warn her, but perhaps it had been only a ploy, an excuse to get what he wanted from her.

No, I wanted Devan to make love to me, and he made me feel alive. Sex with Steve hadn't made me feel like that in years. Does sex after almost thirty years of marriage have to be boring? Was sex with Steve boring for Karen? Did he act as sterile with Karen as always did with me? I doubt it. Karen would have been a new and exciting toy. Depending on how long they had been together, it was quite possible he would have gotten tired of her as well.

Her thoughts turned to all of the late meetings, the out of town trips, which had accelerated over the last four years. *Was Karen the mysterious new client he talked about so much? Anything could be possible, especially since I never pried into Steve's business life.*

"Hi, Julie," Meg's voice cut into her thoughts.

"So, who spread the good news to you?" Julie snapped.

"Aren't we touchy today?" Meg replied.

"Wouldn't you be?" Julie countered. "I feel a bit woozy and I end up in the hospital."

"Just how long have you been feeling 'a bit woozy'?"

Julie lowered her eyes to escape Meg's gaze. It pained her to admit to any defect, but there seemed no point in denying what everyone would soon know to be true. "Off and on for the last few months. It's just never been this bad before, since I haven't passed out. It's just something I've learned to live with. Every once in a while, the floor seems to drop out from under my feet. I feel strange for a couple of minutes and it goes away."

"So what made today different?"

Julie felt her temper flare. "I would have thought our dear friend, George, would have filled you in by now. Didn't he tell you how Jerry, so thoughtfully, spilled the beans about Steve and Karen? You did know about them, didn't you?"

"Yes, I knew."

"I thought so. It seems his deep dark secret wasn't very well kept. Everyone knew... everyone but me, that is. What's wrong with me? My own husband couldn't stand to be anywhere near me."

"Stop it, Julie! You know better than that."

"Do I? Then why was he having an affair with Karen Gaines?"

"Look, Honey, Jim and I both tried to talk to him. I even went so far as to threaten to tell you. He only laughed at me. He said he knew I could never hurt you that way. He was right. It seemed better for you to believe everything was okay."

Julie nodded. *How could I have been so blind? Can I even remember the last time Steve whispered I love you, without me saying it first?* "So, now what?" she asked, the fight gone from her.

"First, you change into the nightgown I brought for you, then you concentrate on getting out of this place. I went over to your house and got some things I thought you might need, and I called Jill."

"Please say I didn't hear you right. I didn't want the kids to know."

"I thought she should be home. Jim went to Madison to pick her up when I left for here."

"But, Meg, she can't afford to come home again so soon after Christmas."

"Jim and I sent her the tickets, but enough of that. Devan wants to know when he can come and see you?"

"Devan?"

"Jim says he seemed terribly worried about you. Is something going on I don't know about?"

Julie smiled weakly. "Would you think I'm terrible if I told you I asked Devan to spend the night with me on New Year's Eve?"

Meg laughed. "I'd think you were finally acting like a woman. Did he agree?"

"Yes, and we made love. I should be ashamed of what I did, but I'm not. At this point shame can't hold a candle to confusion."

"Do you want to see him again?"

Julie shrugged her shoulders, her smile gone. "I thought maybe we'd find something special. After what I heard about Steve, I have my doubts. I don't suppose I can stop him from coming to the hospital. We do have to talk. Of course, George says I should have lots of company to keep my spirits up. I guess Devan is as good as anybody."

"Just give him a chance. Let's change the subject. George says you're taking six weeks off work. Think of all the great shopping we can do."

"George says a lot of things. Shopping is fun, once in a while, but six weeks worth? I don't think so. I really don't want to take that much time off."

Meg nodded. "What about a vacation? You know, some place warm and exotic."

"Maybe, but this is such a busy time at work. I have résumés to read, hiring to do."

"You're going to stop thinking about work and everything else, including Steve," George said, as he entered the room.

"Well," Meg began, "now that you're here, I can see Julie doesn't need me, and I have to get ready for Jill to arrive. I'll see you tomorrow. Give some thought to what we talked about."

As though on cue, Meg left the room and George turned his attention back to Julie. "Jerry made a grave mistake in telling you so long after Steve's death. You were just getting your life together. Maybe it was for the best, though. It gave me an excuse to give you a good physical."

Julie thought for a moment, contemplating George's words. Jerry had made a mistake, but it wasn't inadvertent. He knew exactly what he was doing. He'd saved the information he'd imparted for a time when he could hurt her. If she hadn't passed out, she would have put him on probation for the next six months. It would have meant no raises, no promotions, and no affairs with his co-workers.

"Are you listening to me, Julie?" George questioned.

"I guess I wasn't. I'm sorry. What were you saying?"

"I said, we should have your test results in the morning. For now, I want you to rest."

"Whatever you say, Doc," she replied. She closed her eyes and thought about the day's events. Everyone seemed concerned, and yet they had all known about Steve. If they knew, why hadn't anyone told her?

"I've come to one conclusion," George continued, causing her to open her eyes and concentrate on what he was saying. "The weight loss may have originally been from grief, bit it's gotten out of control. The technical term could be Anorexia. You've dropped a lot of weight, but you're not in any danger... yet. I strongly suggest you get some counseling."

"I am seeing a counselor, George. The kids insisted on it over Christmas. He feels I'm making good progress and so do I."

"Do you mind if I contact him?"

"Sure, why not? Let's bring everyone in to poke and probe. His name is Dale Bentz."

"Dale's good, there's no doubt about it. I'll have him come in and see you tomorrow."

~ * ~

Devan entered the hospital. Why had Julie been different from the other women he'd dated since the divorce? In the past, he could easily make love to a woman one night and barely remember her name the next. He'd been with Julie for one night and now she haunted his thoughts.

At the information desk, he obtained her room number before taking the elevator to the second floor. Checking the number against those posted on the wall, he found Julie's room at the end of the hall.

He almost bumped into George as he came out of the room. "It's good to see you, Devan. Julie can use the company."

"She's alone? I thought Meg would be with her."

"She was, but when I showed up, she went home. She wanted to get ready for Julie's daughter, Jill. She's due in soon and will be staying with Jim and Meg."

"What happened?"

"She passed out."

"And for that you hospitalized her? There has to be more to it."

"There is. I wasn't happy with her color at the party the other night, and her episode this morning confirmed my suspicions."

George continued to explain the situation until Devan felt sickened by what he heard. *How could anyone, especially Jerry, hurt*

Julie so badly? Hadn't they called themselves The Four Musketeers? Weren't they close friends, sworn to be there for each other, no matter what? If Jerry's wife and Steve were having an affair, why throw it in Julie's face a year after Steve's death?

"How could Julie not know what was going on?" he finally asked, trying to comprehend the situation.

"Don't get me wrong, Devan, I think the world and all of Julie, but she's little more than a child. She's a grown woman with a responsible job, but she's also as trusting as she was thirty years ago. Until today, she believed in Once Upon A Time and Happily Ever After. She'll never be that trusting again. I'm afraid you won't see the same woman you met the other night. Be patient with the one you do find."

George left Devan outside the room. For a moment, Devan wondered if he should enter Julie's world or turn around and leave.

Hesitantly, he opened the door. Hoping George was wrong, he glanced toward the bed, only to confirm his worst fears. Although he'd seen her yesterday, she looked frail and exhausted. Without her make-up he could see for himself what George meant about her color. "May I come in?"

Julie turned toward him. "Sure, why not? Thank you for the flowers, they're beautiful. Your florist bill must resemble the national debt. I received the roses this morning."

"I hope someone remembers to bring them over for you," Devan said, for lack of anything else to say.

"It doesn't matter. I've received my payment. Isn't that what they were, Devan, payment? Isn't that what men do, they have a one night stand, send her flowers, then never see her again? Did you consider me a one night stand?"

"No. If you recall, I warned you about the consequences of our actions."

"And I told you I didn't love you. At the time I believed it. Unfortunately, by the time the night ended you'd turned my life upside down. How many times did you cheat on your wife before the divorce? Did you always leave your conquests thinking they couldn't survive without you?"

"I never cheated on Missy."

"Oh, really? Haven't you heard? Everyone does it, just ask Jerry."

"We need to talk, Julie. You've been hurt."

"So, you knew it, too. How nice for you. What did Steve do, take out an ad in all the major papers or did he just put it on CNN?"

"Stop it, Julie! I wouldn't have known anything, but I ran into George in the hall. He told me about Steve. I'm sorry this happened to you, but I can't change it. I honestly didn't have a mistress, at least not in the conventional sense. My mistress is and was my work. Missy couldn't compete. I thought taking promotions, relocations, would be the way to insure our future. Instead, I drove her away."

"So, you became an experienced lover of women who expected no commitment."

"You might say that, at least until I met you the other night. I can't explain it, but you've become very important to me. I want you to be part of my life."

"Please understand, I don't know what I want. I'm not sure I know who I even am. I could easily allow you to be come important to me, to depend on you, but I'm scared. Does anything I'm saying make any sense?"

Devan sat beside her on the bed and lifted her hand to his lips. "Unfortunately, I understand all too well. I don't want to lose you, but I do understand. When you're ready, you have my number. I promise, I'll always be there for you."

He took her into his arms and kissed her. The passion, the urgency of two days earlier, was replaced by concern. "Promise me you will call," he said, holding her just a moment longer than necessary.

"I promise. As soon as I find Julie, I'll give Devan a chance."

~ * ~

Jill Lansing prepared for the plane to land in Madison. She knew Jim Preston would be there to meet her. Meg's call hadn't been completely unexpected. She'd been worried ever since Christmas.

Although she and her brothers persuaded their mother to begin counseling, Jill continued to worry.

After talking with Meg, she'd placed a call to Mark. Honolulu seemed a million miles away, but she felt he should know what had happened in Minter.

As for Lance, she hadn't known what to do. His vacation would end tomorrow and he'd be home in another day or two. What difference would a couple of days make?

At last, the plane rolled to a halt and she joined the crush of passengers making their way toward the exit. When she entered the baggage claim area, she easily located Jim. He stood off to one side, waving to her.

"Do you have much luggage, honey?" he asked, after giving her a fatherly kiss on the cheek.

"A little, it should be coming in soon. What's going on with Mom?"

"I can't tell you much. All George said when he called was she'd collapsed at work and he hospitalized her."

"There's my bag," she said, pointing at the carousel.

Jim picked up the bag and led the way to the car. "We'll get you something to eat, then you can go to the hospital."

"I'd rather go and see Mom first. I had something on the plane, so I'm not hungry."

"Did you call the boys?" Jim inquired.

"I don't know where to find Lance, but I did call Mark. I promised to keep him informed."

"Meg wants you to stay with us. We've got your Mom's car for you as well. Her secretary called to say she would be dropping it off at our place."

Jill nodded, before lapsing into a silent contemplation of the day's events.

They finally arrived at the hospital, and Jill hurried into the lobby to check her mother's room number before going upstairs.

She easily located the private room at the end of the hall and saw a man leaving. From the expression on his face, she realized how worried he seemed.

"Have you been in to see my mother?" she asked.

"You must be Jill. My name is Devan Yates, and yes, I just left her. She'll be pleased to have you here with her." He extended his hand to Jill.

"I'm pleased to meet you, Mr. Yates. Have you known my mother long?"

"Since high school. We met, accidentally, at Jim and Meg's New Year's Eve party."

"I see," Jill replied, remembering her mother telling her about the man she'd met, the man who walked her home and stayed for coffee. "How is she?"

"She's confused, very confused."

"Confused? I don't think I understand."

"She should be the one to tell you about it." He reached into his coat pocket, produced a business card, and wrote something on the back. "If you or your mother needs me, here are my home and business numbers. Please don't hesitate to call." With that he turned and left.

For a moment, she stood holding the card and watching him make his way toward the elevator. What did he mean to her mother? He readily admitted they'd only reestablished their relationship on New Year's Eve, yet he looked worried and depressed.

Putting the thoughts of the man whose card she held to the back of her mind, she entered the room. "Mom," she said, when she stood next to the bed, "are you awake?"

Her mother turned to face her. "Oh, Jill, I wish they hadn't called you. This is so ridiculous."

"No, it's not." She bent to kiss her mother's cheek. "I just ran into a man in the hall who looked like he just lost his best friend. He told me his name is Devan Yates. Is he the man who brought you home on New Year's Eve?"

"Yes."

"What did you do to him? He's absolutely devastated."

"I told him I didn't want to see him for a while."

"You're letting a hunk like him get away?" She watched her mother's expression, trying to understand what could have prompted her hospitalization. "Mr. Yates said you would tell me what happened. He thought it best if you explained everything. What is there to explain?"

Jill waited for her mother to take a deep breath before she began. "Devan and I went to high school together. I haven't seen him in almost thirty years, and if you must know, we spent the night together."

"Good for you, Mom. I think you needed that. As a matter-of-fact, I think you need him. What I don't understand is why you're here?"

"Maybe it's best you hear it from me. After today, I'm certain there will be enough gossip going around."

"Gossip? What gossip?"

Jill listened as her mother told her about the morning's confrontation with Jerry, shocked by what she heard. "Not Daddy," she whispered, when her mother finished.

"Yes, Jill, Daddy. Everyone knew, everyone but me. Maybe now you can understand why I asked Devan to wait. I need time to sort out my feelings. Right now, men seem to be pretty low on my list of priorities."

Four

Mark Weston hung up the phone. Jill's voice continued to ring in his ears. "Mom's in the hospital, Mark. I'm flying to Madison in a couple of hours. I'll keep you posted."

Now he weighed this conversation against the one with his mother, less than twenty-four hours earlier. He remembered well the New Year's Day call. She'd seemed so excited about the man she met at Meg's party. She sounded happier than she'd seemed in a year. Her laughter certainly came easier than before.

What did this man do to her? How did he hurt her? Those two questions outweighed everything else in his mind.

He contemplated the situation. He knew what his recommendation would be if one of his men came to him with these concerns. He would tell them to see the chaplain and help them arrange for emergency leave. Of course, he'd just been home, just returned to work this morning. Had he stayed longer he would have been there. Could he have changed what happened? Postponed it, perhaps, but not changed it.

Pushing aside the work on his desk, he made his way to the office of his superior officer, Commander Jackson.

"Come in, Captain, what can I do for you?" Kurt Jackson greeted him.

"It seems I have a problem, sir, a real problem," Mark began, standing stiffly in front of Kurt's desk.

"Sit down and tell me about it."

Mark seated himself in the leather chair facing Kurt. Outside the office, they were good friends. He'd met Kurt in March, when he first arrived in Honolulu. Even with the difference in age, they'd formed a close friendship. In the office, of course, formality seemed mandatory.

He rested his elbows on the arms of the chair and clasped his hands, studying his locked fingers for just a moment before he began to speak.

"I realize I just got back from being home," he paused again, to search for the right words.

"I know you've been worried about your mother, but at the party yesterday, you indicated she was much better," Kurt said, as if trying to read Mark's expression.

"Things were different yesterday. I just received a call from my sister. Mom is in the hospital. Jill said she collapsed at work and they called the paramedics."

"Do you want to go home?"

"I don't know. I'm certainly not needed there, but I'm so far away here. If one of my men came to me with this problem, I'd recommend emergency leave."

"Is that what you want me to recommend, Mark?"

"I don't know what I want," he confessed, still contemplating his clasped hands. "I want to find out about the new man in my mother's life. I want to know what part he played in this. If I find he's the one who brought this on, I want to punch him out."

"I certainly can understand your feelings," Kurt agreed, "but I think you should withhold judgment until you know the whole story. I'll take care of your emergency leave, you make reservations for this afternoon's flight to Chicago. You'll be no good here, with your mind in Wisconsin."

"I guess I needed to hear someone else say what I've been telling myself. Thanks, Kurt. I'll keep you informed as to what is going on."

Once Mark made his reservations, he cleared his desk and drove to the apartment he shared with Keoki. He'd met the Polynesian girl shortly after his arrival in Honolulu. By last Thanksgiving, she'd agreed to marry him and they moved in together. Their wedding, set for April, would be the first time she'd meet his family. Now, worry over his mother's condition made him wonder if she would be able to make the wedding.

"Mark! What are you doing home?" Keoki asked, when he entered the apartment.

He took her in his arms, feeling the need of her body close to his before he could speak. "I have to go back to Wisconsin for a little while, Honey."

"You just got back," she said, pulling away slightly to look into his eyes.

"I know. I got a call from Jill. Mom is in the hospital. Jill said not to come, but I feel the need to be there."

"Of course, you should be there. I'll miss you terribly, but if it were my mom, I'd feel the same way."

"I wish I could take you with me," Mark said, holding her tighter.

"You can hardly afford the flight yourself. Besides, isn't it cold there?"

Mark laughed at her comment. "If you're going to marry me, Keoki, you'd better get used to it. Who knows where we'll be stationed next?"

"I hope it's somewhere warm," she teased.

He held her a moment longer, before he swept her into his arms and headed for the bedroom.

He needed to feel her body beneath him, to vent his emotions by making love to her.

~ * ~

To Mark's surprise, he found himself able to sleep on the flight home. Perhaps his body decided to use this time to steel itself for the days ahead. It was more likely he merely gave in to the exhaustion of his last trans-pacific flight only days earlier.

The touchdown at O'Hare came shortly after five in the morning. By the time he collected his luggage and rented a car, the winter sky had already begun to lighten.

Snow flurries filled the air and he wondered if another blizzard would be hitting soon. Everywhere he looked, snow piles dominated the landscape.

By eight, he pulled into the Prestons' driveway. His ringing of the bell brought Meg to the door. "Mark? What are you doing here? I thought Jill said you weren't going to come home."

Mark kissed Meg's cheek. "That's what I told her, but I had to be here. I couldn't stay in Honolulu, not knowing what could be happening. Have you heard anything from Mom today? Do you know how she's doing?"

"George won't have any blood work back until this morning. Last night he mentioned Anorexia, but I think he was grasping at straws. Come on in. You must be exhausted and hungry. I'll fix you some breakfast."

Mark accepted a cup of coffee and sat at the table while Meg made French toast. He'd forgotten about Meg's French toast with its touch of vanilla and cinnamon. His mom always fixed bacon and eggs or pancakes, while Keoki's idea of breakfast was fresh fruit and English muffins. He promised himself he would teach her the delights of Mid-Western breakfasts when he returned to the islands.

"Where's Jill?" he asked, once Meg set a plate of food in front of him. "I thought she'd be staying with you."

"She is. You just missed her. She left for the hospital at seven forty-five. She has a meeting with George at eight-thirty. He wants to check her over. You know George, he's worried about her overdoing it so early in her pregnancy."

Mark nodded, his mouth too full to make a verbal comment.

"Will you be staying with us, too, Mark?"

"No. Lance will be home in a couple of days, and I'll be more comfortable at the house."

He turned his attention inward, to his own private thoughts, while he finished eating.

"That tasted great, Meg," he said. He leaned across the table and took hold of her hand.

"On New Year's Eve, you set Mom up with someone. Who was he?"

"What does that have to do with anything?"

"I want to know, so I can talk to him."

"Talking to Devan Yates isn't going to do you any good."

"What do you mean?"

"Devan had nothing to do with what happened, nothing at all. He's the best medicine your mom could have right now. When he turned out to be old friend from high school it worked out well. They were comfortable with each other from the first minute Jim introduced them. She laughed and smiled, she seemed closer to her old self than she's been in a year."

Mark shook his head. Ever since he'd received Jill's call, he'd been content to blame the unknown man his mother mentioned on New Year's Day. "So what did happen to Mom?"

"I think you should ask your mother that question," Meg replied.

"Don't beat around the bush, Meg. Tell me what happened."

He watched as she took a deep breath. It made him wonder if she needed to prepare herself before telling him anything. "Your mom had a meeting at the plant with one of the men. In anger he told her what most of us already knew. He informed her your dad had been having an affair for the last three years before he died."

"Dad?"

"Yes, your father. It's not the kind of thing you wanted to hear, is it?"

"Not really. Who in the hell could be so rude as to tell her something like that when the man has been dead for a year?"

"Does it matter?"

"Of course it matters. What good did he think it would do to tell her? Why put her through it?"

"It was a means of retaliation. It's a long story and it doesn't really matter. It only brought to a head, what we knew would happen eventually."

"How can you say that? Mom collapsed. She seemed to be doing so well at Christmas. I just don't see how—"

"Of course, you can't see how something like this could affect her so badly. You saw her for a week. In that time you talked her into getting rid of you dad's clothes and personal belongings. You convinced her to see a counselor and go for a couple of sessions. You didn't see what has been evident to everyone else. You didn't do anything about her physical condition and it finally caught up with her. Believe me, Mark, finding out about your father could turn out to be a blessing in disguise. It's gotten her to take a good look at herself and give George a chance to give her a complete physical."

Mark sat, his hands on his temples, listening to what Meg told him. "I should have taken the full two weeks, I should have been here," he commented absently.

Meg shook her head. "Listen to yourself. Of course, you know what you should have done. It's always so easy to look back and say if only, but things like this rarely come to the forefront when everyone is around. No matter how long you stayed, she still would have collapsed and you'd still be concerned."

"I do want to talk to Yates. Where can I find him?"

Meg sighed deeply. "He works with Jim."

"Now, are you, or are you not, going to tell me who told Mom about Dad?"

"I don't see what good it will do, but it was Jerry Gaines."

Mark clenched his fist and pounded the table, making Meg jump. "I should have known. I never liked him. I remember when him and Karen used to come to the house when we were kids. Jerry and Mom would talk about the things they did in high school. He always made Mom sound like some kind of a wild kid. After they left, Dad always got mad about the things he said. He acted like a bastard then and it doesn't sound as though he's changed much."

"You'd better withhold judgment until you find out how your mom feels about him. They've always been close friends. The worst part of this whole mess is that your dad had his affair with Karen."

Mark sat silently for a moment. How could he accept the things Meg just told him? "Thanks for breakfast," he said, as he pushed back his chair. "I have several things I need to do before I go and see Mom."

~ * ~

Julie awoke. By the light of day, she realized she would have to come to some decisions. Steve was gone and Jerry's revelation had been meant to hurt her. Well, it did. Now she must put all of it behind her. She had to move past the hurt, the betrayal and the lies. She needed to find a way to move past everything and everyone she ever knew in Minter, but move to where? Where she would go, what could she do?

It wasn't like she felt tied to Minter. Anyone could do her job. If she sold the house and the cottage, maybe she could start over somewhere else. It didn't matter where, just so long as no one knew the humiliation she felt over the lie her life with Steve had been.

Over this past year, she'd been able to save a little money. She could take some time off and decide what to do, without being hurt financially.

She would begin by planning a vacation. *Much as I hate to admit it, George is right. A vacation will do me a world of good. Once Jill goes home I'll begin planning in earnest. Jill will have to realize I can care for myself. I've done so for the past year, even though I haven't done a good job of it. As a matter of fact, all I've managed to do is feel sorry for myself and in the process become sick. That will all have to change. The time has come for me to make myself well.*

"Good morning," George said, interrupting her train of thought.

"Well, good morning, Dr. Martin," she replied, flashing a brilliant smile. The small gesture reminded her of the Julie who existed just over a year ago. Until recently, she had begun to think she might have forgotten how to smile with sincerity.

"My, aren't we formal today? It's good to see you smiling," George said, taking her hand in his.

"It feels good to smile. I spent last night making some much-needed decisions about the future. I can't change anything about the past, but tomorrow is a blank slate and only I can fill it. I plan to make all of my tomorrow's positive."

"I couldn't be more pleased. As long as you're changing things, we're going to change your lifestyle as well."

"My lifestyle? You must have my test results. No more needles, I hope."

"I can't promise you anything like that. The tests show you have diabetes. It shouldn't have come as much of a shock to me, but it did. All I had to do was pay closer attention to you on New Year's Eve. As I recall, you were drinking a lot of water, you spent a lot of time in the powder room, and, of course, your weight loss. Those are all signs, which should have tipped me off right away. Your blood sugar is three hundred and forty-two. Normal is in the ninety to one hundred and twenty range."

"But it can be controlled, right?"

George nodded. "I'm going to keep you here for a while and see which medications work for you. If pills don't do it, you'll learn to give yourself injections. You'll be meeting with a dietitian. She'll be changing your eating habits. You'll also start getting plenty of rest, exercise, and eat meals at regular times. These things are all important, but eating on time is especially so. I don't want you skipping meals."

Julie nodded in agreement before George continued. "So, now, what conclusions have you come to?"

"I don't plan to fight you on any of this. I'll do as you say. I'll not let Jerry's hateful words throw me into a tailspin again. It's over, it can't be changed, and I'm certain Karen has gone on to new conquests by now."

"I'm pleased to hear you talking sensibly. I heard Jill got home last night. As a matter of fact, I plan to check her over in a few minutes. What about the boys? Will they be here soon?"

"Jill didn't try calling Lance, he's due home tomorrow or the next day. As for Mark, she told him she'd keep him posted."

Julie studied George's face. Even before he said anything she knew he wondered about Devan.

"You don't have to ask. Devan stopped in last night. He's another of those things I have to come to a decision about, but not right now. He'll have to wait and if he doesn't, well, he doesn't. He woke me up, showed me life is worth living to the fullest."

"Were you careful? You haven't started the change yet."

Julie laughed at the comment. "Believe me, Devan took all the necessary precautions and I plan to do the same. Contrary to the general opinion, I haven't been living in a vacuum this past year. I know the single life ain't all it's cracked up to be, especially the dating scene. I intend to enjoy life, but I plan to do it safely."

"You have changed," George said, approval sounding in his voice. He checked her chart, and continued. "Let me see, you have an appointment with the dietitian at nine and one with Dale at eleven. In between, we'll start your medications and do several more blood tests. As for me, I have sick people to see."

Julie watched him leave the room and lay back against the pillow. Until George mentioned diabetes, she hardly knew what the word meant. Now she felt certain she would soon become an expert on the subject.

~ * ~

Lance hit the button on the garage door opener and watched as the door lifted, almost instantly. Long ago he'd stopped marveling at the mystery of technology. As a child it had been his fascination. With age and education, the magic seemed to disappear.

Having left the Michigan resort yesterday afternoon, he drove throughout the night to get here. The empty garage made Lance laugh at the premonition, which made him cut his vacation short.

As the garage door closed, he decided not to take his skis from the roof just yet. He could do it later, after he showered, had something to eat and grabbed a couple of hours of sleep.

He almost tripped over the box of ornaments in the hall and turned to look out the window. He hadn't noticed the tree at the curb when he drove in, but now he saw it waiting for the trash pick up. Annoyance with his mother began to build. Hadn't they agreed she should wait until he got home to take down the decorations and let him do the heavy work?

Before going upstairs, he checked the refrigerator and smiled to himself at the amount of food. More than likely, his mother stocked it especially for him. Her weight loss attested to the fact she didn't eat properly. He made himself a ham sandwich and took it, along with a can of soda, when he headed upstairs for a shower.

His hunger somewhat satisfied and being refreshed by the shower, he pulled on a pair of jeans and a sweater.

As he left the room, he thought he heard someone downstairs, but dismissed the idea as soon as it entered his mind. No one could be here. He had the house entirely to himself.

Thinking of the skis on his car and the ornaments sitting in the hall, he hurried down the stairs. To his surprise, he came face to face with his older brother.

"Mark? What are you doing here? What's wrong?" Lance asked, noting the exhaustion and concern in his brother's eyes.

"You don't know?" Mark's question came as a surprise.

"Know? Know what? Has something happened to Jill? To Mom?" Lance felt the shock of seeing his brother turn to panic. For what unknown reason had Mark returned home?

"Mom's in the hospital. She collapsed at work yesterday. I just left Meg's house. She hadn't heard any reports since last night, though. There's not much more I can tell you. Jill's here, she spent last night with Jim and Meg, but I'm certain since we're both home she'll move over here tonight. Of course, she thinks I'm still at the base, but I just couldn't stay away and not know what's going on with Mom."

"At least someone called you," Lance said, his voice betraying his disbelief. "How come no one thought to call me? She's my mom too, or have you all forgotten that minor detail?"

"Jill knew you were expected home tomorrow or the next day at the latest. She didn't want to spoil your vacation," Mark replied.

"So what triggered this collapse? I talked to her on New Year's Eve and she sounded like she was on top of the world. What happened?" Lance could hear the anger in his own voice, but he couldn't contain it.

"Calm down, Lance," Mark began. "She had a meeting yesterday at work. There was a discussion that became heated and she collapsed."

"Do I have to guess who she had the discussion with, or are you going to tell me?" Lance demanded when his brother paused for a moment.

"I wasn't planning to keep anything from you. Mom had the meeting with Jerry Gaines."

"That bastard!" Lance spat. "I suppose he had the balls to tell her about Dad and Karen."

"You knew?" Mark shouted.

"Sure, who didn't?"

"Mom, Jill, me, why didn't you tell me? How long have you known?"

Lance stared silently at his brother for a moment. "Come out to the kitchen, Mark, I'll make us some coffee and we can talk about this."

Although Lance knew his brother wanted to protest, he started for the kitchen. He needed time to put his thoughts into coherent words. He could feel the electricity in the air, the questions he knew Mark wanted to ask.

"How long have I known?" Lance repeated his brother's question, as he set two cups of coffee on the table. "I've known for three years now. I heard rumors when I came home for Christmas vacation my freshman year. I didn't say anything then, because I didn't want to believe something like that about Dad.

"By summer vacation, I couldn't ignore them anymore. I confronted him when he took me to Devil's Lake camping for the weekend. Dad called it a real guy thing, even though he knew how much I hate camping and hiking."

"So what did he say? How did he handle it?" Mark probed.

"He told me it was none of my goddamn business, he'd do what he wanted, when he wanted. When I asked him about Mom, he said she had her work and he needed more."

Lance paused again, watching the impact of his words on his brother's face. Although Mark remained dry-eyed, Lance could hear the tears in his voice.

"I always thought Dad was the greatest guy in the world. I just can't believe Mom never knew.

"I know what you're saying. I never felt the same about him after that weekend. As for telling you and Jill, you were just too far away. Besides, if the two of you knew, Mom would have found out. I was positive she didn't know about it. Otherwise, she wouldn't have stayed."

They both sat, each lost in his own thoughts, until they finished their coffee.

"I'm going up and take a shower," Mark said, before pushing his chair away from the kitchen table.

While Mark showered, Lance poured himself another cup of coffee, then sat down in the living room to contemplate the situation

In his mind, he relived the camping trip to Devil's Lake. His father had been so smug about the affair. "Grow up, Lance," he could hear his father saying. "This is the nineties. Fidelity went out with *Father Knows Best* and *Leave It To Beaver*. Men have been cheating on their wives since time began. No man should be chained to one woman for a lifetime. That's a wedding ring she gives you, not a ball and chain."

When he had remained silent, his father continued. "Don't look at me that way, boy. You're no angel and neither is your brother. I'm certain you've both laid more broads than you care to count."

"Low blow, Dad. I'm single, so is Mark. It doesn't make it right, but at least I'm not married. Twenty-five years of marriage, doesn't that mean anything to you?"

"Of course, it does. It means I'm bored as hell. Your mother is a great woman and she throws one hell of a party, but in bed she's a lump. I need excitement and Karen gives it to me. As long as your mom doesn't know, who am I hurting?"

Lance took a long drink of coffee, feeling again the anger of three years ago.

"Damn you!" he shouted. "Damn you to hell. Why?" Without thinking, he threw the coffee mug against the bricks of the fireplace.

~ * ~

Mark finished dressing and stood on the top step, when his brother's words preceded the sound of shattering glass. Hurrying down the stairs, he saw Lance leaning against the fireplace, his shoulders shaking as he sobbed.

"Are you all right, Lance?" Mark asked, placing his hand on his younger brother's shoulder.

Lance turned to face Mark, his cheeks streaked with tears. As Mark stared into his eyes, he remembered how Lance had stood dry-eyed at the funeral, while both Jill and himself cried.

"Why Mark? Why did Dad feel he had to cheat on Mom?" Lance asked, not bothering to wipe his eyes.

"I don't know. It's past history now. Are you ready to go?"

Lance looked down at the remains of the shattered ceramic mug on the brick hearth.

"We can clean this up later," Mark assured him. "Let's go."

"Go?" Lance repeated. "Oh, yeah, to the hospital. Sure, I'm ready."

"Not to the hospital. I want to go to the plant first. I need to see Jerry Gaines."

Lance came to full attention at Mark's words. "Are you sure?"

"Positive," Mark replied, pulling on a ski jacket from the hall closet.

Both men kept to themselves as they drove across town and at last parked in the space marked *VISITOR* in the parking lot.

Inside the building, in the reception area of the office, they were surprised to be met by Tom Randall.

"Mark? Lance? When did you two get in?"

"This morning," Mark replied. "Where will we find Jerry Gaines?"

"I don't think it's wise for you to see him," Tom cautioned.

"I do. Will you find him for me, or will I have to go out into the plant and find him myself?"

"You and Lance go up to your mother's office. I'll have him paged."

Mark thanked Tom, and with Lance, headed for the second floor. Inside the office, he half expected to be greeted by his mother rather then Roxie.

"Mark, Lance, I certainly didn't expect to see you here. Jill said—"

"I know, Jill told you I wouldn't be coming home and Lance wasn't expected this early, but we're here."

"Jerry Gaines, Jerry Gaines, green line," Tom's voice came over the P.A. system.

"I wonder what Tom's paging Jerry for?" Roxie asked absently.

"Mark asked to see him," Lance said, answering the question for which they knew she expected no answer.

"Do you think that's wise?" she inquired.

Mark checked his anger. If one more person questioned his reasoning or his right to be here, he might just lash out.

"Maybe not, but he's the reason Mom's in the hospital. I have to talk to him."

"Whatever you say," Roxie said, shaking her head in disagreement. "You can wait in her office."

When they were alone, Lance started to voice his own concerns, but Mark spoke, interrupting him. "Look, Lance, I know what you're going to say. Maybe everyone is right, but until I have some answers, I can't even begin to rationalize this situation."

Before he could say more, he saw Lance looking intently at something on the desk. Turning his attention to follow his brother's gaze, he noticed the arrangement of roses, the card still secure in the forked plastic holder. He reached out to take the card and read the note. The name Devan jumped out at him and seemed to mock him. "This whole fiasco began with a man named Devan Yates," he said, hardly realizing he'd put voice to his thoughts.

"Who?" Lance asked.

"Devan Yates. Mom's date for New Year's Eve. Everything was just fine until—"

"Until she met him?" Lance finished Mark's statement as a question "I don't think so. I talked to her on New Year's Eve and she sounded great. I think he's good for her."

"You didn't even know his name until I mentioned it just now," Mark snapped.

"Maybe I didn't know his name, but I do know she sounded happy for the first time in a year. Mom needs more than us and this job. She needs to get out and meet new people. I, for one, hope Devan Yates becomes very special to her."

Mark contemplated his brother's words. "Do you think they..."

"Slept together?" Lance asked, laughing for the first time. "Not our Mom, she's too straight."

"I don't know, look at this card. It doesn't read like he came for tea and crumpets to me."

Before Lance could look at the card, Jerry entered the room. He nodded his acknowledgment to both young men. "How's your mother?" he asked.

"We don't know. We haven't been to the hospital, yet," Mark answered.

"I'm sure you both know what happened yesterday. I honestly thought Julie knew what went on between your dad and Karen. It wasn't a secret, for God's sake. Julie was coming down hard on me and I knew she planned to put me on probation. I thought I had to do something to stop it, so I retaliated the only way I knew how."

"Do you think she would have stayed with him if she knew?" Mark snapped.

"I don't know. I stayed with Karen, if that gives you any indication. Sometimes it's easier to stay with the familiar rather than strike out on your own. I hope neither of you ever has to experience anything like this first hand."

"Is that how Karen feels about your affairs?" Lance questioned.

"Right now, yes it is."

"Does she know what you did to Mom?" Lance continued, his usually calm voice having an edge of anger.

"We talked about it last night. We both agreed your mom has no good reason to like me right now. I honestly expected one of you to land the first punch. Just remember, Julie and I go back a long way. We went to high school together. We even got in trouble together, her and me, and Sandy and Devan."

Mark exchanged a questioning look with his brother. *There it was,* Mark thought to himself, knowing Lance's thoughts to be the same, *the name Devan Yates.* "Just who the hell is Devan Yates?" he demanded.

"One of the nicest guys you'll ever get to meet. I hope he and Julie get together. They were close friends in school and now he's back in town. I think he's good for her. Look guys, I'd do anything in the world to take yesterday back, but I can't. Yesterday is over and what was said can't be changed. The only thing I can do is hope everything goes well for her. Maybe, someday, we can be friends again. Do you have any idea what I'm trying to tell you?"

Mark studied Jerry's face. The concern appeared to be genuine and knowing his mother's loyalty to her friends, he knew what transpired the day before had been equally devastating for both of them. "You know, Jerry, I think I do."

Jerry tentatively extended his hand and Mark accepted it, his own grip firm and reassuring. "Tell Julie I'm sorry. I'm not going to try to go to the hospital. Just tell her I'm thinking about her."

"We're sorry we pulled you out of work, but we had to clear the air. I'm sure you can understand our motives," Mark replied.

Jerry nodded, then left the room without saying anything more.

Mark turned toward the desk and reached for the vase of roses. Earlier, he had returned the card to its plastic holder. Now he pulled it free and put it in his pocket. "We'll give these to Roxie. I'm certain she'll enjoy them. If we try to take them to the hospital, they'll freeze."

When they got back in the car, Mark looked at Lance. "Did you really look at those flowers? A dozen roses, assorted colors, they had to cost an arm and a leg. I think the next place I want to go is to meet Devan Yates."

"What good will it do?" Lance asked. "I think we should go to the hospital."

"Not just yet. Jill's there and Mom doesn't know we're in town. We won't be missed."

They drove across town in silence until they reached the building that housed Devan's office.

"Is Mr. Yates in?" Mark asked the receptionist.

"May I tell him who's here?" the girl asked.

"Mark and Lance Weston."

"Do you have an appointment?"

"Of course we don't," Lance said, leaning across the desk. "If we did, we would know if he was in. Now, it's very important we get in to see him. He'll know who we are."

They waited while the girl placed a call to Devan's secretary.

"You're to go right up," she said, when she hung up the phone. "Take the elevator to the third floor. It's the fourth door on your left."

They thanked her and headed for the elevator and the confrontation with Devan.

~ * ~

Devan sat at his desk waiting for Julie's sons to come to his office. He knew what they'd ask, what they'd want to know. What would he tell them? It certainly wasn't his place to inform her sons they'd spent New Year's Eve, as well as New Year's Day, together.

He contemplated his feelings for Julie. In his thoughts, he professed his love for her. To his surprise, it seemed natural. Perhaps he'd always loved Julie Morgan. In high school, they'd been close friends, confidants. Maybe love was being comfortable with someone; being able to talk to them, having them understand what you were talking about; to be your friend, no matter what. If that were the case, then the physical thing could be an added bonus.

He turned his thoughts to Missy. The physical thing had been all they shared, and in the end it wasn't enough.

"Mark and Lance Weston are here to see you, Mr. Yates," his secretary's voice sounded over the intercom.

Devan picked up his phone to give his reply. Even though he could have responded without ever picking up the receiver, he hated talking on speakerphones. "Send them in." He hung up and took a deep breath to steel himself for the meeting to come.

The two men who entered the office struck him as confident individuals. They both stood well over six feet tall. As he remembered, Steve had been tall and slender, like the younger of the two men. The older man was heavier, more like Julie's brother, Jack.

"Mark, Lance," Devan said, getting to his feet and extending his hand. "Your mother has told me a lot about both of you."

"I wish we could say the same," the older man said, his voice sounding authoritative.

This man, Devan decided, *was used to command.*

"Until today, we didn't even know your name. Just what happened on New Year's Eve?"

"I honestly don't think you have any right to ask that question. What happened on New Year's Eve is between your mother and me. If you're thinking I did something to hurt her, you're wrong. Julie's

56

special, very special. If anyone hurt her, it was your father. Unfortunately, we're all suffering because of it." He watched the impact of his words on the two of them. Surely, they knew the cause of Julie's hospitalization and with that information maybe they had even met with Jerry by now. If that were the case, he wondered if they saw the roses and read the card?

As though Mark could read his mind, he said, "We saw the roses you sent her. They're beautiful. It's the card that bothers me."

Devan looked at the younger man. Had he read the card and his brother's use of the word 'me' stood for them both, or was he ignorant of the words he chose when he sent the flowers?

"The card meant exactly what it said. I'd been invited to a party, which I knew would be terribly boring. To my surprise, I saw a beautiful woman and she turned out to be your mother. To become reacquainted with someone from the past, someone who had been my best friend in high school, became my good fortune. She made the evening special, very special. I'd hoped we would again become good friends, now I don't know where I stand."

"Where do you want to stand?" Lance asked.

"I'll be honest. I've missed a lot by not having Julie in my life. Your father was very lucky to have had her."

"Apparently he didn't think so," Lance commented, his voice laced with sarcasm.

"Let me rephrase that, then. He was a very lucky man and he didn't even know it. Julie is a beautiful, sensual woman, and he was a fool to cheat on her. I can't change that anymore than I can change what you're thinking about me."

"Maybe you can't," Mark said. "I still want to know what you're thinking about Mom?"

Devan took a deep breath. Could he put into words what he knew to be the truth? "I'm falling in love with her. I love her so much, that if she wants me to step aside, I will. Does that answer your question?"

"You expect us to believe you've fallen in love with her in just three days?" Lance asked.

"I don't expect you to believe anything."

"So where were you all these years?" Mark inquired. "If you and Mom were so close, why haven't we ever heard her talk about you?"

"I've been living my life. There was college, marriage, family, career, all of which meant very little in the end. My education found my wife and my career lost her. As for my sons, I wish they felt as close to me as you do to Julie. She's very lucky to have you. I hope she realizes it. I think you need to go to your mother now. She needs you. Just don't push her on this."

For the first time, Mark seemed to relax, and Devan saw Julie's smile duplicated. "Thank you for being frank with us. I have to admit, I've harbored some nasty thoughts about you in the past twenty-four hours."

"I would imagine you did. I know Julie told you about meeting me. If she were my mother, I'd feel the same way. She's a very special lady and I'd never hurt her for anything in the world."

"I hope you're right, Mr. Yates," Mark said. "I never thought my dad or Jerry would hurt her either, but they did. No one can say never and mean it. Never is a long time and we can't predict what might happen tomorrow."

Devan marveled at the wisdom of the words. "You're right, of course. I do want you to know I care deeply for her. I would appreciate it if you'd call me Devan."

Both young men stared at him, their features softened a bit from when they first entered the office.

"Even if I don't hear from Julie," he continued, when his statement met with silence, "I'd appreciate being kept informed. I promised her I'd stay away until she's ready to see me. It won't be the easiest thing I've ever done, but I gave her my word."

They spoke for several more minutes, every mention of Julie, every word of concern tore at Devan's very being. Why had he come back to Minter? Why had he met her on New Year's Eve? Why had he allowed himself to fall in love with her?

When the young men left his office, he asked himself more questions. Could he give up Julie as easily as he made it sound? Did he want to give her up? In his heart, he knew the answer to both questions had to be no. Unfortunately, he'd put the ball in her court, and now he must abide by her decision.

Five

Julie waited for Jill to arrive and contemplated all the information George and the dietitian had given her. She realized diabetes meant a change in lifestyle, a change in diet, but it wasn't nearly as bad as it could have been. She could live with the diet, and as for the change in lifestyle, she'd just have to adjust.

How insignificant these adjustments seemed compared with the ones she made this past year, these past days. If anyone would have told her she would survive so many tragedies in so short a period of time, she would have never believed it.

Turning her thoughts to the here and now, she hoped Jill remembered the things she asked her to bring, especially her book. In the few short minutes she'd been alone, she found daytime television not to her liking. Although the news shows were informative, every talk show seemed to feature men who cheated on their wives, lonely widows who craved affairs, and women whose friends tried to protect them from the hurtful actions perpetrated against them.

"Good morning, Mom," Jill said, entering the room.

"Good morning, honey. Did George give you a clean bill of health?"

Jill leaned over and kissed Julie's cheek. "I'm just fine. George is over cautious."

"It makes him feel better. You know he always thought you were special."

"He told me you have diabetes. How are you handling it?"

"I'm not hysterical, if that's what you mean. I'm putting it into perspective. I still have miles to go and lots to learn, though."

"You'll do just great. Remember Kelly, my roommate in college?"

Julie nodded, thinking of the slightly heavy girl with auburn hair. As she recalled, Kelly maintained high grades and always seemed to be active in sports.

"She has diabetes. I learned a lot about it when we lived together. I'm glad I was receptive to what she was going through then. I feel prepared to help you through this now."

Julie agreed. Although she had originally been distressed to see her daughter, she knew she needed her in Minter and not fifteen hundred miles away in Denver.

"You said you called Mark," Julie commented, changing the subject. "Did you ever reach Lance?"

"No. I decided to wait. He'll be home tomorrow or the next day. Why ruin his last Christmas vacation?"

While she had been talking, Jill reached into the bag she carried and pulled out nightgowns, soap, shampoo, and two books.

Once her personal articles were put away, Julie tried to explain her thoughts to her daughter.

"I'm planning to take some time off, a six-week leave of absence from work. I need to put things into their proper perspective. I'm also planning to sell the house."

"Sell the house?" Jill echoed.

"Don't sound so surprised. It's far too large for me. Why do I need five bedrooms with you kids all grown and settled? The house needs a family and kids. I think I'm going to get a condo."

"A condo? It does sound like a good idea, but isn't it going to take six months to buy a condo?"

"No, but it might take me six months to decide where to buy a condo. I don't know if I want to stay in Minter. Maybe I'll do some traveling, find out what life is like somewhere else, and find out who Julie Weston really is."

The look on Jill's face became one of bewilderment. "I don't understand, Mom."

Julie smiled. How could she expect Jill to understand what her life had been like? "When I turned eighteen, I graduated from high school on Thursday night and got married on Saturday afternoon. From then on, I became used to being referred to as Steve's wife or the kids' mother. When I went to school and got my job, I became a real person. Now I'm not so certain I know who or what I became."

"So how do you plan to find yourself?"

"I'm not sure. I do know once you go home, where you belong, I'll be doing some heavy duty planning."

"Why not go to the cottage? It would be the perfect get away for you. There certainly wouldn't be anything or anyone to distract you."

Julie sighed. "Of all places, not the cottage. I'm trying to get away from your father, not run into him. I don't expect you to understand."

Before Jill could reply, they heard a rap at the door. "Good morning, Julie," Dale Bentz said, entering the room

"It's good to see you," Julie replied. "Dale Bentz, this is my daughter, Jill Lansing."

"It's a pleasure, Jill," Dale said, shaking her hand. "Here's my card. Please contact me soon. I'd like meet with you and your brothers before you leave. I need to talk to you about what's going on in your mom's life right now."

"I see no problem with seeing you, along with my brother, Lance, but my older brother, Mark, is stationed in Honolulu and won't be coming home."

Dale knotted his eyebrows. "It might mean a phone call, but I can arrange it."

Jill nodded, then leaned over to again kiss her mother's cheek. "I'm going down to call Karl.

"Have a good session."

Once Jill left the room, Dale pulled a chair next to Julie's bed. "So, what's been going on?" he asked.

"I thought George would have filled you in by now." She found herself surprised by the lack of sarcasm in her voice.

"He did. Now I want to hear how you feel about what happened. How do you view the last couple of days?"

"I'm hurt, angry, betrayed. I won't kid you, I have a lot of bad feelings about Steve and Jerry, about all men for that matter, and I'm scared."

"I can understand your apprehensions. What do you plan to do about it? You can't go on hating men, so what's the first step you plan to take?"

Julie looked at Dale's tape recorder and weighed her words carefully. "I don't know. Sell the house, for starters."

"It sounds like a positive move. It isn't safe anymore, is it?"

"It certainly isn't. I haven't given it much thought, but you're right. I guess you could say the same thing about the cottage at the lake."

"A lake cottage? It sounds like a nice getaway."

"It sounds like hell."

"It does? Why don't you tell me about it?"

Julie laughed, "Tell you about it? Where should I start? The cottage, like everything else in our marriage, belonged to Steve, for Steve's enjoyment. I've always thought about it that way, but I've been afraid to say it out loud. I thought Steve and I were the perfect couple and things like this were better left unsaid. I guess I didn't want to rock the boat." She paused, the relief she'd experienced at saying the words surprised her.

"It all started on our honeymoon. I thought we were going to Chicago or Milwaukee or Madison, to stay in a hotel. Instead, Steve used our wedding money to buy camping equipment and we went to Devil's Lake. When the kids started coming along, he bought a camping trailer.

"When they got older, he came home one day with a cottage."

"What do you mean he came home with a cottage?" Dale interrupted.

"Steve had been out of town on business, when he came home on Thursday night, he announced he planned to sell the trailer. I thought he'd decided to take us on a real vacation for a change. Let the kids see the Grand Canyon, the Black Hills, or Yellowstone. Instead he threw a packet of pictures on the table. Horrified is the only word I can think of to describe my feelings. 'The Cottage' is almost as large as my house here in Minter. It came completely furnished and even had a washer and dryer. It became an obsession with Steve."

"What do you mean, an obsession?" Dale again interrupted.

Julie never hesitated in her answer, as though talking about the cottage would lessen the load she carried. "Steve liked to fish and so did the boys. Jill liked the boys she met on the beach. During the summer, we spent every weekend as well as our vacation there. Before I went to work, I would pack the car on Friday and unpack on Monday. Once I started working, I did it on Thursday nights and Monday nights. It became part of my job, something Steve expected of me. In the winter we would go up for at least two or three weekends as well as part of the week between Christmas and New Years. Steve and the kids loved the cross country skiing and the ice fishing."

"What did you do at the lake?" Dale asked.

"I unpacked the car, cleaned the cottage, and kept up the lawn. A few summers I even got to paint the damn thing. Of course, in my free time, I did a lot of reading, fancy work and sometimes, at night, I'd go swimming. You must remember I certainly couldn't have been called a beauty in a bathing suit. Fifty pounds makes quite a difference."

"So, what would you have preferred your vacations and weekends to be like?" Dale inquired.

"Something more exciting than housework, lawn work and chasing kids. I always wanted to go to New York City, or Florida, to see the natural wonders other than the Dells or Devil's Lake and to go away without the kids. Needless to say, Steve couldn't understand why I wanted to do anything other than relax at the cottage!"

~ * ~

Jill wondered why Dale Bentz would want to meet with her and Lance. Understanding her mother's condition seemed to be a lame excuse.

Still considering Dale's words, she placed a call to Karl's office. She promised to call this morning and inform him of George's findings, both for her mother and herself.

"Hi, Honey," Karl greeted her. "How are things this morning?"

Jill paused, just a moment. *How are things,* she asked herself. "Better, I guess. Mom's spirits are much higher than they were last night."

"I hear a but," Karl said.

"I guess you do. I should start from the beginning. George found Mom has diabetes. I should have considered it when we saw her at Christmas. He told her she'd need to change her lifestyle and she took him seriously. She's planning to take a vacation and wants to sell the house."

"Sell the house?" Karl asked, repeating her words as a question.

"She dropped her little bombshell on me when I first walked into the room. I can understand her decision. After what she told me last night, it would be hard for her to stay there. It's just that I've never known any other home. I can't imagine her living anywhere else."

"Just remember, everyone has to change," Karl assured her. "Has Lance gotten home yet?"

"No. I told you, I have no reason to expect him for another day or two. As soon as we hang up, though, I do plan to call Mark and update him."

"I know how hard it is for him," Karl said. "I wish I could be with you and your mom right now. I know he must feel the same. Honolulu is so far away when there's an emergency like this. I hate to hang up, but I do have to get back to work. I miss you like crazy, but I want you to stay as long as is necessary. Give Mom my love."

"I will," Jill promised, before ending the conversation.

She hung up the phone and started to search in her purse for Mark's office number. She jumped when someone touched her shoulder. She turned, startled to see Mark standing behind her. After embracing him, she found her voice. "I can't believe you're here. I was just getting ready to call you."

"I couldn't stay away. I noticed you standing here when I started toward the desk to get Mom's room number. So, what's going on?"

"Mom's very lucky. George found diabetes. She's already met with the dietitian and she's having a session with the counselor right now."

"How about you?"

"I'm healthy as a horse and so is Junior. George insisted on checking me over this morning."

"Since we can't see Mom right now, let's go down to the cafeteria. Lance is already down there, he says he's starving."

"Lance? Is he home, too?"

"He got in about the same time I did. He said he had a funny feeling and cut his vacation short to get home."

Jill allowed Mark to escort her to the cafeteria, but all the while her mind spun. How could she tell her brothers what brought on their mother's collapse? How could she explain their father's affair or the significance of Devan Yates in their mother's life?

Once they filled their plates, they saw Lance already occupying a table near the windows. Before they sat down, he got to his feet to embrace Jill.

Again the questions about their mother were asked and answered. When Jill finished relaying the information to Lance, she broached the subject, which so bothered her.

"There's something else you should know," she started.

"It you're talking about Dad's relationship with Karen Gaines and Mom's date with Devan Yates, we already know," Mark assured her.

"How?"

"I've known about Dad almost since the beginning of the affair," Lance said. "Mark stopped at Meg's this morning and she told him the rest. We've already seen Jerry as well as Devan."

"Did you cause a scene? You two didn't do anything foolish, did you?"

Mark laughed. "Of course not. Jerry honestly thought Mom knew about the affair. He figured she planned to come down on him for his own affairs and thought her actions hypocritical if that were the case."

"So," Jill said, "Jerry, explained his actions to your satisfaction. I don't think I can accept his story so easily. Changing the subject, what did you think of Devan Yates?"

"I must say," Mark began, "he's an interesting man."

"Very interesting," Jill agreed. "I don't think Mom's being fair to him."

"Do you think—" Lance began, Jill's laughter stopping him mid sentence.

"Do I think they slept together? I don't have to think about it, I know they did. Mom told me so."

"Well, you seem unconcerned. I suppose you approve," Mark said, his voice sounding instantly angry.

Jill reached across the table and took his hand in hers. "Be realistic, Mark, this is the twenty-first century. You and Keoki sleep together, don't you?"

"Of course we do, but we're different."

"Just how are you different?" Lance asked. "I've slept with girls I've just met, so have you. Mom's still young, why should she be alone for the rest of her life?"

"Okay! Okay!" Mark said, holding up his hands. "I never could stand up to the two of you when you ganged up on me."

"So," Jill said, "what do you think of Devan?"

Mark shook his head. "I don't know. I came prepared to hate him and instead I found I like him. I actually feel sorry for him. When he talks about Mom, he looks like a hurt puppy."

"I know. I saw it last night when he left her room."

Lance finished the last of his pie, before he spoke again. "I'm still confused about all of this. I don't know what to make of the man. I just hope he doesn't try to hurt her. Dad's done a good enough job without having a stranger do the same thing."

~ * ~

Julie tried to concentrate on her book, but found herself dwelling on her conversation with Dale.

The discussion about the cottage caught her off guard. Over the past months she had thought about the cottage, even considered selling it, but Steve always stood in her way. As much as she disliked the place, it had been Steve's pride and joy. When she thought she still loved him, she couldn't bring herself to part with it. How quickly things changed. How relieved she felt after making the break and admitting her true feelings.

"Hi, Mom, I'm back," Jill said, interrupting Julie's thought. "I brought you some more company."

"Who did you run into in the hall? Is Meg prowling around out there?"

"No, Mom, she ran into us," Mark said, as he and Lance entered the room.

"But I thought—"

"We weren't coming home. I know, so did everyone else. I couldn't stay away and Lance had a premonition and cut his vacation short."

"I don't know why," Lance began, "I just knew I had to get home. I left late yesterday afternoon and drove all night. Finding out you were here made me certain I'd come to the right decision."

"What am I ever going to do with you? You certainly don't need to be hovering at my bedside, you know. I don't plan to do anything drastic like die on you. Of course, since you're here, Jill must have told you everything that's been going on."

"I already knew," Lance said, "and Meg told Mark when he first got here. We've been to see Jerry and your friend, Devan. We wanted someone to blame and they seemed to be the most likely choices.

Instead, we found out what I already knew. There's no one to blame but Dad."

"I wish Lance had told me about this months ago," Mark began, "maybe I could have..."

"Could have what, Mark?" Julie asked. "Knowing wouldn't have changed anything."

She wished she could erase the ugly words her children had heard, wished she could change the things their father did, but she couldn't. From the corner of her eyes, she saw the expression on her younger son's face. His eyes, those expressive eyes, hid nothing. "How long have you known about your dad, Lance?"

"Too long, Mom. Maybe I should have told you, saved you this pain, but I didn't want to be the one to hurt you. When Dad died, I thought it didn't matter anymore. I shouldn't have let sleeping dogs lie."

Julie's eyes filled with tears. From the expressions on her sons' faces, she knew Steve's actions had hurt more than herself. Mark's anger boiled over into his stormy disposition and Lance's look of depression said more than words.

"Let's drop the past for a minute," Mark suggested. "Jill says you want to sell the house. I don't understand why."

"How can I explain it to you? Your father built the house, just like he bought the cottage. Both places hold a lot of memories. A week ago, those memories were so precious and now they hurt too much to remember them."

"What are you trying to tell us, Mom? Are you planning to sell the cottage as well as the house?" Lance demanded.

Julie looked toward Jill. "I thought you realized I wanted to sell the cottage when we talked earlier."

"But why?" Mark persisted.

"Why?" Julie echoed. "Surely you knew I never enjoyed going there. You kids and your dad thought it a great get away because you could swim and fish and lay in the sun. It became the perfect retreat, but I never saw you mowing the lawn or weeding the flowers. None of you even helped me when I had to paint it."

"Daddy always said you enjoyed the gardening and—"

"And what, Jill?" Julie interrupted. "Your dad knew how much I wanted a real vacation, he just didn't want to give up his pleasures for me."

"We never knew," Lance said, comforting her as the tears rolled down her cheeks. "We always thought you loved the cottage as much as we did. When you didn't want to go up there last summer, I thought you... oh, never mind. We can't change the past, but together we can make the future better."

Julie wiped her eyes. "You bet we'll make things better! We'll start by you kids going back to where you belong. Lance, you need to get back to school; Jill, you have my grandchild and your husband to worry about; and Mark, you need to get back to Keoki and plan your wedding."

"We will," Mark promised, "but before we do, we want to spend some quality time with you. We all need to take the time to get to know each other again."

Six

Julie waited for Mark and Lance to come to her room. Dale had left several minutes earlier. She'd reluctantly promised she would make an appointment as soon as the kids went home and her life returned to normal. She didn't know why he thought she still needed his help.

Hadn't she faced the reality of Steve's death as well as his infidelity? What could Dale possibly do for her now? She had to work these things out for herself, but since both Dale and George insisted on visits, why not humor them?

"Are you ready to go home, my lady?" Lance's voice broke her concentration. She focused on the wheelchair he pushed into the room. "Your chariot awaits."

Julie laughed at the sight of the chair, then sobered when she saw the expression on Mark's face. "Do I have to be wheeled out of here?" she asked.

"Hospital regulations, Mom," Mark assured her. "Lance can go back and get a cart for your flowers, then we'll be ready to go."

When they pulled into the cul-de-sac, Julie shuddered. Nothing had changed. The house she shared with Steve looked no different than it did just days earlier. She wondered what she expected. Should she have seen ghosts streaming from the windows or jagged spears of lightning striking the house the way she remembered one of the scenes from *Psycho*?

Although she hadn't seen Mark reach for the garage door opener, she knew he'd pushed the button when the double door went up. Once they parked, she hesitated for just a moment before getting out of the car and entering the kitchen.

Jill stood at the stove, stirring a bubbling pot of chili and Julie noticed the neatly set table with a freshly baked loaf of bread on a plate in the middle.

"You look wonderful, Mom," Jill said, embracing Julie. "Lunch is ready. Once the boys get your bags and flowers in, we can eat."

Conversation at lunch remained light, but Julie knew her kids well enough to realize they had more on their minds than idle chatter.

Once they finished lunch and the dishes were loaded into the dishwasher, Julie relaxed in the living room. Someone had laid a fire in the fireplace. Outside the patio door a light snow shower dropped sparkling crystals onto the already snow covered lawn.

"You three look like you did when you were little and had done something wrong. What's up?" Julie finally asked.

"We called Bill and Evelyn last night," Mark said. "We want you to go to the cottage with us next week. Bill said he'd open it up for us."

"The cottage?" Julie questioned, her mind racing. She hadn't thought about Bill and Evelyn Moore, the people who owned the house next to the cottage, in the past year. Mentally she tried to remember if anyone called them when Steve died, if they even sent a card.

"Yes, Mom, the cottage. We want to see it again and get some things before you sell it. We talked to your counselor and he agrees you should go with us."

"I suppose you're right," she sighed, knowing herself to be outnumbered. "If I intend to sell it, I'll need to clean things out."

~ * ~

The trip to the lake resembled no trip they had ever taken previously. Mark insisted an early start would not be necessary and the packing could be done leisurely in the morning. When Julie said she could help, Lance escorted her into the living room and insisted she relax.

Midmorning passed before they left Minter. Instead of the hurried pace Steve always set, Mark took his time, allowing them to enjoy the winter wonderland around them as they traveled.

The trip Steve prided himself upon making in less than an hour and a half stretched into more than two hours.

After stopping in town for lunch, they took the road to the lake. With each familiar landmark, Julie tensed. She knew she was being ridiculous, but she couldn't help herself. The cottage was only a house, an inanimate object, but it terrified her.

Mark pulled the car into the already clean driveway and waited for just a moment, giving her time to assess the house in front of her.

"Are you all right, Mom?" Lance asked.

"I think so. Let's go in," Julie replied.

Julie led the way up the sidewalk to the front door. As she did, she hunted in her purse for her key. Before she could fit it into the lock, Mark took it from her hand.

"Let me open it, Mom," he said.

When the door swung open, Mark led the way into the already warm house.

Julie closed her eyes, momentarily, remembering the last time she'd been here. Although she'd been exhausted from Jill's early December wedding as well as the holiday preparations and parties, Steve insisted they go to the cottage for Christmas. He said since only Lance would be home, it would be fun to be at the cottage. While Julie worked preparing Christmas dinner in the small, less well equipped kitchen, Steve and Lance set up the artificial tree. At the time, she told herself Christmas at the cottage would be an adventure. Now, she saw it as hard work.

Before going into the living room, they hung their coats in the hall closet. As Julie rounded the corner, the decorated Christmas tree caught her attention. It seemed to mock her in its domination of the living room. It stood, bathed in the weak light of the January afternoon, a tree with bright balls and tinsel, standing in contrast to the natural beauty of the snow covered lawn leading to the frozen lake. It became a blatant reminder of her last visit to the cottage.

Lance put voice to the words everyone wanted to say. "Why didn't you take it down?"

"Your father said we'd have plenty of time to do it the next time we came up, only we never had a next time." Julie seated herself in a comfortable chair and studied the tree, reliving the memory of her last visit to the cottage.

"Whatever prompted Daddy to come to the cottage for Christmas Day?" Jill asked.

"You and Mark were on your own, Christmas with just the three of us was meant to be an adventure, a time to change old habits. He thought this would be fun for a change. He did some cross country skiing and I had plenty to do to keep me busy."

"You always had plenty to keep you busy up here," Jill said. "As I look back on it, I never saw you relax."

"I know you didn't," Julie replied. "I never enjoyed coming here. I knew there were too many things at home to do and too many places I wanted to see. I longed for a real vacation. My parents used to take your Uncle Jack and me on wonderful trips when we were young. As I think about it now, we went on a shoestring, camping out rather than staying in expensive hotels, but I have wonderful memories of those days. We went to the Grand Canyon and the Black Hills and enjoyed the natural beauty of this country. I wanted to take you kids to places like those, but this cottage always got in the way."

"Well, I know why he wanted to come up here for Christmas," Lance said, his voice laced with anger. "Why do you think I left on the twenty-sixth?"

"What do you mean?" Mark questioned.

"Karen and Jerry went to Florida for the holidays last year. Dad didn't hide the fact from me. He didn't want to be in Minter without her. I bet if you check the phone bill, you'd find several calls to Florida, made from here."

"Is Lance right, Mom?" Mark asked.

"I wouldn't know. I never saw any of the household bills. As a matter-of-fact, I still don't. I have no idea what it costs to live in my own house. The firm takes care of it."

"When you get back, I think it's time you made some changes," Mark said. "I don't like the idea of Dad's firm knowing your every move. It seems like they know more about your business than you do."

Julie looked down at her clasped hands. "I guess they do. They administer your father's income from the firm, as well as his profit sharing. They also pay all the household expenses, just as your father did before he died."

"What about your paycheck? What does it cover?" Lance asked.

"Clothes, food, my life and car insurance, and my car payment. Like I said, the household bills go directly to the firm."

Mark shook his head. "When we get back, we'll change a lot of things. I wonder what the payments on this place actually are? I guess we'll find out soon enough. I thought you knew about your finances. I thought—"

"You thought your father and I shared everything?" Julie questioned, punctuating her words with a sarcastic laugh. "He always said he wanted to spare me the financial worries."

"As soon as this phone is working, I'll call Minter," Mark insisted. "When we get the car unpacked, I'll go over to Bill and Evelyn's and call the phone company to hook us up."

Lance crossed the room, picked up the receiver and listened to the dial tone. "Don't bother Bill and Evelyn," he said. "It's never been disconnected before, why should now be any different? I hadn't given it a thought, but Mom's been paying for a phone she hasn't been using."

Mark's eyes flashed with an anger Julie had seen all too often over the past few days, as he snatched the receiver from Lance. Even from across the room, she could hear the abuse he gave the push buttons when he punched the number of his father's former office.

"This is Mark Weston," Julie heard him say. "Yes, it's good to speak with you, too. I need to talk to John. We're up at the cottage... right, Mom intends to sell it. I want a complete accounting of Mom's finances... you heard me, complete. I want to know what she owns and what she owes. To start with, why hasn't this phone been turned off? Don't give me any of your crap, no one has been here for the last year. You should have suspected as much by the bills. I want a complete accounting of the last two, no make it four years. I'll be back on Friday morning and in your office in the afternoon. She'll be needing her income from the firm. She's taking a leave of absence from work. I'll also need the pay off on the house and this place, so we can put them on the market."

Julie became attentive as Mark continued to list the things he wanted to know. To her surprise, the list included personal loans, assets and investments. All things she had never concerned herself with before this.

"Do you think all this is necessary?" she asked, when he hung up the phone.

"Yes, Mom, it's necessary. You need to know what you're worth. It never crossed my mind you didn't know these things."

"It never seemed important before. Your father always handled the finances."

"Well," Lance said, putting his hands on her shoulders, "it's important now. I can't believe the control he held over your life. It's almost like he brainwashed you."

Julie said nothing. As much as her son's words hurt, she knew they were right. It had been too easy to allow Steve to run their lives, to remain ignorant of the issues she needed to understand and address. Steve had been a CPA, he owned the firm his father established. He always pointed out her shortcomings in anything mathematical.

"You look tired, Mom," Mark said. "Why don't you and Jill go and lie down for a while? Lance and I can get the car unpacked."

Julie admitted she was tired. The trip always exhausted her, but never before had she been allowed the luxury of rest once they arrived. There had been the car to unpack, the kitchen to stock, and the cleaning to be done before she could rest. As for Steve, he needed to become reacquainted with the neighbors, check the lake, or wax his skis, important manly things.

The bedroom stood, as she left it, neat in its appearance. The only thing out of place was the sweater she'd given Steve last Christmas. It lay crumpled on the bed. She picked it up, surprised to catch the scent of Steve's aftershave, which still clung to the fibers.

She still clutched the sweater when she noticed the blinking of Steve's answering machine. He'd installed it in the bedroom so he could handle business calls privately.

She wondered what good it would do to listen to a year old message. Whatever it said no longer mattered. Business had continued as usual, after Steve's death. This call had, most surely, been answered and addressed months ago.

Absently she pressed the play button. To her surprise, the voice belonged to a woman. "Hello, darling. It's the thirtieth at two in the afternoon. I tried to reach you at the house, but I didn't get an answer. Jerry and I got back this morning and I can hardly wait to have you make love to me. Call me as soon as you get in." The message ended with the sound of Karen blowing a kiss into the receiver.

Julie listened as the machine beeped twice. Steve had missed the call by fifteen minutes. They'd left the cottage at one forty-five. Did he call Karen when they got home? She assumed so, since he barricaded himself in the study while she unpacked the car.

As much as she wanted to smash the machine against the wall, she restrained. It would do no good. It certainly wouldn't change the words she'd just heard.

A light rap at the door brought her back to the present. When she acknowledged it, Mark brought her suitcase into the room.

"What's wrong, Mom? You're white as a sheet."

"Play the message on your father's machine. Then you'll know what's wrong. I can't listen to it again." She threw the sweater back onto the bed and hurried out of the room.

Just hearing Karen's voice relaying the year old message hurt her. She never considered their lives so unhappy, never thought she'd given Steve reason to stray. Didn't men have affairs because their wives were cold in bed, unwilling to satisfy their needs? She could never remember ever saying no to Steve, but over the years he seemed to lose interest in sex. No wonder, he had Karen to satisfy those needs.

"I thought you were resting," Lance said, when she entered the kitchen.

"I needed a glass of water," she said.

Lance took a glass from the cupboard and began to fill it, when Mark's profanity laced shout preceded by the sound of the answering machine smashing against the wall.

Seven

The visit to the cottage, which began on such a sour note with the message from Karen, ended on a more positive one. Clothes and personal belongings were sorted, packed and shipped home, given to Goodwill, or put out for the trash.

They spent as much time as possible with Bill and Evelyn as well as their daughter, Nancy, and her husband. To Julie's delight, Nancy told them she'd recently gotten her realtor's license.

With Nancy handling the listing of the cottage, Julie relaxed about the sale of the property. Nancy would find the proper buyers and get the best price. By eleven on Friday, they arrived back in Minter. The few things Julie brought with her from the cottage were quickly unloaded and put away.

"We're going to Dad's office this afternoon," Mark said, when they were eating their lunch. "Do you want to go with us?"

Julie thought for a moment before answering. "No, I think I'll go down to Minter Realty and talk to Patti about listing the house. I know I should go with you, but I don't think I'm up to facing the office just yet."

"I can understand your concerns," Jill said. "I'll come with you. When you're done, we can go shopping."

They continued to eat in silence, but something nagged at Julie's mind, something that ate at her. "Would I be wrong to consider selling the firm?" she finally asked.

"It's a thought," Mark said, "but it does provide you with an income."

"An income I've never seen," she reminded him.

"Let's wait until we see where you stand first. Once you have all the facts, you can make a more logical decision. You don't even know what the profits will turn out to be. With taking some time off, you should know if you can live off what you're making, or if you should plan to go back to work earlier than you want to."

~ * ~

Julie debated taking the kids out for dinner, but purchased steaks at the market instead. They would have too much to talk about to do so in a restaurant. It would also be the last time they would all be together in this house. In the morning, Lance would leave for school and drop Jill at the Madison airport on the way. By the time they were in Honolulu for the wedding, the house, hopefully, would be sold.

They agreed not to talk about what the boys found at the office until they finished dinner. Julie knew it was an excuse, made up by the boys, to keep the table talk light.

"So, what did you find at the firm?" she asked, once they were in the living room, enjoying their coffee.

Mark and Lance exchanged worried glances. "Dad has about a million five, between his profit sharing and investments. From what we can determine, the money is well invested and making enough for you to live comfortably off the interest. As for the house and the cottage, you own them both free and clear."

"What else did you find?" she probed, when Mark stopped to take a breath. By the look on his face, she knew there had to be more.

"Your income from the firm is close to five thousand dollars a month. Over a thousand goes for taxes. Another thousand pays for the utilities on both places, as well as the condo."

"Condo!" Julie echoed. "What condo?"

"Dad bought a condo a few years back. At the time, he took out a loan for two hundred thousand dollars. Between the loan payments and insurance it costs you about two thousand a month. The other thousand is put into a non-interest bearing checking account."

Silence hung in the room like a thick cloud. For a moment, Julie weighed her options, she could become hysterical or she could laugh at the entire situation. To her surprise, she chose to do the latter.

"I don't see anything about this," Lance said.

"Don't you? By the terms of your father's will, I am sole heir to any and all of his assets. He wrote it twenty years ago, for my protection, he said. He never expected to die so young and so he didn't bother changed it. I'm certain the condo, like his affair with Karen, became a well kept company secret."

"I agree with Lance," Jill declared. "I see nothing at all funny about any of this."

"Maybe not," Mark replied, "but facts are facts. Our father certainly didn't qualify for Husband of the Year. He led a life which didn't include any of us and we've found out about it."

"I don't think we'll ever understand any of it," Julie commented. "What I want to know, is how he could afford two lives on a thousand a month?"

"Before he died, he worked with several clients, and besides commissions and fees, he received the income from the firm," Mark explained. "His salary, for the past several years, has been in the six figure range."

"A hundred thousand plus a year?" Julie questioned in disbelief. "I scrimped and saved for all those years to have the things we couldn't afford and he made over a hundred thousand a year?"

"Well, I'm sorry," Jill said getting up from the couch. "I can't sit here and listen to all of this. We're not talking about some character from a soap opera. We're talking about Daddy."

Julie saw the look on Mark's face, as Jill left the room. She knew he wanted to make her understand exactly what they'd uncovered along with the ramifications involved. When he stood to follow her, Julie stopped him.

"Let her go, Mark. You know she always idolized your father. She's not having an easy time with this. There are some more things I want to know. To begin with, why didn't anyone ever mention the condo to me, and why did I continue to pay for it?"

"John told me everyone considered it one of the perks of the company. They benefited from it, used it to entertain clients. Since Dad's office always paid the bills, nothing changed with his death. Why should anything change? No one questioned it."

"I want to see this condo for myself," Julie said. "What are the chances of going there?"

Mark's smile told her she'd played right into his hands. "We'll take you there tonight, Mom. John gave us a key this afternoon."

~ * ~

The complex of condominiums sat in a fashionable neighborhood of the newly expanded North side of town. The row of homes, separated by spacious garages, stood elegantly illuminated by the carriage lights burning beside the garage doors.

Mark pulled into the driveway of the complex with the number *2392 Wexford Lane* displayed on the garage door.

"So, this is it," Julie said, her voice hardly more than a whisper.

Lance led the way, and together they entered through the front door. The foyer sprang to life when he turned on the overhead light. A highly polished wood parquet floor reflected the light shed from the crystal chandelier suspended from the ceiling.

The living room carpeting, a light peach in color and a deep pile in texture, accented the furnishings, which were equally elegant. Heavy oak pieces, upholstered in rich damask complimented the expensive stereo that took up one wall, and the white brick fireplace with its marble mantel on the wall opposite.

"Steve and his fireplaces," Julie mused.

"What did you say, Mom?" Mark asked.

"Nothing really, just thinking aloud. I should have expected to find a fireplace here. It seems they were your father's passion. With the exception of our first apartment, every place we ever lived had one."

Before she could say more, Lance called to them from the master bedroom. "Wait until you see this."

Julie followed her son's voice, stopping just outside the bedroom door. Had she gone mad? What had she become? These rooms were where Steve betrayed her, and yet their very existence excited her. Unable to enter the room, she turned, almost bumping into Mark.

"Jill's right," she said, "I shouldn't have come here. This place only confirms—"

"This place belongs to you, Mom, like the rest of Dad's assets. You have to know what's yours and do with it as you deem fit. If you've seen enough, we'll go home. You do look tired to me, but come Monday everything here will be in your name."

Julie took a deep breath and allowed the impact of Mark's words to sink in. Everything here did belong to her and with each object she saw she could hear Steve telling her about all the things they couldn't afford. The furnishings alone would have easily paid for Lance's education, while Steve insisted the boy, like his sister, go heavily into debt to finance it. Only Mark escaped the burden of debt, having received an appointment to Annapolis.

"Mom's seen enough," Mark said.

Julie turned to face her younger son and caught a glimpse of something glittering in his hand.

Focusing on the diamond and emerald necklace he held, she experienced a sinking feeling, then dizziness before the room began to close in on her.

"Mom, Mom," she heard Mark say. She could feel a damp cloth on her forehead. "Are you all right, Mom?"

"I-I think so. Did I faint?"

"Yes. Maybe we should take you to the emergency room," Lance suggested.

Julie moved to a sitting position. "I don't think it will be necessary. I'll take my sugar count when I get home. George said I might experience something like this if it got too low. If it is low, I'll have a glass of orange juice and everything will be fine."

Neither of the boys accepted her explanation until they confirmed her self-diagnosis at the emergency room. Even George agreed, the excitement could have dropped her sugar level and caused her to faint.

Eight

Wednesday morning, Julie found herself sitting at Meg's kitchen table talking over coffee, the way they did before she went to work. "I certainly am relieved to have the kids gone. Mark took off for Chicago about six this morning. Don't get me wrong, I needed them here, but I also need time for me."

"I can't believe Steve owned a condo and you never knew about it," Meg said, as she poured them each another cup of coffee. "Whatever happened to the truth in lending law? Don't they have to tell you when your husband borrows money?"

"I'm sure if you saw the original paperwork, you'd find my signature. Steve had a habit of bringing home papers and telling me to sign. I gave up asking him what they were all about years ago. His answer was always the same, 'It's business, you wouldn't understand'."

"Why?" Meg pressed.

Julie fell silent for a moment, contemplating Meg's question. How many times, over the past few days, had she asked herself why? How many times had she wondered whatever happened to Julie Morgan, the fun loving teenager, who would have taken nothing for granted? When had she become Julie Weston? When had Steve turned her into a timid, dominated housewife who did whatever her husband demanded?

"Steve always made a big deal about my not knowing anything about figures. It started as a casual thing, and little by little, I began to believe him. I thought he wanted to protect me. I certainly pegged him wrong."

"So, what did you find in the condo?" Meg asked.

"Where do I start? Let's see, there's a ten thousand dollar lead crystal chandelier in the foyer, furnishings worth at least another ten thousand, fifty thousand dollars worth of antiques, and enough expensive jewelry to start my own store. I put the condo on the market for three hundred and ten thousand minus the antiques, furnishings, and jewelry. The realtor says it's a good price. I hope so. I honestly don't care what I get for it. I just want the damn thing *sold*!"

Julie sipped her coffee slowly. She didn't mention the journal she'd found hidden in one of the dresser drawers. What good would it do for Meg to know Karen hadn't been the first, nor would she have been the last of Steve's lovers? Steve's journal documented sexual conquests and the list included secretaries and call girls, as well as clients. By the time Julie read the journal, it seemed as though she was reading a novel and the main character was a cad. Steve's life, away from home, certainly didn't resemble the life of Steve Weston, husband and father.

~ * ~

By eleven thirty, Julie pulled into her parking space at the plant. The biting January wind assaulted her face as she hurried across the lot to the sanctuary of the warm building.

For a moment, she stood in the reception area of the lobby, feeling almost alien in the familiar surroundings. She'd spent eight to ten hours a day, five days a week, here for the past twelve years, but somehow, she knew this part of her life would soon be over for good. In a few minutes she would ask Tom for a six-month leave of absence and for the first time she questioned the rationality of her decision.

Steve's non-interest bearing checking account contained well over twenty thousand dollars and an antique dealer had offered her almost two hundred and fifty thousand for the condo's many treasures. She still waited to hear from the jeweler, but somehow she knew his offer would be equally large. She certainly didn't have to work, but could she spend her days, like Meg, doing housework and volunteering?

"Julie, did you hear me?" Mary Parker, the receptionist, asked for the second time.

"Were you talking to me, Mary? I guess I'm out in Never-Never Land somewhere. It certainly feels good in here. The wind today is wicked."

Mary smiled at Julie's comment and she knew the answer she gave wasn't the one Mary wanted.

"So," Mary continued, seemingly content on receiving the right answer. "How are you feeling?"

"Much better, thank you. Is Mr. Randall in?" Julie experienced a strange sensation in asking Mary about Tom, when normally she would have stopped by his office, unannounced.

"Yes, he's here. Would you like me to tell him you want to see him?"

"No. I have some other things to do first. I just needed to know if he came in today. I'll see him later."

She checked her watch noting the time to be eleven fifty. She made her way toward the first floor assembly area, after hanging her coat on the rack reserved for visitors.

Pete Weber met her at the crib, a small room where the supplies were kept.

"Julie," Pete said, "it's good to see you. What gives with the jeans and sweater? Did Tom relax the dress code for the office?"

"Just visiting, Pete. I need a hard hat and a pair of safety glasses."

Pete handed her the equipment and when she put them on, she continued. "Have you seen Jerry today?"

"Sure. Jerry's here. I can't understand why you want to see him."

"What do you mean, you don't know why I'd want to see Jerry?"

"Well, you know. Everyone in the plant knows what Jerry did to you. Because of him you ended up in the hospital."

"You'd better get your facts straight, Pete," Julie snapped. "Because of Jerry, I got the medical attention I needed. Whatever gossip you've heard or spread, I want it stopped here and now. Do I make myself clear?"

"Perfectly," Pete muttered.

Julie heard his comment, but let it pass. She'd seen Jerry leave the washroom and hurried across the assembly area to talk to him.

Jerry hadn't been looking in her direction and when she spoke his name, he turned abruptly, his look one of shock. "Julie? Are you sure you should be here?"

"Positive," she replied. "You look like you want to retreat back into the men's room, but it wouldn't do you any good, I'd just follow you."

The tension lifted when Jerry began to laugh at her comment. "You sound more like Julie Morgan than Julie Weston. What happened to you?"

"Too much, but it has nothing to do with my reason for being here. It's almost lunchtime. Let's go to the cafeteria where we can talk." Julie slipped her arm through Jerry's and together they left the assembly area, past their astonished co-workers.

As usual, the cafeteria buzzed with conversation, but when Julie and Jerry joined the line to choose their lunch, the room became strangely silent. Before Julie could produce her wallet, Jerry handed the cashier a ten-dollar bill.

"I intended to pay for your lunch," she protested.

"And bruise my fragile male ego? No way," Jerry teased.

He selected a table for two in a quiet corner, and held the chair while Julie seated herself.

"I thought I'd hear from you before this," Julie began.

"I needed to straighten out some things first."

"Damn it, Jerry, talk to me. What's going on here? I don't like the gossip I'm hearing anymore than the cold stares we're getting."

"Come on, Julie, if you've heard the gossip, you know what's going on. There are no secrets here. Everyone knows why you collapsed as well as why Tom put me on probation."

"There you go, just like everyone else, jumping to conclusions again," Julie said. "Do you know why I collapsed? I doubt it. You couldn't have had any idea I didn't know about Steve and Karen. The way I found out could have been a bit more diplomatic, but it forced me to get the medical attention I needed. In short, you saved my life. I have diabetes. Who knows what might have happened if it continued on undetected?"

She watched the expression on Jerry's face. Earlier, she'd noticed his usual defiant attitude had been replaced by one of self-pity, but now it changed to worry." I-I didn't know. Are you going to be all right? Shouldn't you be resting or something?"

Julie laughed at his ignorance of the disease. "I'm getting everything under control with medication. I'm eating right, resting, and getting some structured exercise. All in all, I'm probably healthier than you are."

"How are you handling... well, you know?"

"You mean Steve's other life. What can I say? If he were alive, I'd probably kill him. The only thing I can do is go on. If it makes things any easier, I found his journal and Karen couldn't be called the first, nor would she have been the last. His affairs were perfectly choreographed. He planned his affair with Karen for at least six months before it started. He had decided to break things off just after her birthday last year.

"I think it's time I started living for me and not for someone who puts me behind his own pleasures. I think I'd like to find Julie Morgan again. I'd forgotten the fun we used to have."

Jerry's face brightened as though he too remembered those crazy days called the teenage years. "You were different then," he said. "I guess we all were. Do you remember the great Christmas tree rip off?"

"Remember it? How could I forget it? It all seemed so logical, right up until I saw the fresh stump in Professor Wunderlick's front yard."

"The way I remember it, the whole things started as your idea and, if you recall, the results certainly pleased Margie Lund's family."

Julie sat, for a minute, remembering the Christmas of thirty years earlier. Margie Lund had been a junior at Minter High School, when her younger brother, Tony, was seriously injured in a car accident. The accident forced Margie into the roll of student by day and mother by night, while her parents stayed at the hospital. With three younger brothers and sisters, she knew there would be no Christmas. A week before the holiday, while the staff of the local college attended a Christmas party, The Four Musketeers ventured into the country to Professor Wunderlick's home, to cut down the big pine tree in the front yard. No one ever guessed who did the dirty deed, but when word got out about Margie's special Christmas tree, even the old professor voiced his approval. The sacrifice of his tree gave the Lund family something it needed, a gift from the heart and the true meaning of Christmas.

Jerry reached across the table and wiped a tear from Julie's cheek. "Are you getting maudlin on me?"

"Remembering that night makes me a little sad. I wish we could have done more for them without having to cut down the tree. We were lucky we didn't get caught. My lord, if Steve ever knew what we did, he certainly would never have married me."

"Maybe you should have told him and kept your identity. I hope you find Julie Morgan again. She's a far cry from Julie Weston. As long as you're finding things, have you found Devan?"

"Devan?" she questioned.

"Look, I saw the roses and I read the card. I know he's back in town and you've seen him. He's a very special guy. So where does he stand?"

"I asked him to wait," Julie replied, looking down at her folded hands.

"Don't wait too long. Get to know him again. I think it would do you a world of good."

"I will, Jerry, tomorrow, I promise. Now, you need to get back to work and I have to see Tom. Thank you for lunch."

Jerry held her chair as she got to her feet. "Does this mean we're still friends?"

Julie smiled broadly and kissed Jerry's cheek. "We never stopped being friends. For a while I wanted to hate you, but we've had too many good times to jeopardize our friendship over something like this."

Impulsively she reached into her purse and pulled out a pair of amethyst and diamond earrings.

"According to Steve's journal, these were bought for Karen. He meant to give them to her as a combination birthday and breaking up present. Amethyst is her birthstone, isn't it?"

"Yes, but—"

"I want her to have them. The rest of the jewelry will be sold, but these belong to her. I wouldn't feel right about selling them. They're so beautiful, I want her to enjoy them."

"Are you certain? It isn't necessary."

"Yes, it is, Jerry. It breaks the final link."

"Final link? I don't understand."

"I don't expect you to. I'm seeing a counselor and getting my life together. Steve's affairs hurt me deeply, but I don't plan to let them scar me. Once his love nest, along with everything in it, is gone, I can get on with my life."

"Sounds like there's a lot of counseling going on. Karen and I are getting help, too. After twenty-one years, we're going to try to salvage what's left of our marriage."

~ * ~

Tom Randall paced his office. It didn't take long for word to reach him of Julie's arrival at the plant and her meeting with Jerry Gaines. He'd confirmed it, for himself, when he'd gone down to the cafeteria to get a sandwich and seen them sitting in a quiet corner, their heads together.

Julie entered his office unannounced. "Do you have a minute, Tom?"

"It certainly took you long enough to get up here," he snapped. "What's going on between you and Gaines?"

Tom watched as Julie's eyes flashed with an anger he'd never before seen. "I don't see where it's any of your business."

"You were seen carrying on with him in the assembly area as well as the cafeteria. Do you have any idea how it looked, considering everyone knows what happened the other day. You intended to put him on probation for his affairs and now you're—"

"I'm what?" Julie demanded. "Do you have any idea what the word friendship means?"

"Friendship?" Tom asked.

"You're from Detroit, how could I ever expect you to understand life in a small town like Minter. Did you have close friends in high school? Did you stay close after graduation? I doubt it. When Jerry and I were teenagers, there were four of us who hung around together. We weren't lovers, just good friends who had fun together. After graduation, we all went our separate ways. Jerry joined the army; Devan went to college; Sandy studied to be a nurse and was killed in a car accident; and I got married. When Jerry returned from the service, it seemed as though he'd been gone only days, not years. Whatever happened the other day can't change a lifetime of friendship."

Tom stood, dumbfounded by Julie's tirade. He hadn't considered her friendship with Jerry; hadn't thought how hard putting him on probation would have been for her. "I'm sorry, Julie. I assumed—"

"Didn't anyone ever tell you about assumptions? You're no better than the people in the plant. You thrive on false accusations and rumors. I came here to ask for a six-month leave of absence. Instead, consider this my two-week notice. I'll clean out my things and be out of here within the hour."

Tom caught Julie's arm before she could storm out of his office. "Can't we talk about this? You know I can't afford to lose you."

"You can replace me easily, Tom, and I don't think I can stay on with all of the accusations."

"Sit down, Julie. I'm sorry for jumping to conclusions. Take a month... three months... six months. If you still feel the same way, I'll consider your resignation, but I won't consider it today, not in anger."

Tom watched as Julie's face softened. Her blue-gray eyes only showed a minimum of their prior anger.

"Apology accepted, Tom," she said, her voice noticeably softer as well.

"So, what will you do with yourself, if you're not coming here every day?" he asked, as he directed her to a chair opposite his.

"I'm going to take a vacation, go to Mark's wedding in Honolulu, attend Lance's graduation in Minnesota, and help Jill when the baby comes. By then it will be July. If I'm lucky, all of my property will be sold by then and I can make up my mind about the future."

When they finished their conversation and Julie left, she knew Tom contemplated what she'd said. Perhaps she'd been right. Leaving the company had been what she'd come to do and the six-month leave of absence only an excuse to prolong the inevitable.

Nine

It surprised Julie to have slept so late. Time seemed to fly as it would soon be nine and she'd only eaten breakfast and showered.

She stood before the freestanding mirror in her bedroom, trying to decide what she should wear to Devan's office. Although she planned to see him the day before, her plans were altered. One day would make no difference, she told herself. Devan didn't know she wanted to see him, so if she came on Friday rather than Thursday, it wouldn't matter.

On the bed, the pile of discarded outfits grew larger. At last she settled on a new suit she'd bought while shopping with Jill at Christmas. They'd driven to Madison to visit a small shop a friend of Julie's recently opened. Although she cringed at paying over two hundred dollars for the suit, she'd fallen in love with it the minute she tried it on. The material reminded her more of a tee shirt than anything else, but looked extremely dressy. The background of cream sported a white embossed pattern, mixed with mauve and green flowers. The oversized jacket and matching mid-calf skirt came alive with the waist length mauve tee-top. Julie smiled at her reflection in the mirror, as she added white kid boots to the ensemble then decided on a pair of mauve pumps instead.

"The sub-zero temperatures of the past three days are now behind us," the radio announcer began. Julie stopped and listened to the report. She always kept the radio on these days, for company, she told herself. "The high today is expected to be in the mid-teens with a wind chill of minus ten. There's a possibility of scattered snow showers in the Southeastern sections of the state. The low tonight is expected to be five above zero."

With the end of the report, Julie turned off the radio and methodically hung up the discarded clothes before going downstairs. She heard the grandfather clock strike the half-hour just before the phone rang.

"Damn," she uttered aloud. She wondered who could be calling and hoped it wouldn't be someone who could again ruin her plans.

"Hello," she said into the receiver.

"Julie, it's Jerry."

"Jerry? Are you on break?"

"Only gone two weeks and you've already forgotten the nine-thirty coffee break, how soon we forget?"

"So why waste your precious ten minutes of relaxation on me?"

"I wanted to find out what's going on?" he asked, his voice sounding serious.

"What on earth are you talking about?"

"You promised to see Devan yesterday. Why did you go back on your word?"

"How do you know I didn't go see him?"

"How do you think? I called him last night. Remember you told me I should get in touch with him. Your name happened to come up and he said he hadn't seen you since you were in the hospital."

Julie hesitated a moment before continuing. "You told him I'd planned to go to his office yesterday?" she finally managed to ask.

"Of course, I told him. I didn't think I acted out of line."

"No, I guess you didn't. I got tied up with the realtor and the jeweler. I just finished getting ready to go to his office now and I have to admit, I'm nervous as a cat."

Jerry began to laugh heartily.

"What's so funny?" Julie demanded.

"From what I heard, you weren't very nervous when you were in Tom's office the other day. The word is you gave notice."

"I guess I did. I couldn't take all the accusations and innuendoes. He wouldn't accept it, of course. We ended up agreeing to a six month leave of absence."

"Well, it looks like break time is just about over. I'm glad you and Devan are going to clear the air today. Break a leg."

Julie said good-bye then hung up the phone, smiling at Jerry's comment. Ever since she'd been in the school plays, it became a private joke between them. He told her repeatedly she shouldn't get married so soon, should go to Hollywood and try her luck at acting. How foolish it always seemed. Who in their right mind would cast an overweight teenager, with glasses no less? Her dream of entertaining people became another thing she'd put behind her for Steve.

She glanced into the hallway mirror before putting on her winter cape and beret. Satisfied with her appearance, she went out to the garage. Before going to Devan's office, she would stop at the travel agency and make plans for a vacation. She wanted to go someplace quiet and warm, where she could sort out her feelings and make plans for the future.

The travel agency in the mini-mall by Julie's house displayed a variety of colorful posters depicting exotic location. Anita Brice sat at the front desk. She knew Anita through her husband, Don, who worked as the accountant at the plant.

"Julie, it's good to see you. With all the stories Don's been bringing home, I certainly didn't expect you to come here."

Julie hid her annoyance at the mention of the vicious plant gossip. "I guess you can't believe everything you hear. I need a vacation. It has to be something restful, fun, someplace where I can meet new people, and of course, it has to be warm. Maybe I'd like Key West or Arizona."

Anita winked at Julie before getting up and going to the brochure rack. "Neither," she said, returning to her desk. "I think you'll enjoy this place more."

The pamphlet she handed Julie read *Make It Jamaica... Make It Hidden Island*. "Hidden Island?" Julie questioned. "I've never heard of it."

"It's an all-inclusive resort. At first it sounds terribly expensive, but it's worth it. This is one of the few places a single can go without paying a premium. The price includes everything except souvenirs and side trips. I think it's just the place for you."

Julie looked at the booklet depicting horseback riding, tennis, aerobics, and elegant dining. "All inclusive, meals, drinks, entertainment, cigarettes," Julie read aloud. "It sounds too good to be true."

"You might end up with a roommate, this being the peak season and all, but I think you'll enjoy it."

"Whatever you say. You're the expert. How soon can I go?" She reread the description of the hotel and fantasized about spending a week in a tropical paradise.

"How about a week from Sunday?" Anita asked, breaking her concentration.

"What did you say?"

"I said they have space on the flight a week from Sunday. Should I take it?"

"Yes, definitely."

When Anita finished on the computer, she turned back to Julie. "The flight leaves Chicago at six thirty in the morning. You might want to think about spending the night at the airport."

"Where do you suggest?"

"The Hilton, the Ramada, the Sheraton, the Marriott, they're all good. Think about it. In the meantime, I'll look for a good package deal down there."

Julie wrote the check and left the office. It would take her fifteen minutes to drive across town to see Devan, putting her there at eleven forty-five. She'd be just in time for lunch.

~ * ~

Devan sat at his desk, the surface littered with manila file folders and unread proposals. Every paper he picked up mirrored Julie's face, every word he read echoed her voice.

Ignoring the work, which couldn't hold his attention, he turned his chair toward the window and watched as the wind swirled eddies of snow down the side street just below his office. He removed his glasses and rubbed his eyes, in an attempt to erase Julie from his mind, but the gesture proved futile.

Last evening's phone calls replayed in his head as though he was listening to a tape recording. The first call came from his oldest son, Todd. After several minutes of conversation, Todd finally came to the reason for the call.

"Brandon and I were talking last night," he began.

"Talking?" Devan questioned.

"Did we miss something, Dad? On New Year's Day, you were so excited about this new woman you'd met, but since then we haven't heard you mention her. It's not like you. Whatever happened to my dad, the great lover?"

"I guess he got put on hold. The woman I met turned out to be Julie Morgan Weston, a friend of mine from high school."

"I keep forgetting you grew up in Minter, didn't you?" Todd interrupted.

"Yes, I did grow up here. Anyway, Julie and I were best friends, thirty years ago. She lost her husband about this time last year and I thought we might have a chance at something special, until..." Devan remembered how his voice trailed off.

"Until what, Dad?"

"Until she got sick. She asked me to give her time and I agreed."

"I can't believe you accepted her terms. Either she doesn't mean much to you or she's got you where she wants you. Which is it?"

"It's neither. You don't know Julie. You certainly don't know what's been going on here. She could be special to me, very special. I agreed to her terms out of respect."

"Look, Dad, I don't like the tone of your voice. Why don't you call her? It might make you feel better."

Devan hardly remembered the remainder of the conversation. Todd was right, he'd been a fool to let Julie leave him hanging. When he finished talking with Todd, he dialed Julie's number, only to find the line busy.

He'd still been contemplating his conversation with his son, when the phone rang. To his surprise, Jerry Gaines's voice greeted him.

"How did you and Julie get along today?" Jerry asked, mid-way through the call.

"What are you talking about? I haven't seen or talked to her since the night she collapsed."

"Oh, I thought, well, it's just that Julie promised me she'd talk to you today."

Devan shook his head to rid himself of Jerry's voice. On an impulse, he picked up the phone and called her number. After four rings, the answering machine picked up and Julie's voice came over the line. *Hi, this is Julie. I can't come to the phone right now, but please leave a message. I want to get back to you.* Hearing her voice angered him. He started to leave a message, but after the first three words, he changed his mind and hung up, abruptly.

He picked up the phone again and called his secretary on the intercom.

~ * ~

"Good morning," Devan's secretary greeted Julie when she entered the outer office.

"Good morning," Julie replied. "Is Mr. Yates in?"

"Do you have an appointment?"

"No, just tell him Ms. Weston is here to see him."

Before the girl could announce her, Devan's voice came over the intercom, "Carol."

"Yes, Mr. Yates," the girl answered, after picking up the phone.

Julie waited while the girl listened to Devan's words. "But—" she started, apparently cut short by Devan.

"I'm sorry, Ms. Weston, Mr. Yates just canceled his appointments and asked not to be disturbed."

Julie debated for a moment, then started toward the door leading to Devan's office.

"Ms. Weston," Carol said. "I just told you, Mr. Yates doesn't want to be disturbed. If I let you in, I could lose my job."

"I'll make certain he doesn't blame you. If he gets mad, it will have to be at me. I'll take full responsibility."

~ * ~

Devan slammed down the receiver and turned his chair back to the window. He contemplated what Carol started to say, and decided it must have been inconsequential or she would have pursued the subject further.

As he looked out the window, he began to plan his strategy. As soon as he ate lunch, he would drive over to Julie's house. If he didn't find her home he would wait for her. She'd have to come back sometime. When he did see her he'd...

The opening of the door broke his concentration. "Damn it, Carol," he said, turning the chair toward the door. "I thought I told you..."

To his surprise, he saw Julie standing in front of the now closed door.

"I'm not Carol, Devan, and for Pete's sake, don't blame her for letting me in here."

"Julie? I've been sitting here thinking about you," he said, as he got out of his chair and moved to her side.

"I thought you might be. I'm sorry I didn't make it yesterday, sorry Jerry talked to you before I got a chance to see you."

"Did Jerry call you, too?"

She nodded. "This morning. Look, Devan, we can't talk here. Let me take you to lunch."

Devan tried to read the thoughts behind Julie's blue-gray eyes, but found it impossible. As much as he wanted to take her in his arms, he restrained. Being unable to read her mind, he decided it was better to stay at arm's length and give her time to make the first move.

Once he retrieved his coat from the closet, Julie continued. "We can take my car, it's already warm."

Devan didn't argue. "Where would you like to go for lunch?"

"I don't know. I've been away from downtown for so long, I couldn't tell you what's good anymore. What do you suggest?"

Devan noticed her smile, but didn't allow himself to be lulled into hopefulness by it. "Do you still like Chinese?"

"Sounds good to me. Is Kim Fong's still downtown?"

Her question startled him. As he recalled, Kim Fong's had always been her favorite restaurant. "Then Kim Fong's it is," he said, holding the door open.

"I'll see you on Monday, Carol. Have a good weekend."

They said little as they made their way to the elevator, then to Julie's car. Devan hoped it would prove to be a positive sign.

On the short drive to Kim Fong's, the conversation remained general. Could she tell a difference now, since she started on the proper medication? Did her kids get home all right? Were her plans already made to liquidate her property as Mark said she might?

They were lucky to find a parking place almost in front of the door and hurried into the dimly lit hallway. The steep carpeted stairs led to the private upstairs restaurant.

Once at the top of the stairs and inside the large room, Julie rubbed her hand over the teakwood Buddha, a far away look in her eyes.

At last they were seated in the privacy of a circular booth. "Nothing changes here," she said, wistfully.

"How long has it been since you were here last?" Devan inquired.

"Let's see, it must have been the night of the panty raid."

Devan couldn't believe his ears. "You always loved this place. Didn't Steve bring you here?"

"No. He didn't like Chinese."

Devan sat, stunned. He thought Steve could easily have found something to his liking on the menu that featured a full complement of American dishes.

"Do you still enjoy musicals?" he asked, in an attempt to get to know her better.

"Yes, but it's been years since I've seen a really good production, with the exception of the ones I catch on TV. Of course, I went to all the high school presentations when the kids were in them."

"You said you went to the plays, what about Steve?"

"He never enjoyed plays and certainly not musicals. At the time, I didn't mind going alone."

"My god, Julie, didn't he ever do anything you enjoyed? How could you let him run your life?"

"It all happened very slowly. We were young and he molded me into what he wanted me to be. I didn't ask you out to lunch to talk about Steve. I want to talk about us."

"Can there be an us, Julie, or did Steve wreck that, too?"

"I hope there can be an us, but the terms I need to ask for are difficult."

"I don't understand," Devan said, holding her hand.

She looked down, as though memorizing every line on his hand. "I don't know if I'm ready for a total commitment. I'd like us to be non-committed friendly lovers," she replied, softly.

Devan watched Julie's expression and saw the pained look in her eyes as he considered her request.

"Is something wrong?" she asked. "Of course, there is, I don't know why I thought it would work. Forget I mentioned it."

"Don't Julie, I only stopped to think about all the times I asked the women in my life to be non-committed friendly lovers. I couldn't help remembering the times they said yes when I could see the hurt in their eyes. I never understood why. Now I do."

"I'm sorry, Devan, I shouldn't have asked I—"

"Is this how you reacted to Steve? Were you always the one to say you were sorry, even when something wasn't your fault?"

Julie nodded.

"I'm not Steve. I don't expect you to give into my every whim. When you need to be loved, I'll love you. When you need a confidant, I'll be ready to listen. And when you need a friend, I'll be there for you."

"Thank you, Devan," Julie said. "I don't want to lose us, I want us to become special, I just didn't know how to ask."

"I know what I want to ask," Devan said. "I want to know how you allowed Steve to do this to you?"

"I told you, it happened very slowly. He worked hard molding me to be what he wanted me to be. He had the college a degree, as well as his CPA certification. My high school diploma didn't seem quite as important."

"You were class salutatorian, every college in the state would have done anything to have you register with them."

"It became a little hard to believe when everything I did and everything I said met with Steve's disapproval. He taught me well, taught me to realize my stupidity. He made certain I believed everything he said, so when he started his affairs I wouldn't question his late nights at the office."

"But you went back to school. You got your BA. Didn't it mean anything to him?"

"Sure, it meant I could go back to work to pay for all the things he said we couldn't afford. Once I did go back to work, I didn't have time to worry about Steve's affairs, either financial or extra-marital."

Devan ached at her confession and slid closer to her in the booth, embracing her while she cried. "It's over now. Today you begin a new life and it looks like you're already planning tomorrow. I saw the travel brochures in your car."

"Yes, I booked a vacation for myself."

"Are you going to Jamaica?"

"A place called *Hidden Island*."

"I noticed. Is Jamaica where you want to go?"

"Look Devan, it doesn't matter where I go, the important thing is that I go. I need some time to be alone, and to decide what I want to do with my life. I can't do it in Minter, at least I don't think I can."

"But *Hidden Island*?" Devan continued to protest. "A friend of mine spent his vacation there last year. He said the men were after one thing and one thing only... women."

"And men aren't after women here? Steve carried on affairs with Karen, not to mention the others. Jerry chases everything in or out of a skirt, then there's you and me. From what I saw in the brochures, they want sweet young things, not forty something widows."

After lunch, they spent the afternoon at Devan's apartment, becoming better acquainted. By five, Julie returned home and after a long soak in a hot tub, she placed a call to Jerry, to assure him she did, indeed, keep her promise and clear the air with Devan.

To her surprise, Karen answered the phone. "Hello, Karen, this is Julie," she began. She could hear Karen's voice tense; hear her shock at finding Julie on the other end of the line. "I don't mean to upset you, Karen. I've come to grips with what and who Steve became.

How can I blame you, when I've learned of his passion for the unknown, for women in general?"

She and Jerry talked for almost an hour before she hung up the phone and turned on the TV. She cruised the channels until she found an airing of *Paint Your Wagon*, and curled up in the recliner with a cup of mint tea to watch it.

~ * ~

The ringing of the phone brought Julie to full awareness. To her surprise, she still sat in the recliner and the TV showed Saturday morning children's programming.

"Did I wake you?" Devan asked.

"I guess so. I fell asleep in front of the TV last night. What time is it?"

"It's nine fifteen. What are you doing today?"

"I don't know," she said, punctuating her words with a yawn.

"Good. Get dressed. We're going on a mini vacation. I just got two tickets to *Evita* in Milwaukee for tonight, along with a weekend package at the Hilton. We'll do some sightseeing, see the play,and enjoy this evening."

"I can't believe you got tickets for *Evita*. I've wanted to see it for years. My secretary, Roxie saw it in Chicago a couple of years ago and brought me a tape."

"Then *Evita* it is. Get your bag packed, I'll pick you up in an hour."

Julie hung up the phone and headed for the shower. If she was going away for the weekend she had a lot to do and it all had to be accomplished in an hour's time.

Exactly one hour later, Devan stood at her door. "Are you ready?" he asked.

"Just about. I just have to get my medicine, then I'm sure I have everything."

He stepped into the living room and took her into his arms. "I'm glad you didn't have plans. I really took a chance when I bought the tickets and made the reservations at the hotel."

"You should have known my social calendar isn't exactly filled to overflowing these days."

"That might have been true a few weeks ago. But I'm certain word has gotten out to all of the eligible bachelors in Minter, and it won't be long before they start beating a path to your door."

Julie laughed. "They already have and I'm afraid they've all found Julie Weston to be a bit too stuffy for their tastes. Ever since Steve died, his friends have been trying to set me up. Most of my 'dates' turned out to be toads rather than Prince Charming."

"So much the better for me. I may not be a prince, but I think I'm a far cry from a toad."

The trip to Milwaukee was filled with reminiscences of their teenage years. Every few miles, one of them would begin a sentence with, "Do you remember when we..." By the time the story was finished, they would be laughing uncontrollably.

For Julie, the experience was one she hadn't expected. It seemed as though someone turned back the clock and she hadn't become an adult. All of the old escapades were as fresh in her mind as when they had actually happened.

At last they arrived at the hotel. After checking in, Devan suggested a trip to the Domes. The botanical gardens were ablaze with the colors of hundreds of blooms, growing and thriving in spite of the cold of winter which held the rest of the city in its grip.

From there, they went on to the museum, opting to forego the brewery, considering Julie couldn't have the beer.

By five, they returned to the hotel to get ready for the evening's performance. Devan looked dashing in his dark suit.

"You look beautiful," he said, assessing her long black skirt with its colorful overblouse stitched in gold.

"Why thank you. You don't look so bad yourself, for an old man."

"Old man! If we didn't have reservations to keep, I'd show you old."

"I guess you'll just have to show me after the theater, if you think you're up to it, that is?"

Devan took her in his arms and kissed her tenderly. It amazed her how easily the teasing came, how wonderful it felt to be with him and loved by him.

~ * ~

The music from the play echoed in their minds as they returned to their room. To Julie's surprise, a bottle of champagne, a bowl of strawberries, and a beautiful candle sat on the table situated by the window.

"When did you order these?" she asked.

"Last night, when I made the reservations. I thought it might be romantic."

"It certainly is." She watched while he lit the candle, then opened the champagne. The pop of the cork gave her a feeling of excitement. Although she'd had champagne at parties, Steve never bothered to buy any for her, even though he knew she enjoyed it.

"Not to worry," Devan said, handing her a glass, "it's non-alcoholic. I checked with George to see if you could have this. He told me not to get the real thing and not to have the strawberries dipped in chocolate."

Julie could feel a blush creep into her cheeks at the thought of Devan being so considerate. Steve would have never thought to check on what she could and couldn't have.

Stop it. Devan isn't Steve. Didn't he say as much at lunch yesterday? You have to stop comparing the two of them. Steve is gone and from what you've learned, it's with good riddance. Enjoy Devan. Who knows, something wonderful could come out of it.

"To us," Devan said, lifting his glass and silencing Julie's inner voice.

"To us," she repeated, as the glasses touched.

Ten

Milwaukee proved to be but a prelude to the next weekend in Chicago. Julie was able to change their reservations from one night to two and they left right after Devan finished work on Friday. On the way, they stopped in Rockford for dinner at a restaurant Julie had heard Meg rave about several times. It was after eight when they finally arrived at their hotel. At the desk, Devan upgraded their room to a suite with its own private whirlpool.

"This is sinful," she said, once they were alone in the suite.

"Why would you say such a thing?"

"I know that's a king sized bed, but it looks much larger. As for having this much luxury, I'm afraid I'm going to get spoiled."

"That's the general idea. I'm ready for that whirlpool. How about you?" Julie giggled. "I'm afraid my swimsuits are still in the car. I certainly didn't think—"

Devan's finger on her lips silenced her. "Why do you think I asked for a whirlpool suite? With this amount of privacy, who needs suits?"

A rap at the door interrupted them, leaving Julie speechless. As if on cue, the young man delivered a tray of champagne, strawberries, and a candle. After he left, Devan popped the cork and handed a glass of the sparkling liquid to Julie.

"This is getting to be a habit," she whispered.

"I'd prefer to call it a tradition."

Once they were in the tub, Devan fed her the strawberries, while she sipped the wine. Everything was perfect.

"Enough of the preliminaries, I'm ready for the main attraction," he said, pulling her into his arms.

He started by caressing her breasts, then moved his hand lower, until he cradled the heart of her woman's soul between his fingers. His circular movements made her moan with delight.

Moved to the height of passion, he lifted her from the tub and dried her with the towel. Together they lay down on the bed and made delightful love for longer than she ever though possible.

"Oh, Devan," she whispered. "I wish I wasn't leaving for Jamaica. I could stay in your arms forever."

"Now, that's a tempting thought, but it's quite unrealistic. You do have the reservations, and I agree with George, this vacation will do you a world of good."

"But you said this place has a reputation. What if—"

He silenced her with a kiss. Once they parted, he finished her sentence. "If you should meet a man who stirs your emotions, I hope you have the sense to enjoy it. We've talked about this before. You know I've had several lovers and I know you've only had two. If the opportunity presents itself, why not? As you remember, we agreed to be non-committed friendly lovers."

"But—"

"But nothing. This is a time for you to find yourself again. A vacation romance isn't the worst thing you could do. Believe me I understand. I'm not saying I won't be jealous of the guy, but I do understand."

~ * ~

Devan pulled out of the parking ramp at O'Hare. How could he have ever told her she could have an affair in Jamaica? Why did the words, I do understand, gnaw at his gut? He'd told her he would be jealous, but he never expected the thought of her with another man to eat at him so badly.

As he pulled up to the booth to pay for his parking, then he glanced at the dashboard clock. It read six forty-six. He could hardly believe he'd been able to get to the car and out of the lot in just a little over fifteen minutes.

Being Sunday morning, he found little traffic. After he paid for his parking, he slipped the disc of the soundtrack from *Evita* into his CD player. As the car came to life with the music, he relived the weekend in Milwaukee with Julie. *Evita* so excited her he smiled at the memory of the night. Before they left the theater, he purchased the CD, as if by having it, he could hang onto the memory of the evening forever.

His thoughts turned to what George told him at the hospital the night Julie collapsed. "She's little more than a child. Until today she still believed in '*Once Upon A Time* and *Happily Ever After.*'"

Devan repeated the words aloud and knew Julie no longer believed them. He wondered if he could be the one to change her mind? He wanted to be, but this trip to Jamaica would become the unknown factor.

In the past week, they'd seen each other almost daily. For the first time in his life, he found himself in love. He'd made love to Missy as well as a dozen other women over the years, but he'd never been 'in love' and the prospect frightened him. At the age of forty-seven, the schoolboy feeling of indecision over a woman brought forth an unsettling effect.

He wondered how he would last a week without hearing her voice, without feeling her in his arms, without making love to her. Would she return changed? Would she meet someone in Jamaica? Would she even want him when she did return?

"Don't cry for me Argentina," the star of the musical sang. He contemplated the words and decided he could use those same words to describe himself, if Julie came back with no desire to continue their relationship. "Don't cry for me, Julie Weston," he said aloud, knowing he didn't mean it.

The dashboard clock read nine fifteen when he pulled into the underground parking garage. Pleased with the good time he'd made, he grabbed his overnight bag and took the elevator to his fourth floor apartment.

As he fit his key into the lock, he heard his phone begin to ring. Before he could reach it, the answering machine began its message. He picked up the receiver and shouted over the sound of his own voice on the recording. "Don't hang up, I'm here." He quickly pushed the cancel button. When he did, he noticed several messages blinking.

"Hello," he finally said, when the machine shut off.

"Dad, Dad it's Brandon. Where have you been? I've been trying to reach you all night."

"What's wrong?" he asked, panic rising in his throat. He hoped his voice sounded calmer than his emotions. Brandon was upset and he certainly didn't need his father to be in the same condition.

"I'm in Philadelphia. It's Todd. He's in Intensive Care."

"Intensive Care?" Devan echoed. "What happened? Did he have an accident?"

"No. He was shot. It was a drive by shooting."

"How could such a thing happen?"

"He and Andy were at a party, just arriving, as a matter of fact, when a car drove by and started shooting at the house. I don't understand it all. The police called me right after it happened yesterday afternoon and I got in late last night. I've only seen him once. He didn't get out of surgery until two this morning."

"Where's your mother?" Devan asked, suddenly annoyed with Missy for allowing Brandon to bear the brunt of this tragedy.

"She's in Hawaii. I can't reach her."

"Is someone with you, anyone?"

"Todd's girlfriend, Andy, and the cops."

"If there's an officer with you now, let me talk to him."

Devan waited while Brandon handed the receiver to someone else. He could hear muffled voices and ached with the knowledge of his youngest son enduring this nightmare alone.

"Mr. Yates, I'm Detective Brannigan."

"What's going on out there?" Devan demanded.

"Your son just arrived at a party when a car drove by and shot at the house. We're certain this is drug related, but they targeted the wrong house. We've raided a crack house two doors down at least twice in the past month."

"And my son?"

"He caught a bullet in the back. The surgery lasted well over twelve hours. This all happened about noon yesterday. When can you get here?"

"As soon as I get a flight."

"I'll stay with Brandon until you arrive," the detective assured him. "When you arrange a flight time, call me here and I'll have an officer meet you at the airport. We've already arranged for temporary lodging for you and your son. Since we've finally reached you, we're taking him over there for some rest. The doctors have prescribed something so he can sleep. As a precaution, we're sending an officer with him."

"Why the security?" Devan asked.

"In a case like this, we don't take any chances. We're assuming this is drug related, but since we don't know who the shooters were, we don't know the actual motive. If this stemmed from a grudge against your oldest son, we wouldn't want to put Brandon in danger."

"I see. Can you tell me anything about Todd, about his condition?"

"The doctors aren't saying much. He's still unconscious. Maybe we'll know more by the time you arrive."

After Devan jotted down the number at the hospital, he hung up the phone. Still in shock, he pressed the play button on the machine. The messages from Brandon, the police, and several doctors all said the same thing he'd just heard from Brandon and Detective Brannigan.

When the last message ended, he pressed the delete button, as if by erasing them this horrible tragedy would disappear as well.

After looking up the number for the airlines, he called the reservation desk. "I need a flight to Philadelphia, preferably from Madison," he told the reservationist. "It has to be as soon as possible."

"I have a flight at one fifty. With one stop it puts you in at six twenty."

"I'll take it. My name is Devan Yates," he said, then read the number from his credit card. "Can you make it first class?"

With the reservation made, he hung up the phone. So few people traveled first class any more, with the cost and all, he prayed it would be deserted. He needed the time alone to digest the information he'd just received.

He placed his next call to Jim. "Why, Devan," Jim began, "I didn't expect to hear from you on a Sunday morning."

"I need a favor, Jim. I need you to take me to the Madison airport."

"Didn't you just get back from taking Julie to Chicago? Is something wrong?"

"My oldest son, Todd, is in the hospital. He's been shot. I need to go to Philadelphia right away."

"Of course. What time do you need to leave?"

Devan looked at his watch, surprised to see he'd been home for almost an hour and a half.

"Soon. It's almost eleven. My flight leaves at one fifty. If we leave by noon, we should be all right."

He continued to talk with Jim for several more minutes, trying to sort out his feelings, to understand the confusing events of the few minutes since he'd returned home.

When at last he finished his conversation, he packed a bag and called Julie's house. Her answering machine picked up and he listened to her voice before leaving his message. "Julie, I just got back from taking you to the airport. I've very confused right now. My son, Todd, is in the hospital. I'm leaving for Philadelphia this afternoon. I'll talk to you when I get home. I hope your vacation is great."

He hung up the phone and immediately regretted leaving the message. Julie would return in a week. Maybe he'd be home by then. No matter what the case, she certainly didn't need to hear his depressing news as soon as she arrived. For a moment, he wondered why he bothered to leave a message at all. Of course, he knew the answer, the message hadn't been important; he only wanted to hear her voice.

Eleven

Julie held her breath as the plane made its approach into the Montego Bay airport. She'd never flown before and had no idea what to expect during take off and landing.

When the plane started its ascent, she'd experienced a rush, not unlike the one she felt whenever she rode an elevator. To her surprise, she hardly noticed the slow descent until the wheels touched the pavement of the runway.

Once the plane rolled to a stop, she joined the passengers who were making their way toward the door. Instead of stepping into a jetway, she found herself greeted by the exotic beauty of the Jamaican countryside. A warm breeze kissed her cheek and ruffled her hair, the sweet smell of tropical flowers reached her nostrils, and the sound of reggae music filled the air.

Almost as soon as she entered the terminal, a dark skinned man handed her a glass of rum punch. "Welcome to Jamaica, my lady," he said, his accent very pronounced.

"Thank you," she said. She accepted the glass and took a sip of the sweet liquid. The taste of it reminded her of George's warning about avoiding sugar.

Her expression must have denoted her bewilderment, because the man who greeted her earlier touched her arm. "Wait over there, my lady. Soon your luggage will arrive and when you are finished with customs, you will be free to find the coach to your hotel."

When Julie joined the people waiting for their luggage, she saw her bag on the first cart to come from the plane. After retrieving it, she followed instructions and stood in line with the rest of the tourists.

An official looking man came down the line, randomly choosing people to have them open their bags for customs. She held her breath until he passed by her. The woman standing next to her was not so lucky, as the man asked her to open her bags for inspection.

At the customs desk, she presented her new passport. When the official stamped it, she smiled at the Jamaican imprint gracing its first page.

Once outside the terminal, she again enjoyed the warm breeze and took off her suit jacket to become more comfortable. Across the way, she noticed several busses with the name of the tour company printed on their sides.

Beside one of the busses stood a young Jamaican woman. "May I have your name, my lady?" she asked.

"Julie Weston," she replied, feeling suddenly lonely in this strange land where happy couples surrounded her.

"Of course, Ms. Weston. You'll be taking the far bus, the one to Negril. Do enjoy your stay in Jamaica."

On the bus, Julie made her way to a seat at the center and slid across to sit next to the window.

One by one, other passengers boarded the bus. A young woman, whom she'd seen on the plane, made her way down the aisle and stopped beside Julie. Julie had been watching her so intently she hardly realized she'd paused.

The woman, who couldn't be much older than thirty-five, wore an ankle length skirt of a gauzy material, which sported a bold print, with a matching blouse open to the waist where it ended in a knot. Beneath the blouse, she wore a brightly colored tank top. Her blonde hair, Julie ascertained, had come from a bottle, for she definitely didn't have the coloring to be a natural blonde.

"Is this seat taken?" the woman asked.

"No," Julie replied.

"Good." The woman slid in beside Julie, shoving her bag under the seat in front of her. "I noticed you on the plane. Is this your first trip to Jamaica? It's my third. I come every time I lose a husband."

"Are you a widow?" Julie asked, hardly able to believe this flamboyant character could be in mourning.

"You could say that, my second husband did die, but I divorced numbers one and three. My name is Dorah Rutland."

"Well, Dorah Rutland, I'm Julie Weston." She extended her hand. Against her better judgment, she found herself beginning to like Dorah, almost wishing she were as self-confident and outgoing.

"I pegged you for a first timer when I saw you on the plane. You looked kind of scared. Until today, you haven't flown much, have you?"

"No, I haven't. How did you know?"

"I can spot a first timer a mile away. While they were giving all those safety instructions, you were listening to every word. Anyone who flies a lot already has the book open by then. So, where are you from?"

"A little town you've probably never heard of, called Minter."

"Minter, Wisconsin? Sure I know it. It's the first potty stop north of Chicago."

Julie laughed out loud. "I've never heard it called that before."

"My last husband, Rutty, liked the Big North Woods. He considered himself a great one for camping and all that other happy horseshit. Well, I told him, Dorah doesn't camp, so all the time we were dating I made him rent us a cottage. Like a dope, I even said we could spend our honeymoon there. I should have known better. I caught him in bed with an Indian bitch three days after the wedding. That ended that mighty quick."

"On your honeymoon?" Julie asked, astonished.

"You've got the picture. The bastard could have either been more discreet or at least waited a couple of years. I came back from swimming and there she sat, maybe laid is a better terminology, naked as a jaybird. Well, I just told him, if he wanted his little Indian tail, he could have it, but Dorah wanted a *big* settlement. I got it, too. One of these days I'm going to find a husband who says, 'Dorah, dear, I don't want you to work, I can support you,' or I'm going to make enough on divorce settlements to live comfortably."

Julie wanted to hear more about Dorah. If she asked several questions she hoped the topic of conversation wouldn't turn to her life.

Before she could question Dorah further, the girl she had spoke with earlier joined them on the bus. She announced they were leaving for Negril and mentioned several points of interest to watch for along the way.

When at last, the bus took to the road, Julie continued. "You said he was your third husband, what were the other two like?"

Dorah smiled, as though pleased to have an excuse to talk about herself. "My first husband was J. Worthington Wentworth the third. I met him in New York and he swept me off my feet. He wouldn't make love to me until we were married, because he loved me too much to cheapen me. What a crock! He looked like a hunk, but he was a dud in bed. What he didn't know about sex could fill a book. I mean, at that point you couldn't have called me a pro, but I knew what I wanted, what things should be like. We were married for five years, never had any kids, but that didn't come as any surprise, our sex life was almost nonexistent. Then I came home one day and caught him in bed with the gardener. I found him having great sex with another guy. I said *adios*, packed my bags, and lo and behold, he said he didn't want to give me a settlement. I just said, do you want Daddy to find out about your sex life? You just withhold a settlement from me and I'll call J. Worthington Junior and spill my guts. The old man would have disowned him if he found out about him being gay. Of course, it turned out to be academic, he found out anyway, in the end. I heard J. Worthington the third contracted AIDS about six years ago and died three years later. I got myself checked right away, but thank God, he got it after we split."

"It doesn't sound like you're lucky in love," Julie said.

"Oh, I wouldn't say that. My second husband, now he's still special, even if he is dead. I met him at Hidden Island, right after I divorced dear J. I'd decided to drown my sorrows at the bar and found Jeff there with a group of his friends. We hit it off right away. I even moved to Chicago to be close to him. I got a job with a law firm and about a year later we got married. We had a real marriage, too, not like playing house with J. After two years, we decided we wanted kids, so we bought a little house in Oak Park. The problem came when I didn't get pregnant. The tests showed Jeff to be sterile, but they also showed he had cancer. He lasted two years."

"How terrible," Julie said, wiping away a tear. "Did you keep the house?"

"No, I couldn't stand to go back to it. We were so happy there and I loved Jeff so deeply. I sold it and bought a small condo. I also returned to Jamaica, because I'd promised Jeff I would."

"And that's when you met your third husband, right?" Julie asked, enthralled by Dorah's narrative.

"No. I met him at a party in Chicago about two years later." Dorah paused and gazed out the window.

Julie watched the younger woman and tried to read her thoughts. Undoubtedly, they were of the good times she'd spent with Jeff.

Had there ever been good times with Steve? Two months ago, she could have recalled any number of them, pleasant memories. Now every good thing seemed overshadowed by Steve's planned infidelity.

"Here I've been prattling on about my life and I haven't given you a chance to say a thing," Dorah said, turning her attention back to Julie. "I suppose the guy at the airport is your husband."

"Airport?" Julie questioned before she remembered Devan.

"Oh, you mean Devan. No, he's just an old friend."

"Some old friend," Dorah said. "He looks more like a hunk to me."

"I guess he is," Julie agreed, unable to conceal the confusion in her voice.

"I'm sorry," Dora apologized, placing her slender, well-manicured hand over Julie's. "I sense some painful memories. Is he a cad or is it too much to talk about?"

Julie laughed at Dorah's suggestion. "Devan? Good heavens, no. Like I said, we're friends. Friendly non-committed lovers, as a matter-of-fact. Unfortunately, I met him again, at the wrong time."

"Again?"

"Devan and I were buddies in high school. He moved back to Minter last fall, but I didn't know about it until New Year's Eve. A mutual friend of ours set us up at a party, not knowing we already knew each other. You know how it is, get a date for the poor grieving widow."

"Were you married long?"

"Too long. Steve and I made it twenty-eight and a half years. At least I thought we did. After this past month, I'm not so sure. He'd been cheating on me for about ten of those years. It all made for bad timing between Devan and me. I guess I thought this trip might clear my mind about a lot of things."

"How did you find out? You make it sound like you haven't know about it for long."

"It all happened just after the first of the year. A friend of mine thought I knew about Steve. We were having an argument and he needed a weapon to use against me. We've cleared the air about it, though."

"How could you forgive something like that?"

"At first I didn't think I could. When I heard those ugly words, I collapsed. Fortunately, it forced me to get medical attention, maybe even saved my life."

They continued to talk, to get to know each other and marvel at the beauty of the countryside, until the bus pulled up in front of the massive gates leading to Hidden Island. Almost magically, the gates opened and the bus pulled up the beautifully landscaped driveway.

"It's beautiful," Julie said, with the excitement of a child on Christmas morning. "I certainly didn't expect anything like this."

"It is a bit overwhelming, the first time," Dorah agreed. "Did your travel agent mention you might have a roommate?"

Julie nodded, too awed to say anything.

"Good. If we have roomies, let's see if we can switch and be together."

The idea appealed to Julie and by the time they were met, it had been settled. She'd become comfortable with Dorah and knew the chances of finding someone else as compatible were slim.

Everyone on the staff seemed to know Dorah and was excited to see her again. There had been no problem rooming together and they soon found themselves escorted to a beautiful room with a view of the Caribbean.

"Well," Dorah said, as she plopped down on the bed nearest the door. "What do you think?"

"I've read about places like this, seen them on *Lifestyles Of The Rich And Famous*, but I never expected to come to one. I feel like Alice In Wonderland or Cinderella. If I'm dreaming, please don't wake me." Her comment brought an amusing thought to mind. She may not be famous, but she certainly was rich.

While they unpacked, Dorah explained how the open-air pavilion they'd passed through on the their arrival served as a commons area. Meals, entertainment, aerobics all took place there. To one side, Dorah had continued, a piano bar provided an intimate atmosphere, while a more casual pool bar stood just outside the dining area. Of course, she quickly pointed out the disco a few feet away. It contained a large window that looked out into the swimming pool, and the beach bar allowed you refreshment while you enjoyed the warmth of the Caribbean.

"Are you ready to hit the nude beach?" Dorah asked, when everything had been put away.

"*Nude beach*!" Julie echoed.

"Weren't you warned about that? Oh, well, no biggie. Don't jump into it. Going there certainly isn't mandatory. If you feel uncomfortable don't go. If you decide to give it a try, join me. I try to go for at least an hour every day, it gives me a more even tan."

"Completely nude?" Julie gasped, unaware of anything else Dorah had said.

"Look, you aren't in Minter anymore. You've entered Fantasy Island. Anything you ever wanted to do, do it here. If it's swimming at the nude beach, so be it. If it's getting up to entertain at the guest talent night, more power to you. Here you aren't Julie Weston, widow, or Julie Weston, head of personnel at LisPro. Here you're plain Julie, and Julie is entitled to as good time as anyone else. Just remember, you'll probably never see any of these people again, so have a good time."

Julie sank down on the second bed. "That's quite an analogy."

"I guess it is. Jeff taught me that the first time I came here. Live for today and to hell with tomorrow. My folks have a lot of money. I grew up on Long Island and thought being a goody two shoes would give me the perfect life. What a crock of shit that turned out to be." Dorah paused, as if waiting for her words to sink in. "When I found out about J., it didn't matter that I'd had the most elegant coming out party on Long Island or I'd been the debutante of the year. Nothing matters but today. Jeff taught me how to live like a real person. I thought my mother would have a coronary when I moved to Chicago to be closer to Jeff, but she didn't. Of course, coming here is downright sinful in her eyes."

"Do you ever see your folks?"

"Oh, sure I do. I go home for Christmas as well as a week in the summer, and I do the mandatory call home once a week thing. I won't ever fit into their lives on a full time basis and I honestly don't want to. My lifestyle suits me just fine and it's a hell of a lot more fun."

Julie lay back on the bed and tried to imagine Dorah in high society. It seemed as strange as her own trip to Jamaica must be to Mark, Jill, and Lance.

"You know, my oldest son doesn't approve of my new lifestyle, either. When he found out I'd spent the night with Devan, he hit the roof. He let me know, in no uncertain terms, there were things mothers didn't do, and sex without marriage is one of them."

"He sounds straight... too straight. Is that want Julie Weston is like?"

"It's what she used to be like. Sex, no matter how much I enjoyed it, became like everything else in my marriage, predictable. Get a kiss good night, whenever he came home before I fell asleep, and make love for ten minutes on Friday night."

"Well," Dorah proclaimed, swinging her long, shapely legs over the side of the bed to the floor, "enough about yesterday and to hell with tomorrow. It's time to enjoy today!

~ * ~

Julie spent her first afternoon exploring the grounds of Hidden Island and marveling over the tropical beauty of the resort. As much as she enjoyed Dorah's company, she delighted in the solitude.

Live for today, Dorah's voice echoed in her mind. She wondered if straight, shy Julie could ever abide by those words. Could she possible become as carefree as when she'd been Julie Morgan?

She took great pains in dressing for dinner. She chose the black and white sundress Meg insisted she buy and accented it with red accessories.

"That's disgusting," Dorah observed. "Nobody should look that good. All of the men will be swarming around you and there won't be any left for me."

"I know you're flattering me, but please don't stop. My ego needs all the help it can get."

"Believe what you want, but the way you look you're going to have a great week."

The pavilion had already begun to fill with the guests who tonight were strangers and by next Sunday would be friends. Julie observed the strange mix of humanity. There were the young, both married and single, for whom this resort seemed perfectly suited. There were people you could only call middle-aged who, like herself, were embracing this new lifestyle, and there were older couples that had come here to relive their youth and forget their age.

Dorah led her to the long buffet table and when their plates were filled, a young man escorted them to a table for four where two men were already seated.

Julie judged the younger man to be in his early forties. Undoubtedly, he worked in an office, as his fair skin seemed almost pale next to Dorah's artificial tan from hours spent in a tanning booth.

"Good evening, ladies," the younger man said. "My name is Craig Parker." He held out a chair for Dorah, unable to take his eyes from her.

"And I'm Royd McAlester," the older man advised them, holding the other vacant chair for Julie.

She judged Royd's age to be about fifty and his thick drawl told her he came from Texas.

"Dorah Rutland," Julie heard her roommate reply. "I'm a secretary from Chicago."

"I'm Julie Weston," she said, following Dorah's head and wondering why she ever thought she belonged in a place like this.

"Let's see, your accent tells me you're from the Midwest. Could it be Wisconsin?" Royd asked.

Julie nodded, dumbfounded by his guess.

"Milwaukee, Madison, Green Bay, would you be from any of those lovely cities?"

"Hardly. I'm from a small town you've never heard of. I'm from Minter."

"Minter," Craig commented, joining the conversation for the first time. "Isn't there a company there called LisPro?"

"Yes. I'm a secretary there," she replied, catching Dorah's smile of approval at her white lie, from the corner of her eye.

"I see," Royd said. He put his hand over hers and leaned a bit closer. "How did they allow a beauty like you to get out of Minter?"

"I went to Chicago and got on the plane. No one seemed to be clamoring for me to stay home." As soon as she said the words, she thought of Devan. Although he'd told her to have a good time and assured her he thought this vacation would be a good thing for her, she knew he wanted her to stay with him.

"I doubt that," Royd continued, dispelling Julie's thoughts of Devan. "I bet you've broken the heart of every single man in that fair city."

Julie blushed and looked down at her food, feeling nervous at her small deception.

"So what brings you to Jamaica?" Royd questioned. "A broken heart or just a vacation?"

"Perhaps a little of both," she replied sweetly.

Dinner proved to be a mix of good food and exploratory conversation. Craig and Royd were businessmen who, like Dorah and Julie, had been paired off as roommates. Craig and his wife were separated, soon to be divorced, and he came from Overland Park, Kansas. Royd, on the other hand, proved to be a widower from El Paso.

Julie listened intently to the conversation around her, more than content to allow Dorah to carry on the feminine end of the table talk.

After they finished dessert, Dorah and Craig disappeared into the velvety curtain of the night.

"Would you care to take a moonlight walk on the beach, Julia?" Royd asked.

"My name is Julie," she corrected him.

"But isn't that a shortened version of Julia? I do dearly love the name Julia, and it does suit you well."

"Then Julia it is," she agreed, pleased to be someone different for a few days. "I'd love to take a walk on the beach."

They strolled across the warm sand for more than an hour and, at Royd's insistence, Julie took off her sandals. It seemed as though she was a teenager again and she wondered low long she could extend the feeling.

A light breeze blew in from the water and Julie shivered slightly.

"I think it's time I took you back to your room," Royd said.

As though she'd lost all track of time, Julie looked up, surprised to see they had arrived back at the complex.

"Until tomorrow, lovely lady," Royd said, as he kissed her hand and disappeared into the night.

"Well," Dorah said the minute Julie entered the room, "did he kiss you?"

"He kissed my hand and called me Julia," she sighed.

"That doesn't sound good. Maybe you'd better look for someone else."

"Dorah!" Julie exclaimed, hardly able to believe her ears.

"At least I got to first base, you didn't even get up to bat."

"I can't believe you said that."

"Give it a couple of days if you like. As for me, I can guarantee I'll hit a home run before you do."

"You mean you'd sleep with a perfect stranger?"

"Oh Julie, don't you understand? I've slept with a lot of perfect strangers. I even married three of them. From what you've said, you slept with a perfect stranger for twenty-eight years. Can you actually say you ever knew your husband? The difference is you were acquainted with him, but it doesn't matter, we all have our dirty little secrets."

Julie thought about Dorah's words. Steve had been her friend, her lover, and her husband, yet she'd never known him. Did she know Devan? Of course, she didn't, but it hadn't mattered on New Year's Eve and it certainly didn't matter now.

~ * ~

Julie's first morning in Jamaica began early. At Dorah's insistence, she slipped into a swimsuit and pulled a skirt over it before going to the pool.

"I wondered if I'd see you this morning, or if you were just a wonderful dream," Royd greeted her. He got up from the chaise lounge by the pool and took her hand.

"What are you smiling at, Mr. McAlester?" she inquired.

"You're more beautiful by the light of day, Julia. Are you ready for an early morning swim before breakfast?"

Julie hesitated for a moment and remembered the many times Steve ridiculed her about the way she looked in a swimsuit. She wished he could see her now, could hear the desire in Royd's voice.

"Julia, Julia! Are you all right?"

"All right?" she repeated when she managed to find her voice. "Oh, yes, of course I am. You caught me thinking of another time, another place. Didn't you say something about swimming?"

Julie eased herself into the pool and wondered if she had forgotten how to swim. It seemed a lifetime ago when she, Devan, Jerry, and Sandy had spent their summers at the lake, swimming and sunbathing. She even swam on the high school relay team.

"You do swim, don't you?" Royd asked.

"Yes, but I'm afraid I'm a bit rusty."

"Never fear, beautiful lady, I'll save you if you start to drown."

She moved into the deeper water, and began to swim as though she had done it every day of her life.

After completing several laps, she eased herself to the side of the pool and accepted the towel Royd held out to her.

"You hardly need a life guard," he teased. "What do you mean you're rusty?"

"It's strange, Julie replied. "I haven't done any serious swimming in almost thirty years. I guess it's like riding a bicycle, you never forget how to do it."

Royd helped her to her feet and escorted her to the dining area. "Are you hungry?"

"Starving. I'm not used to this much activity before breakfast. I usually have to leave for work by the time I finish dressing. Seven o'clock comes all too early, you know."

"Do you go to work at seven? I didn't think secretaries started work much before eight."

"Did I say seven, I... ah, I meant eight."

"What are you so flustered about?"

"Nothing, nothing at all. Oh, look at all that food," she said, abruptly changing the subject. "Doesn't it look delicious?"

She began to fill her plate and could feel Royd's eyes boring into the back of her neck, in an attempt to read her thoughts.

The tables, which last evening were filled with soups, appetizers, salads, vegetables and entrees, were now laden with platters of breakfast meats, mounds of fresh fruits, pastries, as well as anything else anyone could want for a morning meal.

Royd led her to a secluded table and held her chair while she seated herself. "You're going to spoil me. I'm not used to being pampered," she said, her words coming a bit too fast as she tried to hide her trepidation at almost being caught in a lie.

"What would you like to do today?" Royd asked.

"I don't know," she replied, beginning to relax. Perhaps Royd wouldn't press her about her slip. "What do you want to do? You seem to be the expert on this place, not me. You know what there is to do here."

"Would you like to go riding?"

"As in horse?" she questioned.

"As in horse," Royd said, then laughed heartily. "You do ride, don't you?"

Julie heard Royd's question, but she didn't answer. Instead Steve's voice entered her mind :: "as in horse? Really Julie, do you *think anyone could find a horse to hold you? Why put a poor animal through the agony and embarrass yourself in the process?"::*

"Julia, Julia, did you hear me? Do you ride?"

Julie nodded her head. "Of course I ride. It's just been—"

"I know it's been a long time. You were somewhere else again, weren't you?"

"I'm afraid so."

"Is it such a terrible place? When I lose you to it, you look so very sad."

Julie nodded. "I'm sorry Royd. I came here to find Julie Weston, but I've started off on the wrong foot." She paused for a moment and took a sip of her coffee. Before Royd could say anything, she continued. "You were right, you know. You caught me in a lie. I'm not a secretary at LisPro. I'm head of the Personnel Department there. In fact, I'm the first woman department head in the history of the company."

"Then why, Julia? Why pass yourself off as a secretary? Why degrade yourself?"

"I guess I'm very naive about the single life. Dorah said men don't like women who are in management. I had no trouble believing her. No matter what I achieved, what I did, I never considered myself more than a secretary. My husband made it quite clear as to what my status was."

Julie's mind spun. She'd said it and she certainly didn't regret her decision. She didn't wear half-truths and lies as well as Steve had. She didn't wear them well at all.

"I don't understand your late husband, Julia. How could he not be proud of your accomplishments?"

"As Steve Weston's wife, my job description read 'to compliment Steve and keep my mouth shut about anything I'd done or become.'"

"This man must have been a fool. Anyone who could provoke such sadness in your eyes could never consider himself worthy of you."

"Don't be so quick to pass judgment, Royd. You didn't know me then. You didn't see me fifty pounds heavier than I am now."

"Did fifty pounds alter your personality? Did it change who you are? I doubt it. I said it before and I'll say it again, he was a fool."

Julie smiled. Royd's words flattered her and at the same time she knew they rang with a note of truth. She'd always considered herself one hell of a woman and Royd just confirmed her self-analysis. Her confession, his acceptance, made her feel confident in her decision to begin a new life.

While Royd arranged for the horses, Julie returned to her room to change clothes. To her surprise, she found Dorah still in bed.

"I thought you got up when I did," she commented.

Dorah propped herself up on her elbow. "I just got up to get you off on the right foot. Did you find him waiting for you?"

Julie picked up the pillow from her unmade bed and threw it at Dorah. "Yes, I found him waiting for me, but this time I handled things my way."

"What do you mean?"

"I told him the truth about Julie Weston and he didn't run away. He thinks I'm great even if I'm not a secretary. We're going riding."

"Riding? As in horse?" Dorah asked, wrinkling her nose in disgust.

"That's right, as in horse. Have you ever gone riding down here?"

"Good heavens, no. I never did fit in with the horsey set. Just give me the nude beach and I'll be happy. Have a good time."

~ * ~

Julia's behavior baffled Royd, until her confession. He tried to envision her heavier and in doing so, he could only see his wife.

LuAnn had been the only woman he'd ever loved. She hadn't worked outside the home, but he'd been proud of her. She, like Julia, had been heavy, but she'd never allowed the weight to bother her. LuAnn had been active, sexy, and beautiful.

Just thinking about LuAnn brought a lump to his throat. The last two years of their life together seemed like a nightmare. The cancer, as well as the chemo, ate away at her body until she weighed less than one hundred pounds. Watching her body waste away had been terrible, but her mind remained sharp and she never ceased being the woman he loved.

He'd asked Julia if fifty pounds made her a different person and she'd said no. Somehow he knew that would be her answer, knew her weight had nothing to do with the woman inside the body.

~ * ~

For Julie, the week passed much too quickly. By Saturday, she'd done things she never envisioned herself doing. Royd took her horseback riding, windsurfing, and on an excursion to the famous Dunn's River Falls. They'd played tennis, swam in the sea as well as the pool, and done aerobics. As busy as their days seemed, their nights were equally full. After the gourmet dinners, they enjoyed entertainment, romantic walks in the moonlight and long talks accompanied by tender kisses and soft caresses.

In the course of a week, Royd told her of his wife, LuAnn, and she could see the love in his eyes. She ached to experience the kind of love that radiated at even the mention of LuAnn's name. As much as Steve's unexpected death devastated her, she knew the experience could not rival Royd's last two years with LuAnn. Her death had not been sudden. Royd had watched her waste away, knowing there would be no miracle cure, no last minute reprieve.

To compensate for his loss, he enjoyed a relationship with a woman named Betty. She could only equate their relationship to the one she shared with Devan. For Royd, Jamaica had become a welcome diversion from the routine of daily life.

As for Dorah, they rarely saw each other. Dorah went her own way and Julie soon became able to sleep through her comings and goings. When Julie retired, Dorah never seemed to be around, but slipped in sometime during the night to become a familiar lump in the other bed the next morning.

Julie had been surprised to find Dorah's bed still freshly made and Dorah nowhere in sight on Saturday morning. She gave the matter little thought as she stepped into the shower. The refreshing needles of water brought her to full alertness. She'd just wrapped herself in a large, soft towel when she heard the door open and someone enter the room.

"Julie, Julie, are you here?" Dorah called.

Julie opened the bathroom door, to allow a cloud of steam to follow her into the room.

"Well, good morning," she greeted Dorah. "You're a little later than usual."

"I guess I am. I had a wild night."

Julie studied Dorah's disheveled appearance. "I bet you did. I think every night you have is a wild night."

"No, really, this time things were different. We stripped all the covers off Craig's bed and slept on the beach."

"You slept on the beach?" Julie echoed.

"We pulled two chaise lounges together and slept there after we made love in the sand. We laid under the stars and held hands all night."

"But on the beach?"

"Well, you and Royd don't make it very easy for us to stay here. You aren't cooperating at all. We thought at least one room would be empty for the night by now."

"I guess we're just a bit slower than you and Craig. We haven't progressed that far yet."

Dorah shook her head. "I told you to find someone else. It's almost time to go home and you haven't even gotten out of the batter's box."

"Are you really a baseball nut or do you still think like we did in high school?"

Dorah flopped down on the bed, convulsed in gales of laughter. "I'm a real, honest to goodness baseball fan, thanks to my husbands. With J. we had champagne and season tickets to see the Yankees. Jeff and I enjoyed soda and the White Sox four or five times a year from box seats. Rutty introduced me to beer, the bleachers, and the Cubs. I cheered for them all, especially the ones with nice tight buns."

Julie joined her laughter. "You said your husbands introduced you to baseball. Didn't your dad ever take you to games?" she asked, her mind filled with memories of Braves' games with her parents and one Brewers' game with Steve and the kids. She'd almost forgotten the fun of cheering on the home team.

"Dear old Daddy doesn't approve of baseball," Dorah said, her voice taking on a much sharper edge. "It's not refined to root for the home team, even if you do it with a glass of Dom Perignon."

Julie allowed the conversation to drop, sensing more behind Dorah's icy tone than she confided.

Her conversation with Dorah delayed her arrival at the pool. When she finally got there, Royd had already begun his morning swim. Without waiting for him to notice her, she moved to the deep end and dove in.

"Good morning, Miss Julia," Royd said, when he swam up to greet her.

"I bet you thought I got lost," she replied.

"To be truthful, I thought you weren't coming, but I'm certainly glad you proved me wrong."

Julie allowed him to take her in his arms and kiss her tenderly. She hardly realized he'd slipped his hands inside the top of her suit until he cupped her breasts and caressed her nipples.

A soft moan of pleasure escaped her lips and she wrapped her arms tightly around his neck.

"I want you, Julia, but not like this. Spend the night with me tonight and let me love you in a more appropriate way."

Julie nodded and in doing so, wondered if she knew what she had agreed to do. With Steve she made love because she was in love and sex was expected. With Devan she'd been lonely and he'd filled the gap, but they had been friends, friendly lovers. She now amazed even herself by planning to make love to a perfect stranger in this tropical paradise.

~ * ~

Royd's room looked exactly like the one Julie shared with Dorah. With all day to contemplate her actions, she'd become a bit nervous. She knew she had no reason for such feelings. She was a grown woman and her decision like the one Mark made when he moved in with Keoki, had been made as an adult.

"Julia," Royd said. He came up behind her and put his hands on her shoulders, then caressed down her arms.

She leaned her head back against his chest and allowed him to enjoy the feel of her body beneath his probing hands. She could feel a slight tug as he untied the straps of her sundress and moaned softly when he pushed the bodice down around her waist, exposing her white breasts.

His touch delighted her and she wanted more. When he turned her to face him, she became aware of his nude body, aware of the desire she'd invoked in him.

His hands moved from her breasts to her waist, then to her hips, until the dress, along with her underwear had fallen to the floor. For a moment, he held her at arm's length and gazed lustfully at her naked body.

"My god, Julia, you are absolutely gorgeous. How could I get so lucky as to meet someone like you?"

She wanted to scream for him to stop making small talk and make love to her, but before she could utter a word, she found herself on the bed, with Royd on top of her. He covered her body with tender kisses then began to probe between her legs with his fingers.

"Oh, Royd," she uttered when to her surprise, he began kissing her stomach and moving lower until his tongue found her most erotic zone and drove her to heights she'd never expected to reach.

Just when she decided she could stand no more, he moved up and began teasing her nipples with kisses, bites, and prolonged sucking while he made love to her. Afterwards, they fell, exhausted, into each other's arms. It didn't take long for them to regain their strength and make love again, until Julie knew she could prolong the ecstasy no longer. At last they fell asleep, until the sun streaming into the window awakened them.

Although they wanted to make love again, they knew time was short. Royd's bus would be leaving at eleven and the clock already read eight. He and Craig would need to pack, and Julie needed to do the same if she were to be ready to leave at one.

Julie slipped from Royd's arms and headed for the shower. To her surprise, Royd joined her.

He took the soap from her hands and began to lather her body. The movement of his hands across her skin proved to be even more sensual than their lovemaking only a few hours earlier.

"I've never had such an experience," she confessed, once she'd dressed. "You're an expert lover."

"LuAnn always thought so. You've never showered with anyone, have you?"

"Considering my size, two of us couldn't fit into such a confined space," she laughed at the joke she'd made at her own expense.

"Don't," he said, as he put his finger to her lips in an attempt to silence her words. "Don't ever put yourself down because of your size."

She wished she could put Steve's ugly words behind her as easily as Royd made it sound, but she knew it would take longer than a week to forget what she had been.

Royd insisted they say good-bye in his room, after Julie helped him pack his bag. Before he left, he took her phone number and address with him. She considered it a nice gesture, since she knew she would never hear from him again. Theirs had been a vacation love affair, one to be remembered fondly, but not something to be prolonged. He would be returning to Betty and she to Devan. He probably would think of her only on evenings when he sat alone with his memories. She hoped she would be as pleasant a memory for him as she knew he would be for her.

"When you spend the night with a man, you really spend the night," Dorah teased, when Julie entered their room. "Do you think you'll see him again?"

"No," Julie said, her voice echoing her sadness. "He has someone at home and so do I. What we shared is but a pleasant diversion. How about you and Craig?"

"He's decided to try and reconcile with his wife. It's for the best. I don't think I could become a Royals' fan. He's a good lover, but a bit stuffy for my taste."

~ * ~

The chartered flight neared O'Hare and Julie realized how far away Jamaica and Royd seemed.

Within minutes, they would be landing and Devan would be waiting to take her back to Minter.

This trip had been meant to open her eyes, help her decide what to do about her life. Instead she'd become more confused than when she left. Jamaica had brought rest, fun and Royd, but precious little time for deep thoughts.

"Oh, look," Dorah said, excitement evident in her voice. "All those lights! We're home! I love flying into O'Hare at night, the lights look like a big Christmas tree."

"I guess they do," Julie agreed. "It's strange to think I'll soon be back in Minter. Speaking of going home, how will you get to your place?"

"If I don't run into someone I know, I'll just get a cab. Maybe I'll get lucky and run into Penny."

"Penny?"

"My roommate. She's a flight attendant. She's due in sometime tonight. This week has worked out well. She's been back every night to keep Mr. Peabody company."

"And just who is Mr. Peabody?" Julie asked, as she suppressed a giggle.

"My cat, silly. I know, Mr. Peabody is a dog in the cartoon, but I love the name and I loathe dogs. What kind of a pet do you have?"

"None, thank you. Steve and the kids thought we needed a pet, so we got a dog. Then one day Jill brought home a cat. When I first found out I hit the roof. To make a long story short, I put up with those two animals for almost ten years. Finally the dog died and the cat decided to go on vacation at the same time we did, only we came back. After that I said no more pets. It just didn't seem fair, we were never home and pets need someone to care for them. Of course, the kids had a fit. I told them when they were on their own, they could have any animals they wanted, but not in my house."

Julie settled back into her seat, just as the Fasten Seat Belt sign blinked on and Dorah dissolved in laughter.

"Really, Julie, you're wasting your time in Minter. You should be in one of the comedy clubs in Chicago. You could come down and stay with me. I could arrange for you to get on one of the amateur nights."

"Don't be silly. I'm almost forty-eight years old, for Pete's sake."

"Look at Phyllis Diller and Roseanne. They weren't twenty when they started. Give it some thought, it would be fun if nothing else."

The plane continued it's descent, and Julie contemplated Dorah's suggestion. Maybe she would go to Chicago and stay with Dorah for a weekend. Devan had understood her need to go to Jamaica. If she decided to go to Chicago, he would have to understand that as well.

The wheels of the plane touched the runway and at last they taxied to a stop. "Welcome to Chicago," the captain announced over the public address system. "The time in Chicago is eight thirty Central Standard Time and the temperature is eighteen degrees above zero."

Julie began to gather her carry on luggage when Dorah stopped her. "Wait a minute," she whispered. "Let those three guys behind us get off first."

"Why?" Julie asked.

"Pot. They're bringing in Jamaican pot. I heard them talking a while ago. We don't need to be anywhere near them when they get busted in customs."

Once inside the terminal, Julie looked around for the three young men and finally caught a fleeting glance of them as they were escorted into another room.

"Hi, Dorah," the customs agent greeted them. "I didn't know you'd gone away. Did you find a new man at Hidden Island?"

"Not this time, Ted. I don't think I'll ever find another Jeff. How are Mary and the kids?"

"They're fine. How about you, do you have a way home?"

Dorah shook her head. "I'll just grab a cab."

"If it weren't for that mess," he began, nodding toward the room where the three young men had been taken, "I'd take you home myself."

"It's okay, Ted," Dorah replied.

When they were at last finished with customs, Julie turned to Dorah. "Do you know everyone?"

Dorah deposited several coins into the coin box on the cart rack and pulled out a luggage cart.

"It seems that way. Ted and Jeff were best friends. Ted acted as our best man and Jeff did the same for him. Later I asked Ted to be one of Jeff's pallbearers. He tries to play big brother, but he's been cool ever since I started seeing Rutty. I'll probably be seeing a lot more of him and his wife now."

~ * ~

"What are you going to tell her?" Meg asked.

Jim held Meg's hand a little tighter. "I don't know, honey. What should I tell her? I can't be the one to break the news about Devan asking for a transfer."

"Of course you can't, but—"

"Shh," Jim cautioned, "here she comes." He watched Julie and a younger woman come from the customs area. The younger woman pushed a cart loaded with luggage and they seemed to be sharing a private joke.

"Julie, over here," he heard Meg call. He watched Julie's face as she crossed the room to meet them. He could see the questions in her eyes and ached with the answers, answers Devan said he would explain.

"Meg, Jim, what are you doing here? Where's Devan?" Julie asked.

"He couldn't come," Jim said, once they'd both embraced her. "He had a family emergency in Philadelphia."

Julie nodded, accepting his answer, and went on to introduce her companion before Dorah left them to catch a cab.

During the trip home, Julie bubbled with the fun she'd had in Jamaica. Jim knew she had questions about Devan, but she didn't voice them. Devan's promise to call her on Monday seemed to be enough to pacify her apprehension over his absence.

Twelve

Julie awoke at nine thirty, happy to be home, to have spent the night in her own bed, in her own house. She put off getting up for as long as possible. She knew she had much to do, but the warmth of her bed invited her to linger and enjoy a few more minutes of her self-imposed vacation. Outside, the wind sounded as though it would blow up a storm, and she wondered if she'd lost a month and come home to March rather than February. Reluctantly, she got out of bed and pulled on her robe and slippers.

Making her way to the kitchen, she realized she needed to go shopping. There were two eggs left in the tray and she found a package of English muffins in the freezer. Together with a glass of orange juice and a cup of coffee, they would make a suitable breakfast. She made a note to stop at the store and pick up some groceries.

When she finished eating, she took her coffee to the living room. Passing the dining room table, she noticed the neat stack of mail Meg had placed there for her. They arrived home so late the previous evening, she'd taken no notice of the mail or the messages which her answering machine noted with its digital read out.

She sat down in the recliner and thought about Devan's unexpected trip to Philadelphia. She'd come back to Minter because it was her home, but mainly because of him. She could have planned another vacation, planned to be gone for weeks on end, but Devan beckoned her home.

She found out in Jamaica she could do quite well on her own. Royd definitely found her attractive, enjoyed her company. Certainly other men would find her equally attractive.

Forcing thoughts of Devan and Royd from her mind, she sorted through the mail. It seemed strange to see envelopes from the phone and power companies. These were the bills, which had, for so many years, been delivered to Steve's office. Half way through the stack, she came across an envelope from the accounting firm. To her amazement, the figures on the enclosed statement attested to the firm's prosperity. Her share of the earnings came to more than six thousand dollars for the month of January, without taking into account the accumulated interest on her numerous investments. She would never have to worry about her financial future at this rate.

With the last of the mail read, she pushed the play button on the answering machine. The first message came from Devan, telling her of his plans to go to Philadelphia. His voice sounded so hurt, so confused, she ached at his tone.

The next voice she heard belonged to Evelyn. "Hi, Julie, it's Evelyn. I told Nancy I'd be giving you a call. She thinks she has a buyer for the cottage. She wants you to meet with him next weekend. They're coming up on Thursday. We'd like you to come on Wednesday and spend a few days with us."

Again the machine beeped and the last message began. Jill's voice sounded full of excitement. "Hi, Mom. It's Sunday night—ten o'clock. I didn't know exactly when you'd be getting home, but I wanted to be the first one to welcome you back. I hope you had a great trip. Please call me tomorrow. Karl and I have wonderful news. I can hardly wait to talk to you."

Julie pushed the erase button, but before she could pick up the receiver to call Jill, the phone rang, startling her.

"Good morning," she answered.

"Julie." She recognized Devan's voice immediately. She couldn't recall ever hearing him sound so depressed, so exhausted.

"I'm so sorry about your son. How are things going?" she asked for lack of any better conversation opener.

"About the same. The doctors say as well as can be expected, whatever that means."

"What do you say?"

"I don't know. Todd regained consciousness on Friday, but he has no feeling in his legs. I still find it all too bizarre to believe. A drive-by shooting just doesn't happen to kids like Todd."

"It happens to anybody anymore, Devan. I, for one, should know about all the things that can't happen but do."

"How much did Jim tell you?"

Devan's question caught her off guard. "He told me about the shooting and your trip to Philadelphia. Is there something else I should know?"

"Yes, there is. I asked for a transfer." Devan's voice sounded flat, as though the words meant nothing to him.

"A transfer? Are you telling me you plan to stay in Philadelphia permanently?"

"I'm sorry, Julie. I guess our timing wasn't right. My son is twenty-three years old and for the first time in his life, he actually needs me. Can you understand why I have to do this?"

"I think so."

"Good, because I don't. All I know is I have to be here. I have to be with him, help him get through this. I wish we would have met at a different time, in a different place. I can't ask you to wait, because I don't know how long the wait might be."

"I understand," Julie replied, knowing she didn't mean the words she knew Devan wanted to hear.

"Do you Julie? I doubt it. You can't fully understand in five minutes what I still don't understand after a week. You see, I don't know if I'm ever coming back to Minter."

Tears sprang to her eyes, but she didn't allow them to sound in her voice. "Will he be paralyzed?" she asked, trying to get back on neutral ground.

"For now, it's a possibility. The doctors say it's too early to tell." Devan paused, then continued. "So, how was your vacation?"

"You're changing the subject, Devan."

"I know. I need to hear something positive. Did you have a good time?"

"I had a wonderful time."

"Did you... ah... did you meet someone special?"

Julie remained silent for a moment and took a deep breath before continuing. "Yes, I did."

"I'm glad," he replied, his voice having a bit of an edge to it. She wondered if he could possibly be jealous. If he were, he had no right to be. This time, he asked her to wait, pushed her out of his life.

"Will you see him again?"

"No. He has someone at home and so do... well, he has someone back home."

"For God's sake, Julie, don't hide in your shell again. You've made such progress. Don't make the same mistakes you did before."

"I won't, I promise. Is there anything I can do, anything at all?"

"The movers will be at my apartment tomorrow morning. I'd appreciate it if you'd be there to supervise. There won't be much to do. It's just a furnished apartment. My stuff is still all in storage. I'd planned to find a house while you were gone and get ready to move in. I guess my priorities got screwed up this week."

"I know. The same thing happens to me all the time. You will keep in touch, won't you?"

"Sure. I'm staying at Todd's apartment for the time being."

"Is anyone else there with you?"

"No. Brandon came out last weekend, but I insisted he return to school. Of course, Missy was on vacation in Hawaii when all this happened. Her flight didn't get back to Seattle until late last night. She called as soon as she got home and heard the message on her machine. She's coming out later today."

When they finished the conversation, Julie sat a while, staring out the patio doors, contemplating Devan's words. What had she expected? Devan needed to be in Philadelphia, but she thought he'd be returning to Minter soon. To make such a drastic decision in a week boggled her mind, especially since she'd made no decisions about her own life in the same amount of time.

She ached for Devan. He sounded so torn. Torn between his needs and those of his son. Of course, his son had won out, but what of her needs? She needed someone, something, but what?

For now, she would forget about Devan and Royd. She'd spend the weekend with Bill and Evelyn, then make plans to visit Dorah. Maybe in Chicago she could become an entirely different person.

As much as she wanted to go on, she knew she had to talk to someone. She had to have someone who really knew her say she'd made the right decision.

Before returning Jill's call, she dialed the number for the plant. "Could I speak to Jerry Gaines?" she asked, as soon as Mary answered the phone.

By the time Jerry picked up her call, she'd begun to feel foolish about calling. "Hi, Jer, it's Julie," she said, hoping her voice sounded cheerful.

"Welcome back. Did you have a good trip?"

"I had an absolutely wonderful time. Can we talk about it later? I hate to drag you away from work, but I need a friend, someone to talk to, really bad."

"You know you can count on me, but what about Meg?" Jerry asked, concern sounding in his voice.

"No, I need someone who understands me, someone who knows who I've been and who I became. You and Devan are the only people who know both sides of Julie."

"You mentioned Devan—"

"I can't talk to him. I'll explain everything when I see you."

"Of course," Jerry said, his voice sounding more concerned as the conversation progressed. "When can we meet?"

"How about tonight, after work?"

"Name the place."

"There's a coffee shop on Locust," she began.

"The Coffee Cup?" Jerry interrupted. "I know where it is."

"Good. Meet me there at four and I'll treat you to pie and coffee." She tried to make her voice sound a bit lighter than before.

"We'll see. I'll be at the Coffee Cup at four. See you then."

Julie hung up the phone and wondered if she'd done the right thing. What could Jerry do about the situation Devan had put her in? Even if her decision proved to be wrong, she needed someone to talk to. Whether right or wrong the die had been cast. She, and she alone, would face the consequences.

The clock struck eleven before Julie called Jill. With the call from Devan and her call to Jerry, she had, momentarily, forgotten her daughter's earlier enthusiasm.

"I decided to give you another half hour to return my call, then call you," Jill greeted her. "I'd started to get worried."

"It's been a little crazy here," Julie began. "First I slept in until nine thirty, then the phone started ringing off the hook."

Jill inquired about the trip and Julie went on to tell her about the fun she'd had and the people she'd met. She described Dorah and Royd in detail, purposely saying nothing about spending the night with Royd. After the kids' reaction to Devan, let them draw their own conclusions. If Royd had been special, he'd ceased to be once he returned to Texas.

She wondered why she'd told Devan she considered the man to be special. Had it been to make him jealous or to make him miss her all the more? Could it be she'd hoped he would change his mind about his transfer?

When Jill questioned her about Devan, she went on to relate the story of Todd's accident and Devan's hasty departure from Minter. She tried to sound as though it didn't matter, to hide her own disappointment and confusion.

Jumping from the depressing subject of Devan, she told Jill about her plans to spend the weekend with Bill and Evelyn at the lake.

"It sounds like Nancy has sold the cottage. You should be getting a call from your Realtor in Minter soon, saying your house is sold as well."

"When did you become psychic?" Julie teased.

"When Karl and I put a bid on your house last week."

"You what?" Julie asked, too stunned to say more.

"We put a bid on your house. Karl hasn't been happy out here. The job isn't what he thought it would be. He started answering ads out of the national business paper before Christmas. Two weeks ago, he received a call from a company in Fort Atkinson who wants to hire a plant manager. He took personal day and flew out for an interview. They hired him last week. He'll be starting April first, so he won't be going to Mark's wedding with me, but at least he'll be happier."

"I can hardly believe it."

"Would you be upset if we bought the house, Mom?"

"Of course not. I know how much you love it here."

"We put in an offer of a hundred and fifty thousand."

"I would have taken a hundred and thirty."

"We think it's worth what we offered. We want you to stay with us as long as you need. The house is large enough for the three of us and I'll need your help when Junior comes."

"I'm thrilled for you, but are you certain this job is what Karl wants? I've seen a lot of people change jobs, just to find out they haven't given it enough thought."

"They offered him everything he wanted and more. This time, he isn't taking a job just to have one. He doesn't have to leave where he is. If it hadn't been right, he wouldn't have considered the move."

When Julie finished her conversation with Jill, she prepared to go out for the afternoon. Her lunch consisted of a TV dinner, since her cupboards had been emptied before the trip and she needed to restock.

As she made her way to her first stop, the Realtor's office, she realized the storm she thought might be blowing up never materialized. In its stead, the wind had died down and the day became beautiful.

Mackenzie Nicholson, her realtor, told her of the offer Karl and Jill submitted and of one she'd received on the condo. She'd been pleased with the bid of over three hundred thousand and instructed Mackenzie to accept both of them. By the weekend, she would be out from under all three of the properties that so reminded her of Steve and the way he'd deceived her.

~ * ~

Jerry stayed for a moment in the small office reserved for supervisors. He contemplated the phone call from Julie. The sound of her voice, the urgency of her need for someone to talk to worried him.

He'd never before heard such an edge in her voice. If she needed someone to talk to, why him? The comment about Devan hadn't escaped him either. Had there been a blow up after she returned or had the weekend in Chicago gone sour?

"I'm sorry, Jerry," Rich Webster said, when he entered the room. "I didn't know you were in here."

"I'm just leaving," Jerry said as he got up from the desk.

"Of course, I heard you paged for a phone call. Nothing serious, I hope."

"No, ah, just a meeting I've been trying to set up. We've been able to make plans for this evening."

Jerry left the office and returned to the line. Rich's comment annoyed him and the small lie he'd found himself telling about his meeting with Julie nagged at the back of his mind.

The remainder of the morning passed quickly and soon the bell rang, signaling the lunch hour. He grabbed a sandwich, then made his way to the pay phones to place a call to Karen at her office.

"This is a shock," Karen greeted him. "You never call me at work."

"I know. I needed to talk to you. I received a very disturbing phone call from Julie this morning."

"Julie? Of course, she got back from her vacation last night, didn't she?"

"Yes, but I don't think she called to show me her vacation pictures. She said she needed someone to talk to. I didn't like the tone of her voice. I said I'd meet her at the Coffee Cup after work."

"I'm glad the two of you remained friends," Karen commented. "I wouldn't blame her if she never wanted to see either of us again."

"I know. I tried to get her to talk to Meg Preston, or Devan, but she brushed off the suggestion."

"Look, Jerry, I don't think you should meet her at the Coffee Cup."

"What do you mean?"

"It's a very public place. If she wants to talk, you should go somewhere a little less crowded. Why don't you take her somewhere nice for dinner? Tonight's the board meeting and I have to take minutes. You'll have to do something about dinner alone anyway."

"It's Monday, I guess I'd forgotten you wouldn't be home. Maybe I'll take her to the new place, what's it called, The Blue Olive?"

"I don't think so. Why don't you go to the Minitree?"

"Why there?"

"Because I know Julie wants to go there."

"How could you know such a thing?"

"Steve used to take me there."

The mention of Steve still bothered him, but the counselor told them they needed to discuss the relationship. "I see, if it was good enough for you and Steve—" he stopped mid-sentence. He hadn't meant the cutting tone.

"I don't think you do. He used to say Julie kept nagging him to take her there, but it was *our* place. Of course, after what Julie told you and what I've heard, talk is all he had going for him. He would have never left Julie. Just take her to the Minitree. It's secluded. You'll be able to talk there."

"Thanks, honey, I needed to hear someone else say meeting with Julie would be a good idea."

"It's been a long time since you called me honey. Maybe we are making progress. Anyway, whatever we can do to help Julie will be worth it in the long run. Right now, I'm certain she's confused. She doesn't really know what's going on, she needs a friend. She needs you. She and I may never be close, but give her my love anyway."

When the conversation ended, Jerry called the Minitree before going back to work. He'd never before been there. It seemed to be one of those places you didn't take your wife, and none of his conquests were important enough to him to warrant such an expense. An old mansion with secluded rooms hardly seemed the place for old married people or one night stands.

The afternoon seemed to drag, more so than any afternoon he could remember. At last the three thirty bell rang, signaling quitting time. Instead of lingering, like he usually did, Jerry joined the *early birds*, as he called them, and headed for the door.

"Must be quite a meeting," Rich said, when he joined Jerry at the time clock. "What's her name?"

"It's just a meeting, Rich. As for the other crap, it's all over with."

"I see," Rich replied, his voice saying he wasn't convinced. "So, you and Karen are really trying to make a go of it. I never thought I'd see it happen."

"Well, it has, thanks to Julie."

"Thanks to Julie?" Rich echoed, phrasing the words as a question.

"Yes, thanks to Julie. If I hadn't said the things I did to her, I would have never been down enough to get counseling and try to make my marriage work. It's funny, Karen and I have found we have a lot in common. As a matter-of-fact, you might say we're falling in love all over again."

"What about her affair with Steve?"

"It was unfortunate, but so were my affairs. We're growing past those days. We've got kids and grandkids to consider as well as ourselves. As for Julie, we cleared the air the other day."

"So you said."

"Look, Rich, my personal life is really none of your business. I know you think I acted like a real bastard to Julie. I guess I did. You have to remember, sometimes things happen in friendships. Julie and I've had some long talks and we've decided not to sacrifice a lifetime of friendship over one unfortunate incident."

"Well, good for you. The way you're talking about Julie, is she the person you're meeting tonight?"

"How did you know?"

"The look in your eyes when you talk about her. It's not love, but genuine concern. I wondered about the relationship the day she came to see you."

Rich's eyes said more than his words. Jerry could sense his worry over Julie. He smiled a bit, thinking Rich's concern seemed to focus in another direction. He hadn't heard the tone of Julie's voice on the phone a few hours ago. His worry centered on her reputation after being seen in public with the notorious Jerry Gaines.

Jerry hurried across the parking lot to his metallic blue Durango. He looked at the line of traffic leaving the plant, annoyed with Rich for keeping him talking so long.

Although the traffic seemed heavy near the plant, once he turned onto one of the main arteries, he made good time. He arrived at the Coffee Cup within ten minutes and searched the lot for signs of Julie's car. To his surprise, she hadn't arrived yet. He'd never known her to be late for anything. This uncharacteristic tardiness bothered him momentarily, but he dismissed it. Everyone ran late on occasion. He parked his vehicle and went into the shop to wait for Julie.

The place had begun to fill up. Jerry found two empty seats at the counter and ordered a cup of coffee. Time seemed to pass slowly, until he finally saw her pull into the lot. He watched as she stepped out of the lot and entered the shop. Dressed in jeans, ski jacket, and boots, she hardly looked like the perfectly groomed Personnel Director he knew so well.

"I'm sorry, Jer," she said, as she sat down on the stool next to his. "I meant to be here on time, I really did, but I had this meeting. I didn't think it would ever end."

"You don't have to explain."

"I just hate being late, especially for an appointment I set up myself."

"Can I interest you in a cup of coffee?" the waitress asked, interrupting Julie.

She nodded. When the girl left, she continued. "I'm glad you started without me. I bet you're starving."

"Not really. I'm worried about you more than anything else."

"Me? I'm just me, nothing to worry about."

"Nothing to worry about? I don't think so. It seems your exact words were, I need a friend, really bad."

"Oh, you mean this morning? Things look different this afternoon."

"I don't believe you. Let's not get into it here. I have reservations at the Minitree."

"The Minitree," Julie repeated. "What will people say?"

"Do you honestly care?"

"Of course not, but—"

"But nothing. Finish your coffee so you can go home and get ready. Our reservations are for seven."

"Do I have a choice?"

"None at all. Karen thought we should go somewhere a little more private than this. I agree with her."

When they finished their coffee, Jerry put money on the counter and held open the door for Julie. "I'll pick you up at six thirty," he said, as she got into her car.

~ * ~

Julie stepped out of the shower and wrapped herself in a big towel. After drying her hair, she returned to her bedroom to dress for the evening. She had just chosen a black jersey dress with a designer scarf when she heard the phone ring.

"Julie," George said, when she answered, "we saw your lights. Shirley wondered if you'd like to join us for dinner."

"Thanks for the invite, but I'm on my way out for the evening. As a matter-of-fact, it's a good thing we don't have phone-o-vision. I'm standing here wrapped in a towel. Of course, it's nothing you haven't seen before."

George laughed. "I guess it isn't. How about tomorrow night? Can you make it then?"

"I guess so, but it will have to be an early evening. I'm leaving for the lake on Wednesday morning."

"Sounds like you've gone from a turtle in its shell to a social butterfly. We'll see you tomorrow night about six."

Julie ended the conversation and wondered if George's call had been purely social or if the doctor had taken over. Whichever, it didn't matter, the phone call made her late. She still had a lot to do to be ready before Jerry arrived at six thirty.

When at last she finished her hair and make-up, Julie opened her jewelry box to find her antique watch, with its heavy chain. Reaching for it, the sparkle of her engagement ring caught her eye. She picked up the ring and heard Steve's voice.

I know it's small. When we can afford it, I'll get you a larger one.

Bitter tears stung Julie's eyes. "Sure Steve," she said aloud. "Me and how many others? I found your love nest and I've seen the jewelry. It doesn't matter anymore. You've left me a very wealthy woman. I've sold this house, accepted an offer on the condo, and am ready to do the same on the cottage."

::Yes, Julie, but what else do you have? I'm the only one who has ever loved you. The only one who ever will. Sure, Devan said he loved you, but he's in Philadelphia. Then there's Royd. You were nothing more than a one-night stand for him. Just what does that make you, Julie? I'd call it a whore, just like the women I dated.::

"Maybe I am, but this is the twenty-first century, Steve. I'm going on and doing so quite nicely, thank you."

The ringing of the doorbell silenced Steve's mocking voice. Not too long ago, hearing Steve's words would have devastated her, shoved her deeper into her shell. Today, rather than devastating her, they became a challenge.

~ * ~

Jerry pulled Karen's white Concord into the cul-de-sac. Julie's porch light illuminated the driveway and sidewalk to the front door.

He waited, only momentarily, after ringing the doorbell for Julie to answer. "You look beautiful," he said, kissing her cheek in greeting.

"You look quite handsome, yourself," Julie replied. "Come in while I get my coat."

Jerry stepped into the warm foyer. It had been years since he'd been in this house. When he'd first returned from the Army, he and Karen spent several enjoyable evenings with Julie and Steve. When the relationship ended, he couldn't remember. He did know if it had been after Julie started at the plant. More than likely about the time Steve became interested in pursuing his numerous affairs.

"It's been a long time," he said, aloud.

"Yes, it has," Julie replied. "We did have some good times when we were younger, didn't we? It seems like a hundred years ago when we were so young and naïve."

Jerry helped her to put on her coat before escorting her to the waiting car.

"Remember when we were kids, and we thought the Minitree was a haunted house," Julie said, as they drove toward the lake.

The restaurant came into view. The large home built in the late nineteenth century seemed ablaze with lights. Legend told how a millionaire from Chicago built the house as a wedding gift for his beautiful bride. While on their honeymoon, they had taken a sailboat out onto the lake. Before they could get safely back to shore, a storm blew up, capsizing the craft.

Their bodies had washed ashore several months later. The house had been boarded up and left to stand as a silent guardian, waiting for its young lovers to return.

In 1980, a young couple from Minneapolis purchased the house. Upon closer inspection, they found it completely furnished, as it had been a hundred years earlier. They'd worked hard at refurbishing the property, until now the first floor contained a kitchen, banquet room, and a public dining room. The second floor boasted several small private rooms with an atmosphere of formal dining mingled with the intimacy of private sitting rooms.

The hostess greeted them at the door and escorted them to one of the upstairs rooms.

"Now, what's been going on?" Jerry asked, once their order had been taken.

"Like I said earlier, things looked a lot different this morning."

"I didn't believe you then and I don't believe you now. You asked for a friend and you won't get rid of me with your flip answers. Talk to me, Julie."

"How do I say it? How do I tell you my feelings? When I went to Jamaica, I did so knowing Devan would be waiting. He said he loved me and I asked to remain non-committed, friendly lovers. While I was there, I met a man and by the end of the week, we'd become very friendly. I had no trouble saying good-bye to him, because I knew Devan would be waiting for me when I got home. I could have easily extended my holiday, followed Royd to Texas, but I came home. I came back to Devan. The man I'd decided I wanted to get better acquainted with, maybe even spend the rest of my life with."

Jerry studied Julie's face, when she paused, while their salads were served.

"I don't think I understand. Has Devan changed his mind?"

Julie nodded, her eyes filled with sadness. "Devan's son was involved in a drive by shooting a week ago. Devan went to Philadelphia to be with him. Now he's transferring there. I can understand why he made such a decision, but I'm hurt. What about me, don't I need attention too?"

"Look, Julie, if Devan is the one you want, you'll have to ride out the storm. Remember, he's not the only man in the world. He's just the first to pay serious attention to you since Steve's death. You've been through a lot these last few months. Take your time making up your mind. Enjoy your freedom. The things you do, the people you meet, might surprise you. Don't make up your mind about what you want until you experience more of what life has to offer."

Thirteen

Julie pulled out of her driveway and headed toward the interstate just prior to nine. In the hopes of driving all thoughts of the events she'd endured the past few weeks from her mind, she put a cassette of an audio book into her tape deck. She'd been promising herself to actually read the book for months, but never found the time. In desperation, she bought the tape, especially for this trip.

The February sun seemed especially brilliant, and its reflection on the newly fallen snow made Julie dig into her purse for her sunglasses.

Listening to the tape made the miles melt away, and by eleven, she found herself turning onto the country road leading to the lake. For the first time, in the many years she'd been coming to the lake, she saw its beauty. Ice fishing shanties dotted the frozen surface and many of the yards contained only the tracks of an occasional rabbit.

Bill and Evelyn's house came as a welcome sight. Evelyn sat in the rocking chair, by the picture window, doing fancy work and watching for Julie's car. She saw Evelyn wave and returned the gesture.

Before turning off the engine, Julie glanced toward the house next door. Fresh show lay atop that which had fallen earlier in the season. The piles of snow marred the scene, where the snow blower dispensed the accumulation from the driveway and sidewalk.

::How can you even think of selling the cottage, Julie? This has always been our place.:: She heard Steve's voice say.

"It was never *our* place," she replied aloud. "This was *your* place. Just like everything else, the cottage belonged to you, for your enjoyment, not mine. As for selling it, I found it very easy. The cottage, the house, the condo, the antiques, the jewelry, I'm selling it all, including my memories of you."

The words she spoke with such bitterness led to silence. Maybe she would win this battle after all. The first time she'd heard Steve's voice, she'd been upset. The second time, she'd been angry. Today she experienced satisfaction. Maybe she'd finally driven home her point as Steve's voice disappeared as quickly as it had come.

She smiled to herself before switching off the ignition. Once she did, she stepped out of the car into the brisk February air, opened the trunk, and took out her weekender and overnight bag.

"Julie," Evelyn called. "Is anything wrong?"

"No," she replied, hurrying up the walk. "I had to take a few minutes to think about what I'm doing."

"I thought I saw you talking to someone while you were in the car."

Julie embraced Evelyn. "It's a long story. I've been hearing Steve's voice at the most inopportune times. At first I tried to ignore it, but I've started talking back. My counselor says it's natural. There's more involved, though. I want you and Bill to know everything, but I'll only tell it once."

Evelyn didn't press for answers and Julie appreciated the consideration.

Once Julie settled into the bright guestroom, she joined Evelyn on the sun porch for lunch. "So, where is Bill?" she asked, while she waited for her chili to cool.

"He went ice fishing," Evelyn replied. "He told me he thought we needed some time for 'girl talk'."

All through lunch they talked about inconsequential things.

"So, have you been seeing anyone?" Evelyn asked, while they cleared the table.

"For a while," Julie replied. "I met an old acquaintance on New Year's Eve, and thought something might come of it, but of course, nothing did. He had family obligations and moved to Philadelphia during my stay in Jamaica."

"Sounds rather sudden to me," Evelyn said.

"Yes, very sudden. His son was the victim of a drive-by shooting. I'm afraid he's paralyzed. Devan decided he had an obligation to be with the boy."

Evelyn didn't pursue the subject and Julie breathed a sigh of relief. Talking about Devan and his abrupt decision depressed her. Had his son been only a convenient excuse? Had their non-committed relationship been something he'd been unable to handle? What was it he said had at the restaurant? He'd asked other women to be non-committed lovers and now he knew how much it hurt. *Had the hurt been too much?*

"Why don't you lie down for a while, Julie," Evelyn said. "It's such a long drive up here, you must be exhausted."

"I should help you with dinner."

"Nonsense. I have everything under control. I'm going to take a little nap and you should, too."

Until Julie actually lay down on the bed, she didn't realize how tired she'd become. The last few days had taken their toll. Devan's disappearance from her life, as well as Steve's invasion of her thoughts, robbed her of the rest she needed. Today she'd silenced Steve. Could she so easily forgive Devan's departure and go on with her life?

In Julie's dream, she appeared as a teenager, enjoying various escapades with Devan, Jerry, and Sandy. Always, in the background, sounded Steve's voice. *::Grow up Julie. You're going to be my wife. You must be dignified. No one appreciates your frivolous attitude.::*

The slamming of a car door awakened her. It took only a few moments for Julie to get her bearings. The darkened room told her the short nap lasted longer than she'd planned.

From the living room came voices. Nancy and her husband must have arrived. Julie switched on the small lamp on the bedside table, then rubbed the sleep from her eyes before running a brush through her hair.

When she opened the door, she followed the sound of the voices and joined her friends in the kitchen.

"I hope we didn't wake you," Nancy said, before kissing her cheek.

"Your mother shouldn't have let me sleep so long," Julie replied.

"If you slept, you must have needed the rest," Bill said.

Julie allowed him to give her a hug. "I'm certain you're right. I took a vacation to rest, but I kept too busy to do it. When I came home, I found too much to do to even think about resting."

"Well, I'm certain Mom will make sure you get the rest you need," Nancy said.

The conversation at supper centered on Julie's vacation. When, at last, they went into the living room with their coffee, Julie broached the subject of the sale of the cottage.

"How did you ever find a buyer so quickly?" she asked. "I thought the asking price would have scared off everyone."

"I keep telling you, Julie, the price is fair, too low if anything. The places in this area are selling for a hundred and fifty thousand and up. The hundred and eighty you're asking is well within reason.

"As I told you, we advertised it locally for two weeks before we put it in the *Chicago Tribune*. The listing ran a week ago Sunday and I had the first contact with Mr. Moran on Tuesday. I Federal Expressed pictures on Wednesday and he called back on Friday to ask for tomorrow's meeting."

"It all seems so sudden. I thought it would take months, maybe even a year to find anyone who would be interested," Julie commented.

"What you forget is lake property comes at a premium, and as close as we are to the Dells, it becomes all the more in demand," Bill added.

"There is something I want to know, Julie," Nancy began. "Are you selling the cottage because of Steve's... ah... behavior?"

Julie's heart skipped a beat. What did Nancy know about Steve's behavior? Had word of his escapades followed them to the lake?

"Steve's behavior?" Julie watched Nancy closely for some indication of what her words meant.

"You didn't know, did you?" Nancy asked.

"Oh, I knew. Steve had been having affairs for the past ten years, but of course, I've only learned about them recently. I didn't think he had the guts to bring his conquests up here."

"Conquests? Affairs? I don't know anything about those, although I'm not surprised," Nancy said. "What I'm talking about is the way he came on to me."

"Oh, dear Lord, no. His affairs with strangers were one thing, but you could have been his daughter. When did all of this happen?"

Julie watched Nancy take a deep breath before she began her narrative. From the look on the faces of those in the room, Julie knew they'd heard the story before.

"It happened the summer of my senior year in high school, the summer before Mark went to college. As you certainly remember, Mark and I spent a lot of time together that year. I don't recall why, but for some reason we were alone. We'd decided to go sailing and I came up to your place for sodas and towels. I'd gotten on my knees to get the towels from the bathroom cupboard when Steve came into the room. He wore only a terry wrap. Before I knew it, he knelt beside me and began to fondle my breasts. I told him to stop, but he began kissing me. I wasn't dumb. I knew what he wanted. I could feel him pressing against me. He only stopped when Mark came into the house and called my name."

Julie could feel tears threatening to spill from her eyes, but her anger forced them back. She indeed did remember the summer to which Nancy referred. It had been the summer when Steve insisted she go on a sunset sail with him.

The memory of her only ride on Mark's sailboat still made her cringe. How the boat capsized, she never knew. The hour she spent clinging to the hull seemed to last a lifetime. She could still feel the bone chilling cold of the water, still hear Steve telling her to hold on to the hull, while he tried to swim for shore and get help. The twenty-four hours spent in the hospital worked to further embitter her toward the cottage as well as the lake.

The decision to sell the boat, she now realized, had been meant as a punishment for Mark for interrupting what could have been a rape.

The sailboat was Mark's pride and joy. Like everything else in Steve's life, the accident had been well planned.

"Did you ever tell Mark what happened?" Julie finally managed to ask.

"No. I told him I didn't feel well. I just couldn't believe Steve would do such a thing. I didn't want to tell Mark what happened. He loved his father and I had no right to taint him in Mark's eyes."

Julie remained silent for a long moment. How many more times would Steve slap her in the face? Had he made advances to or had affairs with any other friends of their kids? What about their own friends? Had he come on to the women in the cul-de-sac? He never mentioned them in his diary. Of course, he'd never mentioned Nancy. Maybe it had been a one-time thing, maybe he'd been ashamed of it, but she doubted it.

"Julie, Julie, are you all right?" Bill asked. "You're white as a sheet."

She shook her head. "I'm fine, just a bit shaken. Every time I think I've learned all of Steve's deep, dark secrets, something like this comes up. I thought he loved me, but I can see now how he deluded me."

Julie continued to relate the details of Steve's life. The life she thought, until today, hadn't touched the cottage.

~ * ~

Julie left for home mid-afternoon on Sunday with mixed emotions. Brad and Connie Moran had seen the cottage on Friday morning and asked to meet with her in the afternoon. Although she wanted to meet the people who would be living in her house, she'd expected a written offer first.

"I know this meeting is unusual, Mrs. Weston," Brad told her, "but we would like to settle as much of this as we can this weekend."

Julie noted Connie's advanced pregnancy and smiled at Brad's concern. She knew the doctor would soon curtail a trip of this length.

"We have some questions," Brad continued. "Would you be receptive to selling the place with the furnishings?"

"I've already taken everything I need out of there. If you want the furnishings, I'm certain we can negotiate them into the price."

"We saw a boat lift and Nancy said she thought you had a speed boat as well as a pontoon boat in storage. Would you consider an offer on them as well?" Connie asked.

"I don't see why not. I hadn't thought much about them. They're in storage at Laursen's on the other side of the lake. You're welcome to take a look at them. I'm sure Mr. Laursen can give you a fair estimate of their worth."

By Saturday, they'd agreed on a price and set a closing date. She would soon be free of the cottage, the furnishings, and the boats. The realization exhilarated her and at the same time saddened her. The kids had grown from awkward children to responsible adults by spending summers and weekends at the cottage. Now, in a matter of weeks, it would belong to someone else.

Flashing lights ahead of Julie brought her back to the reality of the road and the traffic on the interstate. She slowed to a crawl, then a stop. Four or five cars were stopped in front of her and she saw a State Patrol Officer coming toward her. When he motioned his need to talk to her, she depressed the button that controlled the electric window.

"There's been an accident up ahead, ma'am. We're rerouting traffic back to the last exit. If you'll just follow the cars ahead, we'll get you on your way as soon as possible," the officer said before moving on to the next car.

Julie rolled up the window and wiped a tear from her eyes. If anyone knew how fragile life could be, it had to be her. She prayed no one had died in the accident. Following the lead of the car ahead of her, she pulled her own vehicle into the left hand lane, crossed the median, and headed back the way she'd come.

Once off the interstate, she pulled into a small truck stop. Before going into the restaurant, she removed the map from the glove box. She'd plan her alternate route over a bowl of soup and a cup of coffee.

"What's the scanner got on about the accident up on Ninety, Mable?" Julie heard a man ask.

"It must be bad," the middle-aged waitress replied. "They just called for Med Flight from Madison and said they're rerouting traffic."

The woman moved down the counter and greeted Julie. "What can I get you, honey?"

"What kind of soup do you have?" Julie inquired.

The woman turned toward the menu board. "Like the sign says, bean 'n ham and chicken noodle."

"I'll have a bowl of the bean and ham and a cup of coffee," Julie said, pulling the map from her purse.

"Were you on Ninety?" the man who had spoken earlier asked.

"Yes. I was heading toward Minter and they turned me back. I thought I'd better stop in here and decide on the best way home."

The man moved down to the stool next to Julie as she looked at the map. "It must have been bad up there, turning around traffic and all. Look, I'm leaving for Madison soon. Why not follow me? Once you get to the city, you should be okay."

"Thank you," Julie replied, "but I wouldn't want to put you out."

"Nonsense. I'm taking my son back to Madison. You'll be following us. I'm Wayne Arnold."

Julie accepted his outstretched hand. "It's nice to meet you, Wayne. I'm Julie W—Morgan."

A boy Julie judged to be about ten came out of the restroom and Wayne went back to his own stool. The quiet of the restaurant ended as more diverted travelers stopped for coffee and directions.

Julie finished her soup and coffee and wondered why she hadn't given Wayne her correct name. She wasn't in some big city, where she should be wary of strangers. She sat in a small cafe in rural Wisconsin.

"Are you ready to go?" Wayne asked.

Julie nodded. After leaving money on the counter, she followed Wayne and the boy out to the parking lot.

"Are you lost?" the boy asked.

"I guess I am," Julie replied. "I usually just take the interstate home."

"We never take that," the boy continued. "We like the back roads better. Sometimes we even get to see a deer in the woods. As soon as I'm old enough and take the hunter's safety course, my dad's goin' to take me deer hunting."

"It sounds like fun," Julie said, holding back her feelings of revulsion at what she considered Bambi Bashing.

Following Wayne and his son, she envied the boy. If she and Steve would have divorced early in their marriage, she knew he wouldn't have remained close to the kids.

She shook her head, wondering why Steve could so easily invade her thoughts, when she tried so desperately to bury him.

~ * ~

When she at last entered her house, she breathed a sigh of relief. The accident on the interstate, as well as the unplanned detour, had delayed her by two hours. Instead of five, the clock now read seven.

Leaving her weekender in the hall, she went straight to the kitchen. The soup and coffee she'd eaten earlier had long since worn off and now she wanted something more. From the cupboard, she took a bag of popcorn and put it in the microwave. While she listened to the popping kernels, she rummaged through the refrigerator for a can of diet soda and the makings of a salad. Once she prepared her makeshift dinner, she put everything on a tray and made her way to the living room.

She kicked off her shoes and settled into the recliner. The house seemed so quiet she turned on TV to break the silence. Perhaps something on A&E would take her mind from the events of the weekend.

Beside the chair, the answering machine blinked insistently. The blinking digital read out told her there were eight messages waiting for her. She wished the kids had never gotten it for her for Christmas, wished Lance had never hooked it up while she was in the hospital, wished she'd never promised to keep it plugged in. Being tired, the blinking light annoyed her.

Everyone knows I went out of town for a few days, she thought. *Who could have left eight messages?*

She depressed the play button and to her amazement, the first two messages were hang-ups, which only annoyed her further. If they wanted to call and talk to her, why hang up without leaving a message?

As she did at work, when she listened to her messages, she sat with a pen and pad to jot notes. It's a habit, she told herself as Devan's voice came over the recorder.

"Hi, Julie, just wanted to let you know my things arrived safely. Thanks for your help. Things here aren't much different. I don't know what I expected, but it certainly wasn't this. I miss you."

Devan's words were followed by a beep, then two more hang-ups. As Julie listened to the dial tone on the machine, she reread the note she'd written. *Call Devan. How can I call Devan? He didn't give me a phone number for Todd's apartment.*

Another message began. "Hi, Julie. It's Dorah. I just thought I'd see how you survived Hidden Island. Are you going to come down and stay with me for a while or what? Give me a call." Dorah repeated her phone number and Julie made note of it while she listened to the last two hang-ups. Absently, she hit the erase button, her mind wandering.

"Technology," she said aloud. "What a line of crap. Devan can call me, and leave a message, but I can't even talk to him. In the meantime somebody keeps hanging up. It doesn't make any sense at all."

She checked the area code for Philadelphia and dialed information. "I'd like the number for Todd Yates, please," she told the operator.

After a short pause, she heard a prerecorded message. "At the customer's request, the number you have requested is non-published."

"Well, thank you," she said, to the sterile recording. Angry with everyone in general, she slammed down the receiver.

"What's wrong with me?" she questioned. "Why can't Devan stand to be near me? Did he have the number unpublished? Did he plan to break contact with me entirely?" She didn't try to hold back her angry tears. "If this is the way you want to play the game, Yates, it's okay with me! I'll give you one try at the office then it's good-bye Charlie. You aren't the only man in the world. There must be someone out there who can love me."

The ringing of the phone startled her. She grabbed a tissue from the box beside the chair, wiped her eyes, and blew her nose. The phone rang a second time before she answered. Positive she'd hear Devan's voice on the other end of the line, she tried to sound cheery.

"Julia," Royd's voice startled her. She'd never expected to hear from him.

"Why, Royd, what a surprise."

"I've been tryin' to call you all week."

"So, you were the hang-ups," she said, with a nervous laugh.

"The what?" Royd replied.

"The hang-ups on my machine. I came home to six dial tones out of eight messages."

"All from me, I'm afraid. I hate talking to a machine. Were you on another vacation?"

"Not really. I had a buyer for my lake cottage and went up to meet with him."

"Did you reach an agreement?"

"Yes, we did."

"I'm glad. When we were in Jamaica, you seemed certain you'd have a hard time finding a buyer for it." Royd paused for a moment, then continued before Julie could think of anything appropriate to say. "Julia, you don't know how much I miss you."

Royd's words startled her. "You hardly know me."

"I realize that. I've told myself the same thing hundreds of times since the plane left Montego Bay. I also know you have a special friend, but you said you were non-committed friendly lovers. Without commitment, come and visit me."

"What about Betty?" she asked, surprised to even remember the woman's name.

"Our agreement has always been if one of us should find someone—"

"Is this how you left it with her?" Julie interrupted.

"No. It's how she's leaving it with me. It wasn't a shock. I've known about John for a long time. When she told me they were getting married, I wished them well."

"I see," Julie replied. Her mind spun. *He must think I'm better than nothing.*

"Would you please come down?"

159

"I don't know. It certainly wouldn't look proper."

"I'll give you all the proper you want. The house has a guestroom and I told you my daughter lives with me. How much more proper do you want?"

"I'd prefer to stay at a hotel."

"Why waste the money, Julia? The house is huge. You can have all the privacy you need."

"I'll consider it, Royd, but I'll need time to think about this. Can I call you tomorrow evening with my answer?"

"Of course, but... ah, let me be the one to be doin' the callin'. You save your money."

Julie shook her head. Luckily, Royd couldn't see the expression on her face. He had no idea how wealthy she'd become in the past few weeks. "All right, you can call me at nine. I'll have an answer for you by then."

"Nine o'clock," Royd repeated. "I'll look forward to talking with you tomorrow."

"I won't guarantee you'll like my answer. I don't know if I'm ready for this."

When Julie hung up the phone, she contemplated the conversation. What wasn't she ready for? She'd already had an affair with the man.

The phone rang again. With her mind still reeling form her conversation with Royd, she answered it.

"You finally got home," Dorah greeted her.

"Sorry I missed you earlier, but I went up to the lake. Nancy found a buyer for the cottage. Have you ever heard of a lawyer named Brad Moran?"

"Heard of him! He works for the same firm I do. He's only one of the best young legal eagles in the city. He's filthy rich, absolutely gorgeous, and disgustingly married. Why do you ask?"

"He's buying my cottage."

"I hope he's paying you well."

"He is. More than I thought it was worth, to be honest. He even bought the furnishings and the boats."

"It must be a relief to be out from under on at least one of your properties."

"More than one. I've accepted an offer on the condo and my daughter and her husband are buying the house. By summer, I should be free and clear. I just don't know what to do with all of this new found freedom."

"So, what happened at the airport?" Dorah asked, changing the subject. "I've been dying to find out. Why wasn't the hunk waiting for you?"

"Devan got called to Philadelphia on family business. During the week when I planned to make my monumental decisions, he made them instead. He decided to leave Minter and transfer to Philadelphia permanently."

"He moved to Philadelphia?"

"I helped pack his things on Tuesday and even watched while they hooked his car behind the moving van."

"What a jerk! I can't believe anyone would do something like that. Oh, well, he's not the only fish in the sea, you know."

"I know. I just thought he'd be waiting for me here. Before I could adjust to Devan's decision, I got called to the lake. When I returned home, I received a call from Royd."

"Royd? As in Royd McAlester?" Dorah questioned. "What about his friend in Texas?"

"It seems she's getting married, only not to him. Sort of like Devan deciding to move on. He wants me to come down and visit him. He says he wants to get to know me better."

"Are you going?"

"I don't know. I'm so confused. I told him I'd give him my decision, tomorrow night."

Fourteen

Julie settled back into the seat on the bus. From the window, she saw Meg standing on the sidewalk, next to the terminal. Meg had driven Julie to the bus and they stopped at Perkins for something to eat. It had been over breakfast when Meg questioned her trip to Texas with its stopover in Chicago to see Dorah.

"I told you when I got home from the hospital, I need this six months to find me. To find out what I want to do, and it doesn't matter to me what anyone else thinks."

"Running off to Texas to see a man you hardly know, I just don't understand your reasoning. Of course, this Dorah character sounds anything but stable to me," Meg protested.

"Maybe I'm a little unstable, myself," Julie snapped. "Let's face it, I'm free of the things that reminded me of Steve and who knows, I might find I'd like living in Chicago or Texas. I don't have to stay in Minter for the rest of my life."

"I wouldn't think you'd want to be moving away now, with Jill and Karl coming home and the baby on the way."

Julie shook her head at Meg's comment. "I told you, I don't know what I'll do or if I'll do anything. As for the kids, they're due in sometime next week. Keep an eye out for them."

Meg seemed to ignore Julie's last statement and continued with her negative viewpoint. "I just don't approve of this trip."

"I'm sorry you don't approve, Meg. This is something I have to do. I don't know how I can say it any differently to make you understand. Steve certainly left me without any other alternatives, and neither did Devan."

"Have you even tried to call Devan?"

"Tried is the right word. He's never given me a number where I can reach him at Todd's, and when I called information, I learned he has an unpublished number. I've called his office twice. Both times I had the feeling he stood right next to his secretary when she said he just stepped out of the office. He doesn't want to talk to me. Maybe this gave him an excuse to get out of Minter. I'm trying my best to forget him."

"So, you're running off to another man right away."

"It seems to me," Julie countered, knowing her voice held an edge, "when I told you I spent New Year's Eve with Devan, you said, 'welcome to the twenty-first century'."

"I only said that because I thought you and Devan were so perfect together," Meg replied, her voice softer.

"I know, too perfect. I wanted it to go on forever and grow into something wonderful. Of course, what we want and what we get are usually two different things. Maybe it ended with my trip to Jamaica, but I did need to get away. Jerry put it quite plainly when he said if this is meant to be, we'll weather the storm. If it's not, it won't be the end of the world."

Julie now looked out the window of the bus and waved to Meg before she scurried to the car to get out of the biting wind.

Things are moving too fast, Julie thought to herself. Her agreement to visit Royd came before she knew Jill and Karl were arriving early. At first she'd debated calling Royd and postponing the trip, but then decided it would be for the best. The kids needed some time alone to settle into their new home.

The bus driver started the engine, and as the coach drove out of the terminal, Julie turned her attention to the present as well as the future. When the bus pulled onto the interstate, she produced Dorah's detailed instructions from her purse.

> *Take the bus to the downtown depot then take a*
> *cab to my place. The doorman, Tony, knows you're*

coming. I told him you'd be here by noon. He'll let you in. Just make yourself at home. I should be there shortly after you arrive. I've taken off Thursday afternoon and Friday so we can have a special weekend. Don't worry about a thing. I've made all the necessary plans.

Julie reread the last sentence. *All the necessary plans*, she thought. *What plans are necessary? Knowing Dorah, I almost dread the idea.*

After making several stops, including one at O'Hare Airport, the bus arrived at the depot near the Loop. Once Julie retrieved her luggage, she hailed a cab and gave the driver Dorah's address.

Neighborhoods changed rapidly from bustling downtown, to crowded inner city, to fashionable lake front addresses, until at last they stopped in front of Dorah's building. Although Dorah called it a condo, Julie saw it as nothing more than a five-story apartment building. When the cab rolled to a stop, a young man hurried to the curb to open her door.

"You must be Dorah's friend, Julie," he shouted over the stout wind. "I'll get your luggage. You get in where it's warm."

Julie paid the driver, then stepped out onto the sidewalk. She fought the urge to help the young man with her bags and hurried up the steps into the warmth of the building.

Again the door opened, and Tony came into the lobby carrying her bags. "Dorah wants me to take you right up to her apartment," he said, pushing the button to summon the elevator.

"Dorah calls it a condo," Julie commented.

"Condo, apartment, what's the difference? When I was a kid, these were all apartments, fashionable apartments. A few years ago, the owners went condo. It seemed like the thing to do back then."

"Are you from around here?"

"Not really. We could never afford to live like this. I'm from the burbs."

"The burbs?" Julie questioned, not familiar with the terminology.

"You know, the suburbs. At Christmas, my folks always brought us out here to see the lights and decorations. My mom gets into those things. Now I work here. In another year and a half, I'll be graduating from college and this will all be behind me."

"What's your major?"

"Business Administration. I'm lucky, most of my classes are at night and the day classes I do have, I compensate for by working weekends."

The elevator doors opened and they entered the cubicle. When they arrived at Dorah's floor, he carried her bags across the hall to the apartment. Opening the door with a passkey, he set her bags in the foyer.

"I hope you enjoy your stay in Chicago," he said, before he left her alone in the apartment.

Julie looked around the spacious rooms. The decor definitely reflected Dorah's personality. Instead of the dainty crocheted doilies and hand embroidered dresser scarves that graced Julie's tables, bright serapes from Mexico and flowered cloth from Jamaica were everywhere.

From the bedroom, Julie saw a large yellow tomcat enter the room to scrutinize this stranger who had entered his domain. "You must be Mr. Peabody," she said, kneeling down to pet the cat. His contented purr told her he'd accepted her. After a moment, he turned and went back to his bedroom refuge.

Returning her attention to the place Dorah called home, she noticed the patio doors. They looked out onto the lake and a balcony triggered thoughts of summer cocktails with whatever beau captivated Dorah's attention.

While she stood, mesmerized by the crashing waves of the turbulent lake, Dorah entered the apartment. "Good, you're here," Dorah said, the sound of her voice startling Julie.

She turned to face her friend. "How do you ever leave this view to go to work?"

"After a while you get used to it. Even forget to look, if you know what I mean." Dorah crossed the room to embrace Julie. "Now we have to hurry. I'll set the table while you get the cold cuts from the refrigerator."

Julie followed her into the small kitchen. In the small fridge she found a plate of perfectly arranged cold cuts, as well as a dish of raw vegetables and two diet sodas. "So what's the hurry?" she asked.

"We have an appointment at The Spa and the limo will be here at one."

"Limo?" Julie echoed.

"It's part of the fun. I go four times a year. It's something I enjoy, so I thought I'd treat you today. They pick you up in a limo, then you get a sauna, massage, facial, new hairstyle and they redo your make-up. You come out a whole new person."

"And a whole lot poorer, I bet," Julie teased.

"It's not bad. They charge two hundred and fifty a session and once a year I get a freebie. I always take a friend, since I work the cost into my budget. It's less than the cost of a pack of cigarettes a day."

Julie put down her sandwich. "Why not let me treat you?"

"No way!" Dorah exclaimed. "I look forward to introducing my friends to Marie's magic. I may cry hard times, but Jeff left me comfortable and my other two husbands have contributed to my assets. Besides, I make damn good money. I've worked for Forbush, Allen, Clay & Moran for the past eight years and I'm considered one of the best legal secretaries in the city."

Julie sipped her diet soda and saw Dorah in a whole new light. In Jamaica, she'd been a frivolous young woman who appeared to be a scatterbrain. In Chicago, she became a good businesswoman, who knew exactly what she wanted.

A buzzer sounded, followed by Tony's voice over an intercom. "The limo is here for you, Dorah."

Dorah went into the living room and pushed a button beside the door. "We'll be right down."

~ * ~

Julie stared into the mirror hardly able to believe her normally salt and pepper hair had turned to a rich silky brown. The new style complimented her as well.

"I'll never be able to do this," she lamented.

"Of course you will," Marie assured her, as she turned Julie's chair around.

Julie heard water running in the sink behind her. Once Marie had again wet down her hair, she handed Julie the blow dryer and brush.

"Now, you do it."

"You're kidding. I don't know how to use these things. The blow dryer, yes, but the curling iron and brush, I've never been able to master either of them."

"You blow it dry," Marie began. "Then I'll show you how to use the other two."

At first Julie worked, awkwardly. To her surprise, with Marie's expert guidance, she found using the tools to be quite easy. "I didn't think I could do this. No one ever took the time to show me before."

"I know. Most shops aren't willing to take the time. They give you a good cut, a nice style, but not the skills to maintain it."

"I like what I see," Dorah said, interrupting their conversation, as she came into the room.

Julie turned toward Dorah's voice, surprised to see her hair had been dyed a rusty red. "I never expected red, but it looks great on you."

"It should," Dorah agreed. "This is my natural color. I've been considering going back to something less brassy. Since I met Bob, I've decided... well... I think he'll like it."

"Bob?" Julie questioned.

"I met him on a blind date just before I went to Jamaica. I didn't think much about it. When I got back, I found him kinda waiting for me and we've been an item ever since. I never thought I'd find anyone like Jeff again, but Bob runs a real close second."

"I hope it works out for you."

"Speaking of Bob, we'd better get going. The guys are picking us up soon."

"Guys, as in plural?"

"Turn about is fair play. My boss set me up with Bob and I arranged for Frank to take you out tonight."

"I see," Julie said, trying to sound annoyed with Dorah. "So, I have a blind date with your boss. This guy must be pretty desperate."

"Definitely not. I think the two of you will get along great."

Julie tipped Marie and followed Dorah from the shop to the waiting limo. As the car pulled into traffic, she again addressed the situation.

"What are you doing to me? I'm on my way to Texas for a week with Royd and you're setting me up with some guy here."

"This guy is Frank Allen and I promise you'll like him. It's just a date, for Pete's sake. I don't expect you to jump in bed with him. Knowing you, something like that could take weeks. As for Royd, it's a game of wait and see. People aren't always what they appear to be when they're on vacation."

Julie nodded. She'd seen this in Dorah. The flamboyant character she'd roomed with in Jamaica had become a completely different person in Chicago.

~ * ~

Once back at the apartment, Julie began to unpack and Dorah scrutinized each outfit. "This one," Dorah said, holding up the mauve suit, "will be perfect for tonight. Of course, most of these clothes will never do for Texas."

"What do you mean?" Julie asked looking at the clothes she'd had altered to fit her smaller frame.

"I'm certain your winter wardrobe is great, but you've never replenished your summer clothes. Sure, you bought a few things before you went to Jamaica, but you need more. Tomorrow, we're going shopping. You can certainly afford it and you deserve it."

When Dorah went to her own room to change, Julie thought about her words. The things she'd brought did seem outdated, homemade, and dowdy. After changing for the evening, she continued to study the clothes, which were scattered across the bed, until she heard Dorah talking with someone on the intercom.

By the time she reached the living room, Dorah and two men were engaged in conversation.

Julie quickly assessed them and surmised the younger of the two had to be Dorah's date, Bob. The older man took a step toward Julie and extended his hand. "You have to be Julie. Dorah didn't do you justice. I'm Frank Allen."

"It's a pleasure," Julie said, gripping his hand firmly.

For a moment she could hear Steve's voice. *::A good, firm handshake is important in business, Julie.::*

::No, Steve, this is definitely not business. By the looks of this man it will be nothing but pleasure.::

"If you girls are ready, we have reservations at seven and we wouldn't want to be late," Bob said.

Once in the car, Dorah and Bob occupied the back seat, leaving the front to Julie and Frank.

"Looks like we're on our own for conversation," Frank said, after glancing into the rear view mirror. "Dorah tells me you're from Minter. What do you do there?"

"Right now, not much. I usually work as the Personnel Director at LisPro. Of course, for the next few months, I'm trying to find out who I am."

"I'm impressed," Frank replied.

"Dorah tells me you're a lawyer. Do you enjoy it?"

"It puts the bacon on the table. I might as well be up front with you, Julie. On the weekends, I run a comedy club called Allen's Alley. The ten-hour days I work through the weeks allows me Friday, Saturday, and Sunday to play. Running the club is what I do for relaxation. It started out as my wife's dream. She'd been a struggling comedian for as long as I knew her. I opened the Alley for her ten years ago. When she died, I started spending more and more time there to keep her memory alive. Before I knew it, I got hooked. I love the place."

Julie remembered Dorah's comment about her appearing at a comedy club and wondered if she'd been setup.

"What are you getting at?" she finally asked, almost afraid of the answer.

"Dorah thinks you'd be perfect for amateur night."

Julie took a deep breath. "Dorah exaggerates," she said quickly.

"Not about comedians."

"I'm afraid this time she's wrong. You don't even know me. How can you take Dorah's word about this?"

Frank laughed, then continued. "When it comes to comedians, I know better than to not take Dorah's word. She's more than just my secretary. One evening a week, she auditions potential amateurs to perform at the club. I value her opinion highly. She hasn't steered me wrong yet. She thinks you'll be good."

"But, I don't think I'm—"

"You don't think you're funny. Maybe this business needs more people who don't think they're funny. She's been telling me about The Four Musketeers of Minter. Even second hand your material is wonderful."

"I don't have *material*. Those stories are just that, stories. They certainly aren't anything an audience wants to hear. They want mother-in-law jokes, how bad someone's wife is, or how small a town they came from."

"Not anymore, sophisticated people want to hear stories about things they did themselves or wish they had. The crazy things kids do, how they handle situations, memories, that's what people want today."

"And you think—"

"I don't think, Julie, I know. There's room for you on Saturday night's show. What do you say?"

Julie thought for a moment. Could she actually do something so crazy? Could she even consider getting up in front of an audience again after all these years?

Why not, a small voice within her said. *You'll be in front of a bunch of strangers. If you bomb, no one will know but you. You'll never have to see these people again.*

"This has to be the craziest thing I've ever agreed to, but it might be fun. I did say I took these next few months to find me. If I don't try something like this, I'll never know if I could have done it."

~ * ~

Jerry lay on the bed of the hotel room. The spur of the moment trip the counselor suggested three days ago, became a needed shot in the arm for his strained relationship with Karen.

Since the plant had gone to a four day, forty hour week just after the first of the year, he'd had all Friday morning to plan the kidnap of his wife from work. He'd even remembered to leave a note, just in case one of the kids happened to come home for the weekend.

Karen's boss had been receptive when Jerry told him of his plans to take her first to lunch, then to Chicago.

He'd packed only a few toiletries and Karen's make-up case. The weekend would be a completely spontaneous happening. Whatever they needed, they would buy. Whatever sounded like fun, they would do.

The hotel Anita suggested, when he visited the travel agency, provided the perfect romantic setting. Situated close to shopping and sightseeing, their package included a suite with a whirlpool, the use of the pool, dining coupons, and tickets to one of the comedy clubs in the area.

His thoughts came back to the here and now, when he heard the shower turn off and Karen's blow dryer start. At last, Karen came out of the bathroom wrapped in a large fluffy towel. Jerry looked up at her, then pulled her down onto the bed beside him, the towel dropping to the floor.

"Let's skip the comedy club thing," he said. "We could stay here and make mad passionate love." He ran his hand up her firm belly and caressed her ample breasts.

"Oh, Jerry," she said, removing his hand. "We have all the time in the world to make love. I thought you were excited about going to the comedy club."

"I'm more excited about you." He rolled her onto her back and soon they were intertwined. He loved her the way he'd loved other women, the way it seemed almost obscene to love your wife.

After they climaxed, they lay, for several minutes, in each other's arms. "I'm going to have to shower all over again," Karen whispered, wriggling to be free of his embrace. Her giggles assured him she'd enjoyed their interlude as much as he did.

"I'll join you," he said, remembering the woman who insisted they shower together. He'd been awkward, as he knew Karen would be now.

They stepped into the shower and he began to lather her body with shower gel. It didn't take her long to relax in his arms.

"This is wonderful," she whispered in his ear. "We should have thought of it a long time ago."

They stepped from the shower and while Karen dressed, Jerry stood before the mirror, shaving. "What time does the show start?" he called, through the open door.

The tickets say seven-thirty."

"What time is it now?"

"Just a little past six."

"See, I told you, we have plenty of time." Jerry entered the bedroom and began dressing. "How do we know we'll even like a comedy club?"

"The girl at the desk said the show is great."

"I don't believe it. My wife, Miss Skeptical herself, actually believed the girl at the desk," Jerry teased.

"It's something different. Something we've never done before. Why not give it a shot? She said everyone is an amateur and tonight is ladies night."

"Women comedians," Jerry quipped. "What's this world coming to?"

"Women are everywhere," Karen said, in defense of her gender. "Besides, you always liked Phyllis Diller and Roseanne."

"I guess I did. So, we're going to have a good time, but we won't get a chance to eat."

"They serve munchies and the show is over by eight-thirty or nine. We can eat then, unless you want to stay for the late show."

Jerry pulled her into his arms. "I'd rather have a late show here, with you. Why would I want to sit through the same show twice when I could bring you back here and ravage you?"

"Because the second show is a professional one, with the exception of the winner from the first show. Of course, we have to pay for it and it runs two hours."

"Sort of a gotcha?"

"I guess you could call it that. Give it a chance. You might find you like it."

Allen's Alley reminded Jerry of a storefront speakeasy he'd seen once in a movie about the Roaring Twenties. Once the hostess seated them at a table for two toward the center of the room, a waitress came over and took their drink order.

"Look at these names," Jerry said, scanning the photocopied ballot, which lay on the table. "The first three sound like the Stepford Wives and the last one must be a real bimbo. Who, in their right mind, would ever name a child Jewel West?"

"It's probably just a stage name. If they weren't good, they couldn't have made it this far."

Their waitress returned with the drinks and a basket of chips. "You're right," the girl said. "I didn't mean to eavesdrop on your conversation, but these girls are good. The first three have appeared here before and been asked back."

"What about the last one?" Jerry asked. "Can someone named Jewel be any good?"

"Your guess is as good as mine. It's been the sixty-four thousand dollar question around here all night. The gossip is, she's a personal friend of Mr. Allen and he convinced her to be here."

"Well, that explains a lot," Jerry said, once the girl left their table. "A personal friend of the owner. Is that something like being that new guy in your office, Justin? Didn't you say he is your boss's brother-in-law?"

"Who knows? I guess we'll just have to withhold judgment until we hear what this girl has to offer."

Jerry grinned at Karen's statement, then held out his glass in a mock toast. "It ought to be an interesting evening. What do you say we drink to that statement?"

The lights dimmed and a man dressed in a tuxedo took the stage. "Welcome to Allen's Alley. I'm your host, Frank Allen, and I hope you enjoy the evening. For you first timers, you'll be seeing four talented ladies this evening and their futures lie in your hands. When they've all finished, please grade them from one to four on the ballots we've placed on your tables. Now I know you didn't come here to listen to me, so let me introduce Miss Janet Karsted. Please give her a warm welcome."

Jerry and Karen enjoyed the monologue of each of the first three women. "How do we decide which one is best?" Karen whispered in Jerry's ear. "They're all great."

"I know what you mean. I can't make a decision, either. Maybe this Jewel West will be a real flop and it will make everything easier."

Again Frank Allen took the stage. "To make your decision just a bit more difficult, we have one more young lady to entertain you. Unlike the first three, she hasn't graced our stage before. She tells me she's a bit nervous, so please make her feel welcome. It gives me great pleasure to introduce, Miss Jewel West."

Jerry and Karen watched in disbelief as Julie came out onto the stage. Karen found her voice first. "It can't be, it just can't be Julie Weston."

"Why not Julie?" Jerry replied. "We knew she was planning to come to Chicago this weekend. As for the name, the spelling is different, but I always called her Jul in high school. Sometimes I still do. West only seems natural. Why not?"

"Her hair, it's all wrong," Karen whispered back.

Jerry studied the woman on stage. She looked enough like Julie to be her twin. The only difference was her hair. It didn't contain Julie's distinctive gray and she appeared to be much younger. As soon as she began to speak, all questions ceased to exist.

Jerry, as well as everyone else in the audience, laughed at the antics of The Four Musketeers of Minter. Had they been quite so funny thirty years ago, or did Julie merely have a knack for storytelling?

Time seemed to fly, and soon Julie's allotted ten minutes ended. After a moment of silence, the room seemed to explode with applause. Jerry and Karen joined the others in the audience as they enthusiastically gave Julie their support.

When at last the curtain closed, the room again became quiet. With the silence, another young woman took the stage. Jerry judged the attractive redhead to be in her mid thirties.

"Well, ladies and gentlemen, this concludes our first show of the evening. Now, it's up to you. One of these talented young ladies will be our guest as a paid performer at the second show. It will be her chance of a lifetime. For the other three, there will be cash prizes and a chance to return at a later date. Their future is in your hands. Please mark your choices one through four, and the waitresses will collect them when you're finished. On behalf of Allen's Alley, thank you for your support this evening."

"Whom are you voting for as number one?" Jerry asked.

"Julie, of course," Karen replied. "Do you think she has a chance of winning?"

"It's hard to say. Not everyone here has known her as long as we have. We may be prejudiced in thinking she's the best."

Jerry looked around the room and tried to read the minds of those seated at the other tables. No one seemed to take very long to make their choices and he wondered whom they considered the best.

He and Karen thought Julie deserved their number one vote, but as he told Karen, they were prejudiced.

"May I take your ballots?" the waitress who served them earlier asked.

"Of course," Karen said, handing the girl their two slips of paper. "I wonder, would it be possible to meet Miss West?"

Jerry came to immediate attention at Karen's question. He would have never expected Karen, of all people, to ask such a question. Before he could say anything, he became aware of the waitress' surprised expression. "I don't know," she replied. "It's against house policy."

"It's all right," Jerry quickly added. "My wife just thought maybe we could see her, since we're personal friends."

"Well, since you're friends, I'll ask Miss Rutland, but I can't promise anything. The policy, as well as the right to change it, is decided by her and Mr. Allen."

Jerry nodded as the girl continued on, collecting ballots. When she could no longer hear them, he turned his attention to Karen. "Did you mean it? Do you really want to see Julie?"

"Of course I do. She made a very generous gesture when she gave me the earrings. She's even called me a couple of times. She said she didn't blame me for the affair and she wanted to be friends. At first I didn't know if I could accept her friendship, but seeing her tonight has changed my mind. I can't just sit here and not tell her what a great job I thought she did."

Jerry took her hand and held it to his lips. Not long ago, he'd considered divorce, even thought of how to do away with Steve, without hurting Julie. The only thing he'd done had been to become the Romeo of Minter, to flaunt his affairs to Karen the way she had to him.

Before he could say anything, he saw the redhead making her way toward their table. He pushed back his chair and prepared to stand, but she motioned him to remain seated.

"Please don't get up," she said, extending her hand. "I'm Dorah Rutland. Tracy said you wanted to meet Miss West. I'm afraid it's against policy. We've had some trouble in the past."

"Trouble? What kind of trouble?"

"We've had people who said they knew the performers, then tried to hurt them. One man even pulled a knife on someone because he didn't like the monologue. We just don't take chances anymore. I am sorry."

"Don't be. Policy is policy. We just wanted to tell Julie what a great job we thought she did."

"Julie?" Dorah questioned.

"It's her name isn't it? Julie Weston."

Dorah smiled broadly. "You do know her. Around here only two people, other than myself know who she really is. Everyone else only knows her as Jewel West. How do you know her?"

"I'm Jerry Gaines, and this is my wife, Karen. Judging by the name, you have to be the Dorah from Hidden Island."

"So, you're Jerry Gaines. I thought for a minute you were going to tell me you were Devan Yates. I certainly wouldn't have allowed him backstage. Of course I knew you weren't Devan. I saw him at the airport. As soon as the winners are announced, I'll have Tracy bring you backstage. Julie will be delighted to see you."

"I hope so," Karen said. "She certainly isn't expecting us, but we do want to see her.

~ * ~

Julie finished her monologue and stood for a moment in the blinding glare of the foot lights.

176

Instead of applause, her offering met with silence. Even polite applause would be better than this. She'd been a fool to listen to Dorah, to get up on this stage and open herself to humiliation. Before the lump in her throat could turn to tears, the applause began. She wondered if she imagined it, or if it was louder for her than for the other women.

Once the curtain closed, Frank came to her side. "You were fabulous, Julie. Did you hear the applause?"

She nodded, unable to think of anything to say. For the first time in her life, she was absolutely speechless.

"Overwhelming, isn't it?" Frank asked, as he escorted her into the wings, allowing Dorah to go out on stage.

"I don't know if overwhelming is the right word, but it's good enough for me."

Frank put his arm around her shoulders, kissed her cheek, then winked broadly.

"Who do you think will win?" she asked.

"You can't be serious. Everyone but you knows you'll be the winner."

"You're sweet, but the others were all good. They're polished, they know their material; they're comfortable out there. As for me, I'm terrified and out of place. Couldn't you hear my knees? They sounded like two sticks knocking together. These girls out class me by a country mile."

"You're too hard on yourself. The only way we'll convince you is when the votes are in."

Julie rolled her eyes. Winning didn't matter. She thought of the applause and warmly remembered the parts she'd played while in high school and how much she'd enjoyed them.

For a moment, she became seventeen again, playing Annie to Devan's Frank Butler; she'd become the star of the show. She relived basking in the limelight. Why had Steve been so important to her when he was so appalled by her love of entertaining?

"Julie, Julie, did you hear me?" Frank asked.

"I guess I was somewhere else. What did you say?"

"I asked if you'd like a soda or something?"

"No, I'm fine. While there's a lull, I'd like to thank you," she said, kissing his cheek as he had kissed hers earlier.

"Thank me? For what?"

"For tonight. I'd forgotten how good it is to hear the applause of an audience."

"Forgotten?"

"I did some plays in high school."

"I see," Frank said, nodding his head. "I suppose Jerry, and Sandy, and Devan were there, too."

She nodded, then turned when Dorah returned to the backstage area.

"I've got the results right here," she said, holding up an envelope.

Julie joined the other girls and Frank on stage. Uncontrollably, her stomach began doing flip-flops as soon as the curtains parted.

Frank now held the envelope in his hand and made a great show out of opening it. He took so long in announcing the third and fourth place winners Julie wondered why he was prolonging this agony. With each announcement, Dorah presented the girls with an envelope containing a cash prize as well as a single long stemmed red rose.

Each time Frank announced a name other than hers, she felt herself breathing a sigh of relief. She'd done this as a lark, knowing she didn't have a chance in the world. Being one of the last two remaining on stage made her heart pound with wild anticipation.

"In second place," she heard Frank say, "is Janet Karsted."

Julie had been ready to accept the single red rose, to enthusiastically congratulate Janet on her first place win. Instead, Janet offered Julie her congratulations and Dorah handed her a bouquet of a dozen roses. From the audience came thunderous applause, laced with cheers.

Julie still had trouble believing what just happened. She could only stand, in a state of shock, as Frank held up his hand for silence.

"Ladies and gentlemen, tonight is a first for the Alley. Never before have I been able to say an entire audience has voted for the same person. There were two hundred and eighty-five ballots cast and each one marked Jewel West as number one. Considering this is her first attempt at comedy, she made quite an impression on everyone here. The second show begins at ten. I hope you can come back and join us. If you can't, thank you for coming and drive safely."

The curtain closed and the audience again began to applaud. Backstage, the other contestants offered Julie their sincere congratulations.

"I don't understand any of this," she told them. "You are all so polished, you've practiced and worked hard on your lines, while I'm just a novice."

One of the girls took her hand. "It's not how much practicing you do, its how much talent you have and believe me, you have plenty."

"She's right, you know," Dorah said.

"I still don't believe it. I can't believe I've won first place." Julie said. "What about the people who came for the other girls?"

"If they hadn't thought you were good, they would have voted differently. The people who come here know comedy and they know what they like. Tonight, they like you. Just wait until the second show and you'll see what I mean."

"I'm still skeptical. How much influence did you and Frank have in all of this?"

"None. We can't vote and neither can the staff. It's entirely up to the guests."

Before Julie could reply, she heard a familiar voice behind her. "It looks like the guests loved you."

Surprised, she turned and came face to face with Jerry and Karen. "What are you two doing here?" she asked, before she hugged them both.

"We decided to take a second honeymoon. I kidnapped my wife on Friday, brought her to Chicago, and took her to a posh hotel. I almost didn't come tonight. It would have been easy to stay at the hotel for a night of pleasure. You'll never know how glad I am I didn't do it. God, Julie, you were great. We're thrilled for you."

"You certainly were," Karen agreed. "We're very proud of you. I can hardly wait for the second show. I'd forgotten how much fun you guys had in school. As I remember, I always wished I were older, so I could be in your group."

"What's this?" Frank bellowed, when he joined the group. "Why are there guests backstage? Where is Dorah?"

"Right here," Dorah said. "I take full responsibility. Frank Allen, this is Jerry Gaines, and his wife, Karen."

"*The* Jerry Gaines? One of The Four Musketeers of Minter? Who else will we find lurking out in the audience? Sandy? Devan?"

Jerry's grip tightened on Julie's hand at Frank's words. "I wouldn't count on it," she replied, her voice sounding a bit shaky. "Sandy died in a car crash five years after we graduated. As for Devan—well—you can scratch him, too."

"Devan's—"

Julie interrupted Frank, finishing his question. "Dead? Hardly. He's just not very receptive to me these days."

"Well, I would like to be receptive to you," Julie heard an unfamiliar voice say. Looking up, she saw a man, about Frank's age, coming toward her.

"How did you get back here, Greg?" Frank asked.

"I walked. No one stops me when I want to go backstage. You know I come to as many of these things as I can."

"I also know you almost never come backstage. Apparently, my talent isn't good enough for you."

"It's usually not the caliber I'm looking for, but tonight, well, you must know why I'm here."

Frank smiled. "I certainly do. I just didn't expect you to be as convinced as I am."

Frank turned to Julie. "Jewel West, this is Greg Lauer. Greg is one of the top agents in the country."

"Agent?" Julie questioned.

"I represent comedians," Greg said. "I come to a lot of the amateur nights. I keep hoping to find another Phyllis Diller or Eddie Murphy, but they just don't seem to be out there. At least I didn't think they were until tonight. Your performance was exceptional, Miss West. I'd like to represent you."

"I'm sorry, Mr. Lauer. I'm not a comedian. I did this as a lark, something fun, something different."

"I'd like you to do something fun and different professionally," Greg offered.

"Professionally? You can't be serious." Julie replied, her mind spinning, as momentarily she envisioned herself back on stage, listening to the applause, as well as the laughter of the audience.

"I'm very serious, Miss West. I've never attended an amateur night where one contestant received every first place vote. I've never seen anyone make the hit you did on the first time out. People were talking about you after your performance. Everyone knew you were a winner from the minute you stepped out onto the stage and opened your mouth. Who writes your material?"

"No one writes my material. I don't have any material. The things I talked about were just things I did as a kid. You know, teenagers growing up in a small town, just a bunch of really good friends, getting into a lot of trouble, and thankfully not getting caught."

Greg smiled and took Julie's hand in his. "My dear Miss West, maybe more people need to hear about just a bunch of friends from a small town. Your style reminds me of Bill Cosby."

"If I'm dreaming, please don't wake me," Julie said.

"Then you will consider signing with me?" Greg asked.

Julie looked from Frank, to Dorah, to Jerry. Each nodded, but Frank was the one to speak up. "Think about it, Jewel. I've known Greg a long time. He only hires the best. Believe me, he wouldn't be here if he didn't recognize your talent. I've been doing amateur nights for years. I can tell you Greg has only been backstage once before tonight. Of course, I know he's usually in the audience."

"Then you aren't putting me on?"

"Good heavens, no," Greg assured her. "I'd never consider putting you on. I recognize your talent, even if you don't."

Jerry moved closer to Julie and put his arm around her shoulder. "The man is right, Julie. I've always known you were talented, I'd just forgotten what being on stage did to you. Tonight I saw Julie Morgan standing up there, just like she used to stand on the stage of Minter High. Didn't you tell me you took six months off to find out who you are? How do you expect to find out if you don't give it a try?"

"You seem to forget, I'm leaving Monday morning for a week in Texas."

"Good," Greg said. "A week will give you time to think, and me time to have my lawyer draw up a contract. I'll expect you in my office a week from Tuesday."

"Why not?" Julie said. "Jerry's right. I took this time to find myself and I'll never know if I don't try. I'll see you in your office a week from Tuesday. Just don't expect too much. Maybe tonight will turn out to be a fluke."

Greg pulled a card from his wallet and wrote something on the back. "Until a week from Tuesday, nine o'clock sharp. I'm certain you won't regret your decision and I won't be disappointed either."

When Greg left the club, Julie found herself the center of attention. Here, with Dorah and Frank, as well as Jerry and Karen, her future seemed so bright. Would she feel the same way after spending a week with Royd?

Fifteen

Monday morning came all too quickly. Once Dorah left for work, Julie started packing. By the time she finished, she heard the door buzzer and let Frank up.

She'd been surprised when he insisted on driving her to the airport. His announcement had come late on Sunday evening, after they'd spent most of the day together. The day began discussing the review of Julie's performance in the *Chicago Tribune*, over brunch. The article came as a surprise but Frank assured her one of the reporters for the entertainment section often came to the amateur nights, in the hopes of stumbling onto some undiscovered talent.

Throughout the afternoon, they saw Chicago the way Frank saw it. Not as a glittery tourist town, but the city where he lived and worked, where Allen's Alley had been born.

Frank entered the apartment and gave Julie a friendly hug.

"I told you yesterday, Frank, you don't have to take me to the airport. I'm perfectly capable—"

He put his finger to her lips to silence her. "I know you're perfectly capable of taking a cab. I'm certain you're perfectly capable of just about anything. I want to take you to the airport."

"Don't you have to be in court or something?"

"There are no court appearances scheduled for today and the something can wait. This is one thing I want to do. You see, I have this fabulous new client, Miss Jewel West, and she deserves my undivided attention."

"How can you be so sure of this new client? She's not entirely sure of herself. I don't know how I ever let you and Dorah talk me into doing something so crazy in the first place."

"I'm just glad we did. This trip to Texas will give you time to think. Once you get used to the idea, you might even come to enjoy being Jewel West. Dorah had a great idea when she thought up the name. It fits you. You are a perfect Jewel, whether you know it or not. I only hope you won't forget the Alley, when you become rich and famous."

Julie looked intently into Frank's brown eyes. "I'm already rich, Steve saw to that. As for the other, I doubt I'll ever be famous. Of course, if I ever am, I could never forget the Alley, or Frank Allen for that matter. This weekend has changed my life in so many ways. I don't know what the future will bring, or if there will ever be a Jewel West to contend with. I do know I owe everything to you and Dorah."

Frank put his arms around her waist and pulled her toward him. It seemed comforting to be in his arms, to have him kiss her.

"I'm sorry," Frank said, releasing her. "I know you're going to Texas to meet another man."

Julie sadly agreed. "Yes, I am, but I'm not certain I know exactly what I'm doing anymore. I don't even know this man. I thought I knew Dorah, but here in Chicago, she's a different person. I realize I'm a different person, too. I don't know what I'll find there."

~ * ~

The plane taxied to a stop and Julie took a deep breath. Before she'd gone to Chicago, she'd been excited about this trip. Now with so many decisions to make, apprehension overshadowed her excitement.

She certainly wasn't the Julie Weston who left for Jamaica a month ago. Today she'd become more confident about herself as well as her future.

Once she claimed her luggage she searched the area for Royd. When she didn't see him, she began to panic.

"Are you Julia?" a young woman asked, when she approached her.

Julie looked intently at the heavyset woman. She wore faded blue jeans, a plaid shirt, and a white Stetson. Julie judged her age to be about twenty-five or twenty-six and noticed her strong resemblance to Royd. "Yes, I'm Julie Weston."

"I'm Tori McAlester. Daddy's been called away on business. He said to tell you he's sorry, but he'll meet you at the house before we go to dinner."

"We?" Julie questioned.

"Daddy made reservations at a restaurant in town. Monday is the only night we can all get together. He wants you to meet the entire family."

Julie nodded and followed Tori to the baggage claim area. "Are these yours?" Tori asked, when Julie pulled her luggage off the carousel.

She bit back a tart answer of 'I wouldn't be taking them if they weren't mine.' The fact the girl even asked the question amazed her.

When Tori made no move to help her with her bags, she picked them up and trailed along behind the girl to the parking lot. Once there, Tori pointed out a beat up pick up truck.

"This is great," Julie said, hefting the bags into the bed of the truck. "I thought you'd be driving some little sports car with no room for my things. I never expected anything so practical."

"Well," Tori said, once they were in the cab and the engine came to life, "you aren't exactly what I expected, either."

"Just what did you expect?"

"I don't know. I guess it's the fact you don't look exactly like what Daddy described. I always wonder about the women Daddy meets when he goes on vacation. You're the first one he's ever brought home."

"Look, Tori," Julie began, trying not to sound annoyed. "I'm not a stray cat. I'm here at your father's invitation. I'm sorry if you're unhappy about it."

Tori stopped to pay the parking fee, then pulled out onto the highway. "Don't get me wrong, Julia. My father has been very lonely since my mother died. You certainly must be aware of the fact he is very well off."

"The fact hasn't escaped me. I assure you, I'm not here because of his money. I came because he asked me to come. Had it been for his money, I would have been the one to make the first overture."

Julie's comment met with Tori's stony silence. Instead of trying to initiate further conversation, she sat back to enjoy the scenery. It didn't take long for city to become country and soon Tori turned from the main artery onto a two-lane road.

"This is beautiful country," Julie finally commented.

"We've always thought so."

They drove, again in silence, until Tori turned into a gravel driveway. Ahead of them, Julie saw a large gate with a sign above it, which read *Slanted M*.

"The Slanted M," Julie mused. "Is it a registered brand?"

"What do you know about registered brands?" Tori questioned, her voice belying her astonishment.

"Not much, but I am a history buff. Especially the Old West. My dad loved western movies and books. I guess I inherited his love and took it a bit further. I minored in American History in college and have done a lot of research on the subject."

For the first time, Tori laughed. "You'll find real life ranching is a far cry from the way Hollywood depicts it. The Slanted M was established when Mexico still owned Texas, by the first McAlester to come here. It's only a shell of what it was, since Daddy and Michael have no interest in ranching. I rent out what land I don't need for my horses."

"In other words, you love it," Julie said. "I remember feeling the same way about my grandpa's farm. I'd forgotten it until just now. My uncle stayed, and of course, Mom married and moved into town. My cousin, Gene, runs a big operation out there, but I never seem to find time to drive the thirty miles to go and visit. Thank you for reminding me of what I've been missing."

The truck stopped in front of a sprawling house, which reminded Julie of a Mexican hacienda. Before she could get out of the truck, a young man appeared and pulled her luggage from the back.

"I'll take these up to the guestroom, Tori," the young man said, his voice sounding with a worried urgency. "I'm certainly glad you're back. Lady Blue is having trouble with her foal. I've called Dr. Harris, he'll be here soon."

Tori's face softened as the man's concern became her own. "I'm sorry, I have to get out to the barn. You'll find your room upstairs. It's the second door on the left."

"Tori," Julie said, stopping the girl in her tracks. "If I change my clothes, do you mind if I come out and watch?"

"Suit yourself. The barn is down there. I don't have time to show you the way." Without further comment, she started running toward the well-kept, white building.

Julie hurried up the stairs and easily found her room. The young man had put her bag on the bed. She quickly opened it and found jeans, a shirt, and tennis shoes.

The clothes looked and felt stiffly new as she hurried down the stairs and out the door. At the barn, she saw a truck pull up and a man rush into the building. She quickened her step so as not to miss the procedure.

"Can I help?" she asked.

"Have you ever helped a mare foal?" Tori questioned skeptically.

"When I was a kid, I spent a couple of weeks every summer with my uncle on the farm. He used to let me watch when the cows had their calves."

"If you think you can handle it," Tori said, "hold her head. We've got a breech here. We've got to turn the foal."

Julie climbed over the wooden half door to the stall and knelt beside the mare. The horse seemed weak and Julie positioned herself so she could hold its head in her lap and gently stroke the animal's nose. The mare seemed to appreciate Julie's concern. She could feel it begin to relax, allowing those trying to help turn the colt to do the work.

Julie lost track of time. In an attempt to calm the mare, she continued to speak in a low voice, talking about everything from her kids to her flight without changing her calming tone.

"We've got a filly!" Julie heard Tori exclaim. "She's a beauty!"

For the first time, Julie diverted her attention from the laboring animal to the perfect foal. When Tori finished wiping down the baby, it found its wobbly legs and began to call for its mother.

"We did it," Tori said, enthusiastically pumping Julie's hand.

"No, you did it. I only watched."

"If you hadn't kept her calm, we wouldn't have gotten the foal turned," Dr. Harris said. "We could have never done it without you. If she hadn't stayed calm, we might have lost them both."

Tori checked her watch. "We'd better get you cleaned up. Daddy will skin me alive if you're not ready when he gets here."

~ * ~

Julie stepped from the shower, still awed by the miracle of birth she'd been allowed to witness in the barn.

The clock radio reminded her of the time. *I'm late in eating supper,* she told herself. *I'm already starting to feel dizzy. I don't know if it's because I need to eat or if I'm taking George's warnings too seriously.*

She hurried to finish applying her make-up before going downstairs. When at last she approved of her appearance, she prepared to go to meet Royd. To her surprise, when she opened the door, Royd stood, ready to knock.

"Royd," she said. "I was just coming downstairs to meet you. I've had such a wonderful afternoon."

"So I heard," he replied flatly.

His tone made the smile on her lips fade. She could tell by his voice, her afternoon's activities annoyed him.

Instead of taking her in his arms, as she had expected, he put his hand to her hair and absently stroked the dark strands. "You look," he hesitated, as if searching for the proper word, "lovely."

"Thank you. I've been looking forward to being here." As soon as she spoke the words, she realized how lame they sounded. Nothing here had been what she expected. Royd appeared cold, stiff. Had she won over Tori only to alienate Royd?

Julie closed the bedroom door and followed him down the staircase. She had become painfully aware of her need to eat, but considering Royd's present mood, she said nothing.

When they were seated in the car, Royd broke the silence. "I'm sorry I wasn't at the airport to meet you, Julia."

"I understand. I can't expect you to ignore business for me. It gave me a chance to get to know Tori."

Even in the darkened car, she saw Royd's grip on the steering wheel tighten. She wondered how much it would cost her to change her ticket and return home early.

The parking lot of the restaurant stood almost empty and Julie remembered Monday evenings were usually a quiet night to eat out, even in Minter.

Once inside, she noticed two couples sitting at a table near the freestanding fireplace. As she and Royd made their way toward the group, the two men stood to greet them.

"Looks like you got an early start," Royd said, shaking hands with both men.

"Not really, Daddy," one of the men replied. "We just got here."

"Julia," Royd said, "this is my son, Michael, his wife, Brianne, my daughter, Morgan, and her husband, Jack Pate."

Julie took Michael's hand and hoped he wouldn't notice the slight tremor she had begun experiencing earlier.

"Let's see, Michael," she began. "If I remember correctly, you and your wife are doctors, and Morgan, you and your husband run a night club."

Michael looked surprised. "I'm impressed. I didn't think you would remember something so trivial. Now what can I get you to drink?"

Royd ordered a Brandy Manhattan, giving Julie a moment to consider what she wanted. "I'd like a glass of orange juice," she said, when Michael turned to her.

"Just plain orange juice? Wouldn't you like some vodka in it or perhaps a little sloe gin?" Royd asked.

"No thank you, plain orange juice is all I want." She watched Michael turn toward the bar, pleased she'd remembered George's advice about drinking orange juice when she didn't eat on time or began feeling light headed.

"Are you all right, Julia?" Brianne asked from across the table. "You're trembling."

"I'm a bit over excited and I guess I'm a little late in eating."

"You should have told me," Royd said, taking her hand. "We could have had a bite to eat before we left."

"I didn't think it necessary at the time. I'll be just fine, once I have some juice."

Michael reappeared at the table with a tray of drinks and handed the first glass to Julie. She took a long drink, then another before realizing how overly sweet the juice tasted. She looked up at Michael, suspiciously.

"I had the bartender put some sugar in your juice," he said, as though he read her mind. "Have you ever experienced a drop in blood sugar before?"

"A what?"

"A drop in blood sugar. It's what happened to you just now. Has it happened before?"

"No, of course not," she lied. "The food on the plane didn't appeal to me and it has been an exciting day."

"So I heard. I ran into Kip Harris at the gas station and he told me about Lady Blue. I assume she's the reason Tori is late."

Royd nodded, noticeably annoyed with his youngest daughter. "You'd think Lady Blue was Tori's child, the way she carries on. She did say she'd be here in time for dinner, though."

"You're too hard on Tori, Daddy," Morgan countered. "She's got a lot invested in Lady Blue. Something must have been terribly wrong if she had to call Kip."

Michael nodded. "Kip said the foal didn't turn and they were worried about a breech birth. He also said Daddy's friend, Julia, made quite a midwife."

Julie could feel the color begin to creep into her face. She'd never dreamed her part in this afternoon's drama would be discussed over dinner. "I didn't do anything, really," she protested.

"Didn't do anything!" Michael exclaimed. "Me thinks the lady doth protest too much. Kip said she has the knack. She calmed the mare like a pro."

"It wasn't anything spectacular. I only talked to the poor thing. As a matter-of-fact, I was born and raised in Minter. I'm a dyed in the wool city girl. What I don't know about animals could fill volumes."

"Minter?" Jack asked, picking up on the name of her hometown. "Do you know someone from Minter by the name of Jewel West?"

Julie almost choked on her juice at the mention of the woman she'd become over the weekend. She hadn't intended to say anything to Royd about what she'd done until she'd had time to decide the best way to broach the subject. "Ah—Jewel West—well..."

"Jewel West, of course," Morgan said. "Julia Weston, Jewel West. You're Jewel West aren't you?"

"Yes, but it's nothing, not really."

"Nothing?" Morgan echoed. "It didn't sound like nothing in the *Chicago Tribune*. You were a hit at Allen's Alley and Greg Lauer wants to sign you to a contract. I certainly wouldn't call that nothing."

Before Julie could respond, Tori entered the room and the focus of the conversation turned to Lady Blue and her new filly. To Julie's relief, all talk of low blood sugar and Jewel West had been forgotten.

Dinner consisted of large steaks, baked potatoes, which Julie declined, and generous house salads. Around her, the members of Royd's family talked about their daily routines and Julie enjoyed the temporary reprieve from responding.

"Can I interest you in dessert?" the waitress asked, before handing each person at the table a small dessert menu.

Everyone ordered rich, gooey desserts, until the waitress stopped beside Julie. "What kind of flavored coffee do you have tonight?"

"We have pecan, Irish cream, and hazelnut."

"I'll have the pecan with cream, thank you."

"You should have a better desert than coffee, Julia," Royd encouraged her.

"The coffee is perfect. As much as I'd adore one of those desserts, I'm afraid they aren't on my diet."

"Diet!" Royd exploded. "You certainly don't need to diet."

"Yes she does, Daddy," Michael said. "Julia has diabetes."

Julie appreciated Michael again coming to her rescue. His diagnosis of her problem, though, caught her off guard. "How did you know?" she asked.

"I guessed as much when you ordered the juice and I saw you trembling. Of course, then you declined your potato and now no dessert. How long have you been diagnosed?"

"I found out just after the first of the year. I guess my doctor put the fear of God into me about my diet. I remember how I felt before he diagnosed me and if diet can make such a difference, I guess I can do as I'm told."

"Do you keep track of your blood sugar?" Brianne asked.

"I wouldn't dare not to. George is much more than my doctor. He's also my neighbor. If I don't check in enough to suit him, he shows up on my doorstep. I even had to promise I'd call him on Wednesday and let him know how I'm doing."

"Why don't you stop by my office on Wednesday and I'll call him," Michael suggested.

"Speaking of stopping by," Jack said, "Would you consider performing at the club Wednesday evening? We rarely get top talent down here. I'd like to be able to say you were here before you became a star."

"I don't think—"

"It might be interesting, Julia," Royd said, his voice laced with sarcasm. "I think we ought to see the other side of you."

Royd's tone put Julie on edge. In spite of her annoyance with him, she agreed. If the *Tribune* thought she'd been great, why not prove it to Royd and his family?

~ * ~

The alarm went off at seven. The soft music, which came from the clock radio, was a soothing wake-up call, even though Julie didn't need it. The night seemed to drag on forever. If she'd received an hour of sleep it would have been nothing short of a miracle. The events of Monday had combined to chase sleep away.

To her surprise, the jeans and shirt she'd worn the day before were clean and neatly folded on the bed when she'd returned last evening. After a quick shower, she pulled them on and went down to breakfast.

Hearing voices, she followed the sound until she stood outside of the dining room. She waited for a moment before entering and caught a bit of the conversation, apparently not meant for her ears.

"Honestly Daddy, I couldn't believe the way you acted last night. If I were Julia, I'd be on the first plane to Chicago," Tori said.

"You're a fine one to talk. Just a few days ago, you were telling me how much you disapproved of Julia coming here," Royd replied.

"I hadn't met her then. She's not at all what I expected. Michael, Morgan, and I all think she's wonderful and we can't understand your attitude."

"I'm not asking you kids to understand anything. What I do is of no consequence to you."

Royd's last comment met with silence and Julie cleared her throat to make her presence known before entering the room.

"Good morning," she said, pretending she hadn't eavesdropped on their conversation.

"Julia," Royd acknowledged her, getting to his feet and coming to her side to kiss her cheek. "I didn't expect you to be up so early. I thought you'd take advantage of being able to sleep late."

"I'm able to sleep late every morning. I want to see the ranch and go horseback riding."

Tori smiled broadly. "Then I'll excuse myself and go out to finish my chores. As soon as I'm done, I can take you for a tour, since Daddy has to go to work."

When they were alone, Julie turned to Royd. "You have to go to work?"

"I'm afraid so. I'm learning not to take a vacation without leaving the state. Are you certain you'll be all right?"

"Don't be silly. I'll be just fine. It will give me more of an opportunity to get to know Tori."

Royd pulled a chair away from the table and held it for Julie. As she lowered herself into it, she caught a glimpse of something to make her blood run cold.

"That picture," she gasped. "Is it of you and LuAnn?" She concentrated on Royd as he looked toward the eleven by twenty portrait hanging on the wall.

"Why yes, it is. I didn't think it would upset you so."

"You didn't think I'd be upset! How could I not be upset? It could have been a picture of me a year ago. Add fifty pounds to my weight, take the color out of my hair, and we could be twins. Is this the reason you asked me to come down here? Did you think you could get LuAnn back? I'm not LuAnn! I'm Julie, not Julia, Julie!" She pushed her chair back and got up. She knew she had to get out of the room and away from Royd.

Surprisingly, Royd put his hands on her shoulders to stop her from leaving. "Maybe I haven't been completely honest with you, but have you been honest with me? Why didn't you tell me about your diabetes or this Jewel West thing?"

Anger rose within Julie as she pulled away from Royd. She had just turned to leave, when a young woman entered the room. "There's a telephone call for you, Mrs. Weston."

"Julia," Royd called to her. "We have to talk."

Julie nodded, without turning back. To talk to Royd now could easily override her common sense. In the heat of anger, they might both say things better left unsaid.

"Julie," the voice on the other end of the line said. "This is Dan Conklin, from the *Ledger*. I had the strangest call from Jerry Gaines last night. He asked me to read the article about Jewel West in Sunday's *Tribune*. He said if I called you at this number, you'd explain everything and give me an exclusive."

"Jerry certainly didn't waste any time," Julie commented. She continued talking, telling Dan the story, which still seemed too incredible to be true. "You can add this little note to your story," she finally added. "Jewel West will be performing here on Wednesday evening. I'll be at a club called Morgan's Den. Of course once I get back home, I'll have to make a decision about the future of this new person who seems to have taken over my body."

When she finished, she returned to the dining room. Royd had left and the room seemed large and empty. Instead of remaining there, alone with LuAnn's picture, she wandered into the kitchen.

"Mrs. Weston," the woman doing dishes greeted her. "Are you ready for breakfast?"

Julie nodded and sat down on a stool at the counter.

"What can I get for you?"

"Anything simple. Toast and coffee will be fine."

"Eggs and bacon sound better. Mr. McAlester insisted I fix you a good breakfast. How do you like your eggs?"

"Over easy, but please don't fuss."

~ * ~

The barn bustled with activity when Julie arrived. Grooms were busy with the horses as well as cleaning out the stalls.

"Are you ready to go riding?" Tori called from the loft.

"Whenever you are. I thought I'd like to check on Lady Blue first. How's Lady Blue's filly this morning?" She looked up toward the loft and saw Tori swing her legs over the side.

"You mean Jewel? She's great."

Lady Blue nickered, as if agreeing with Tori's statement.

"Jewel? What kind of a name is that for a horse?"

"What kind of a name is that for a comedian?" Tori countered, as she climbed down the ladder.

"*Touché*," Julie replied when Tori stood in front of her.

Lady Blue nickered again and Julie went over to the stall. "Do you remember my voice, girl?"

The horse nuzzled Julie's hand, as though looking for something.

"She wants this," Tori said, placing a sugar cube in Julie's hand.

"Are you certain she should have it?"

Tori nodded, and Lady Blue greedily took the sugar from the palm of Julie's hand.

"I'm almost ashamed to admit it," Tori began, "but I heard what went on between you and Daddy this morning."

"I don't see how you could have helped but hear us. I'm certain people in the next county heard us."

"What's going to happen?"

"I don't know. Your dad says he wants to talk. I couldn't even consider it this morning. Seeing the picture of your mother shocked me so badly, I knew I'd say things I didn't mean."

Julie watched the expression on Tori's face. Should she mention how she'd eavesdropped on the conversation between father and daughter just before her own confrontation with Royd?

Deciding against it, she continued in a different vein. "So much makes sense now. Your father told you I looked exactly like your mother, didn't he?"

Without waiting for an answer, she continued, "It's the reason you looked so surprised so when we met at the airport. Of course, I can understand your concern about my wanting his money. You had no way of knowing my husband left me very comfortable."

"You're right about the money, as well as Daddy's description of you. In your place, I'd be booking a flight back to Chicago and not sitting here, calmly talking to some stranger."

Julie laughed. "I had those same thoughts this morning, but I can't leave here without at least talking to him. It wouldn't be fair to Royd, and I did promise Jack and Morgan I'd be at the club on Wednesday evening. I never go back on my word. Playing Jewel West will help me make the right decision when I get home."

"Your horses are ready, Miss McAlester," a young man said, interrupting them.

Julie followed Tori from the barn and easily mounted the chestnut gelding who waited for her.

"You seem quite comfortable with your horse," Tori said, once they were away from the barn. "Daddy said you could ride, but I've been skeptical."

"I guess I don't blame you. I know how my kids feel about all the new things I've been doing lately. I haven't been riding since I graduated from high school. I used to be good at it, but I did feel rusty when we rode in Jamaica. It is something you don't forget, though. Did your mother ride?"

"Oh yes, I'm a lot like her. She loved this ranch and found riding the only acceptable way to enjoy it."

"Acceptable?" Julie asked.

"Mother was a lady, or so Daddy thought. Ladies don't run ranches, therefore she knew her place and it wasn't in the barns."

Julie wanted to ask further questions, but Tori's tone closed the door on the subject.

They rode for almost an hour and Tori assured Julie they had seen only a minute portion of the Slanted M.

"It's getting colder," Tori said, when she reined her horse to a halt. "Look off to the West, there's a storm brewing. We'll have to hurry back to the house or we'll get soaked."

~ * ~

Julie relaxed in the steaming tub. The promise of hearty homemade soup, combined with the hot water, helped to ward off the chill from the soaking rain. The combination worked to make her drowsy.

"Are you almost done?" Tori called from the hall.

"Soon," Julie answered, suddenly jolted from the brink of sleep. She eased herself from the tub and shivered slightly at the chill of the air against her overly warm body.

She pulled on her new yellow sweatsuit with matching socks and tennis shoes, then hurried down to join Tori in the kitchen.

The woman, who served her breakfast, now placed a steaming bowl of soup in front of her.

"I can't believe the two of you let yourselves get caught in the storm," she said. "When Mr. McAlester finds out you were soaking wet, he'll have a fit."

"And just how will he find out, Peggy?" Tori countered. "I doubt if either of us will be telling him." She punctuated her comment with a giggle.

The woman turned from the table and returned to the stove at the other end of the room.

"Peggy is a gem, but mark my words, Daddy will know about us getting caught in the storm within ten minutes of walking in the door," Tori whispered. "She's always been an old mother hen when it comes to us kids."

"Be glad she loves you," Julie said.

The remainder of the afternoon passed uneventfully. Tori went into town right after lunch, leaving Julie to entertain herself.

A short nap served to refresh her, and by four she found her way to the library at the far end of the house. In the fireplace, logs had been perfectly laid in the grates and the fire took the chill from the room.

Julie chose a book from the shelf and had just sat down in one of the big leather chairs when a young woman came into the room. "There's a phone call for you, Mrs. Weston. You can take it in here."

She picked up the phone, surprised to find Jill on the other end of the line.

"Congratulations, Mom," Jill greeted her. "I didn't know you were a comedian."

They talked on for several minutes. Jill told her about their trip home and learning about Jewel West from Meg. It seemed as though all of Minter knew about her new personality.

Julie went back to the book she'd chosen feeling more relaxed than she had earlier. In the back of her mind, she had worried about the trip from Denver to Minter in the middle of winter. Storms could come up so quickly and with Jill's pregnancy, they didn't need to be stranded on the highway.

Curling up, catlike, in the chair, she continued to read. It took her only minutes to become completely enthralled by the story. How long she read, she didn't know, but an involuntary shudder gave her the uneasy feeling of being watched. She looked up and instantly relaxed at the sight of Royd standing in the doorway, a plate of hors d'oeuvres in his hand.

"Am I welcome?" he asked.

"It's your home, Royd. Of course, you're welcome."

He seemed to relax, and crossed the short distance between the door and the chair, setting the hors d'oeuvres on the table next to her.

"Peggy says dinner will be a bit delayed. She thought we might enjoy these."

Julie looked from Royd to the plate he held in his hand. "I wish you wouldn't pamper me. I know my limits. If I need something, I'm able to get it."

"You didn't take care of yourself last night, or this morning for that matter."

Julie stiffened at Royd's words, though not at his tone. The edge his voice carried last evening as well as this morning had been replaced by genuine concern.

"No, I guess I didn't. I take it you heard about Tori and me getting caught in the storm. Last night, I was too worried about your reaction to me to take the warning signs seriously. Today, the storm blew up so quickly, we had no time to get back." She watched his face for confirmation of his annoyance, but sensed none of the tension she'd expected.

"Julie, I'm sorry," he said, kneeling in front of her chair. "I'm so very sorry. I fell in love with you instantly, or so I thought, when we were in Jamaica. When I came home and compared the pictures I'd taken of you with the portrait of LuAnn, inwardly the two of you became one in the same. I knew how wrong I'd been as soon as I saw you last night. Can we start over?" Royd's eyes were downcast, as though he couldn't meet her gaze.

"Of course, we can," she said, her words bringing eye contact. "I, too, have a confession to make, something which needs to be said before we can begin again."

Julie took a deep breath and paused just a moment to choose her words carefully. "When I returned to Minter, my friend, Devan, had been called to Philadelphia on family business. When I spoke with him, he told me he'd decided to stay in Philadelphia, permanently. His son had been badly injured in an accident and he thought he should stay to care for him. At first, I became devastated. It took a while for everything to sink in. When it did, I realized I didn't even have a number where I could reach him. I couldn't just let him disappear from my life, so I called his office. I knew he stood right there and yet wouldn't take or return my calls. Then the devastation turned to hurt. In the meantime, I'd accepted your invitation. I accepted because someone wanted me and I needed to be wanted. I'm rebounding from Devan, and trying to find out who I am. I'm afraid it's not fair to you."

Royd got to his feet, pulling her up from the chair and into his arms. "I asked you to come here without commitment. The offer still holds. You aren't LuAnn, my children have made the fact painfully clear to me today, and I'm not Devan. We're just two lonely people. For one week, let's be lonely together. There will be no more calls back to the office, I promise. We'll do anything you want to do."

"Anything?" Julie asked.

"Anything," Royd repeated. "Is there something special you'd like to do or see?"

"I'd like to see San Antonio and the Alamo, and I've always wanted to go to Mexico." Julie surprised herself by expressing her desires to Royd. Her wants, her requests always remained buried as in the past she tended to defer to Steve.

"Let's see," Royd began, "Michael is expecting you in the morning and tomorrow night you'll be at the club. Thursday morning we'll take my plane and fly to San Antonio, then Friday we'll go on to Cancun. We can spend Friday, Saturday, and Sunday at my friend's condo, then come back on Monday in time for your flight to Chicago."

"I didn't know you flew," Julie said, already envisioning herself returning to a tropical paradise.

"There's a lot we don't know about each other. I've always enjoyed going to Mexico, especially the Yucatan. You'll love the ruins at Chitzen Itza."

"Chitzen Itza?" Julie questioned.

"It's a beautiful tribute to the Mayan civilization. You'll understand once you see it. The Mayans, like the Aztecs, were light years ahead of their time. Theirs is the true legacy of Mexico. Unlike the border towns, the Americans haven't exploited the area, yet."

"It sounds wonderful. I've always been fascinated by ancient history. I must admit, I concentrated mostly on Europe and the Far East. I've never considered the ancients of the New World to be as civilized."

Royd laughed. "Then you'll be pleasantly surprised. Dinner should be ready, then I'll have you all to myself for the remainder of the evening."

Julie felt Royd pull her tighter into his arms and allowed herself to become lost in the sensuality of his kiss. When they broke apart, Royd picked up a cracker from the plate and handed it to Julie. "Peggy will have a fit if you don't eat at least one of these."

~ * ~

Wednesday afternoon Julie returned from Michael's office and went up to take a short nap before they were scheduled to leave for Morgan's Den. When she awoke, the bedside clock read four. Alarmed by the lateness of the hour, she took a quick shower then slipped into slacks and a sweater. Before going downstairs, she picked up her make-up case and chose the outfit she wanted from the closet.

"I thought I should come and get you up," Royd greeted her, when she reached the base of the stairs. "Peggy has prepared a light supper for us. Morgan isn't planning her buffet until after the first show."

"I wish they wouldn't fuss so," Julie replied. "For me tonight is going to be fun."

"I don't think they're fussing, nor do I think this is just for fun," Royd assured her. "I'm afraid I've lost you to the stage and tonight will help you make your decision."

Julie cringed at how close Royd came to the truth. "I've never been yours to lose. I do admit, until last weekend, I hadn't thought about a career on the stage, but it seems so natural, so easy, I have to try."

"I'll reserve judgment until tonight is over. You see, I tend to be a bit skeptical," Royd teased. "I find nothing about you to be funny."

~ * ~

Morgan's Den, like Allen's Alley, didn't appear to be overly impressive at first glance. A storefront theater came alive inside with a raised stage and intimate tables with seating for almost two hundred people.

"I'm so excited about tonight," Morgan greeted them. "Help yourself to the bar, Daddy. I'll take Julie backstage."

Julie took just a moment to assess the sights around her, before following Morgan.

"This is the way to your dressing room," Morgan said. "The others will be here soon."

"Others?" Julie questioned.

"There will be three comedians tonight. You'll each get about twenty minutes."

Julie nodded and followed Morgan around the maze of tables and through a door beside the stage. Before closing the door behind her, she glanced at Royd as he engaged Jack in conversation at the bar.

Down the hallway were four closed doors, each with a star painted on the center panel. Julie raised her eyebrows. "Stars?"

"We want everyone who performs here to feel like a star," Morgan assured her, as she stopped in front of the first door.

As she stepped inside the room, Julie's knees weakened and her stomach began to churn. Three large floral arrangements dominated the small area. Of the three, the vase containing a dozen roses of assorted colors caught her eye. Devan became foremost in her mind.

No, she thought, Devan couldn't have sent them. *He has no idea where I am and even if he does know, he doesn't care."*

Are you all right, Julie?" Morgan asked.

"Oh, yes," she replied. "I'm just overwhelmed. I never expected anything like this."

Absently, she reached for the card from the roses, almost dreading the knowledge of the sender.

An exceptional bouquet for an exceptional lady.

Royd and family.

She breathed a bit easier and wondered why she inspired bouquets of roses in assorted colors.

Morgan reached for the card on the second arrangement and handed it to Julie.

"We're all so proud of you, Mom—Love Mark and Keoki, Jill and Karl, and Lance," Julie read aloud.

"Your kids?" Morgan asked.

Julie nodded. "They shouldn't spend their money so foolishly."

"I don't think it's at all foolish," Morgan said, handing Julie the last card.

"Guess it's all in how you look at it," she replied, as she opened the envelope.

We can't believe everything we're hearing—best of luck with your new career.

Jim and Meg, George and Shirley.

"My neighbors," Julie said, after reading the card.

"Well, enjoy your flowers," Morgan said. "You've got about an hour to fix your face and dress. I'll send in one of the waitresses to help you, in a few minutes."

Julie nodded and experienced a sense of relief to be alone in the small room. For a moment, she stared at the roses. What kind of power did Devan hold over her? Just the sight of the flowers brought thoughts of him to her mind. Unbidden tears sprung to her eyes and she buried her face in her hand.

A knock at the door brought her to full attention. "Just a minute," she called, reaching for a tissue.

Before she got to her feet, the door opened. "I'm sorry," she said, without looking up at the girl who had come to help her with her hair. "I haven't even started getting ready."

"So I see," a man's voice sounded from behind her.

Julie turned quickly and got to her feet. To her surprise, Frank stood in the doorway, a tray with a carafe of orange juice and a glass in his hands.

"Frank? What on earth are you doing here? How did you know? How did you get here?"

"One question at a time, pretty lady," Frank said, setting the tray on the dressing table. "First you're to drink this."

Julie watched Frank pour a glass of juice and hand it to her. "I don't need this," she protested.

"Funny, I heard an entirely different story just a few minutes ago from the good doctor. Now drink it."

"So, how did you get here?" Julie asked, once she drank enough juice to satisfy Frank. "How did you know about tonight?"

"I've known Jack and Morgan for about three years now. They called me yesterday. I decided not to stay away, since you might say I discovered you. Dorah and I flew down this afternoon."

"Dorah's here, too?"

203

"I couldn't get away without her. Besides, this is a business trip. Greg dropped by my office today with an informal proposal. He wants me to lobby for him."

Julie laughed. "I don't think he has to worry. No one else is beating down my door. I'm beginning to wonder if he knows what he's talking about."

Frank took the glass from her hand and set it on the dressing table before he pulled her into his arms. "Believe me, he knows. Everyone knows, but you. Maybe tonight will convince you."

Dorah came into the dressing room and insisted Frank leave and give Julie some much needed time alone.

"What am I doing, Dorah?" she pleaded.

"What do you mean?"

"I came here to see Royd, but I know he's not the one I want. Frank only confuses the matter. I'm more confused now than before. I want to forget Devan and get on with my life, but I don't think I'm ready for another relationship. What would you do in my shoes?"

"I'd relax. Frank knows you're not ready to jump into anything. So does Royd. As for Devan, you have to forget him. He's gone on with his life, you should, too."

Sixteen

Devan returned home, the hour too late for a decent supper. He stopped in the lobby, to get the mail from the locked box, before making his way to Todd's second floor apartment. These last few weeks had been trying. When not at work, he spent his time at the hospital. His usually quiet life had been turned upside down.

Tonight, he'd left the hospital earlier than usual. Todd had been tired. At the insistence of the doctor, Devan left before visiting hours were over. He, too, needed to get some rest, to get to bed early enough to get at least a few hours of sleep before the alarm jarred him back to reality.

It would be over soon. This evening, the doctor announced Todd would be coming home in a week.

Physical therapy could continue at home and Todd could return to work. His boss had insisted on installing a drafting table, a computer terminal, and a FAX machine at the apartment. He had been without Todd's input too long already.

The elevator doors opened and Devan stepped into the mirrored cubicle. For the first time, in weeks, he studied his reflection. To his surprise, he faced a stranger. Dark circles beneath his eyes gave him a haunted look and he had definitely lost weight. Even his hair belonged to someone else. His normally dark strands now sported more streaks of silver.

The apartment, as usual, remained deathly quiet. Before he tossed the mail on the table, he scanned its contents. A letter with Jerry's return address had been forwarded from his Minter apartment and his copy of the *Minter Ledger* were the only pieces in the stack for him.

It seemed strange how special Saturdays had become. On Saturday, he received the *Ledger*. He should have dropped his subscription, he usually didn't recognize many of the names, but for some reason, it became a link to home, to Julie.

When the mail hit the table, it became momentarily forgotten. A gnawing sensation in his stomach reminded him lunch; a sandwich from the machine in the cafeteria at work had been over nine hours ago.

He opened the refrigerator and checked its contents. He found a chunk of cheese, full of mold, and a loaf of bread, which didn't look too bad. He could eat it if he took slices form the center where it hadn't turned green yet. He put a pan on the stove to heat, while he cleaned the mold from the cheese, so he could make himself a grilled cheese sandwich.

The sandwich sizzled in the pan and he thought a glass of milk sounded good. Checking the refrigerator, he found only a can of beer.

"Grilled cheese and beer," he said aloud. "How much more Wisconsin can you get?"

He sat down at the table and picked up the letter from Jerry, slitting open the envelope with the knife he'd used to butter his bread.

> *We're having our 30th class reunion, July 10, 7 p.m., at the Minitree. The cost includes dinner, with choice of prime rib, shrimp, or chicken Kiev, free beer, and a D.J. for your dancing enjoyment. Couples $50 - Singles $25 Please RSVP by June 6th.*

The names of Jerry and two other classmates, with addresses and phone numbers, were listed at the bottom of the page.

A *couple of months ago, the class reunion seemed so important, now nothing is important, except Todd. How can I attend the reunion and face Julie?*

With no further thoughts of its contents, he lay the letter aside and picked up the paper. The headlines seemed to scream at him: *Local Woman Wins Contest At Comedy Club.*

"No one I know," he said aloud, before turning his attention to the article.

> *Julie Weston pleasantly surprised an audience of almost three hundred Saturday evening in Chicago. Julie, a lifelong resident of Minter, touted a unanimous victory, with her stories of growing up in a small town and being a member of The Four Musketeers of Minter.*
>
> *'I've never seen anything like it,' commented Frank Allen, owner of the club, Allen's Alley. 'People just don't win these things by a unanimous vote. She's very lucky Greg Lauer, one of the top comedy agents in the country, saw her. He wants her to sign a contract with his office.'*
>
> *Jerry Gaines, who first contacted our office with the story, told us he and Karen had been in Chicago for the show. 'We didn't go to Chicago because of Julie,' he commented. 'Tickets to the show were part of our hotel package. Imagine our shock when Jewel West turned out to be Julie Weston. Her material took us quite by surprise, since I never thought growing up here to be very funny.'*
>
> *We finally reached Julie, as she vacationed in Texas. She told us she had thought the experience to be a lark and her future plans were uncertain. She did say she would be performing at a club, called Morgan's Den, on Wednesday evening.*
>
> *When Julie will again return to Minter is unknown, but we do wish her luck!!*

Devan put down the paper and concentrated on Julie and The Four Musketeers. So much had happened in their lives, they could never go back to those carefree days. Why did people have to grow up? Why couldn't life remain as simple as it had seemed thirty years ago?

He glanced at the clock. *Nine-thirty,* he thought to himself, *it's only eight-thirty in Minter.*

He picked up the phone and placed a call to Jerry, hoping he'd get more than a machine. Karen answered and called Jerry to the phone at Devan's request. While he waited for Jerry, he wondered about the necessity of the call.

"Jerry, this is Devan," he said, acknowledging Jerry's greeting.

"Devan? You're the last person I expected to hear from."

"I just got this class reunion thing in the mail, as well as my copy of the *Ledger.*"

"I see," Jerry replied. "So, it's Julie you're calling about, not the reunion."

"You might say as much. According to the paper, she's good."

"Good isn't the word, she's fantastic. Of course, she always has been. Greg Lauer's offer attests to it. You might say it's all thanks to you."

"What do you mean, thanks to me?"

"If you hadn't walked out on her, she wouldn't have gone to Texas to meet Royd McAlester."

"Who?" Devan interrupted.

"Royd McAlester. I thought the mention of his name might perk you up a bit. She met him in Jamaica and accepted an invitation to visit him. I guess he wanted her to meet his kids. Of course, if she hadn't decided to take the trip, she wouldn't have spent the weekend with her friend, Dorah, in Chicago, and she wouldn't have performed at Allen's Alley."

Devan fumed at Jerry's attitude. "Maybe I ought to set you straight on a few things, Jerry. I didn't walk out on Julie. You just don't understand what I've been going through, here."

"Don't give me your shit, Devan. I know exactly what you're going through, only my son wasn't living on his own. He was six years old when a hit and run driver ran down his bike. Julie came to the hospital every day and even took care of our other kids so we could be with Timmy. When he died, Julie and Steve were the first ones at the funeral home and the last ones to leave. All she wanted was to help you, to know you care, and you shut her out. She told me about Todd's unlisted phone number and how you wouldn't return the calls she placed to your office, so don't tell me about poor misunderstood Devan. By the way, how is Todd? Julie will be interested when I tell her I talked to you."

"He's coming home a week from today, but don't tell Julie. Okay? It sounds like she's got her life together, which is more than I can say for me. I'm sorry about your son, I didn't know."

"It's all right. It all happened twelve years ago. I didn't tell you about Timmy for sympathy. I was trying to make you understand Julie. She cares for you. She only wanted to help you, but you pushed her away. Wake up, Devan. Give her a call. Talk to her, let her help you."

"I don't think so, Jerry. If she signs with this Lauer guy, she'll have a whole new life to build. She doesn't need old baggage to contend with. It's been good talking to you."

Devan heard Jerry start to say something, but he couldn't listen any longer. Instead, he hung up the phone.

I've screwed up royal. I've misjudged Julie, even alienated her, but what else could I have done? Unable to answer the question he'd just asked himself, he poured the rest of the beer down the drain, dumped the sandwich in the trash, and went into the living room.

After slipping the disk of *Evita* into the CD player, he relived the weekend in Milwaukee. The feel of Julie's body, the smell of her perfume, the sound of her voice, invaded his mind and dominated his dreams as he drifted off to sleep in the recliner.

~ * ~

"The nerve of that guy," Jerry said, once he hung up the phone. "The sonofabitch hung up on me. I thought I knew him, thought we were friends, not just Devan and me, but Julie, too. I know he's going through hell, but at a time like this he needs us the most. Just who does he think he is, anyway? We don't hear from him for almost thirty years, then he shows up, turns Julie upside down, only to fall off the face of the earth again."

"Maybe you don't want to hear this, but didn't we do the same thing to her?" Karen asked. "I had an affair with Steve and you rubbed it in when she'd just started to recover from his death. The difference is, we stayed in Minter to face the consequences of our actions."

Jerry pulled Karen to her feet and held her tightly. He understood the truth in her words. They'd all hurt Julie, but miraculously she rebounded.

His only concern now came over Julie's feelings for Devan. No matter what she said, no matter how she acted, he knew her too well. Her non-committed relationship with Devan had been a safety net. Deep down, Jerry knew, she loved Devan and would be hard put to set aside her feelings.

Seventeen

Julie prepared to board her flight to Chicago as soon as her row number was called. She hugged Royd and made her way with the other passengers through security. Before leaving the security area to get to the departure gate, she turned for one last look at Royd. He waved and blew her a kiss, then turned to leave.

She wiped a tear away and hurried toward the plane. Royd's parting gesture told her he, too, knew theirs could never be a lasting relationship. They had been a pleasant diversion for each other. Two people who met on vacation and would think of each other often, each thought bringing special memories.

She settled onto the plush seat in the coach section of the 737 and snapped the buckle of her seat belt into place. Around her, businessmen were beginning their workweek with flights to Chicago. She, too, would be flying to Chicago to begin the workweek, to meet with Greg and secure her future.

The flight attendant began giving the safety instructions and Julie closed her eyes in an attempt to relive the last few days.

Her appearance at Morgan's Den had convinced not only herself, but Royd as well, that Jewel West would become someone very special. Frank made Greg's contract sound exceptionally good, and Julie now knew what would transpire once she arrived in Chicago.

Rather than thinking about the future, she continued to dwell on the past. Her thoughts turned to the last time she saw Frank and

Dorah. Since their flight corresponded with Royd's scheduled departure, everything worked out perfectly.

"I'll pick you up at the airport on Monday," Frank assured her, while Royd filed their flight plan.

"It's not necessary, you know."

Frank placed his hands on her shoulders. "Will you stop with the it's not necessary, already? Just look for me on Monday."

Royd reappeared in the waiting area and Julie found no time to argue further. Within minutes Frank and Dorah were on their way to Chicago and Julie and Royd were airborne.

The weekend became everything Royd promised. They explored the beautiful city of San Antonio and saw The Alamo before going on to Cancun.

Julie fell in love instantly with the beautiful beaches, the clear blue waters of the Caribbean, and the trip to the ruins at Chitzen Itza. The only thing missing was the intimacy between herself and Royd. He promised her proper, and proper is exactly what he gave her.

After she learned about her amazing resemblance to LuAnn, she welcomed the detachment. She'd known, early in the week, she'd been a fool to think she could replace Devan so easily in her life. Perhaps she would never care for anyone the way she did for him, but it didn't matter.

Having a fling on a tropical island had been one thing; hoping the moment would continue once they returned to reality, quite another.

"We're making our final approach to Chicago," the pilot's voice came over the public address system, driving all thoughts of tropical paradises, ancient civilizations, and Royd from Julie's mind.

The plane taxied to a stop and Julie smiled at the snow flurries in the air. She'd definitely arrived home. She'd returned to the unpredictability of winter in the Midwest.

Around her, the other passengers prepared to deplane. She saw no point in joining the mad rush for the door. A delay of a few minutes would make little difference. The last of the passengers passed her before she stood to retrieve her cape from the overhead compartment, as well as her carry-on from under the seat.

At the door the flight attendants greeted her and she began the short walk down the jetway and to the future.

"I thought you might have missed your flight," Frank commented, before kissing her on the cheek.

"You couldn't get so lucky. I just prefer to let the other passengers join the mad rush and get off leisurely. Did you get me a hotel room for tonight?"

"Sure, right at the Hotel Dorah. For now, we're going back to the office and go over Greg's contract. He sent it by courier this morning."

After collecting her bags, Julie followed Frank from the terminal to the parking ramp. Soon they were speeding along the freeway with the rest of the Chicago traffic.

Frank's office occupied the entire fourth floor of a downtown high-rise building.

"I'm impressed. This is a far cry from my office in Minter," Julie observed.

"Julie! Welcome home," Dorah said, hurrying to give her a hug.

"I'm not really home yet, but the snow outside certainly looks familiar."

Julie listened as Frank and Dorah discussed business and marveled at how different they appeared in this professional setting. Of course, if they met Julie Weston in the personnel office of LisPro, they would have trouble recognizing her as well.

"I have some calls to return," Frank said, addressing Julie directly. "I'll be back later if you have any questions."

Greg's contract looked long and wordy, but Dorah easily sorted out the main points. "You'll be working five days a week, Tuesday through Saturday, at a salary of five hundred dollars a week. You'll be doing two shows a night and, according to this sample schedule, you'll be in one state or area for the entire week. Greg's office will pick up the cost of transportation and hotels. You'll be expected to take care of meals, etc. You'll be traveling with three other newcomers. He expects you to respect his no drinking, no drugs policy. Everything looks to be spelled out quite plainly."

Julie agreed and continued to read the lengthy contract. The wording, at first glance, had been confusing, but became clearer the more she read.

"So," Dorah said, "how did things go in Texas? I couldn't tell anything while we were there. Royd seemed pretty non-committal about everything."

Julie laughed and told Dorah about her week with Royd.

"It wasn't what you were expecting, was it?"

"Not really, but I think it's what I needed. I'll carry some fond memories of Royd, but we both know we aren't destined to be together."

~ * ~

Greg's office, although smaller, impressed Julie, as had Frank's office the previous day. As she and Frank waited for Greg to arrive for their appointment, she allowed her mind to wander.

What am I doing in such an alien setting, talking about this stranger named Jewel West, and discussing contracts and show schedules?

At last they were escorted into Greg's private office. "So, have you had time to read everything over?"

Julie nodded. "I think everything sounds fine."

"Do you have any problems with the conditions of the contract?"

"I don't foresee any, considering I don't smoke, drink or take drugs."

Greg laughed at her statement. "It's not funny, but most of my clients aren't quite so straight forward."

"I don't see any reason not to be straight forward with you," Julie replied.

"Good, because before we sign these contracts, I intend to find out everything there is to know about Julie Weston. If it seems harsh, it's because it's meant to be. I think it's necessary. I know what the press can do to you. They usually crucify anyone new. If there's some deep dark secret in your past, they'll find it, especially if you make it big, and I have no doubt that you will. So, you see, I need to know everything about you, starting with day one."

"Day one?" Julie echoed.

"Well, maybe I'm being a bit extreme. Let's start with Minter High. How about The Four Musketeers? Who are they, where are they now, what are they doing, and how close are you to them?"

"The Four Musketeers," Julie mused. "Let's see, I guess I should start with Sandy Sullivan. She and I were best friends in school. She attended vocational school after graduation and got her LPN. She was killed in a traffic accident about five years after we graduated. Her death hit me pretty hard."

Greg nodded his head, while he furiously jotted down notes on Julie's narrative.

"You met Jerry Gaines and his wife, Karen. You might as well know: Karen and my husband, Steve, had an affair for three years. Jerry and I had a confrontation about it in January, which landed me in the hospital."

"And you're still friends?"

"You don't throw away over thirty years of friendship because of something over and done with for a year. We've worked around it. We've had some tense moments, but we're getting back to where we were. Jerry and I have always been close."

"I see. What about Devan?"

Julie stared down at her folded hands. From the beginning of the interview, she knew his name would come up and now she needed to face what he'd meant to her.

"Good question. I think Devan is a ghost. His name is Devan Yates. Of the four of us, he's the only one who went on to college right out of high school. Just after he got his degree, his parents were killed in a terrible accident outside of town. We talked a bit, at the time, but I'd been married for several years and I had Mark by then. Steve and I went to the visitation. Of course, Sandy was working in Milwaukee and Jerry was still in the military and couldn't be there. Devan dropped out of sight and I didn't hear from him again until a couple of months ago."

"How come? You were all good friends in high school. Why the break?"

"Devan broke not only with me, but with Jerry and Minter."

"What do you mean, he broke with Minter?"

"I don't know how to put it to you, but I guess he didn't want to be reminded of what happened to his folks. Like I said, we both went our separate ways. I got wrapped up with my family and he with his career. We met, quite by accident, on New Year's Eve. It seemed like we'd never been apart. He made me feel comfortable."

"Comfortable enough to sleep with him?"

"You don't have to answer such a question, Julie," Frank cautioned.

"It's all right, Frank. I have nothing to hide. Devan and I spent New Year's Eve together. I thought it would be a one-night stand. I'd been feeling especially lonely. You might say I used Devan. I wanted a man in my house and in my bed. Devan was handy."

"You certainly are a breath of fresh air, Julie," Greg said. "Most women would contend they were the one to be used. I wish the women I date were more like you. I think I've heard enough about The Four Musketeers. What about Julie Weston?"

"What about Julie Weston?" she repeated. "I hardly know where to start. I graduated from high school as a member of the National Honor Society, Salutatorian, as a matter of fact. My husband, Steve, graduated from college a month earlier and held a job with his father's accounting firm in Minter. We were married two days after graduation and he began to mold me into a dignified wife. Within a few years you would never have recognized me. I did the wife and mommy thing as well as the usual volunteer work. Steve insisted I go back to school at our local college, once the kids were in school. When I received my degree, I landed a job with LisPro and within three years, I became the first female department head. I've been head of personnel for the past ten years."

"Impressive," Greg commented. "Very impressive. Brains, beauty, and talent all in one package."

Julie beamed at the compliment, then continued the most difficult part of her narrative. She chose her words carefully. It still hurt to talk about Steve's affairs, to admit how naive she'd been. She watched Greg's face as she described the cottage, the house, the condo, and the furnishings she'd found at Steve's love nest.

"How did he die?" Greg inquired once she finished.

"I didn't kill him, if that's what you're getting at," she quipped. "He had a massive heart attack a year ago, just after midnight on New Year's Day. Of course, I didn't know about his double life then. That's where Jerry came in. We were having a confrontation about his affairs when he told me about Steve and Karen. He thought I knew, everyone else did. I guess you could say he saved my life."

"Saved your life? What do you mean?"

"I'd known I wasn't well for months, but I kept ignoring the warning signs. When he gave me the news, I collapsed and they took me to the hospital. The diagnosis came as a shock. I have diabetes, so maybe you'd like to reconsider your offer."

Greg laughed. "I don't know why. Mary Tyler Moore has diabetes, it certainly doesn't stop her."

"I'd forgotten about her. I just wanted you to know exactly what you're getting."

"What I'm getting is an agent's dream come true, but let's get back to you personally. I know you just returned from Texas and a week with a man named Royd McAlester, so what happened to Devan?"

"I took a leave of absence from LisPro to find out who I am. The first thing I did was book a vacation to Jamaica. Devan agreed I needed to get away and he knew I might meet someone at the resort. Of course, I did. I met Royd. I don't think I need to tell you what we did while we were there. After a week in paradise, I came home, convinced about my feelings for Devan. I wanted him in my life, only he didn't want me. During my stay in Jamaica, he'd been called to Philadelphia to be with his son. Todd had been involved in a drive-by shooting, which left him paralyzed. Devan went out to be with him and decided to transfer, permanently. He broke off the relationship. I realized I'd acted like a fool, thinking I could be special to someone like him."

"Didn't you try to contact him, at least to talk to him?"

"Of course, I did. He called me once and we talked. Other than the one time, I've had only two messages on my machine, then nothing. I tried to call him, but his son's number is unlisted. I also called his office twice and he ignored my calls. I certainly couldn't go to

Philadelphia and barge into the life of someone who obviously doesn't want me."

Greg nodded, his gesture one of understanding. "I heard about your trip to Texas and the hit Jewel West made at Morgan's Den. Is there anything else I should know about your visit?"

"I don't think so. Royd and I realized just how little we have in common. I enjoyed a lovely vacation, nothing more."

"Good, because now I need you to do a few things for me. I need a complete commitment if this is going to work. You'll need to quit your job and get a physical."

"I see no problem there. My next door neighbor is my doctor and he'll insist I see him as soon as I get home. As for my job, I think I'd decided to leave in January when I requested my leave of absence. I've been looking for my place in life, and I think I've found it here."

Julie watched Greg intently, her comment had been meant to compliment her prospective agent and she could tell she'd succeeded.

"Well, it looks like we're ready to sign on the dotted line. Before we do, I want to know if there are any days you need to take off? I can't expect you to completely give up your personal life on a moment's notice."

"I appreciate it. My son, Mark, is getting married the first weekend in May, in Honolulu. I have tickets to fly out there on April 22nd and return on May 2nd. Of course, I thought—"

"You thought I'd make you miss something so important? You underestimate me. I would like to book you into a couple of clubs in the islands, though. There are some owners there who would like to book my talent, but they can't afford the extra expense to fly them in. Your trip would benefit both of us. Now, is there anything else?"

"Over Memorial Day weekend, Lance will be graduating from college. There are functions planned for Friday evening as well as Saturday. Then there's my high school class reunion over the Fourth of July weekend."

"I see no problem with any of those dates. We don't book anything for the holiday weekends. I think we'll have a good working relationship. All we have left to do is sign the contracts. You'll be opening in Rockford a week from today. Do you know where the Clock Tower is?"

"Of course, I do."

"Good. Once your signature is on this piece of paper, you're free to go home for a while. I'll meet you at one next Tuesday at the Clock Tower."

Julie signed the document Greg gave her, then handed it to Frank to witness.

"You know," Greg said, "this couldn't have happened at a better time. I got a call last week from FOX, and they want Karlie Jade for a sitcom. To be honest, when I first approached you, I had no idea when you'd be able to start, but then this thing came up with Karlie. They want her in Los Angeles next week, so everything is working out perfectly."

Eighteen

Jill Lansing finished the last of the lunch dishes before joining her husband, Karl, in the living room. With leaving Denver earlier than expected, he wouldn't be starting his new job for another two and a half weeks. The thought pleased her, as his help in settling the house would be invaluable.

As she looked at her mother's furnishings, she longed for her own belongings to grace the familiar rooms. "When do you think our stuff will get here?" she asked Karl.

He looked up from the book he'd been reading. "What did you say, honey?"

"I asked when you thought our furniture would be here?"

"I checked with the movers this morning. They assured me we'd have everything by the end of the week."

Karl went back to his book, and Jill sat down in the recliner to watch television. She knew once the furniture arrived they would have several decisions to make. For now decisions could wait. She'd be content to lose herself in the characters of her favorite soap opera and work on her knitting.

The words Special Bulletin flashed across the screen and she paid closer attention. "We interrupt this program to bring you a special news bulletin for the Channel 3 News Room. An Airport-Link Bus, traveling between Chicago and Madison has overturned on I 90, just outside Marengo, Illinois. We have no casualty reports, although area ambulances have been called to the scene. Icy conditions, caused by the freezing rain which is falling in the area, are being cited as the cause of the accident. Stay tuned to Channel 3 for further updates. Complete details will be available on the six o'clock news."

"It has to be the bus Mom planned on taking," Jill gasped, in a half whisper.

"But she didn't," Karl reassured her. "We're lucky her friend, Mr. Allen, insisted on bringing her home."

"I know. I just wish she would get here. Is it doing anything outside?"

Karl got up from his chair and drew open the drapes. "It's snowing, but no freezing rain.

"Don't worry. They'll be here soon."

Jill knew Karl experienced the same dread as she did. His attempt to put her at ease only worried her further. If the road had become bad enough to overturn a bus, how much trouble would a small car have in negotiating the icy conditions?

The phone rang, and Jill jumped at the intrusion. Her heart pounded wildly as she answered, dreading the worst.

"Is this Jill?" the woman on the other end asked.

"Yes," Jill replied, her voice shaky.

"This is Dorah Rutland, your Mom's friend from Chicago. Have she and my boss arrived yet?"

Jill relaxed a bit. "Not yet. Is there a problem?"

"When they left, we were only having rain, but we had a quick drop in temperature and everything turned to ice. I've closed the office and sent everyone home. When they get in, have Frank call me at my place."

When Jill hung up the phone, she began to cry. "What's wrong, honey?" Karl asked, getting up from the couch to kneel beside her chair.

"I just know something terrible has happened. They're having an ice storm in Chicago. The call came from Mom's friend, Dorah. She thought they'd be here by now. Where are they? Why aren't they here yet?"

~ * ~

"Let's stop in Marengo," Frank suggested. "If we have some lunch, maybe this rain will let up while we're eating."

"It sounds good to me," Julie replied. "I don't like driving in the rain."

Frank pulled off the interstate and within minutes parked outside a small restaurant. "You take the umbrella," he insisted. "We don't need our star getting soaked and catching pneumonia."

"I think this umbrella is big enough for both of us. Why don't you take it then come around to my side? That way, neither of us will risk getting sick."

Lunch consisted of steaming bowls of baked French onion soup, thick slices of homemade bread, and large house salads.

"Something tells me you've been here before, Mr. Allen," Julie teased.

"I have. I come here every chance I get. It's a good place to hideout and the food isn't bad, either."

Once they finished lunch, they lingered over coffee. "You haven't said much about this morning's meeting," Julie began. "What kind of an impression do you think I made?"

"I think you answered a lot of questions you shouldn't have been asked. He had no right pressing you about such personal things."

"Yes, he did, Frank. I think he knows what he's doing. I can see where trouble could arise if he didn't know everything about his clients. I just wish I could ask questions like his when I hire people. As it is, all I have to deal with are rumors. In this day and age there's plenty of trouble out there."

A waitress came to replenish their coffee and when she left, Frank questioned Julie's statement.

She never hesitated in her answer. The story of Jerry's affairs and the scene that followed her accusations seemed to surprise him. Whether Frank understood or not, she couldn't tell, but soon the conversation turned to other things and Julie's personal life seemed less important.

"Do you know we've been talking for almost two hours?" Frank asked, checking his watch. "We'd better get you home." He picked up the check, and helped with her cape.

"Was everything all right, Mr. Allen?" The woman at the cash register inquired, after she ran his American Express card through the machine to verify the charge.

"Perfect, as always. Hopefully, the rain has let up a bit so we can get back on the road."

"I wouldn't recommend driving if you don't have to," a man said, from behind them.

Julie turned to face the two State Patrol officers who had just entered the restaurant.

"The rain you're worried about turned to ice about an hour ago and a half ago and now it's snowing," the second officer said, as if anticipating Frank's question. "The interstate looks like people are playing bumper cars. We've got a bus overturned just north of here and cars are in the ditch from Chicago to the state line. If you don't have to get to where you're going tonight, I'd suggest you get a motel and stay here."

"Here?" Julie echoed.

"There's a motel, just up the road," the woman at the register said. "I'll call and make a reservation for you."

"But Frank," Julie protested, "what about the kids?"

"You can call Jill from the motel. The man's right, there's no sense risking our lives just to get you back to Minter tonight."

The motel was small, perhaps forty years old, but extremely neat and clean. When at last they were shown to their room, Julie flopped down on one of the double beds. "I can't believe you signed the register as Mr. and Mrs. Frank Allen."

"What did you want me to do? They only had one room left. How would it have looked if I'd signed us in as Mr. Frank Allen and Miss Jewel West?"

"I don't suppose it would have looked very good. It's just..."

"Are you afraid of me? Believe me, I have no ulterior motive. Even if there weren't two beds in here, you'd be perfectly safe."

Julie laughed. She hadn't considered herself to be in any danger with Frank. It would be fun to have a fling, but it wouldn't be practical. She didn't need a man to complicate her life, unless of course, it was Devan.

"I'm sorry, I shouldn't have laughed. I'll call Jill now." Julie knew her words sounded lame, but she had blurted out something in the hopes Frank wouldn't guess her feelings for Devan. She'd tried for weeks to convince herself Devan's departure from her life hadn't devastated her, but she'd been unsuccessful. No matter what she told people, what she said aloud, she missed him.

How could she have allowed him to become so important when Steve hurt her so badly? Why had she jumped in feet first? Did she need someone so much she'd closed her eyes to the pitfalls of a serious relationship?

~ * ~

"Are you certain you don't have to stop somewhere for breakfast?" Frank asked, when they pulled off the interstate.

"I told you, I'll fix us omelets when we get home," Julie replied.

Following her directions, they took the country roads into Minter. The traffic seemed a little heavier than she would have expected. She glanced at the dash clock and noted the time to be seven-thirty, rush hour. It was time for people to go to work.

"Turn right after you crest this hill," she instructed, "then take the third right into the cul-de-sac."

"Cul-de-sac? I'm impressed," Frank teased.

Julie let Frank's words pass without comment, concentrating on the traffic. *What did you expect, a fire engine and police cars, with sirens blaring the way they meet the winning football or basketball teams? Who do you think you are anyway? Have you let your minor triumphs cloud your judgment and make you overestimate your importance?*

As soon as they pulled into the driveway her inner voice became silent. To her surprise, the garage door opened and Karl came out to meet them.

"Welcome home, Mom," Karl greeted her, when he opened the passenger door and embraced her.

"What are you kids doing up so early?"

"Waiting for you. Jill couldn't sleep and I've been trying not to get into the habit of sleeping late."

"You must be Karl, I'm Frank Allen," Frank said, coming around the car, to shake Karl's hand.

"I'm sorry," Julie apologized, "I should have made the introductions."

"Don't worry about it," Karl assured her. "I'll help Mr. Allen with your bags. You get into the house."

Julie heard Karl and Frank as they continued talking but didn't listen closely. She wanted to see Jill, to be home.

"I'm so glad you're finally here," Jill said, when Julie entered the kitchen. She wiped her hands on a dishtowel and hurried across the room to hug her mother.

"You look wonderful," Julie stated, when she stepped back to make a better assessment of her daughter. She smiled at the slight bulge visible under the loose fitting sweatsuit. Before she could comment, Frank and Karl entered the kitchen with her bags and she made the necessary introductions.

"I still didn't get to cook for you," she teased Frank when they finished eating the breakfast Jill prepared.

"I have no doubts about your culinary talents," Frank replied. "I have no doubts about any of your talents."

"Speaking of talents," Karl interrupted, "are you certain about this comedy thing? It sounds pretty iffy to me."

Frank laughed. "I'm certain you have doubts, as well as questions. Let me assure you, Julie's talent is immense. I ought to know, she gave her first performance at my club and I've never seen anything like it. No matter what she thinks, we put her up against the stiffest competition we could find. She has a very bright future."

"Maybe she does," Jill commented, "but I can't help worrying about her health."

"I am still here," Julie said, waving her hands for attention.

"I never doubted your presence for a moment." Frank gave her hand a reassuring squeeze.

"Look, Jill," Julie continued, "the agreement I made with my agent says I'm to continue my counseling when I'm home, and see George for a physical. I made no secret about my weaknesses, everything is out in the open."

The clock struck nine and Frank pushed his chair away from the table. "I'd better get going. I have a busy afternoon and I'm sure you have a lot to do as well."

Julie accompanied him to the door. After retrieving his coat from the closet, he unexpectedly took her in his arms and kissed her.

"Now, Mr. Allen, you shouldn't have done such a thing," Julie said, the act catching her completely off guard.

"Why do you say that?" Frank asked, keeping her encircled in his arms.

"I'm not certain how I'm feeling about a relationship right now."

"I don't care how you're feeling. I enjoyed kissing you, having you in my arms. I wish I could convince you it's all right to be kissed. It doesn't have to lead to a sexual relationship. Unfortunately that would take time and I have to go. I'll see you a week from Friday at the Alley."

"I'm looking forward to it. Being at the Alley will be like coming home, comfortable."

"Hold onto that thought," he said, kissing her again.

Julie relaxed and enjoyed Frank's attentions, until he broke the embrace. She stood in the doorway watching him walk to the car, then waved until he turned the corner and disappeared from sight. Frank could become special in her life, if only thoughts of Devan didn't lie so dangerously close to the surface.

"Mr. Allen is a very nice man," Jill said, when Julie returned to the kitchen.

"Yes, he is," Julie replied, wistfully.

"What went on last night? Anything I should know about?" Jill teased.

"Nothing really. The room had two double beds."

"You only had one room?"

"It's not what you think. They only had one room. People were coming off the interstate in droves."

"I see," Jill mused, her voice as well as her eyes filled with accusations.

Before Julie could reply the phone rang. "Good morning," she answered, relieved to have an excuse to end the conversation with her daughter.

"Welcome home, stranger," Tom Randall's voice greeted her.

"Tom, it's good to hear from you."

"I expected you to call me yesterday when you got in. Didn't Jill give you my message?"

"I just got in this morning. We got caught in the ice storm coming up from Chicago and had to spend the night in Marengo. I haven't had time to even ask about messages."

"I know this is short notice, but I need to meet with you. Can you be in my office at say eleven-thirty? I'll take you to lunch in the cafeteria."

"Sure, no problem. I'd planned to call for an appointment, anyway. It's nine-thirty now, so I'd better get going. I'll see you later."

Julie had hardly hung up the phone when the doorbell rang. She paid little attention until she heard Meg and Shirley talking with Karl.

"We waited until we saw *his* car leave," Meg said. "We want to hear about everything."

"I hate to rush you," Julie retorted, "but I have an appointment at the plant."

"You're off the hook for now," Shirley agreed, "but tonight we want you to come to dinner. It'll be just the neighbors. We're all anxious for the details."

"What time do you want me?"

"Let's say six. It's not too late for you, is it?"

"I don't think so."

"Can you and Karl make it, Jill?" Meg asked.

"Not this time. We're leaving soon for Madison. We're meeting friends there. We're planning to do some shopping then go out to dinner. Afterwards they have tickets for a concert or something."

Julie experienced a twinge of jealousy. Tonight would be her first night in the house with the kids and they wouldn't even be there.

Upstairs, Julie scanned her wardrobe. If she were only going to be stopping at the plant, jeans and a sweater would be acceptable. Of course, she had planned to go to Steve's old office. In the back of her mind, she wanted to look her best. She chose a light cream suede suit with a chocolate brown blouse and gold accessories. *Professional, not overdressed. At least they'll know I mean business.*

She took a long look at her reflection in the full-length mirror. Had it been less than two weeks ago when she'd seen a graying woman who didn't know what she wanted in this very glass?

The woman who stared back at her looked confident, poised, even radiant, but she remained a stranger.

"You look great, Mom," Jill said, from behind her.

Julie saw her daughter's reflection before she turned to face her. "Thank you."

"I didn't get a chance to comment on your hair earlier, but I love the color. You should have done it years ago. It makes you look much younger."

"I know, I think so, too, but your father certainly would never have approved."

Jill said nothing, and Julie sensed her daughter's reluctance to discuss the man who had, so easily, destroyed their lives a year after his death.

~ * ~

Julie arrived at the plant with a few minutes to spare and took her time going to Tom's corner office. She paused in front of the door marked *Julie Weston - Personnel Director* and traced the gold plated letters with the index finger of her right hand.

How much am I giving up for this? This office, this building, they both mean security. My past is here. My future could be, too. Have I done the right thing to walk away from it, to follow this crazy notion of becoming Jewel West? Now certainly isn't the time for regrets. I've signed Greg's contract, committed myself to a year, a year that doesn't include LisPro. Right or wrong, I've said yes, I've changed my life with the stroke of a pen.

Reluctantly, she put her thoughts aside and moved down the hall toward Tom's office.

"Julie, it's good to see you," Tom's secretary, Pam, said, when Julie entered the outer office. "Congratulations."

"Thanks Pam, I think."

"You think? Don't tell me you're having second thoughts about all of this?"

"Don't we always? Remember when I took the promotion to Personnel Director? I recall being scared to death."

"Yes, I remember, but everything turned out okay. This will, too. Tom's waiting for you."

Julie rapped lightly at the door separating the two offices, then entered without waiting for a reply from within.

Tom crossed the room, then kissed Julie on the cheek. "You look radiant," he complimented her. "I'm sure you know why I asked you to come."

"I know, you need my resignation so you can start looking for my replacement."

"Actually, it's to try to persuade you not to leave."

"Please don't try. I'm committed. I signed the contract yesterday. Face it, Tom, we knew I wouldn't be coming back in January when—"

"When we had our blow up. I'd hoped you'd let me apologize. I can see your mind is made up. I assure you I do understand. I just want to wish you luck."

They talked for several minutes, made small talk, almost as though they were strangers. Finally, Tom took her hand in his. "Are you excited?"

"I'm excited, scared, and totally convinced I've lost my mind. Good grief, Tom, I'm almost forty-eight years old. Don't you think I'd have more sense than to pull a harebrained stunt like this?"

"Like what?"

"You know, starting a new career, being a comedian. I've never been funny a day in my life."

Tom began to laugh. "That's not the way Jerry tells it. He says you were a hit."

"So they tell me. I guess they know more than I do. Let's just drop the subject. It seems you asked me out to lunch. Why don't we go down to the cafeteria? When we get done I have some people I want to see before I go on to the rest of my appointments."

"No wonder you seem to be overdressed. Another trip to Steve's office?"

Julie nodded. "I should at least try to make them think I'm a business woman when I go over there. If this thing flops, they will be supplying me with my income for the rest of my life."

"If this flops, you know you'll always have a place here, even if I have to fire your replacement to make room for you."

"You're sweet, but we both know it won't work."

They walked out of Tom's office and Julie noticed Pam had already left for lunch. "That's strange, Pam usually doesn't go to lunch this early," she commented.

"She said she had a meeting and asked to leave early. I told her it would be all right."

They took the back stairs down to the cafeteria. Once on the ground floor, Tom opened the door and allowed Julie to enter ahead of him.

To her amazement, the room overflowed with people, all applauding and a sign on the opposite wall read GOOD LUCK JULIE! Several flashes of light came from the cameras of people anxious to capture her surprise on film. To her left stood what could be described as a head table, decorated with a floral centerpiece and flanked by candles. Jill, Karl, Jerry, and Frank stood in front of the table smiling at her.

"Just what is going on here?" she asked, in disbelief.

"We wanted to show you how we feel about your new career," Tom replied.

Julie made her way toward the table speaking with old friends as she did. She embraced Jerry first. "You brat," she whispered in his ear. "Something tells me you're behind this."

She became aware of more flashes when she stepped back. "And you," she said, accusingly, when she faced Frank. "I thought you had a big meeting in Chicago this afternoon."

"I never mentioned Chicago. I had some pretty tense moments. Jerry asked me to make sure you got home on time. I planned to spend the night up here, but the storm altered our plans a bit."

From Frank, she looked to Jill and Karl. "Aren't you missing out on a big shopping trip to Madison?"

"Oh," Jill said, putting her hand to her mouth to surpass a giggle. "Did I say we were going today? I meant we have plans with our friends for Saturday. It was all part of the secret, Mom. Were you really surprised?"

"Shocked is a more appropriate word."

By three o'clock, only Julie and Jerry remained in the cafeteria. Jerry brought them each another cup of coffee, then seated himself opposite her.

"Thank you for a lovely party," she said.

"You deserve it. I heard about Texas. You have to know you were great."

"I guess I do. I'm just not sure about any of this."

"Are you sure about Royd McAlester?"

"Royd, well, it's a long story. He wasn't—"

"Wasn't Devan?" Jerry interrupted.

"Those are your words, not mine. What I started to say is he wasn't impressed with the new me. With my gray hair, I could have been his dead wife's twin. He wanted another LuAnn McAlester, not Julie Weston, on the verge of becoming Jewel West."

"I'm sorry. I'd hoped maybe he'd fill the gap, make you forget our former friend."

"Former friend? Are you talking about Devan?"

"Who else?"

"Look, Jerry, Devan hurt me, but so did you. If I ever get the chance, I'll confront him about it, but I won't have you making my decisions for me about something like this. I just wish I could talk to him."

"No, you don't. He's not the same. He's very bitter about what happened to his son."

"Then you've talked to him. How did you reach him?" she asked, trying to hide her excitement about perhaps getting his number.

"He called me about the reunion."

Julie's excitement disappeared. It seemed as though Jerry had slapped her in the face with Devan's lack of interest. His mention of

Devan had raised her hopes. She'd expected him to say Devan had called because he'd heard of her success. Had he even mentioned her name? Of course, the reunion, I'd almost forgotten."

"Don't look so sad. He only used the reunion as an excuse. He wanted to hear about you."

"But not enough to give me a number where I can call him or an address so I can write. You don't have to say anything. There's nothing more to say. Let's change the subject."

Nineteen

Julie glanced back at the house and saw Jill standing at the living room window, waving good-bye. At breakfast, she used the excuse of wanting to stop at a small shop in Beloit for her early start. Now she wondered if Jill and Karl had actually believed her white lie? It didn't matter what Jill believed, she needed some time alone before she embraced this new lifestyle.

She'd been trying to find the time to think ever since her talk with Jerry at the party. She needed this time to put her feelings for Devan in perspective.

"Oh, Devan," she said aloud. "How could I let you do this to me? How could I stand by and let you turn me upside down? Jerry says you might care, but he doubts it. Do you? Damn it, I care for you. Jerry was right when he said Royd wasn't you. Frank wants more, but he isn't you either. He at least understands. I don't think Royd ever could. Get out of my mind. Steve got out, why can't you do the same?"

I must be going crazy. I'm driving along and talking to myself. If I'm going to talk to myself, I might as well practice my monologue.

Julie cleared her throat, then ran her tongue over her lips before beginning. "I grew up in Minter—Minter, Wisconsin, small town USA. I had three of the greatest friends anyone could hope for. We

233

were The Four Musketeers, Jerry and Sandy and Devan and me—And Devan And Me—*And Devan and me!"* she ended up screaming.

She pulled the car over to the shoulder of the road, put her head against the steering wheel and took several deep breaths while she waited for her hands to stop shaking.

What can I do? I can't change my monologue. I can't pretend Devan never existed. I'll just have to accept his decision and put him behind me. I've done it before with Steve and I'll do it again with Devan.

She waited for a break in the traffic, then pulled back onto the interstate. Raindrops splattered against the windshield, reminding her of the ice storm only a week earlier. Within ten miles, she drove out of the rain and back into the bright sunshine.

March, how unpredictable the weather during this month can be in the upper Midwest. It's almost like the unpredictability of life.

Another light shower began just prior to the state line and stopped by the time she reached the tollbooth. Once she threw the coins into the hopper, she knew there would be no turning back.

The parking lot of The Clock Tower seemed surprisingly crowded. At last she found a parking place at the far end of the lot, then took her baggage from the trunk. After tonight's show, Jill and Karl would take the car home and her means of escape would be gone.

Once inside the hotel, Julie set her bag next to the registration desk. "May I help you?" the clerk asked.

"You're holding a reservation for me. I'm Jewel West," she said, feeling funny using her new name so easily.

"Of course, Miss West, you're in room two thirty-five and I have a message for you." The girl placed the electronic key on the counter and handed Julie a small manilla envelope.

Before she could pick up the key, a young man took it as well as her luggage. "Just follow me, Miss West," he said.

As he requested, she trailed behind him across the lobby to the elevator. When it stopped on the second floor, they went down the hall to room two thirty-five.

The young man fit the key into the lock and took her luggage in, setting it onto the luggage rack at the end of one of the double beds.

To Julie's surprise, a piece of hot pink luggage lay on the other rack and a jacket had been tossed across the bed. She thought she'd be the first to arrive and therefore have time to be alone before the others came.

The young man turned to leave and Julie realized she hadn't given him a tip. She opened her purse, but he stopped her. "No need, Miss West. The tip has been taken care of. Enjoy your stay and if there is anything you need, just call down to the desk."

"I see," Julie replied. "Thank you."

When the door closed, Julie took off her cape and hung it, carefully, on the hanger. She turned and caught a glimpse of herself in the mirror. "You don't look half bad, old girl," she said aloud.

She turned from the mirror and remembered the envelope she'd been given at the desk. Taking it from her purse, she noticed the flap had been turned inside rather than being sealed. She flipped it open and removed the note.

> Jewel: Don't Eat Lunch—Meet Us In Room 236
> As Soon As You Get In.
>
>   Greg.

So much for solitude, she thought. She glanced into the mirror again, making certain she looked presentable before she put her key into her purse and left the room.

Greg answered her light rap at the door across the hall. "I'm surprised to see you so early. We weren't supposed to get together until one. Come on in and meet everyone."

"Everyone?" Julie questioned.

"I made certain Faye, Cameron, and Hunter would get here before you did. We were just getting ready to watch a video."

"A video? I don't think I understand you people."

"You will," Greg assured her, as she followed him into the room.

A slightly heavy-set girl in her early twenties sat on one of the beds. Her freckled face and green eyes reassured Julie the girl's red hair came naturally. Next to her sat a young man, a few years older, his long brown hair pulled back into a ponytail. At the table sat a black man whose age seemed hard to determine.

"Everyone," Greg said, "this is Jewel West."

"Hi, Jewel," the girl acknowledged her. The young man next to her raised his hand in greeting and the black man nodded in her direction.

"This is Faye," Greg said, beginning the introductions. "She'll be your roommate. She's just waiting to get to New York so she can have a chance to audition for musical comedy. Next to her is Cameron. He wants to be my associate. I told him if that's what he wants, he'd better learn to be funny. Last, but not least, this is Hunter. He's between projects. For this tour he's your driver. If there's anything you need, any problems you have, talk to him."

Hunter stood and approached Julie, his hand extended. Julie focused her attention on him. On closer inspection, he appeared to be older than she first thought. He seemed nearer to Julie than the age of the two young people who sat on the bed. He also appeared to be familiar, but she couldn't place where she could have possibly seen him.

"Welcome, Jewel," Hunter said, holding her hand in his. "It will be good to finally have a soul sister on this tour."

"Whatever do you mean?"

"It will be a pleasure to be able to talk with someone who speaks my language. I get tired of jockeying around these kids. Just keeping up on the slang is a full time job."

Julie nodded, unable to keep herself from staring at the man standing in front of her.

"Don't try too hard, Jewel. You have seen me before," Hunter assured her.

"I have? Where?"

"Several TV shows, bit parts mostly." He listed several comedies as well as one of the nighttime soap operas.

"So what are you doing on the road?"

"I don't like to be idle. I've been on *With This Ring*, and now they're working on a spin-off for me. They won't be ready to start filming until July. Until then, I need something to occupy my time. I'm lucky to have Greg as my agent. He can always find a place for me."

"With Hunter headlining the show, you can expect a packed house," Greg said, joining the conversation. "You two will have plenty of time to get acquainted. We've got a video to watch, so make yourself comfortable, Jewel."

From the corner of her eye, she saw Hunter pull a chair from the table in front of the patio doors. Once she seated herself, Hunter pulled another chair next to hers for himself. Greg slipped the cassette into the VCR and to Julie's surprise she recognized the interior of Morgan's Den.

"That's The Den," she said, her voice hardly more than a whisper.

Greg paused the tape. "I asked Frank to arrange for it to be made. Maybe I jumped the gun a bit, not having your signature on a contract, but I'm glad I did. I want these kids to see what you have to offer before tonight."

"Maybe it will do me good, too. I have no idea what I look or sound like on tape," she replied.

Greg again started the tape and Julie watched the camera focus closely on her face. Everyone laughed at the now familiar words. Although she could hear her own laughter, inside she cried. She had no trouble in agreeing with all of her friends. She was good. So, why did Devan still lie so dangerously close to the surface?

Up until her talk with Jerry at the plant the other day, she'd given it very little thought. She could easily talk about Devan, because she honestly thought he'd come around, he'd realize he did love her, he'd contact her and ask for her forgiveness. Jerry made it very clear, Devan wanted to forget the past few months in Minter ever happened.

"You won't be on the road long," Hunter predicted, once the tape ended.

"What do you mean?"

"I'm willing to bet Greg has great plans for you. You'll be in Hollywood or New York before you know it."

"I wouldn't count on it," Julie said, laughing nervously. "I don't think I'm the Hollywood type."

"You're a lot more than that," Greg assured her, then turned to the two young people on the bed.

"Will you kids try to convince her she's good?"

"Of course we will," Faye said. "You are great Jewel, just great. I'd kill to have half your talent."

"Greg says you write your own material," Cameron said. "I'm envious. Do you know how much I had to pay a writer to make me funny?"

"How could a writer know what happened to me when I was a kid?" Julie asked.

"Are you telling us there really is a Minter and The Four Musketeers actually existed?" Cameron questioned.

"Believe it or not, yes, and I did do all those crazy things I talk about. Until recently, I'd forgotten all the fun I had as a kid. I guess it's why I'm so nervous about this change in my lifestyle. I have kids older than you and Faye, and I'm going to be a grandma soon. I honestly don't know what I'm doing here."

"Give it a couple of weeks," Hunter said. "This will be in your blood. You'll see, once you get on stage tonight, you'll forget all about your qualms."

Julie nodded. She knew Hunter was right. She'd been on stage twice and once she began the monologue, she became at ease, as though she were talking with old friends.

Greg took them all down to the coffee shop for lunch. "Call me tonight after the show, Hunter," he said as he prepared to leave for Chicago.

"After the show, we're taking Jewel out to celebrate. I'll catch you tomorrow morning at the office."

Greg said his good-byes to the group. Before leaving, he wished Julie well.

"Why does Greg want you to call him?" she asked, once Faye and Cameron left the table and she lingered over her coffee with Hunter.

"To report on how you do tonight. Normally, he'd be here for your first show, but he has an appointment at the New York office early tomorrow morning. I'll be able to reach him there. You see I'm sort of the watchdog for the group during the months I'm not filming. I'll be honest, Greg wants me to keep my eye on you."

Julie put her elbows on the table and clasped her hands together. "Oh, you think so," she said, a mischievous smile coming to her lips.

"I know so, but not the way you think. I'll be showing you the ropes. For starters, do you swim? They have an excellent pool here."

"As a matter of fact I do. I checked out the hotels on the list before I left home, just to be sure I'd find a pool."

"Good, get your suit. I'll meet you there in let's say fifteen minutes."

Julie flashed Hunter a brilliant smile then hurried to her room to change.

"What's going on?" Faye asked, while Julie rummaged through her bag for a suit.

"I'm going swimming," she said, without looking up.

"You should be napping."

"I suppose you're right, but I'm far too excited to sleep. Give me a couple of weeks for the newness to wear off. For now, I'm going down and get some exercise to work off this nervous energy."

"Not me," Faye said. "I'm going to sleep away the afternoon. I suppose Hunter's going with you. He's always in the pool."

"Yes, he is. Of course I'd planned to go swimming, anyway."

"I don't understand older people. Hunter's a great guy. You'll like him. You know I was scared of him when he first came. I come from St. Louis. I never knew many of the black guys at school, at least not nice ones. The guys I knew were in the gangs. Most of them came from broken homes and seemed to be into drugs. Hunter's different. He's from Chicago, his folks still live there and run a Mom and Pop grocery store."

Julie contemplated Faye's words. Coming from Minter, she certainly didn't know many black people either. The closest she came to knowing someone of a different race was the exchange student who had come to Minter High during her senior year from Ethiopia.

"So, you're into swimming," Hunter said, once Julie eased herself into the water.

"You might say so. Until a few weeks ago, I hadn't done any for almost thirty years. You know if the weather in Minter were more conducive to swimming, I'd put in a pool." She paused then laughed at her statement.

"What's so funny?" Hunter asked.

"I don't know where I'd put a pool. I sold my house and just about everything else which ties me to Minter. Everything but my memories. There are days I'd like to be able to put them up for sale as well. I've been through a couple of bad months."

"You don't have to tell me anything. I know all about your life. Greg filled me in about you. Like I said, I'm the watchdog. It's my job to know everything I care about all of the people in this group. I know about your husband, your diabetes, even the man you think about more than you should."

"I'll race you to the end of the pool," Julie said, turning from Hunter and the truth in his words.

He put his hand on her arm and turned her to face him. "I'm sorry you're angry with me, Jewel, but it's best to be honest with each other. We're planning to make you a star."

"What do you mean we?"

"Greg and me. I emcee the show. I go on first. You'll be last. It's not to make you nervous, just to save the best for last. It gives the customers something to remember, something to keep them coming back. You were pretty busy watching the video. I'd already seen it. I watched Faye and Cameron. They know you're good, better than they are. I can see it scares them."

"I certainly don't see why, but if you say so, it must be true. Now, did we come here to talk or to swim?"

"To swim," Hunter said, before using powerful strokes to reach the far end of the pool just ahead of her.

~ * ~

"Are you ready to go?" Hunter asked. He had taken Julie's cape from its hanger and stood ready to help her put it on.

"I guess so, but where are Faye and Cameron?"

"They'll be at the car. I don't worry too much about them being late. This tour is too important to both their futures."

Julie allowed him to put the cape around her shoulders. For a moment, his hands rested on her upper arms. "You're nervous, aren't you?"

"Yes, I am. How did you know?"

"You're trembling. It's not like you haven't done this before. On the tape you seemed so composed, so confident. I certainly didn't expect you to be nervous tonight."

"Neither did I, but this is different. Before I did it for fun and I didn't know anyone in the audience who knew me well. Do you realize half of Minter will be there tonight and they all expect me to either do something great or fall on my face? I know those people. There's no happy medium with them."

"Just relax. You'll do just find, but not if we continue to hang around here." Hunter picked up Julie's make-up case and opened the door. "Don't know why I'm bothering with this case. You certainly don't need make-up. If I didn't know your age, I'd think you weren't much older than Faye or Cameron."

Julie laughed at Hunter's comment. "Isn't it amazing what a little paint and powder can do for a girl? I'm sorry I don't have a quarter."

"Get used to the compliments, Jewel, there will be plenty more to come and you won't have to pay for them, either."

As Hunter predicted, Cameron and Faye already occupied the back seat of a new Dodge Intrepid. "Yours?" Julie questioned.

"No, it's a rental. My car is in Los Angeles. With the amount of miles we put on in a week, we just rent. It's easier. I picked this up at O'Hare this morning." He held open the passenger's side door for Julie, and she slid into the front seat.

"I'm looking forward to tonight," Cameron said. "After seeing you on tape, I'm ready for the real thing."

"I hope you're not disappointed. I'm afraid I'll be a bundle of nerves. A lot of my friends will be there, not to mention my kids."

"All of them?" Faye asked. "I'd like to meet your boys, they both look hot."

Julie laughed. "I never thought about them as hot. I'm afraid they won't be here, but Jill and Karl will. Lance can't miss school and Mark will just have to wait until I get to Honolulu to see what's going on, not that he wants to know."

"Why not?" Cameron asked. "If you were my mom, I'd be proud of you."

"Mark doesn't think moms do things like this, especially not Moms of naval officers. I'm afraid he's quite embarrassed by my antics."

Julie's comments met with silence and she enjoyed the moment of solitude. The drive to the club would take less than fifteen minutes. She needed some time alone to sort out her thoughts and calm her nerves.

"Welcome," the club owner greeted them. "Your dressing rooms are ready. Be prepared, both shows are sold out and Miss West has had some flowers delivered."

"Flowers?" Julie questioned. "I specifically asked everyone not to do anything so foolish."

She took her case from Hunter and hurried backstage. The dressing rooms were larger than the ones she used previously. Each room could accommodate two performers. On one of the dressing tables sat a bud vase with a red rose in full bloom.

"So, who sent it?" Julie turned to see Hunter standing behind her.

"I don't know, I haven't read the card."

Hunter pulled the card from it holder, then read it aloud. "Good luck from your Secret Admirer. Interesting. Who do you think—"

"I have no idea, but I'll find out tonight."

Thoughts of her mysterious Secret Admirer still dominated her mind while she listened to Hunter, Faye and Cameron run through their monologues.

"And now, ladies and gentlemen, we're proud to present Miss Jewel West, in her first professional appearance," Hunter said, holding his hand out to her as she stood in the wings. Julie crossed the stage and allowed Hunter to brush his lips against her cheek. "You'll be great," he whispered, before he left her alone in the bright lights.

"I grew up in Minter—Minter, Wisconsin, small town USA. I had three of the greatest friends anyone could hope for. We were The Four Musketeers, Jerry and Sandy and Devan and me."

She didn't falter at the words, didn't hesitate as she continued her monologue. At several points she paused to allow the laughter of the audience to die down. When she finished, the applause made her head spin.

She took a second bow, and returned to the wings where Hunter, Cameron, and Faye waited for her.

"You were a hit," Faye said, before she hugged Julie.

"You certainly were," Cameron agreed, holding out his arms to congratulate her in a similar manner.

"We'll have plenty of time for this later," Hunter said. "Now it's time to mingle."

"Mingle?" Julie questioned.

"You know, go out and press the flesh, meet the audience. Greg calls it good public relations," Cameron explains.

"But Frank says—" Julie began.

"Frank had an unfortunate experience," Hunter said. "It left him scared. The performer the man attacked happened to be Frank's wife. It had nothing to do with her death, but he's become very protective of the people who appear at The Alley. When we're there, we respect his wishes, when we're on the road, we do as Greg wants."

Hunter gave Julie no time to protest. Gently, he touched her arm and guided her back onto the stage, then down the steps onto the main floor.

To Julie's surprise friends and family from Minter occupied the front two rows of tables. From the stage, she had been aware of the audience, but with the lights in her eyes, she couldn't make out individual faces.

"You were great Mom," Jill said, hugging Julie tightly. "Why didn't you ever tell us any of those stories?"

"Because you father didn't approve of them."

One by one, Julie greeted her friends, her daughter's question and her own answer ringing in her mind. The old Julie Weston respected her husband's wishes. Jewel West enjoyed the rebellion of telling the stories she'd almost forgotten.

"So, did anyone confess to being your secret admirer?" Hunter asked, when they returned backstage.

"No, but I guess I knew they wouldn't. If anyone from Minter would have sent flowers, it wouldn't have been one long stemmed red rose. I think you're making too much of this. It's all very innocent and sweet."

Hunter shook his head and Julie returned to the dressing room. The rose still sat in the vase on the table, mocking her. *No one from Minter had sent it, who else would have been so thoughtful?*

Frank? Dorah? Royd? They were all possibilities. She'd need to talk to each of them. By the end of the week, she would know which one had sent the rose and put Hunter's fears to rest.

~ * ~

By Saturday evening, Juile still had no idea as to the identity of her secret admirer. Dorah and Frank, as well as Royd, had denied sending the rose. Although she wanted to dismiss the incident, Hunter wouldn't let the subject drop.

Friday night, her appearance at The Alley had been a great success. Reporters from several Chicago papers met with everyone between shows and Julie immediately became the center of attention.

Now, for a brief moment, Julie could relax. After spending the day with Dorah, she took a cab to the club where the Saturday night performance would be held. After paying the driver, she stepped into the brisk March wind and hurried to the door of the club, several feet away.

When she entered the warmth of the building, she saw Hunter and Greg engaged in conversation. "I didn't expect to see you," Julie greeted Greg. "I thought you were still in New York."

"I got home this morning. You didn't think I'd miss your first Saturday night show, did you?"

Julie said nothing, for she caught a look of worry on Hunter's face. "Something's wrong, isn't there? Has something happened to one of my kids?"

"It's not your kids, Jewel," Hunter replied. "There's another rose in your dressing room."

"And I suppose you read the card," she accused.

"I didn't have to. Did you find out who your secret admirer is?"

Julie looked from Hunter to Greg and saw Hunter's worry mirrored on Greg's face.

"No, I didn't. I think you're making too much of this. I'm certain there is nothing to worry about and I refuse to allow you to scare me like this."

Greg put his hands on her shoulders. "Look, Jewel, maybe you should be scared. This secret admirer thing could easily get out of hand. Today it's roses, but if we're dealing with a psycho, who know what will happen next?"

Twenty

The weeks flew past and Julie found towns, hotels, and clubs blended into one another. One thing stood out in her mind. Every Saturday night a perfect long stemmed red rose waited for her in her dressing room.

"I can't believe we're actually on our way to Honolulu," Jill said.

Julie turned from the bus window and her private thoughts to smile at her daughter. "I know, but it's a shame Karl couldn't come with us today."

"He's disappointed, but this new job is too good to jeopardize by taking a week off right after he starts. As it is, they're allowing him to be gone long enough for the wedding and to come home with us."

They engaged in small talk for several miles before they each opened a book. Julie enjoyed losing herself within the pages of the paperback and became aware of the passage of time only when the bus stopped at the United terminal.

After checking in their bags curbside, Julie suggested they stop at the coffee shop for a bite to eat. When she turned toward the restaurant, she almost ran headfirst into Hunter.

"Good grief, what are you doing here?" she asked.

"It looks like I'm taking two lovely ladies for coffee," he teased.

"No, really," Julie pressed, "is something wrong?"

"You might say so. We'll talk about it at the restaurant."

Julie exchanged a puzzled glance with Jill, as they followed Hunter.

"So, what's up?" she asked, once their order had been taken.

Hunter handed her the paper he'd been holding. She scanned the headlines of the grocery store gossip sheet and became sick at heart.

> *Jewel West Stalked By Secret Admirer—Friends*
> *Fear For Her Safety.*

"Why didn't you tell us, Mom?" Jill asked.

"Because it isn't... it didn't seem—"

"What your mother is trying to say is this hasn't gotten out of hand. Greg and I have been worried, but so far she's only received a rose every Saturday. We've kept it quiet. Publicity like this could be very damaging. An innocent rose could turn into something dangerous if the wrong person reads this."

"If you've kept it quiet, how did something like this get published?" Jill probed.

"Who knows?" Julie replied. "We've all talked about it, anyone could have overheard us."

Their food came and for a few minutes they concentrated on light table talk. "You still haven't answered my initial question," Julie pressed. "Why are you here and not Greg?"

"Greg called me last night and asked me to come out. He's in the Islands, trying to set up an office there."

"He's in Honolulu? Are you sure he's not out there to keep his eye on me?"

Hunter laughed. "A little of both. When he booked you in for this week, the club owners convinced him an office might not be such a bad idea. He's considering taking Dave Soby out there. It would open a position for Cameron in Los Angeles. Of course, the trip could take place any time, so why not during your stay?"

Julie nodded. No reply would be necessary. Even if she had thought of the right words, a reporter and cameraman joined them.

"Miss West," the reporter began, "is there any truth to this article?" The man held out the same tabloid Hunter showed them earlier.

Julie noticed the concerned looks on both Hunter and Jill's faces. "What do you think?" she replied.

"I have my doubts."

"So do I," Julie quipped. "It's true, I do have a secret admirer, but the only thing he or she does is send me a rose once a week. I think it's more of a kindness than a threat. Believe me, I'm in no danger."

~ * ~

Mark Weston paced the airport waiting area nervously. His mother and Jill would be arriving soon. The joy over them coming to the wedding had been marred by the headlines he'd read in the grocery store checkout line this morning.

He'd be the first to admit, he hadn't been happy with his mother's choice of a new career. She should be enjoying the money his father had inadvertently left her. If she didn't want to work at LisPro any longer, so be it. She could travel or just live off the interest. She would never have to touch the principal. So, why had she joined this traveling freak show of comedians?

Jill and Lance had both assured him his mother was good, the papers called her a hit, but what did it all mean? *I can't imagine anyone calling my mother a hit. Why can't she just be Mom?*

"Would you please sit down, Mark?" Keoki asked.

Mark turned to face her. "I can't. I'm too nervous. What does Mom think she's doing, anyway? This foolishness of hers is putting her, as well as Jill, in danger."

"Good grief, Mark, how many times do we have to go over this? The article didn't appear in any of the reputable papers, like the *Chicago Tribune* or one of the trades. It appeared in a gossip rag, for Pete's sake. You know what those papers do. They crucify stars. Your mother's just one of many who have received this kind of unwanted publicity."

"Star," Mark mused. "My mother a star, I find it hard to believe."

"Why can't you?" Keoki snapped. "You've been reading the Honolulu papers about her coming out here to perform. If you don't believe them when they say she's great, you should at least believe your own brother and sister. As a matter of fact, everyone you've talked to has assured you she's wonderful. Why can't you give her the benefit of the doubt? Why can't you say, yes, maybe she is good? You haven't even seen her act."

"I don't think I want to see her so-called *act*."

Keoki's brown eyes flashed angrily. "Well, you will see it tomorrow night and again in Maui. When I called to make the reservations, they were already holding tickets in our name."

"Just tell me how you can be so excited about this? She's coming here for our wedding. Doesn't she think maybe, just maybe, we don't want it turned into a three-ring circus? How can she even consider performing while she's here?"

"Do you think she had a choice? Would you start a new job by asking for a week off to go to a wedding? Karl certainly didn't and you wouldn't either. If I were her agent, you can bet I would take advantage of her being in the Islands and book her into a couple of clubs."

Mark looked deep into Keoki's eyes. In his heart, he agreed with her, but he had a problem picturing his mother on stage at his favorite comedy club. He'd become so engrossed in his own thoughts he didn't notice the man who approached them.

"You must be Captain Weston," the man said.

Startled, Mark turned. "Why, yes, I am, but I don't know you."

"I'm certain you don't. My name if Greg Lauer. I'm your mother's agent."

"I see. So you're the one who built up Jewel West," Mark said, his words dripping with venom.

"You bet I am, and I'm damn proud of it. You should be, too."

Mark reached into his pocket and brought out the newspaper article he'd clipped earlier. "If you're so proud of it, why subject her to something like this?"

"I didn't plant the story. As a matter of fact, I'm still trying to find out who did. I assure you, Jewel was met at the Chicago airport, as she will be here."

"By you!" Mark snapped.

"And you," Greg retorted. "I'm only here to talk to the press. After I spoke with Rob Hunter this morning, I don't think I have to worry about them at all. He says Jewel handled herself very well."

"How much danger is she in, Mr. Lauer?" Keoki asked.

"Now this is the first sensible question I've heard today. The article makes it sound much worse than it really is. I've begun to agree with Jewel, it seems rather innocent. At first, we were all concerned about someone we didn't know sending her roses. Luckily, it's never gone any further, and we have no reason to believe it ever will. We're definitely not worried about someone stalking her. It's all probably very innocent."

"Probably?" Mark said, picking up on the word.

"No one can be one hundred percent about anything, Captain. Hunter and Cameron both keep their eyes on her. She's destined for very great things, we wouldn't let anything happen."

"Of course not. Why kill the goose that lays the golden egg? I'd expect someone like you to think about lining his own pocket before he thought about my mother's safety."

"I can't believe I'm hearing you right, Mark," Keoki said.

"It's all right," Greg assured her. "The captain is entitled to his own opinion. Of course I'm making money from her performances, but so is she. The contract she signed is fair, even her lawyer agrees. She wouldn't have signed it, if she didn't want it. I gave her plenty of chances to back out.

"On the road she makes about a thousand a week. From that I get a commission, pay for lodging, transportation, and taxes, leaving her with five hundred free and clear. She's been performing in some of the best clubs in the Midwest. After May first, she'll start on the East Coast Circuit. When I booked Honolulu, I offered to pay for her flight over, I even tried to upgrade her and your sister to first class, but she declined my offer. I did pick up the tab for her Inter-Island flights, though. Now, Captain, is there anything else you want to know?"

Mark stared into Greg's eyes. They looked as defiant as he knew his own eyes looked. Maybe he'd misjudged the man, maybe his mother would be a star in the near future, maybe he should rethink his feelings before her flight arrived from Chicago.

~ * ~

"Do you think Mark read the article?" Jill asked.

"I hope not, but somehow I'm certain he has. If he disliked my career change before, he'll be even more opposed to it now."

"Give him time, Mom. Remember, Karl and I were skeptical, too. Once he sees tomorrow night's show, he'll change his mind."

The plane taxied to a halt and soon Julie picked up the carry on luggage, in preparation to deplane.

"Let me take one of those bags, Mom," Jill offered.

"Nonsense. Your ankles are swollen from the flight. It's only a short way to the terminal and Mark will be waiting for us."

They made their way toward the exit with the other passengers. Over and over again they heard the flight attendants saying the same phrase. "Aloha. Thank you for flying United. Enjoy your stay in Hawaii." She again heard them repeated only this time they were directed toward herself and Jill.

"Thank you," she said.

"I knew it," one of the girls said. "You are Jewel West, aren't you?"

"Guilty as charged."

"I caught your show in Minneapolis. You're great! Are you going to appear in the Islands?"

Julie gave the girl the name of the clubs where she would be appearing, then hurried into the terminal. It had been a long flight and she suddenly realized its exhausting side effects.

At the baggage claim area Julie easily spotted Mark and Keoki. She wondered if she should be surprised to see Greg standing with them. She heard Jill call to her brother and watched as Mark hurried to place leis around their necks.

"Aloha, Mom," he said, lovingly. "This is Keoki."

"I would have known you anywhere, dear," Julie said, embracing the girl.

Keoki moved closer to Jill, to talk with her future sister-in-law and Mark drew Julie aside.

"Are you all right, Mom?"

"Of course I am, honey," she said, putting her hand on Mark's cheek. "Please don't look so worried."

"I won't deny it. I've been worried ever since I saw the article this morning at the grocery store. I couldn't believe it. I even bought the damn paper. I've never bought one of those things in my life."

"There's no need to worry. Those silly papers blow everything out of proportion. There's hardly a word of truth in the entire article."

"So your friend told me," Mark said, inclining his head toward Greg.

"I saw him and decided you'd met each other. I'm sorry the story broke at this time. I never meant for Jewel West to spoil your wedding."

"Don't give it a thought, Mom," Mark replied. He gave her a hug and held her a moment longer than necessary. "I think there's someone else waiting for you." He patted her hand then joined the girls.

Julie took a hesitant step toward Greg before he moved to her side. "Am I expected to pretend I'm surprised to see you here?" she asked when he took her hand.

"It's not necessary. I spoke with Hunter a couple of hours ago. He said he told you I'd be here. If you want to talk about surprises, let's start with how tired you look. I haven't seen you in the last couple of weeks. You're exhausted. Is the road too much for you?"

"Of course not. This weekend has been too much for me. We didn't get done until late Saturday and I didn't get home on Sunday until mid-afternoon. I still had some last minute shopping and some packing to do. Of course, we ended up taking an earlier bus to O'Hare than we'd planned. How Hunter knew when our bus would get in is still a mystery."

"Well, I can clear that one up. He called your son-in-law at work to find out your arrival time. Of course, Hunter's news didn't do you any good. I can tell you didn't sleep on the plane."

Julie nodded her head. "Jill slept for most of the flight and I told her I slept as well."

"She'd have to be blind to believe you. I'm beginning to think I should never have made the bookings here in the Islands. I'm afraid it's too late to back out now, though."

"Nonsense. No matter what's going on around me, once I get on stage I come alive. You'll see, everything will be fine by tomorrow night. I promise I'll look much more rested and if I don't, make-up can cover a multitude of evils."

Greg laughed and put his arm around her shoulders. "I wish I could sweep you out of here and get you to the hotel, but the press is here."

Julie sighed and looked toward her children. How could she tell them there were reporters waiting? How could she persuade them to go to the hotel without her? How could she protect them from the prying questions of the press? "I don't think I'm ready for this."

"I'm sorry, Jewel, but you have no choice. The press is waiting whether or not you're ready."

"I know. You warned me. I just lived believing it wouldn't happen to me. You know how it is—my life will begin with Once Upon A Time and end with She Lived Happily Ever After. No matter how many times life slaps me down, I still want to believe it." Julie wiped away the tears from her eyes. They were tears of disbelief over the tabloid article, as well as tears of exhaustion.

"Is something wrong, Mom?" Mark asked.

"Not really. The press wants an interview. You kids go on to the hotel. Greg will bring me there once we're finished here."

"I don't think so," Mark said. "If you're going to meet the press, we'll be with you."

"I thought you didn't want any part of Jewel West."

Mark took her hand in his. "Hey, you're my mom. What affects you, affects me. What is the quote I want, 'United We Stand'?"

Julie nodded, unable to express her relief at having her family by her side for the press conference.

Greg led them to a small room where several reporters and cameramen were waiting. Julie allowed him to make the introductions, before she fielded the inevitable questions.

"We're here, live at the Honolulu Airport, with Miss Jewel West," a reporter, who acted as a moderator, said into his microphone. "With her are her agent, Greg Lauer; her son, Captain Mark Weston, of the US Navy, his fiancée, Miss Keoki Mallu, of Honolulu, and Jewel's daughter, Mrs. Jill Lansing, of Minter, Wisconsin."

"Miss West, what brings you to Honolulu?" the first reporter asked.

"I came for my son's wedding."

"Is there any truth to the reports of you being stalked?"

"Of course not. I do have a secret admirer who sends me roses, but I'm not being stalked. I don't think the roses represent anything more dangerous than a gift of love."

"Captain Weston, are you concerned for your mother's safety?"

"Of course I am, anyone would be. I'm the first to admit, I've been skeptical about her new lifestyle. Since I've met Mr. Lauer, I've become convinced my mother's safety is of primary importance. I have no cause to worry."

"How do you feel, Mrs. Lansing?"

"I have an edge over my brother. My husband and I have seen several of Mom's performances and met the people she works with. I'm very proud of her. It's very difficult for a widow to change her lifestyle. Jewel West and the people who have helped create her is the best thing that could have happened to my mother."

The questions continued for several more minutes. When at last they made their way toward the car, Mark asked Greg to join them for dinner. Although, initially he declined, he finally accepted the invitation.

With dinner over, Julie allowed Greg to take her to her room. "I hope you don't mind," he said. "I took the liberty of upgrading you and Jill to a suite on a secured floor."

"Do you think it's necessary?"

"Not really. I took care of it as soon as I knew where you were staying. I thought you might be more comfortable with the additional privacy."

Twenty-one

Julie awoke and took a moment to familiarize herself to her surroundings. The darkened room gave no clue as to the time of day.

Little by little, the memories of yesterday's events came back to her. She wondered how long she'd slept. *It must be late, I feel rested so I most certainly overslept.*

Lazily, she got out of bed and opened the heavy drapes. Outside the patio doors, the sun shone brightly. The clock on the bedside table gave the time as nine-thirty.

After showering and washing her hair, she pulled on a swimsuit and skirt to begin the day. The choice of clothing reminded her of the casual dress she'd adopted in Jamaica. As a last minute thought, she added a short sleeved camp shirt to the outfit, knotting it at the waist as she remembered Dorah doing.

A note lay on the table in the living room of the suite.

> *Went to breakfast with Keoki, then shopping. I'll meet you back here at four.*
>
> *Love, Jill.*

For an unknown reason, the note came as a relief. For weeks she'd looked forward to spending time with her daughter. Now the thought of solitude delighted her.

After breakfast, she set out to explore this tropical paradise. Although she'd promised herself leisurely days of relaxing on the beach and playing in the surf, she'd become too restless to spend the day in idle relaxation.

The beach in front of her hotel sported a population of young men and women with perfectly tanned bodies. Julie knew she certainly didn't fit in with this crowd. In an attempt to clear her thoughts and put yesterday's events in perspective, she began walking along the shoreline, allowing the water to lap at her ankles. At last she came to a small, secluded cove. The expanse of water before her made Julie feel very insignificant in the overall scheme of things.

"You shouldn't be out here all alone, pretty lady," a man said, from behind her.

Julie jumped, startled by the realization someone had followed her. She turned to come face to face with a rather unkempt man of approximately forty years of age. "I guess I shouldn't have come so far," she replied, nervously.

"I know who you are," the man said, taking a step closer to her. "I'm your secret admirer, Jewel."

"You-you are?" she stammered.

The man nodded. "You said the flowers were sent out of love. You were right. I love you. I enjoyed sending roses to all those glamorous cities—Los Angeles, San Francisco, Las Vegas. I pictured you dressing and undressing in front of them, in front of me."

"Thank you. I've enjoyed them. It's been nice meeting you, but I have to get back to the hotel, now."

She moved to go around the man, but he moved as well, pulling her roughly into his arms and kissing her. Everything she had ever read about date rape flooded her mind along with everything she'd told Jill about such circumstances. Without formulating a plan, she brought her knee up with as much force as she could muster and slammed it into the man's crotch. The force of her blow brought a scream of pain from the man's lips and made him loosen his grip. She seized the opportunity and began running back toward the hotel. The curve of the beach and her safety loomed ahead of her. She kept her eyes on her destination and not the terrain of the beach. She felt the tug of a piece of driftwood as she lost her balance, falling face forward onto the warm sand.

Behind her, she heard the man's heavy breathing. Her fall had given him a chance to catch up. Quickly, she scrambled to her feet. Before she could run, his hand tightened on her arm and he spun her around to face him.

"Don't run away from me," he said, breathless. "I love you."

Without warning, he slapped her and she again lost her balance, landing hard on the beach; her head slammed against a piece of driftwood.

Although she felt dazed, she heard voices from around the curve of the beach and could see the man standing over her, taking off his shorts. She debated only a moment before she heard someone begin to scream. To her amazement, the screams belonged to her.

The man knelt, naked, straddling her legs. "Stop it," he yelled, hitting her again.

"Hey you!" she heard someone shout. "What's going on here?"

The man began to run, but two men caught up with him. Someone helped Julie to her feet and led her to a big boulder to sit down.

"It's all over now," the young man assured her. "He won't hurt you."

"I love her, just ask her," the man shouted.

A police officer appeared and to Julie's surprise, Greg accompanied him.

"Jewel!" Greg exclaimed. "When I heard about an attempted rape, I got worried. I've been combing the beach looking for you."

"Oh, Greg," she sobbed, getting unsteadily to her feet. "He followed me, he tried... he tried—" she couldn't finish, hysterical tears cut off her words.

"You're safe now, Jewel." Greg's voice was reassuring as he took her in his arms. "Did he hurt you?"

Julie shook her head and sniffed loudly. "No. He slapped me and I hit my head when I fell, but it could have been so much worse. I'm more frightened than anything. I don't know why I ever came out here alone."

"I do. It's not easy dealing with instant fame. I honestly understand your need to be alone. Maybe this will work out for the best and you'll realize you must be more careful."

A woman officer approached them "Can I get a statement?"

"Of course," Greg replied, taking the initiative and relieving Julie from answering. "You can have all the statements you want, just as soon as I have Miss West checked over at a hospital."

Julie stood back and allowed Greg to deal with the officer. The scene before her reminded her of a movie or a news program on TV. She'd become merely a spectator. As the tension of the moment drained, she became acutely aware of her mounting headache.

She glanced to her left and saw the man, who only moments before had posed such a threat. Handcuffed and draped in a towel, he looked more pitiful than menacing.

"Jewel, Jewel," Greg said, touching her arm to attract her attention.

Julie jumped at the intrusion on her thoughts. "Were you talking to me?"

"Yes. We're taking you to the hospital. The officer will question you there. I want you checked over to be certain you're all right."

Julie nodded, as she did, panic began to rise within her. "Mark, we have to call Mark."

"We're contacting your son, Miss West," the officer assured her. "He'll be meeting you at the hospital. The paramedics will be her soon."

"Is that necessary? The paramedics, I mean. Can't Greg take me there? I only have a headache, it's not like I'm seriously injured."

"We'll let the experts decide," Greg said. "You have a cut lip and there's blood on the back of your head. I don't want to take any chances."

Julie didn't argue. Greg made sense. Why take unnecessary chances with Mark's wedding only days away?

~ * ~

Jill and Keoki returned to the hotel at noon in the hopes of finding Julie for lunch. Around them, they heard snatches of conversations about an attempted rape on the beach, just a short distance from the hotel.

"No one is safe anymore," Keoki commented. "When I was a kid, you could walk anywhere in the city, even at night, and not worry. It's not the same now, but then the world has changed."

From the corner of her eye, Jill saw the desk clerk talking to a police officer and pointing toward herself and Keoki.

"Are you Mrs. Lansing?" the officer asked, when he approached them.

"Yes, I am. Is something wrong?

"I'm Officer Blake, Honolulu Police Department. Would you and your companion mind stepping into the office so we can speak privately?"

Jill nodded, and with Keoki, followed the officer into the office of the hotel manager.

"Please, make yourselves comfortable," Officer Blake said.

"You didn't answer my question," Jill pressed, refusing the chair the officer motioned toward. "Is something wrong?"

"I'm afraid there is. This morning an attempted rape occurred on the beach."

"We heard about it when we came in," Keoki said.

"The victim was your mother. We've taken her to the hospital. I've been sent here to take you there to meet her and your brother."

"Not Mom," Jill whispered, as she sank down into the nearest chair.

"How badly is she injured?" Keoki asked.

"I'm sorry. I don't know. I just need to escort you to the hospital."

~ * ~

"I'm sorry, Greg, really sorry. After the article yesterday, I should have known better," Julie said, as she sat on the edge of the examination table. Greg sat across from her, his expression one of concern rather than condemnation.

"Don't be too hard on yourself. The police told me you aren't the first person he's attacked. This is just the first time he's been caught. As for you, you're not used to being a celebrity. You'll learn to be more careful. It will just take time."

A knock at the door interrupted them. The doctor who had examined her earlier entered, accompanied by a young woman.

"Everything looks good, Miss West. Head wounds tend to bleed profusely, even small ones. You'll have a headache and I do want you to consult a physician if it lasts more than a day or two. I also want you to speak with Miss Jackson, she's our rape counselor."

"Rape counselor?" Julie questioned. "I don't know why. Nothing happened."

"Nothing physical," Susan Jackson replied, "but you were raped mentally. No one can go through an experience like this and not suffer from it. I've been told your son and daughter will be here soon, but we can talk for a few minutes and perhaps get together again later."

"I have a performance tonight and I leave for Maui tomorrow," Julie explained.

"You should have no problem carrying out your plans and enjoying your vacation. Now, if your friend will excuse us, we'll talk for a few minutes."

~ * ~

Mark drove from the base to the hospital, his anger threatening to boil over. He knew he had to keep his emotions in check. He'd seen his mother's distress over his condemnation of her chosen career change last night. Causing a scene this morning would only disturb her further. As Jill and Keoki had pointed out, repeatedly, his mother's happiness meant more than his opinion of her choices.

Just ahead of him a police car pulled into the parking lot, but he paid little attention. He parked his van and got out before he again focused on the official vehicle. Two women got out of the back seat and to his surprise he recognized his sister and Keoki. He knew he shouldn't be shocked. It would be foolish to think someone hadn't contacted them.

"Did they tell you what happened?" Jill greeted him, when he joined them in the waiting are.

"No, they didn't know anything. They just said to come here." Mark glanced up and saw Greg entering the room. "Maybe I don't know anything, but I think I see someone who does." Mark left the girls standing by the door and walked toward Greg. Before Mark could cross the lobby, a young woman dressed in the uniform of the Honolulu Police Department joined Greg.

"Mark Weston, this is Officer Lewis," Greg said, making the introductions.

"Captain Weston," the woman acknowledged him, extending her hand. "When your sister and fiancée arrive, we'll go to a room where we can talk."

Mark glanced over his shoulder. "They're already here. Did you say there was somewhere private where we can talk?" He motioned to the girls to follow them and went down the short hall to a small office.

"Since you and Miss Mallu live here in Honolulu, Captain Weston, I'm certain you've heard of the Wednesday Rapist. He attacked your mother, not because of who she is, but what she is."

"What do you mean what she is?" Jill questioned. "Who is the Wednesday Rapist?"

"He's the man we now have in custody. His name is John Gillard. For the past eight weeks he has been attacking attractive, middle aged tourists, like your mother. Don't look so worried, nothing happened this time."

"Are you certain?" Mark asked.

"Positive. Julie Weston, Jewel West, whatever you prefer to call her, is a very brave woman. She did what none of the others could. She fought back. We'll be contacting the other victims, but I don't think it will be necessary. Mr. Gillard has already confessed to the rapes. We think he wanted to be caught."

"If nothing happened, why is Mom here?" Mark asked.

"Because I insisted on it," Greg replied. "He didn't rape her, but he did slap her twice and she fell hitting her head. The doctor assures me she's more shaken than injured. As soon as she's released, she can go back to the hotel."

Twenty-two

Devan's alarm went off and reluctantly he got out of bed. He'd never been a morning person, but since Todd's return home, he'd begun rising at five to give himself an hour and a half before waking his son. He enjoyed the time alone. Although Todd made daily progress, Devan still needed to help him from bed to chair, then assist him in dressing after he cleaned up for the day.

Each week, he found less to do, but still the task of helping his son recover took most of his at home hours.

By five-thirty, Devan waited for his English muffin to pop up from the toaster and the microwave to beep, signaling his coffee water had heated. He switched on the eleven-inch kitchen television and found Headline News. With an hour, he could catch up on the world's news and not have to depend on the newspaper he no longer found time to read.

He paid little attention to the stories as he buttered his muffin. If he heard something he thought interesting, he could always catch it again during the next half-hour.

"Miss Jewel West arrived in Honolulu yesterday afternoon, amid stories of stalking and secret admirers," the commentator said.

Devan heard the knife he'd held in his hand clatter to the floor, but ignored it. Instead of returning it to the table, he turned up the volume on the TV.

"Within hours of denying the article which suggested she feared the man who sends her flowers weekly, she became the eighth victim of the Wednesday Rapist. Her quick thinking saved her from the fate of his last seven victims."

Julie appeared on the screen, undoubtedly from her dressing room. "I only reacted," she said. "I guess the silly story he told me about being my secret admirer gave me a moment to think."

"How did you know he wasn't your secret admirer?" the reporter asked.

"He said he sent flowers to Los Angeles, San Francisco, and Las Vegas. I've never been to those cities."

The camera shot returned to the studio and the commentary ended with the announcement of Julie's scheduled performance tonight in Maui, as well as Mark's wedding. Devan turned down the volume and sat for a moment, holding his head in his hands. He'd never meant the flowers as a threat. He knew how much Julie loved roses. He only wanted to somehow hold onto a small portion of their relationship.

Without considering the time, he picked up the phone and dialed Jerry's number.

~ * ~

Jerry finished his coffee. He'd soon have to leave for work, but as usual, he took a few minutes to monitor the morning news on TV. The story about Julie caught his attention and he studied her face. The strain of the past few days showed in her eyes. He'd been aware of the tabloid article and worried about it, but he'd never anticipated an attack.

The news report ended and Jerry sat, deep in thought. Maybe he should place a call to Julie's hotel, make certain no harm had come to her.

Before he could come to any decisions, the phone rang. He answered it just after the first ring ended.

"Jerry?" he barely recognized the voice as belonging to Devan.

"Devan? What are you doing calling at this hour?"

"Have you heard about the attack on Julie in Honolulu?"

"Yes, just now. Of course, I read about her secret admirer and the stalking in the tabloids."

"Good God," Devan said. "I'm the one responsible for all of this."

Devan's words sounded ridiculous. "Sure you are, so am I, don't be so hard on yourself. The last time we talked I told you you'd hurt her, but I did, too. It doesn't make either of us responsible for what happened."

"You don't understand, Jerry. I'm Julie's secret admirer. I sent her the flowers. I wanted her to feel special, not threatened."

"You've got to let her know you were the one, if for no other reason than to put her mind at ease."

"You're right, of course, but I can't call her. If I hear her voice, I don't think I can stay calm. If you must know, I miss her more than I ever thought possible. I'm hopelessly in love with someone I can't have."

For a moment, Jerry could think of nothing to say. He hadn't expected Devan to be in love with Julie. He knew Julie believed Devan when he told her he loved her, but Jerry had remained skeptical. He remembered telling her boys he considered Devan a great guy. He also remembered telling Julie to give the man a chance. He had changed his mind when Devan disappeared.

"Why are you telling me this?" Jerry finally asked.

"I have to tell someone. I can't tell Julie, not now. At first I told myself I'd done the right thing, I'd saved Julie from this hell I've been living these past weeks. I've always considered myself good with the ladies. Love them and leave them, so to say. I never planned to feel this way about a woman, never wanted to become so involved."

"I don't know what to say to you. As much as I wanted to hate you these past weeks, we're friends, but so is Julie. I can't tell you what to do. If you love her, you should let her know."

Twenty-three

Julie sat on the dimly lit plane. Beside her, Lance's even breathing told her he slept, as did Jill and Karl in the row ahead of her.

Hawaii had been an eye opening experience. For the first time since becoming Jewel West, she'd experienced the danger in being a celebrity. Even though the attack had nothing to do with her identity, she'd become painfully aware of just how vulnerable a woman alone could be.

She thought about Mark and how his attitude had so drastically changed from distaste for her new lifestyle to pride after seeing her performance. Just thinking about the show reminded her of the rose sitting on her dressing table in Maui. She closed her eyes and silently relived the evening.

They'd arrived at the club just prior to six. While Jill, Mark and Keoki met Keoki's parents for dinner, Julie went to her dressing room to prepare for the show.

She stepped into the small room and stopped, taking a deep breath. The crystal bud vase, with its red rose, seemed familiar and yet unexpected. She pulled the card from the holder and read the now too familiar words.

Good Luck—Your Secret Admirer.

Her mind raced as the image of John Gillard appeared before her. "I pictured you dressing and undressing in front of them, in front of me," she heard him say.

"No," she whispered. "Don't do this to me. It isn't fun anymore."

"Are you all right, Miss West?" the manager of the club said.

She'd turned abruptly, almost expecting to see Gillard standing behind her.

She looked again at Lance, sleeping beside her, and wondered if she would ever be able to forget what had happened to her in Honolulu.

"Are you sleeping, Mom?" Lance asked, jolting her back to reality.

"No," Julie replied. "Just remembering the events of this past week. We had a wonderful time, didn't we?"

"You can't fool me, Mom. You were thinking about the creep on the beach, weren't you?"

"Maybe, for a minute, but I know he can't hurt me or anyone else. I just wish I knew who my Secret Admirer really is."

"Do you? I'm afraid knowing might be more painful than remaining ignorant."

~ * ~

Once in the Chicago terminal, Julie and her family joined the crush of passengers heading to the baggage claim area.

"Jewel, Jewel," she heard her name being called, but momentarily didn't recognize the voice.

Involuntarily, she jumped when someone touched her arm, then suppressed a scream when she recognized Hunter at her side.

"I didn't mean to startle you," Hunter said, taking her into his arms and giving her a friendly hug.

"What are you doing here?" Julie asked, now more worried about the reason for his presence than surprised to see him.

"Don't look so concerned. I'm here for a good reason this time."

Julie relaxed a bit. "It must be a good reason for you to get here before six in the morning."

"So, what's this good news you have?" Lance asked. Julie could hear the skepticism in his voice.

"I'm sorry, I can't tell you. I've been sworn to secrecy, but I assure you, I'm here for an exciting reason."

Hunter turned to Julie. "I have strict orders to take you somewhere so you can shower and nap before we meet with Greg at eleven-thirty. I have your road bag in the car."

Julie said her good-byes to the kids. They had agreed to take her luggage back to Minter, while she flew to Kansas City to meet Hunter and the others, before he altered her plans.

"So, what's going on?" she asked, when he pulled out of the parking lot.

"I told you, it's a secret. For now, I'm taking you to my folks' place. Mom's fixing us breakfast, then you can catch a couple of hours of sleep before our meeting."

"But—"

"But nothing. I heard about the attack and I can see you haven't rested much in the last week. I wish you weren't performing tonight, but I can't do anything about it."

Julie hadn't paid any attention to the route they'd taken until Hunter stopped the car in front of a small house on a quiet street in Schaumberg.

Inside the well-planned kitchen, Hunter's mother busied herself at the stove.

Although Julie wasn't at all hungry, she accepted the plate of bacon and eggs the woman set on the table in front of her.

"You eat up, child," the woman said. "When you're finished, Rob will take you to your room. You look exhausted. I'd stay here and take care of you myself, but I have to get to work."

~ * ~

"Jewel, Jewel, it's ten o'clock," she heard Hunter say, as he shook her gently.

"Just another few minutes," she protested, pulling the feather pillow over her head.

"I'd love to let you sleep, but you've got about forty-five minutes to get ready."

Hunter's words brought her to full awareness and reluctantly she headed for the shower. The drive downtown took about half an hour and although Julie asked dozens of questions, Hunter remained secretive about her summons to Greg's office.

"Why can't you tell me what's going on?" she demanded, once the elevator doors closed.

"If I told you what this is about, you'd know as much as I do."

"Oh, Hunter, you're being so cruel. I feel like I did as a child, just before Christmas. Mom would put all the presents under the tree and not let me even shake them."

Hunter burst into laughter, just as the elevator door opened. "It won't be long and this Christmas will be here."

They entered Greg's office and Hunter acknowledged the secretary sitting at the desk.

"You're to go right in, Mr. Hunter," the girl said.

"Mr. Lauer is expecting you and Miss West."

Julie entered the inner office. To her surprise, she saw Frank sitting across the desk from Greg. Beside him sat an attractive woman, who Julie judged to be close to her own age.

"Come on in, Jewel," Greg said. "Did you have a good flight home?"

"You didn't get Hunter up at the crack of dawn, so he could drag me down here when I wanted to sleep, to ask me how my trip went. Something is going on here. What is it, another newspaper article?"

Greg smiled, mischievously before turning to the woman seated next to Frank. "Vaureen Parks, this is Jewel West. Vaureen is the producer of *With This Ring* as well as Hunter's new series, *Black And White*."

"It's a pleasure, Jewel," Vaureen said. "I caught your show in Honolulu and again in Maui. Hunter's been pushing me to see you and once I did, I knew he'd been right. I want you to play Sylvie Adams, Hunter's love interest in the new show."

"Me? But I'm not—"

"Black," Hunter said, finishing her sentence. "Think about the title, *Black And White*. My love interest in the show is white. Vaureen's been looking for the perfect actress for the last two months."

"To no avail," Vaureen interrupted. "Everyone I've suggested, Hunter shot down. He kept telling me you'd be perfect. I finally gave in and I'm glad I did. From what Hunter tells me you work well together, and after I saw you, I knew you were meant to be Sylvia Adams."

"You must know I'm not an actress," Julie said. "Sometimes I don't think I'm even a comedian."

"I saw you on stage, not once, but twice. You don't have to act. You're Sylvie, just the way the writers portrayed her. It's almost as though they wrote the part for you, the way they did for Hunter."

Julie contemplated Vaureen's suggestion, while Frank and Greg explained the contract she would need to sign. She hardly believed her ears when they talked about the enormous salary and royalties, should the show become a hit and go into syndication.

When they finished explaining the details, Julie looked to Frank. "What do you think?" she asked.

"I think it's a great opportunity for you. I'd like to see you take it, but it has to be your decision. From a legal standpoint, you've been offered an excellent contract."

Hunter reached over to take her hand. "It's not as rushed as when you're on the road," he said, but it's also not as easy. The show takes a full week to put together and once you finish one, you have to start another. It's not like doing a familiar monologue. Every week it's a new script, new lines to learn. It also takes more than a couple of hours a night. You'll be on the set at seven in the morning and sometimes you won't get home until after six at night."

Julie sat, quietly, for several moments. Hunter wasn't sugar coating anything, Frank thought the contract fair and Greg wouldn't have agreed to this if he though it might be too much for her.

"I won't know if I can do this if I don't try. I can't argue with three such good friends. I might miss the road, but not the late hours. I've always been a morning person, so let's give it a try."

Vaureen smiled, and extended her hand. "Welcome aboard, Jewel. You'll be doing the first two episodes of *With This Ring* to set up *Black And White*. I've got your schedule, so I can Fed Ex the script to you and Hunter. We'll start filming the week after the Fourth of July and the first show will air in September. You and Hunter will have a couple of months together, on the road, to get familiar with the characters."

"Thank you," Julie said, too overwhelmed to think of anything more appropriate to say.

Vaureen stood to leave. "Well, I have a plane to catch. I'll see you in Los Angeles, Jewel. Greg, Frank, it's been good to see you and as usual, a pleasure doing business with you."

Hunter rose and followed Vaureen from the room, while Julie mutely watched them leave.

"I hope you consider this worth missing some sleep," Greg said.

Julie nodded. "It's going to take some time for this to sink in. Am I really going to be starring with Hunter in *Black And White*, or am I still asleep and dreaming?"

"I assure you," Frank said. "This is no dream."

"Definitely not," Greg agreed. "You have Hunter to thank for this one, though. Speaking of Hunter, he called while you were sleeping. Maybe you ought to call your daughter, so she can stop worrying."

"Yes, I should. She'll have a million questions as to why Hunter whisked me away like he did."

Julie entered her home number into the phone and thought about Hunter. She knew he cared, knew he'd become special in her life, but what part, if any, would he play? She cared for him, but not as a lover, maybe more like a good friend, a confidant, like Jerry.

Jill answered on the second ring. Greg and Frank rose to leave the room. Without verbally questioning them, Julie looked up. "We're going to give you some privacy," Greg whispered. "We'll order some sandwiches and be back shortly."

When Julie finished her conversation with Jill, she hung up the phone. Impulsively she picked up the receiver a second time and placed another call.

"Thank you for calling LisPro. How may I direct your call?" the receptionist answered.

"I'd like to speak with Jerry Gaines, please," Julie said.

~ * ~

Jerry glanced at the clock and noticed it read one o'clock. Lunch had been over for nearly an hour, yet it seemed as though the afternoon would never end. Julie's plane landed early this morning and he wondered how the trip went. He missed seeing her on a weekly basis and decided he'd call Jill as soon as he got home.

"Jerry Gaines, you have a call on line five, Jerry Gaines, line five." The sound of his name being called over the intercom startled him.

He left his area and went to the supervisor's office. Closing the door, he picked up the phone and dialed the operator.

"You have a call, Jerry," the girl on the other end of the line said. "I'll put it through. What extension are you at?"

He gave her the number and waited for the phone to ring. He wondered who would call him at work? Had something happened to Karen or the kids? His mind raced and the ringing of the phone made him jump.

"Jerry?" Julie bubbled on the other end of the line.

"Julie, is it really you? Where are you? I thought you'd be on your way to Kansas City by now. Is something wrong?"

Julie's light laughter put him at ease. "Wrong? Heavens no. Everything is great. I had to call you, had to tell someone other than Jill. I'm in Greg's office and I just signed a contract to star in a sitcom with Hunter. I'll be moving to Los Angeles in July to start taping."

"You're kidding," Jerry said. "No, I can tell by your voice, you're not kidding. Are you happy? Don't answer that, it's a silly question, of course you're happy."

"Yes, Jerry, I'm very happy. With luck I'll be home in a couple of weeks and we can talk."

"Is it a secret?" Jerry asked.

"Secret? I don't know."

"Hell no," he heard someone say in the background. "Who are you talking to?"

"It's Jerry," he heard her say.

"Jerry, this is Greg Lauer. Spread the good word. We're making the official announcement in the *Minter Ledger* this week. Its only right Jewel's friends should be the first to know."

They talked for a few more minutes, but Jerry knew he'd never remember the last part of the call.

Before he left the office, he pressed the button on the phone to patch into the PA system. "Attention," he said, into the phone, wondering if this were the right way to spread the good word. "Julie Weston has just signed a contract to do a sitcom in Los Angeles. She wanted her friends to be the first to know."

He hung up the phone and left the office, amid cheers from her fellow workers. She made it big, we knew she would and she'll be great, were the comments he heard as he made his way back to his workstation.

Although Jerry had spread the word, had congratulated Julie, he weighed his own feelings carefully. Where would Julie's new life put Devan? Since their early morning conversation last week, he planned to somehow bring them together before the reunion. Now getting the two of them together, making them happy became unimportant. Julie seemed happier than he'd heard her sound in months. She no longer needed Devan to make her complete. She had a new career, an exciting life opening up to her, and God knew she deserved it.

~ * ~

Julie hung up the phone, her stomach churning, the way it churned when she'd done something Steve disapproved of, and she got caught. "I'm sorry," she said.

Greg gave her a funny look. "Sorry? What do you have to be sorry about?"

"The call to Jerry. I'll pay for it."

Greg took her hand. "Jewel, the least of my worries is a short call to Jerry Gaines made from this office. What kind of a life have you lived? Sorry, is something you have to have instilled in you. I can't believe you'd say such a thing."

"I just remember how upset my husband would have been if he caught me making a long distance call he didn't approve first."

"You do need reeducating. A call to Minter is a minor thing. As a matter-of-fact, my secretary is placing a call to the *Minter Ledger* right now."

"The *Ledger*?" Julie questioned. "Of course, you said something to Jerry about placing an article," she said, answering her own question.

"It's only fitting for your hometown newspaper to have the exclusive story of your new success. I've sent Frank and Hunter for carry out. We'll eat in the conference room. I'd take you all out for lunch, but we have a lot of work to do here before you and Hunter have to catch your plane at four."

"I understand."

"Damn it, Jewel, do you see what I mean? Don't be so understanding. Anyone else would be put out by such an imposition. There are times you act like you're terrified of displeasing me, of being around me."

"I'm not terrified of you. It's just—"

"Just what? What did your husband do to you, anyway?"

"He merely pointed out what I should have known. He let me know I didn't possess the intelligence to make my own decisions."

"How could you believe such a thing? You graduated from high school at the top of your class. You went to college and graduated with honors. Did either of those things tell you anything?"

"Sure, they told me I could make the grade. He called it book smart, but he wouldn't let me take any accounting courses."

"Of course, not, because he considered accounting his specialty. Keeping books on all his women," Greg said, his voice sounding angry.

"It's all past history, Greg," she commented, trying to reassure him.

"I hope so. You're going to be a star, you already are one, but you'll shine even brighter in the months to come."

Before Julie could respond, Greg's secretary entered the room. "Mr. Conklin is on the line, Mr. Lauer."

"Are you ready to meet the press, Miss West?" Greg teased.

"I don't think of Dan as the press. I've known him forever. We went to high school together."

"Just whom didn't you go to high school with?" he asked, as he switched on the speakerphone.

"Dan, Greg Lauer here."

"Of course," Julie heard Dan's familiar voice say. "Julie Weston's agent. What can I do for you?"

"We're calling to give you an exclusive."

"An exclusive? Those things are for the big publications not local weekly papers."

"In this case, it's all yours. The wire services can get it from you for a change. Jewel is sitting right here. She'd like to talk to you."

"Hi, Dan."

"Julie, it's good to hear your voice. How are you? We've all been worried about you. We read the story in that gossip rag then heard about the attack."

"I hope you don't believe everything you read. I'm in no danger. As for the attack, the police in Honolulu said it was because of what I am not who I am. The man was a monster, but it's all over now. I wasn't injured, but this call has nothing to do with the attack."

"So, why are you calling? What's this exclusive all about?"

"I'll let Greg tell you. He's my agent and he handles all my publicity."

Greg smiled broadly and Julie sat back in the chair to Minter to him explain the baffling events of the morning.

"This morning, Jewel West signed a contract to do a new sitcom with Rob Hunter. It will be a spin off of *With This Ring*, called *Black And White*. Taping will begin with two episodes of *With This Ring* in July, making her last road show—ah, let's see, where's my calendar?"

Julie watched Greg shuffle papers on the desk. She hadn't given much thought to the road shows. She'd become comfortable with Hunter, Faye, and Cameron. With this morning's decision so quickly made, she'd given no consideration to its effect on her life.

"Here it is," she heard Greg say. "Her last road show will be on the second Saturday in June, in Philadelphia."

Julie's stomach began to do flip-flops at the word *Philadelphia*. She couldn't have heard Greg correctly. Blocking her own thoughts from her mind, she tried to concentrate on Greg's conversation with Dan.

"I'll have to speak with the club manager there and hopefully we'll put on quite a gala for her last show."

"I think it's wonderful," she heard Dan say. "Congratulations, Julie."

"Thanks, Dan," she managed to reply.

"Now, that wasn't so bad, was it?" Greg asked, once he broke the connection.

"Did I hear you right? Did you say I'd be doing my last show in Philadelphia? I didn't think we'd be going there."

"I guess you couldn't have known. I finalized the East Coast tour last week. Do you have a problem with Philadelphia?"

"Devan's in Philadelphia."

"Damn, I hadn't thought about him. I only booked you for a Saturday night. I should have given you the entire weekend. I can see if I can change your reservations to fly back to Madison on Monday so you can look him up."

"No, it's better this way."

"Why?"

"He doesn't want to be found. Look, he didn't give me a number for his son's apartment. When I tried to get it they said at the customer's request, it was unlisted. When I called his office, he never returned my calls. I have to accept the fact he doesn't want me to find him."

"There has to be more to it. What aren't you telling me?"

"Jerry's talked to him. He's bitter. With all he's been through, I can't blame him. Even though I understand, I'm having trouble accepting it."

"Luncheon is served," Frank said. "We're setting everything up in the conference room. If you two don't hurry up, we'll eat yours as well as ours."

"We'll be right there," Greg said.

When Frank left the office, Greg turned to Julie. "Come on, Jewel, we won't talk about this right now."

Julie nodded and pushed back her chair. *I don't ever want to talk or think about it, now or ever,* she thought to herself.

Four Styrofoam containers sat on the polished oak table in the conference room. Noticing each container held a juicy hamburger and greasy fries, Julie cringed at the thought of such a lunch.

Halfheartedly, she opened her container, delighted to see it contained a chef's salad, with French-Roquefort dressing on the side. "Do I have to guess who ordered my lunch?" she teased.

"I know what you eat," Hunter said. "I even remembered your sparkling water."

"Does she always eat like this?" Greg asked.

"Usually," Hunter replied. "She's the healthiest one of the group. The rest of us live on junk."

"Hey guys," Julie said, waving her hands. "I'm still here. Don't talk around me. You're beginning to sound like Steve."

"Heaven forbid," Greg said. "I hope we aren't eating too late for you."

"No. Hunter's mom insisted I eat a breakfast big enough to choke a horse this morning. I'm still not hungry, but I know I have to eat. Besides, I'm still on Honolulu time."

Julie's statement met with good-natured teasing and she allowed herself to relax. She'd finished about half of her salad, when Greg produced three bulging manila envelopes.

"What on earth?" she asked.

"Fan mail. You can read them on the road. Here's one we'd like you to read while we're with you."

"You read them?" Julie asked, astonished.

"Of course. You didn't think we'd take the chance of not knowing about threatening letters, do you?"

"I guess not. I take it there were no threats."

"None whatsoever. They were all positive. There's even letters from the other women who were attacked by the man in Honolulu, all thanking you."

Julie fingered the white business envelope with her name neatly typed, followed by Greg's office address. No return address graced the upper left-hand corner and the postmark denoted only a postal station.

She slid the neatly folded sheets from the envelope and began to read. She didn't look at the second page of the letter. Being from a fan, it seemed unlikely she'd recognize the name.

My Dear Julie,

> *I never thought I'd hurt you. The roses were meant to give you pleasure. Instead, they brought you pain.*
>
> *Can it be only a few months ago when I assured your sons I'd never hurt you? As I recall they said never is a long time.*

Tears blurred the paper's typewritten words. "Devan," she half whispered. "Devan's my secret admirer." After ripping the pages in half, she pushed back her chair and hurried from the room.

Behind her, she heard three chairs scraping against the highly polished wood floor. She didn't turn back, didn't want to see any of them right now. They'd all known it was Devan and no one told her. Greg even suggested finding Devan during her stay in Philadelphia.

Within a few feet of the sanctuary of the ladies' room, she felt someone grasp her arm. Turning abruptly, she came face to face with Greg.

"You bastard, you knew. You knew it was Devan. Why didn't you tell me? How could you let me go on, worried out of my mind, scared to death?"

"I only received the letter yesterday. You should finish reading it, Jewel."

"Don't call me that!" she screamed.

"What do you want me to call you, Julie? Not in this office. Here you're Jewel West, only now you're acting like a child. We didn't tell you earlier, because we didn't want anything to spoil this morning's meeting. Now come on back and finish reading the letter."

"Why? Why should I bother? Did he give me a number where I can call him, an address where I can write? Did he say he'd answer my calls if I contacted him at work?"

"No," Greg said, his voice low.

"You said you read it, read the whole thing. Well, since you know what it says, there's no use in my reading it. Devan Yates! I thought I loved him, thought he loved me, what a joke."

"Greg's right, you should read the letter," Frank urged.

"I don't have to. Jerry's talked to him, says he's bitter. Well, maybe I'm bitter, too. After what Steve did to me, I don't know why I ever thought I needed another man in my life."

"Everyone needs somebody, Jewel," Hunter said.

Julie ignored the remark. "Excuse me, I need to use the powder room." She pulled free of Greg's grip and entered the ladies' room. Like the rest of the suite, the small room denoted opulence. Behind her, she heard the door latch and absently she pressed the button to lock it.

Across from her stood a couch, pure white against the light pink walls and deep burgundy carpeting. Ignoring the couch, she slid down the solid door to the floor. The plush carpeting cushioned her knees as she covered her face with her hands and sobbed.

"Damn it, Devan," she said aloud. "I do need you and I do love you. How ironic, I thought I loved Steve and he didn't love me either. I must be quite a woman. Well, I'll show you all. I don't need you, or Royd, or Steve, or anyone else to make my life complete. There are three men out there who believe in me. They will have to be enough to keep me going. I'll prove I can be a success without you. I'll make it on my own and I'll never let anyone get close to me again."

She lingered a few minutes longer before getting to her feet. Past the sitting room, she entered the brightly lit lavatory area. The reflection in the mirror showed her what she didn't want to see.

She looked tired, drawn, and her eyes were red from crying. In an attempt to rectify the situation, she splashed her face with cold water.

"No more Julie Weston," she said to the mirror. "Only to my kids and a few people in Minter. From now on, I'm Jewel West and she's someone to be respected."

Twenty-four

In his dream Devan sat brooding on the steps of his parents' new home in Minter. How could they have done this to him? How could they just up and move the summer before he started high school? All his friends were in Milwaukee and here he sat, in Minter of all places.

"Your name Yates?" He heard someone ask. When he looked up, he saw a kid about his own age riding a bicycle up the sidewalk.

"Who wants to know?"

"Jerry Gaines. I live two doors down. My mom said you moved in yesterday. I've been at camp. Just got home last night. You want to go swimming?"

"Where?"

"Out at the lake, of course. Everybody's probably out there already. I would have gone out earlier, but Mom said I should come over and ask you to come along. We can ride our bikes out. It's only a couple of miles."

They arrived at the lake to find the beach full of teenagers. Jerry introduced him to several people, including a cute redhead by the name of Sandy Sullivan.

"Julie's over there," Jerry said, motioning toward a plump girl with dark hair, sitting on a blanket and reading a book. "I'd introduce you, but I've got to talk to Dan."

Devan kicked at a clump of sand and walked over to where the girl sat. "Hi. I'm Devan Yates."

She looked up from her book, her eyes hidden behind big sunglasses. "I heard. I'm Julie Morgan. Do you swim?"

"I'm from Milwaukee," he said, defiantly. He wondered how she could ask such a question.

"I didn't ask where you came from, Yates, I asked if you could swim."

Devan watched her get to her feet. "Of course, I can swim. We lived on the lake."

Julie took off her sunglasses, revealing her light blue eyes. "Let's see how good you are. I'll race you to the raft."

Devan looked out over the water to the raft half way across the lake. "But you're a girl."

"So what? You're a boy. Now that we've gotten the anatomy lesson out of the way, are you, chicken?" She turned and ran toward the lake.

Devan followed her into the water. "You asked for it," he said.

Once they were in waist deep water, they both began swimming with powerful strokes. Devan pulled himself up onto the raft, surprised to see Julie already seated on the edge, her feet dangling in the water.

"Not bad, Yates," she said. "You thought about trying out for the swim team?"

Before he could answer, Jerry and Sandy hoisted themselves up onto the raft. Julie dove into the water and swam for shore with Sandy.

"I should have warned you about Julie," Jerry began. "We all know better than to race with her."

"Why?"

"She swims anchor on the girl's relay team. She's murder in the classroom, too. You find her in any of your classes and you can kiss the curve good-bye. Everybody cringes when she walks in. Just don't ever hurt her. She's everyone's friend, she's special."

~ * ~

Devan awoke, his body drenched in sweat. Had the realization he'd waited too long to get tickets for Julie's show prompted the dream about their first meeting?

He thought about his stop at the club where Julie would be performing in a week. He'd decided to get three tickets. One for Todd and his fiancée, Andrea, as well as one for himself. How could he have known Julie's show would be sold out?

He'd been disappointed, but tried not to let it show. Todd's progress over the past few weeks had been so promising he wanted nothing to upset his son. Todd no longer needed his wheelchair and his doctors were calling his recovery nothing short of a miracle.

In the shower, Devan considered finding his own apartment. Todd and Andy would be getting married in the fall and they certainly didn't need an interfering father-in-law living with them. Until now, he hadn't given much thought to moving, since Todd still needed his help.

Once he finished his shower and shaved, he went out to the living room. He smiled at Andy and Todd sitting on the couch, engrossed in the Sunday paper.

"Good morning, Dad," Andy said. "We didn't think you'd ever get up this morning."

"Guess I overslept. What do you kids have planned for today?"

"Not much," Todd answered. "Andy wants to work on the guest list for the wedding, then I guess we'll order out Chinese for supper."

"Can I get you some breakfast?" Andy asked.

"Just a cup of coffee, but I can get it."

"I'm going out to get us a refill. I'll bring you some, too."

Andy left the room and Devan reached for the consumer section of the paper.

"Dad," Todd began, before Devan could start scanning the ads for rentals. "You're from Minter. Do you know Jewel West?"

The question caught him completely off guard. "Why would you ask such a thing?"

"There's an article about her in today's paper. Do you know her?"

"Not really."

"Come on, Dad, I think you do. She's the one, isn't she?"

"The one? What are you talking about?"

"You know as well as I do. She's the woman from New Year's Eve."

"It wasn't Jewel West, it was someone else."

"Yeah, I know, I've been racking my brain all morning trying to think of her name."

"Whose name?" Andy asked, when she set the tray with three mugs on the coffee table.

"It's not important." Devan said. "If you haven't started lunch, I'll take you out for something."

"Damn it, Dad, it is important. You see, Andy, before the shooting, Dad met a special lady in Minter. Since he's been here, I've never heard him mention her. What happened? Did you leave her behind to be with me?"

"I had a decision to make. I chose my son over a virtual stranger."

"It didn't sound like she was such a stranger when we talked on New Year's Day. You still haven't answered my question. Is she Jewel West?"

"She calls herself Jewel West now, but I don't know the person she's become. I knew Julie Morgan. I'm surprised you even remembered her."

"I didn't until I saw the article. Then it all came back. Have you called her, talked to her?"

"Not since the first week. There's no reason to talk to her. She's become very successful. She certainly doesn't need me interfering in her life." Devan watched his son's reaction to the half-truth he'd told him. He wondered if Todd believed it.

Before Todd could comment further, the phone rang. Devan breathed a sign of relief for the reprieve from Todd's probing questions.

"Yes, he's right here. Just a minute," Todd said.

"Who is it?" Devan mouthed, when Todd handed him the portable phone.

Todd shrugged his reply.

"Hello," Devan said, still wondering who could be calling. Even Jerry didn't have this number.

"Is this Devan Yates?" the man on the other end said.

Devan didn't recognize the voice. Before he answered, Todd and Andy went into the kitchen, giving him some privacy. "You have me at a disadvantage. You know me, but I don't know whom I'm talking to. How did you get this number, anyway?"

"No one is completely inaccessible, Mr. Yates. You don't know me. My name is Greg Lauer."

Devan's stomach knotted, while Julie's picture smiled up at him from the front page of the entertainment section. "Julie's agent. Did she ask you to call me?"

"Why would she? Are you planning to attend the show Saturday night?"

"No."

"For some reason, I knew what your answer would be. You really are a bastard."

"I'm not as bad as you think. I tried to get tickets yesterday. You must know the show is sold out."

"If you had tickets, would you go?"

"Of course, I would. I wouldn't have known about the show being sold out if I hadn't tried to get them," Devan shouted. His statement met with stony silence. "So, what is this call all about?" Devan demanded.

"It's about you coming to the show on Saturday night. If it were up to me, I'd kick your ass out of the club if you came. Unfortunately, it's not up to me. The promoters want a reunion of the surviving musketeers. Jerry and Karen are coming. If you had tickets would you come as well?"

"Does Julie want me there?"

"She doesn't know. It's to be a surprise, a fitting end for her successful road tour."

"Then what I've been reading is true. She'll be moving to Los Angeles after the Fourth."

"It's true. She's an overnight sensation, the kind of performer every agent dreams of representing and seldom finds. I could go on about Jewel all day, but I'm still waiting for an answer to my question. Will you be there on Saturday night?"

"I'll be there."

"Do you want to bring someone?"

"I'd planned to take my son and his fiancée, but I understand the scarcity of tickets."

"I'll Fed Ex three tickets to your office tomorrow. You'll have them by Tuesday morning."

Devan sat quietly for a minute. In less than a week, he would again see Julie. How would he react?

"Who were you talking to?" Todd asked.

"Julie's agent. Would you kids like to see her show next weekend?"

"You're kidding!" Andy exclaimed. "Of course we would, but it's been sold out for weeks. I've done everything but sell my body on the street to get tickets. They just don't exist."

"They do now," Devan replied. "This Lauer guy wants me to be there. He's sending out three tickets tomorrow, so don't make any plans for Saturday night. We'll make it an evening to remember."

"How do you feel about seeing her again?" Todd inquired.

"Worried, scared. She doesn't know I'm coming."

All day, Devan considered the call from Greg Lauer. Had he made the right decision? He'd hurt Julie, would she become angry when she saw him? How would he react? He'd be friendly, but not overly affectionate. He'd let her make the first move.

Impulsively, he picked up the phone and called Jerry. They'd talked several times over the past weeks and he had again found the friend he'd made so many years ago.

"I hear you're coming to Philadelphia," Devan said, after exchanging the usual pleasantries with Jerry. "When does your plane get in?"

"Karen and I are flying in on Friday. We want to do some sightseeing. We've never been East before. We get in just before noon."

"I'll take the day off and play tour guide. It will be good to see you again."

"Are you saying you're going to the show?"

"Yes. I don't think her agent is overly thrilled about me being there, but he said he'd be sending the tickets."

"Do you blame him?"

285

Although Devan had become accustomed to Jerry's biting accusations, the words still hurt.

"Guess not. You know, Jer, this morning I dreamed of the first time we met. Do you remember what you said when you swam out to the raft?"

"About racing with her? I never told you, but we set you up."

"I always thought I gave you a good laugh by racing with her, but that's not what I mean. You told me 'Julie's everyone's friend, don't hurt her.'"

"I'd forgotten. Is that what's eating at you?"

"I guess so. I don't know. I hurt the one person I never thought I would. I'm scared to death to see her on Saturday."

"Karen and I will be right there with you, but we'll be there for Julie as well."

Twenty-five

"I'm never going to learn these lines, Hunter," Julie lamented.

Hunter lay back on the double bed across from Julie. "Relax. It will all fall into place. The only thing you have to worry about are the key cue phrases. There's always a Teleprompter if you get lost."

"You've told me all this before. I just want to be perfect."

"Lighten up. You're Jewel West, not Julie Weston trying to impress her husband. You don't have to be perfect. If you make a mistake, if you ad-lib a line, no one will know except the two of us. All it takes is not letting the audience know you screwed up."

Julie got up and walked over to the patio door. Outside a summer storm raged, giving her a blurred view of the Louisville skyline. She opened the door and stepped out onto the protected patio.

"You'll get soaked out here," Hunter said, from behind her. He put his arm around her shoulder and guided her back into the room.

"Something's eating at you, has been all week. I can't believe it's learning these lines, or leaving the road tour. What is it?"

Julie hung her head, ashamed of what seemed like her foolish fears. Hunter put his finger under her chin and forced her to look into his eyes.

"If you must know, I'm worried about going to Philadelphia. What if—"

Hunter gently captured the tear that ran down her cheek and wiped it away with his finger. "You're worried about Devan, aren't you? What happened to the Jewel West I saw in Greg's office a few weeks ago? As I recall, she said she didn't need any man."

"She lied," Julie sobbed. "I don't know what I want. I want to see him and yet I don't."

Before Hunter could answer, the phone rang. Julie listened to the one sided conversation, trying to identify the caller.

"Just a minute, I'll get her," she heard Hunter say.

Without bothering to ask whom she would be talking to, she took the phone.

"Jewel," she heard Greg say. "How are you doing?"

"Fine. To what do I owe the honor of this call?"

"I thought you'd like to know, we were able to juggle Cameron's schedule so he can be on the show with you Saturday night."

"What about Eddy?" she asked.

"I don't think anyone will mind seeing five comedians for the price of four."

"What's going on, Hunter?" she asked, when she hung up the phone. "Greg just told me Cameron's coming to Philadelphia."

"He thought it would be good for all of us to be together one last time. I'm going to catch a short nap. Maybe you should do the same."

Hunter left the room and Julie lay down on the bed. She knew she wouldn't sleep. The last six weeks had been so eventful sleep had become an elusive stranger. Things happened so quickly with Greg, you rarely had time to adjust to what was happening before something new came up.

Cameron left the show after the last performance in New York in May. His new position in Los Angeles meant he would be handling Julie and Hunter's careers. The idea of Cameron looking out for her interests put her at ease.

Eddy Showers replaced Cameron. Although the audiences loved Eddy, Julie found herself uncomfortable with his monologue. She disliked his use of foul language and wondered why Greg added him to the group.

New York proved successful for Faye as well. Several Broadway producers had seen her performance and she'd been asked to come to four auditions. So far she hadn't heard anything, but Greg assured her these things took time.

With her hectic East Coast tour, Julie found she had little opportunity to get to Minter. Lance's graduation dominated the Memorial Day weekend and Jill's advanced pregnancy captured her thoughts.

The phone rang and she set aside her mental wanderings. "Hi, Mom," Lance greeted her. "How would you like a roommate in Los Angeles?"

"You got the job! When do you start?"

"The first Monday in July. I thought I'd drive out the last week of June and find a place to live. You know kind of get acquainted before I have to start work."

"Will you be in Philadelphia on Saturday?" Julie asked.

"I wouldn't miss your last show for anything. I'll be flying in on Saturday morning. I have a friend from school out there and he's going to let me crash at his place. Are you going to try and contact Devan?"

"You know better than to ask such a question. Why spoil my last show by looking for someone who doesn't want to be found?"

Before hanging up, Julie spoke with Jill. She breathed a sigh of relief when Jill assured her that the doctor had predicted it would be another two weeks before the baby would arrive. She wanted to be there, wanted to hold her new grandchild within hours of its birth.

~ * ~

Devan watched as Jerry and Karen entered the waiting area of the Philadelphia airport.

Jerry waved and made his way to Devan's side.

"You look tired, Buddy," Jerry remarked. "Maybe you shouldn't have met us."

"Nonsense. I've looked forward to today all week. I wish I could say the same about tomorrow night. I don't know why I ever said I'd go to see Julie."

"You're going to be there for the same reason I'm going. You love her. Only with you, it's more than love between old friends. Are you going to tell her how you feel?"

"I already have. I wrote her a letter telling her I'd been her secret admirer. I don't know what I thought she'd do after she read it, but—"

"We have a lot to talk about," Jerry said. "Let's grab our luggage and go somewhere private."

Devan sat at the table in Jerry's hotel room. Karen had, conveniently, decided to go shopping, giving them time to talk.

"This is quite a suite," Devan commented. "Lauer must have paid a small fortune for it."

"He wanted to, but I wouldn't let him. He's not the enemy, you know. He wants the same thing we do. He wants what's best for Julie."

"Is that what we want? I don't know anymore. I thought—"

"You thought she'd call you at work once she read your letter. She might of, if she'd read it."

"Do you mean he didn't give it to her?"

"He gave it to her. She read the first two paragraphs and tore it up."

Devan pushed his chair away from the table and went to the patio door. *What have I done to her? Have I become such a monster? I wanted nothing more than to make her happy. I want to hold her and tell her how much I love her.*

"She tore it up because she thought they'd known you'd been sending her roses and kept it from her. When she asked if you gave her Todd's number or address, they said no. It might be hard to take, but you're responsible for this mess and somehow you'll have to straighten it out."

Devan continued to stare out at the Philadelphia skyline. "I want to change things, but I don't know how. More than anything else, I'm afraid of her reaction. I'm just vain enough to think she still wants me, but my ego is so fragile, I don't want her to reject me."

"Whatever happens, don't expect her to run into your arms. She's been hurt, not once, but three times."

"Three?" Devan asked. He turned away from the window and faced Jerry.

"Three—Steve, you, and Royd McAlester. When Julie got to Texas it didn't take long for her to realize she looked exactly like his dead wife. She won't admit it, but Royd not wanting her for herself hurt."

"Does Jewel West make her happy?"

"It seems to. She's become more confident. It's like she's a different person on stage. Julie Weston becomes Jewel West, who is an older version of Julie Morgan. You'll see, tomorrow night."

Twenty-six

"I can't believe this is the last road show," Julie said, once Hunter parked the car.

"It's a little like high school graduation. You're leaving behind the familiar and standing on the brink of the unknown."

Hunter's choice of words, Julie decided, were certainly not the ones she wanted to hear. High school graduation brought back memories of Devan as well as the reunion. She wondered if he'd be there, or if he'd blow that off as well.

As usual, Julie and Faye went into the hotel, leaving Hunter and Eddy to wrestle with the luggage. Once in their room, they found gowns for this evening's performance lying on the beds. The designer Greg insisted on hiring had fit them over a week earlier and now the finished product left them stunned.

Like excited children, they tried them on. When Faye zipped up Julie's dress, Julie turned to look into the mirror. The form fitting, low cut bodice, with it's scalloped neckline, continued its sleek lines into a long straight skirt with a slit to the knee on the side. The watery lavender print suited her perfectly and gave the dress a summery air.

Julie studied her reflection then saw Faye standing beside her. "It looks like we found a fairy godmother. You look beautiful," Julie said.

"So do you. I certainly could never pull off a dress like yours, but this one is definitely me."

Julie agreed. The blue print complimented Faye's coloring well and the style, mid-calf skirt and bloused top, hid her figure flaws.

They both took off the dresses and began to get ready for the evening's performance.

"It's all yours," Julie said, once she finished her shower. She noticed their luggage sitting at the end of the bed and rummaged through it for a new pair of hose and something to wear to the club.

After dressing in jeans and a blouse, she put the dress back on its hanger and looked into the mirror. "What are you doing here, Julie Weston?" she asked the reflection. The words had no more than passed her lips, than the phone rang.

"Are you girls just about ready?" the man on the other end of the line greeted her.

"Cameron!" Where are you?"

"Waiting for you in the lobby, as usual. I'm almost starved."

"Give us five minutes."

Julie hung up the phone then knocked on the bathroom door. "Are you almost done, Faye? Cameron's downstairs waiting for us."

~ * ~

"Nothing changes," Cameron said to Hunter, when he returned to the sofa. "As usual, we're waiting in the lobby for Faye and Jewel."

Hunter looked up. "It's always worth the wait, though."

"Are you, well, you know, are you falling in love with her?"

"What do you think?"

"I think you've been in love with her since you first saw her in Rockford. Have you said anything?"

"No, we'll never be more than friends. No matter what she says, she's still in love with Devan Yates. If she weren't, she wouldn't have reacted so badly to performing in Philadelphia, in the town where he lives. I'd like to see him for myself, to find out what makes him so special."

"You'll get to meet him tonight."

"Tonight?" Hunter echoed. "I thought he—"

"Never underestimate Greg. He planned a reunion of The Musketeers. Jerry will be here and so will Devan."

Hunter shook his head, his thoughts racing. *How will Jewel react? Why did Greg have to go and find Devan? If Yates would only stay out of Jewel's life, there might be a chance for me to let her know how I feel.* He wished he could rid his mind of such thoughts. He could never tell Jewel of his feelings, never profess his love for her.

"This looks like a serious conversation," Jewel's voice invaded his thoughts. "I heard someone down here wanted to eat. I'm almost starved myself, so what's the hold up?"

Hunter got to his feet and took Jewel's hand. "Can't eat too much, you know. Greg's got a big party planned for after the show."

"I wish he hadn't done that. I'd like to do something quiet. Something with just us. No press or people who don't even know who we really are."

"Well, we can have our party now," Cameron said. "There's a nice restaurant next to the club. You and Hunter can take his car. Faye, Eddy, and I will follow you in mine."

~ * ~

"I can't believe we're actually going to meet the people you grew up with, Dad," Todd commented.

Devan looked across the table at his son. He could believe it. After spending two days with Jerry, the last thirty years had melted away. Now with Julie's show in an hour and a half, his fears about seeing her were returning. "It's no big deal. It's only Jerry and... ah... Julie."

"What are you going to say to her?" Todd persisted.

"Congratulations, I hear you're a star. It sounds appropriate, don't you think?"

"You know what I mean. I know how you feel about her. Be honest with me."

"You want honest. I'm certain you do know how I feel about her, what you don't know is how she feels about me. She thinks I'm the biggest jerk who ever walked the face of the earth. I'm beginning to think she's right."

Andrea reached across the table and touched Devan's hand. "You're not a jerk, Dad. You just made some poor decisions."

Devan nodded in agreement. "I made some poor decisions all right, like coming here tonight and letting Lauer talk me into wearing this monkey suit. I hate wearing a tux."

"Nonsense," Andy reassured him. "I think you look rather dashing."

Devan looked around the room, hoping to see something to help him change the subject. "There's Jerry and Karen. He looks as uncomfortable as I feel."

He watched as they approached their table and stood to greet them.

"Hey, Dev," Jerry said, "don't you look dashing?"

"If one more person tells me I look dashing, I'll be tempted to hit them," Devan replied, trying to make light of the situation.

"Come on, Yates, I thought you business executives liked to get all dressed up and go to fancy parties. You've always been big man on campus, in and out of school."

Jerry and Karen seated themselves, before Devan replied, "I've always hated these things. Missy used to drag me to parties where I had to wear a tux. I remember feeling like a penguin."

"Not me," Jerry said. "I rather enjoy evenings like this. Working at the plant, I rarely get a chance to dress in anything other than blue jeans."

Devan laughed, then made the necessary introductions.

"It's a pleasure," Todd said. "Up until this past week, I can't ever remember hearing my dad talk about growing up. Now we can't shut him up. Are you two actually part of Jewel West's monologue?"

"Part of it?" Jerry echoed. "We're all of it. All the crazy things we did, she didn't leave anything out. Kids today don't have the fun we did. We lived in a different time warp. We weren't boyfriends and girlfriends. We all dated other people. We were just good friends. Kids don't have relationships like ours anymore."

"So, what's everyone going to have for dinner?" Devan asked, in the hope of changing the subject without being overly obvious. "Have anything you want, my treat."

"I think we should go a little light on supper," Jerry added. "Greg is planning a big party after the show. We're all invited."

Devan looked up from the menu. "Party? He planned a party? What does this guy do anyway? Does he make a career out of manipulating people's lives? Do you know him?" He watched Jerry's face and wondered how the questions affected him.

"I know him, but I know Frank Allen better. Does Greg manipulate people? Of course he does. He's Julie's agent. That's what she pays him to do. He also makes certain she's happy and protected."

"Who's Frank Allen?" Andy asked, before Devan could voice the same question.

Karen smiled. "Frank discovered Julie. He runs a club called Allen's Alley, in Chicago. After Greg showed an interest in her, Frank took over as her lawyer."

"Her lawyer?" Devan exploded. "What's wrong with the lawyers in Minter?"

"They don't practice entertainment law," Jerry snapped. "With Greg in Chicago, it's better she have legal counsel in the same city. Frank does a good job of looking out for her interests."

"Is that what they're calling it these days?" Devan asked.

"It's not what you think, Dev," Jerry said. "Heaven knows I wanted Frank to be special to Julie, but she wouldn't let him get close."

"Does she let anyone get close?" Devan questioned.

"No. A lot of people have tried, Frank, Greg, and even Hunter, but they're nothing more than good friends. Anymore, Julie cultivates good friends, but damn it, I wish she'd cultivate a lover. Devan, I wish—"

"Wishes are for fools," Devan interrupted. "I gave up wishing weeks ago. I can't take back yesterday and tomorrow is already arranged."

Jerry laughed. "Now you sound like me. I said those same words to Julie's kids back in January. Maybe we can't take back yesterday, but Julie and I mended our fences. Don't you think it's time you did the same thing?"

Devan's anger began to rise, not at Jerry, but at himself. Every word of what Jerry said hit home. Julie didn't let anyone get close to her because of what he had done. "Order whatever you want," he said pushing back his chair. "I think I need a drink."

Before he could get up, Jerry grasped his arm. "Not tonight, Yates," he said, through clenched teeth. "You're going to be stone cold sober when you see Julie. I can't believe you're a drinker, but I don't think it would take much to push you into it tonight. If you want to drink, wait until the party. I'm sure you'll find plenty of champagne."

"Have you ever been to one of these parties?"

"No. I don't think Julie's ever been to one of them, either."

"I thought it was what people like Julie do. They put on a show, party until dawn and drink themselves silly."

"This must be your frustration talking. You know better than to say anything so stupid. You, of all people, should know what her schedule is like. Sometimes they drive as much as two hundred miles between shows. There just isn't any time for parties."

Devan nodded. He needed to put his own hurt feelings, his shame for what he'd done, on the back burner. Tonight belonged to Julie. With her watchdogs hovering over her, he'd have no chance to make a fool of himself. Things would be better this way.

~ * ~

Julie picked at her food. For the first time in weeks, her stomach churned and tied itself in knots. When she had at last eaten enough to satisfy Hunter, she pushed her plate away.

"It doesn't look like you're going to eat anymore, so we'd better get over to the club," Hunter said. "We can slip out the back door here and get in backstage without running into the press. They'll be setting up the TV cameras."

"TV cameras? What in the world for?" Julie questioned.

"Tonight is special. The Comedy Network asked to tape the show and Greg decided it would be good publicity for *Black And White*," Hunter replied.

Julie signed deeply. She didn't know if she wanted to be the subject of a Comedy Network special. She just wanted tonight to be over so she could go back to Minter and relax for a couple of weeks.

She followed Hunter through the back alley, which connected the two buildings. Inside the club, she went directly to the dressing room assigned to her.

For the first time in weeks, the small room blossomed with floral arrangements. Excitedly, she looked at the cards, expecting to see Devan's name written on at least one of them. When she didn't find what she'd been looking for, she eased herself into the chair in front of the lighted mirror. Out of exasperation with the situation, she covered her face with her hands and began to cry. *Why did I expect flowers from Devan? Why does a single rose in a bud vase seem so important, when this room virtually blooms as though it were a green house?*

~ * ~

Devan followed Jerry and Karen into the lobby of the theater. The club had begun to fill and he marveled at the capacity of the room. It came as a shock when they were escorted to a table close to the stage.

"I thought we were supposed to surprise Julie," he said to Jerry. "How can we surprise her sitting right down front in full view?"

"She won't be able to see us. The stage lights are almost blinding and the audience area is darkened. She'll know the audience is here, but she can't see who they are. Believe me, we'll be a surprise. When I talked to her Thursday night, I wished her luck and told her I'd see her in Minter."

Devan looked around the room. Even though he knew he would recognize no one, he enjoyed people watching. At affairs like this, you saw people at their best and he wondered how others would view him tonight.

Across the room, he saw Jim Prescott lift his hand in greeting. At the same table, sat Meg, George and Shirley, as well as Dan Conklin and his wife. *Minter's elite, all dressed in their best to honor one of their own.*

"Jerry, I'm glad you made it."

Devan looked up at the man who had just spoken.

"You must be Devan Yates," the man continued, extending his hand. "I'm Greg Lauer, Jewel's agent."

"Mr. Lauer," Devan said, taking the man's hand. "This is my son, Todd, and his fiancée, Andrea Schaller."

Devan watched as Greg shook hands with Todd and Andy while insisting they call him Greg.

"Could I have a word with you in private, Devan?" Greg asked.

Devan cringed at how easily the man used his first name, as he pushed pack his chair to follow Greg to a quiet corner.

"I owe you an apology for the way I talked to you on Sunday. I had no right to say the things I did. My only excuse is my concern for Jewel."

"Concern for Jewel," Devan repeated. "You must realize I don't know Jewel West. I hardly know Julie Weston. Thanks to her husband, Julie Morgan, the girl I knew, almost died. Have you read *The Stepford Wives*? I think he tried to turn her into one of them. When we were together, I tried to bring back the person I knew. Jerry tells me you've continued the resurrection. I hope so. She deserves the happiness she used to enjoy."

"You do care for her, don't you? What will happen when you meet her tonight?"

Before Devan could reply, the house lights dimmed, then came back up again. "There's my cue," Greg said. "I'm needed on stage. We'll talk more at the party, later. You will be there, wont you?"

Devan nodded, then watched the younger man go backstage. *What will happen when I meet her tonight? I guess I won't know until the time comes.* He made his way back to the table, just as the lights dimmed completely.

The footlights came up and a young man took the stage. "Good evening, ladies and gentlemen," he said. "My name is Cameron Zimmer and I'm your host tonight. As you all know, we're here to honor a very talented lady, Miss Jewel West. I had the good fortune of traveling with Jewel during the first weeks of her career. In my new position, as an assistant to Greg Lauer in Los Angeles, I will be overseeing her future. Tonight, I, along with Rob Hunter, Faye Tallman, and Eddy Showers will give you an idea of what makes a terrific lady like Jewel tick. To start the evening, Greg Lauer, our boss, would like to say a few words."

Devan watched the stage, as Greg came from the wings to shake hands with Cameron.

"Three months ago, I attended an amateur night at a club called Allen's Alley, in Chicago. When the program consisted of a ladies' night, I wondered why I came. Don't get me wrong, I love the ladies, but without a good mix between the sexes, I get tired of hearing about the joy of childbirth, the pain of menstrual cramps, the depression of PMS, and those beasts called men."

Greg paused until the laughter from the audience died down, then continued. "By the time Jewel West's portion of the program came, I only hoped her monologue would pass quickly. To my surprise, an almost shy lady took the stage and began by saying, 'I come from Minter—Minter, Wisconsin, small town USA, and I had three of the greatest friends in the world. There was Jerry and Sandy and Devan and me.'"

The opening words of Julie's monologue, took Devan back to the Minter of thirty years ago. In his mind's eye, he saw Julie as a teenager; saw her at the lake, planning and participating in the various pranks they played and heard her giving the Salutatorian address at graduation. He found himself jolted abruptly from his memory of the past when the room exploded in exuberant applause. All around him, chairs were being pushed back and enthusiastic guests were getting to their feet. He focused his attention of the stage and saw Julie coming from the wings to join Greg.

~ * ~

"You look beautiful," Hunter whispered. He massaged her shoulders with his hands, while they listened to Greg's introduction from the wings.

"Thank you. I feel scared. I know it's just another show, but it's the last show. It's like you said, this is kind of like graduation. You know, leaving behind the familiar and standing on the brink of the unknown. At my graduation, I gave the Salutatorian address. I remember it word for word. 'Live for today. Reach for your dreams. Celebrate tomorrow. The future is yours, grasp it, mold it, make it better than the past.' Up until now, I haven't lived those words. For the first time in my life, I'm reaching for my dream. Help me hold on to it."

Hunter turned her to face him, the pulled her into his arms. "I love you, Jewel West," he whispered, before he kissed her.

He had taken her by surprise. After three months on the road, she hadn't expected anything like this, hadn't imagined she could so enjoy Hunter's attentions.

"And now, the lady you've come here to honor, Miss Jewel West!" they heard Greg say, just before the deafening applause began.

"What a reception, and it's all for you," Hunter said, bringing her hand to his lips. "Break a leg!"

Julie put on her most brilliant Jewel West smile, winked at Hunter, and made her way onto the stage.

In the bright stage lights, Greg waited for her, his hands extended. Beyond the lights, she knew the audience had gotten to its feet. Greg kissed her cheek, then handed her a second microphone.

"Thank you, thank you everyone," she said. "I never expected anything like this. If I'm dreaming, please don't wake me up."

"Well, Jewel," Greg began, "the best is yet to come. To begin with, we have some very special guests. From Minter, Wisconsin, Mr. Lance Weston and from Honolulu, Hawaii, Captain Mark Weston and his wife, Keoki."

Julie turned to face the opposite side of the stage and saw her sons and Keoki coming from the wings. Mark, in his dress uniform, reminded her of her brother, Jack, and Lance looked equally handsome in his tux.

"We're very proud of you, Mom," Mark said, when Greg handed him the microphone. "Jill wanted to be here, but she's been a little busy this afternoon. Jennifer Jewel, JJ, came into the world at four this afternoon. Karl and Jill called the hotel just before we left to come here. Congratulations, Grandma."

Julie hugged her sons, unable to say a word. Even if she could have thought of something to say no one would have heard her over the applause.

"Just what was it like having Jewel West as your mom?" Greg asked.

"She may look like Mom and sound like Mom, but she's a whole new person," Mark began. "The more I see of Jewel West, the more I love her. It's wonderful to see her so alive and happy."

After Lance said a few words, Greg escorted the boys to chairs at the back of the stage. Cameron took her hand and turned her back toward the audience. "The program is a little different, tonight, Jewel. Hunter won't be leading off. You'll be starting the show, because tonight's your night. All these people have come to hear your monologue and ours are to be only a complement."

"Thank you, Cameron," Julie began. "It's a pleasure to be here. I want to start by thanking all of you." She motioned toward the audience. "Thank you for coming and making tonight special. As you just heard, I'm a grandma. I hadn't planned on it happening for about a week, so I'm a bit overwhelmed. Of course, I'm certain you know my monologue has nothing to do with being a grandma.

"I'm from Minter—Minter, Wisconsin, small town USA." The opening words brought more applause and put her at ease. She began the now familiar lines pausing in places she'd learned produced laughter, which could drown out her next words.

When she finished, she held out the microphone to Cameron. "Not so fast, little lady. You're spending the evening up here, with me. To begin with, we thought this audience would like to meet The Musketeers of Minter, so we invited them to come."

"You what?" she half whispered, forgetting the live mike she held in her hand, as well as the people just beyond the footlights.

"We invited them to come here tonight and they accepted." Cameron turned toward the wings. "Jerry, Devan, come on out and see Jewel."

Julie could feel her eyes widen and her face flush, as Jerry joined her on stage, followed closely by Devan. Jerry took her in his arms and hugged her tightly.

"What are you two doing here?" The audience laughed, but she ignored them. "You're back in Minter, Jerry, I know you are. You told me you'd see me there on Monday."

"You shouldn't believe everything you hear," Jerry teased.

Julie turned toward Devan, her emotions churning, as she allowed him to hug her. "Devan, I didn't expect—"

"I know. We're supposed to be a surprise. Your agent arranged it."

"You certainly are a surprise. I'll have to have a long talk with Greg, later."

Cameron joined the group. "Well, guys, what was it like growing up with Jewel West?"

"We didn't grow up with Jewel West, we knew Julie Morgan," Jerry said. "Everything she says about growing up is true. We did it all. Devan reminded me, just the other day of the first time we met. Tell them about it, Dev."

Devan reached for Julie's hand and locked her fingers in his. "As I recall, I was the new kid on the block and no one warned me about Julie. Being a dumb kid, with a big male ego to boot, I allowed her to talk me into racing her to the raft at the lake. I gave everyone a good laugh, since Jerry neglected to tell me she swam anchor on the girl's relay team."

Julie couldn't help but laugh at the memory. "I would have told you, but you didn't ask, Yates. You were too concerned about racing a girl. I can't help it if you assumed you could beat me. You know what they say about assumptions."

For a moment all the hurts disappeared and they had gone back in time thirty years. They were the good friends who had done all the crazy things she told people about in her monologue. Devan put his arm around her shoulders and she wanted to throw her arms around his neck and beg him to love her again, but she restrained. Had it not been for Greg, he wouldn't even be here.

He continued speaking, forcing her to remember where they were. "You're right, of course, I never could quite measure up, not at the lake or in the classroom. Your success is something we're all so very proud of."

"Thank you, Devan," she said.

"Jerry," Cameron continued, "from what we hear, you know her the best. You stayed in Minter, remained close. Jewel says you two worked together, had some good times, even some bitter arguments."

"We certainly have. I can personally vouch for the good times as well as the rocky ones. She's a perfectionist. If she can't do it well, she won't do it. No matter what she tackles, she gives it one hundred percent, maybe even one hundred and ten percent. It's true with everything from being a terrific mom, to graduating from college with honors while taking care of a house, husband, and three active kids, to being the best personnel director LisPro has ever had."

Jerry turned toward Julie. "By the way, you don't want to come back to work at the plant, do you? Tom's still looking for your replacement."

Julie laughed. "You know I don't believe you. I talked to Tom, just the other day, and he assured me he'd found someone who is very well suited for the position."

"It doesn't hurt to ask," Jerry said, prompting laughter and applause from the audience. Jerry and Devan both were ushered back to the sitting area, while Julie remained with Cameron.

"Don't look so worried, Jewel. This is all in fun and you'll have time to see your friends at the party after the show," Cameron assured her.

"Our first guest this evening is the woman who has shared a room with you for the last three months, Miss Faye Tallman."

Julie stood next to each of her friends as they told stories about her antics while on the road, embellishing each story for the sake of a laugh.

Hunter came on stage as the last, rather than the first, and told his own stories about Julie. He related everything from afternoon swims to finding someone his own age to relate to. He ended his portion of the show with, "and now this lovely lady will be my love interest in our new show, *Black And White*. I thought tonight we could begin rehearsals." Without warning, he took her in his arms and kissed her.

Julie surprised herself by not holding back, but returning his kiss with equal passion. When at last they broke apart, the audience cheered.

Cameron, once again, took over the microphone. "So, ladies and gentlemen, tonight we've given you a taste of what Jewel West is like. You've heard about Jewel West, Julie Weston, and Julie Morgan.

Everyone sees her differently, has different memories and perceptions of who she is. To those of us who hold her future in our hands, she is a star who will shine bright in the heavens of the world of entertainment. I'm sorry to say tonight is your farewell to the road, Jewel. It suited you well. I look forward to representing you in Los Angeles."

Julie took several bows, before stepping from the stage to mingle with the audience. She accepted congratulations and greetings from those she knew and from those who were strangers, while the TV cameras captured it all.

"Miss West," a reporter said. "Were you as surprised as you appeared when you saw Jerry, Devan, and your kids?"

"Yes. I expected to see Lance, but the others were totally unexpected. How Greg got Mark and Keoki here is beyond me. I did know Devan lived in the city, but I didn't expect to see him tonight. It's not like the old days. We don't know each other very well, anymore."

"Is this true, Mr. Yates?" the reporter asked.

Julie turned to see Devan standing behind her.

"Unfortunately, it is. Things are different when you grow up. You're not as carefree anymore. You don't just pick up the phone to say hi. There are too many things going on in your life and not enough time to be friends."

The reporter moved on to interview others, and Julie looked up at Devan. "I didn't think I'd see you here tonight."

"Greg asked me to come," he said, his voice low.

"Otherwise, you wouldn't have been here?"

"The show sold out early. I couldn't get tickets."

"I understand." She started to leave, but Devan caught her arm to stop her.

"Julie," he said.

She turned back and made eye contact. "Don't Devan, please don't. I can't stand to be hurt anymore. We're good friends, right? Let's just leave it that way."

"Jerry says you cultivate good friends, he thinks you should cultivate a lover. I agree with him."

"What would I do with a lover?" She prayed her eyes wouldn't betray the feelings she harbored for him.

"I told you, months ago, you need to be loved and made love to often."

"Right now, the only thing I need is the love of an audience. It's a different kind of love, a very different kind of love. It gives me great satisfaction. Just listening to them, the way they were tonight almost compares to physical love. I've changed. I'm not scared Julie Weston anymore. I'm not mourning my husband, or you, or Royd McAlester. I'm Jewel West, I'm an entirely different person."

"Will you be at the class reunion?"

His question caught her off guard. "Yes," she said, without thinking. "How about you?"

"I debated, but I finally decided it's time I saw everybody again. I guess this is it, there are other people here who want to see you."

Devan melted back into the crowd and Julie watched him disappear. She'd intentionally pushed him away, intentionally said *no, Devan*, when all she wanted was to love him. Now she knew she must live with the consequences. Jerry's words of a few months earlier came back to her, 'if this is meant to be' but how could anything happen when she'd just said absolutely no? *What have I done,* she asked herself.

A sinking feeling, as though the rug had been pulled from beneath her feet, came over her. She shook her head to rid herself of the unwanted sensation.

"Jewel," she looked up to see Hunter standing in front of her, a look of concern on his face. "We think you ought to come over here and sit down for a while."

"Don't be silly. There are a lot of people here I want to see. There's a whole table of people from Minter and—"

"And nothing," Greg said. "They can come to you. You should relax a bit. You've been on your feet all night."

"Not you, too," Julie commented, trying to sound annoyed.

Greg put his arm around her shoulders and she shuddered slightly at his touch. "Come on, Jewel, let's get you over to a chair and have someone fix you something to eat."

"It's not necessary. I've already eaten supper," she protested, her words sounding slurred, as though she was drunk. She knew her friends were right, she was beginning to see the warning signs for herself. If she delayed in sitting down and eating much longer, she would slip away into unconsciousness.

"Sure you did," Hunter said, his words bringing her back to the reality of the minute. "You picked at your food. You only ate enough to satisfy me. I've seen a canary eat more. Now come on and join us."

Julie couldn't argue with Hunter and followed him to a table where Frank and Dorah were already seated.

"Are you okay, kiddo?" Dorah inquired.

"I'm fine," Julie lied.

"You don't look fine," Frank said. "Especially when you were talking to—"

"To Devan? How did you want me to look? Devan's appearance here took me by surprise. The realization he wouldn't have come if Greg hadn't arranged it, hurt."

Greg set a plate of food in front of her and she knew he'd heard her words. "I thought you would see each other and clear the air."

"You shouldn't try to play matchmaker, Greg. It doesn't become you. Don't get me wrong, I'm grateful for everything you've done for me, but Julie Weston's past is something you can't change. I'm the only one who can deal with it."

~ * ~

Devan turned back and watched Julie for a moment. The look on her face disturbed him. He wanted to go to her and take her in his arms, force her to hear him out. Instead, he went back to his own table and she now stood, surrounded by her watchdogs.

"So?" Jerry inquired.

"So what?" Devan said, answering Jerry's question with one of his own.

"How did it go? Did you two clear the air?"

"Julie cleared it. She doesn't want to be hurt anymore. She doesn't want me and I can't blame her. I wish I hadn't said I'd come to the reunion, but I can't back out now. I told her I'd be there. I just don't know if I want to spend another evening with her."

"So, you're giving up on her, just like that," Jerry said. "I told you not to expect her to run into your arms."

"I guess you did. Well, this is a party, isn't it? It certainly isn't a time for long faces. What do we have here? A champagne glass and a full bottle in the middle of the table, how convenient."

Devan poured himself a glass of wine and held it high. "To Julie, to Julie Morgan, to Julie Weston, to Jewel West, to whomever the hell she becomes next. May her star shine bright."

He drank the wine in one gulp, then reached for the bottle to pour another glass.

"Aren't you going to try again, Dad?" Todd asked.

"No. Once is sufficient, more than enough," Devan replied, again emptying the glass.

Twenty-seven

Devan awoke to the ringing of the phone, his head pounding. *How much champagne did I drink last night? Too much, but not enough to block Julie from my mind.*

"Jerry's on the phone for you," Todd said, after entering the room. The open door brought unwanted light into the darkened room. As much as the light hurt his eyes, he knew he had to answer the phone. "Good morning," he greeted Jerry. His tongue felt thick and fuzzy and his words sounded the same.

"I called to say good-bye, Devan." Jerry said.

"Good-bye!" Devan became immediately alert. "What time is it anyway?"

"It's ten. Karen and I are going to take a cab to the airport."

"What time do you have to be there?"

"The flight leaves at two. We should be there at least an hour early."

"I'm getting up right now. I'll be at your hotel by eleven-thirty. Wait for me."

By ten-thirty, Devan had showered and shaved. "Is Andy coming over today?" he asked Todd.

"Later. Are you going to take Jerry and Karen to the airport?"

Devan nodded.

"Are you going to talk to her?"

"I don't know why, but I thought I'd try."

"You'd better have something to eat before you go. You really tied one on last night."

"I'll be fine. I'm going to grab a sandwich with Jerry and Karen on the way to the airport," Devan said, as he poured coffee into a travel mug and headed out the door.

~ * ~

Julie sat at the airport. It seemed as though the entire waiting area was filled with people from Minter. She wished the flight had been non-stop instead of having an hour layover in Detroit. She wanted to get home and away from the events of the past twenty-four hours.

Greg and Hunter sat on either side of her, with Frank and Dorah across from them. Their flight for Chicago would leave twenty minutes after hers for Madison. For a few weeks, they would all resume their normal lives, away from the overwhelming pace set by Jewel West's road show.

"Thank you for last night," she said. "I know you all had a hand in it. I enjoyed every minute of it, especially the surprise of seeing everyone and being roasted. Now I'm looking forward to a couple of weeks of lying in the sun and getting acquainted with my new granddaughter. Then it's off to California."

"I heard Lance got a job in Los Angeles," Dorah commented. "Guess the two of you will be sharing an apartment for a while."

"We thought it would be a good idea. At least for the first few months. We'll go to the firm next week and arrange for a letter of credit then he'll go out there and look for an apartment for us. I'm relieved not to have to be alone when I get there."

Julie sat, quietly reflecting on the changes in her life these last few months.

"What did you say to him last night?" Greg asked.

"What did I say to who?" Julie countered, knowing full well he meant Devan.

"Don't act coy with me, Jewel, you know I'm talking about Devan."

"I don't think it's any of your business."

"I do. We all do. What did you say to him?"

"I told him I didn't want to be hurt again. Let's change the subject. This one doesn't suit me well."

"Maybe it doesn't, but you have to face it."

"Why? It's over. It ended the day Devan moved to Philadelphia and left me behind. I knew his reasons were valid, but he handled it all wrong. I could have accepted his transfer if we could have talked about it first."

Julie searched Greg's face to see if he accepted her explanation. She needed to make everyone believe Devan had become unimportant to her.

"Julie."

She turned at the sound of Devan's voice, her heart pounding wildly in her chest. "About last night," she began, "if I hurt you, I'm sorry."

"That's not what I wanted to talk to you about. Let's go somewhere that we can be somewhat alone." He took her hand and led her across the room to a secluded corner. "I could say I'm sorry for what happened between us from now until the end of time and it wouldn't change anything. Sorry isn't the magic word. We may never be lovers, but I refuse to lose you as my friend. I want you to have this."

Devan reached into his pocket and produced a business card. Julie took it and ran her fingers over the embossed letters.

"Is this a guarantee of friendship, Devan? It seems you refused my calls before."

"I didn't refuse them. Everything was so hectic between starting a new position and running to the hospital, the messages were a week old before I found them on my desk."

"That explains why you didn't return the calls I made to your office, but why didn't you give me Todd's number?"

"I'm giving it to you now. I didn't realize it was unlisted, not at first. I promise, I'll be there for you."

"Todd's home number," she said, turning over the card to read what he'd written on the back. "I'm surprised."

"It's where I'll be for the time being. I'm looking for a place of my own. I know you could have gotten it from your friend, Greg, but it wouldn't have been the same. I want you to have it. If you need me, call. I'll be there for you and if I'm not, I'll call you back, I promise."

Before she could reply, Devan took her in his arms and quickly kissed her. "Have a good flight. Remember, if you need me, I'll be there for you."

As quickly as he had taken her in his arms, he released her and returned to where Jerry and Karen were seated.

Julie watched him go without looking back at her. "The Musketeers," she whispered. "I thought nothing would ever separate us. Whatever happened to our bond? Sandy's dead, Jerry's married, and Devan, thinks nothing of turning away from me."

She looked again at the number on the back of the card. The elusive number she'd tried so hard to obtain, and now she held it in her hand. Would they ever be able to bury the past and be friends again? "Good-bye Devan," she said, half to herself.

"Did you say something, Jewel?" Hunter asked.

She looked up, surprised to see him standing next to her. "Say something? Oh, no, I was just thinking out loud."

"They called your flight. Didn't you hear it?"

"I guess not." She turned toward the boarding area then having second thoughts, turned back. "Come to Minter for the Fourth, Hunter. You can stay with us. I want you to spend the week and take me to my reunion. Please say you'll come."

"If it means so much to you, of course, I'll come."

"Thank you. One more thing. Kiss me. I need to know someone cares."

~ * ~

Jerry watched as Devan and Julie stood talking. After last night, he'd wondered if they would ever speak to each other again. He smiled when Devan took Julie in his arms and kissed her. Maybe he'd underestimated the two of them. He tried to read the thoughts behind Devan's expression when he turned from Julie.

The announcement of the flight to Madison coincided with Devan walking away.

"Guess this is good-bye," Devan said, when he got closer to where Jerry and Karen stood.

Jerry clasped Devan's hand. "It's too bad we don't have more time."

"Time is what it will take, Jer. No one is going to erase the damage we've done to each other in ten minutes. You'd better catch your plane. I'll see you in a couple of weeks at the reunion."

"I'll talk to her, Dev. Maybe by the time the reunion gets here things will be different."

"Maybe they will, but don't count on it."

Jerry turned toward the boarding area and caught a glimpse of Julie talking to Hunter. To his surprise, Hunter took her in his arms and kissed her tenderly.

Ahead of him, Jerry saw Lance enter the jetway and he hurried to catch up. "Are you sitting next to your mother?" he asked.

"Why would that be of interest to you?"

"I need to talk to her. Will you change seats with me?"

Lance hesitated and Jerry guessed the reason. "I'm sitting next to Dan Conklin. You might be more comfortable next to Dan than to Karen."

Jerry seated himself in the aisle seat that had been assigned to Lance, and waited for Julie.

~ * ~

Julie said good-bye to her friends and hurried toward the boarding area. Minter pulled at her like a magnet. Although she would miss the excitement of the road, she longed for the relaxation of being home.

She checked her boarding pass when she saw Jerry sitting in the seat next to hers.

"Someone must have made a mistake," she said, looking around for Lance.

"No mistake, Julie. I changed seats with Lance. I think we should talk."

Jerry stood and allowed her to cross in front of him to take the window seat.

"So, what do you want to talk about? I'm open to any subject except Devan Yates."

"You certainly have a way of limiting a conversation, but like it or not, you'll hear me out."

"I don't like it. I don't like it at all."

"Give him a chance. He's miserable without you and I know you're miserable without him. Why can't you see it?"

"Please, stay out of this. If it's meant to be, we'll work it out. Right now, neither of us is ready to make a commitment. I'm just beginning a new life and he doesn't know what he wants."

Jerry clasped her hand and Julie wondered if she had made him understand. He still held her hand when the plane took off. They sat in silence until the upward climb ended and the plane leveled.

"You look tired, Julie," Jerry said, putting his arm around her shoulder. "Lean against me. Maybe you can catch a nap on the way home."

She moved in her seat and settled easily against his shoulder. Unexpectedly, a lump formed in her throat and tears sprang to her eyes.

"What's wrong?" Jerry asked, wiping a tear from her cheek with his finger.

"I don't think it's anything more than a let down. All those weeks on the road, the excitement of the last show, seeing Devan, being a grandma, maybe it's all too much."

"You need to rest," Jerry assured her.

He held her closer and she slipped off to sleep. Dreams of the future entered her mind before she fell into a deep and restful sleep.

Julie heard Jerry whisper her name in her ear. She had come to semi-awareness when the plane landed in Detroit and again at take off. Now Jerry's voice brought her fully awake.

"You're arm must be almost ready to fall off," she said, as she straightened to a sitting position.

"It's worth it to see you get your rest. I didn't want to wake you, but we'll be landing soon."

She reached into her purse for a mirror, brush, and lipstick. Over the past weeks, she'd learned to appear at her best even when no one would be looking. You never knew when someone with a camera would catch you off guard.

"Just how are we getting back to Minter?" she questioned, once she was pleased with her appearance.

"Karl is coming up to get Lance, and Tom said he'd pick us up."

The plane landed and for some reason, Julie found her friends allowing her to deplane ahead of them. Several Minter residents greeted her when she entered the terminal, holding a banner, which read *Welcome Home Julie.*

Tom was the first to come forward and greet her warmly. "You look great," he said, above the clamor of the crowd gathered to meet her.

"Miss West, how long will you be home?" a reporter asked, once he elbowed his way through the crowd.

"I'll be around until the week after the Fourth of July, then I'll be moving to Los Angeles."

She allowed the questioning to continue for a few minutes then excused herself to retrieve her luggage.

"Welcome home, Mom," Karl said, when he finally made his way to her side.

"Shouldn't you be with Jill and JJ?"

"They're sleeping and I couldn't let you arrive with no ride home for Lance."

Julie agreed then pointed out her bag on the luggage carousel.

"Is this all the luggage you have?" Karl asked, after he pulled the bag from the conveyor belt.

"I've learned to pack light. What didn't fit in this bag, Faye and Cameron are shipping out to me."

"How did it go last night?"

"It was like a fairy tale and I was the fairy princess. Now tell me all about my granddaughter."

"You can look at these on your way home." Karl produced a packet of pictures from his shirt pocket and handed it to her.

She flipped through the pictures quickly, as she followed Karl from the terminal. For the first time, she realized her friends had already left the building.

A long white limo, parked just outside the building, caught her attention. To her surprise, Tom got out of the car and held open the door for her.

Behind the limo, Julie recognized her own car with Lance at the wheel. A line of familiar vehicles had formed a caravan stretching to the furthest reaches of the parking lot.

"What an unnecessary expense," she commented.

"We couldn't let Minter's star ride home in my Jeep, could we?"

"I don't see why not. What about this parade of cars?"

"It's a tribute, Julie," Jerry said, from inside the limo. "Get in, so we can get you home."

Julie slid across the bench style seat to sit next to Tom's wife. Tom got in on the opposite side to occupy the right side of the seat. Across from them sat Jerry and Karen.

"You're all crazy. You know that, don't you?"

"Guess it doesn't hurt to be a little crazy. Look where it got you," Jerry teased.

The miles passed quickly as Julie answered questions about her weeks on the road, the time spent in Honolulu, the contract she'd signed with Vaureen and last night's performance. To her surprise, they pulled into the Oasis at the Minter exit, and the limo, as well as the caravan stopped.

"End of the line, Julie," Jerry said, opening the door.

Julie questioned his actions with a puzzled look. "But we aren't home yet."

"Close enough," Tom commented.

Jerry got out of the car first, then extended his hand to Julie and helped her out of the back seat.

To her amazement, a fire engine with Minter's insignia on the door waited for them, along with two Minter squad cars and several more vehicles.

"It seems to me," Jerry said, "a little bird told me somebody always wanted to be met by a fire engine."

"Frank told you?"

"Sounds about right," Jerry replied. "Now, Miss West, your coach awaits."

"Are you saying what I think you are? You don't expect me to ride into Minter in a fire engine, do you?" She watched as Jerry nodded. "I only said—I guess it doesn't matter what I said. Frank thought it was cute. Coming from a big city like Chicago, he'd never heard about anyone being met by a fire engine."

"We liked the idea," Tom said. "The press liked it as well. They're waiting for you in Minter. Now, up you go."

A light breeze tugged at Julie's skirt as two Minter firemen helped her up onto the back to he truck.

"You too, Jerry," Tom called.

Julie watched Jerry's expression change from Cheshire Cat grin to surprise.

"You're as much a part of this as Julie is," Dan assured him. "You're one of The Musketeers, always were. The rest of us never fit in. It's only right you should ride into town with her."

"I certainly didn't plan on this," Jerry said, as he climbed up beside her.

"Just like the old days," Julie commented. "All that's missing..." she stopped, unable to finish her sentence.

"All that's missing are Devan and Sandy. We could change things, at least in one respect."

Before Julie could say anything, one of the firemen called, "Hang on tight, Mrs. Weston," and the truck lurched ahead. Any attempts at conversation were lost to the blaring of the sirens.

They drove the five miles to the city limits, then slowed to almost a crawl as the parade of cars wound its way through the business district. Although the streets were lined with well-wishers, the faces were no more than an unrecognizable blur.

At last they pulled into the parking lot of the high school and Julie saw several vans from area TV stations. Cameras focused on the caravan and when Julie's feet hit the pavement, reporters came at her from every direction.

"Whose idea was this anyway?" she whispered through clenched teeth into Jerry's ear. "I feel like a sideshow attraction."

"What kind of a star are you, Miss West?" Jerry whispered back. "Everybody in show biz craves publicity and this is the best you can get. This comes from the heart, your hometown loves you."

Inside the gym, the bleachers were full of people she knew, as well as the curious, those anxious to get a look at Minter's celebrity of the moment.

"Welcome home, Julie," Clay Tanner, the principal of the high school greeted her. "Tonight it's Minter's turn to honor her own."

"When I came here as an English teacher, I was impressed with the school as well as its students. In the freshman class, I met a young lady by the name of Julie Morgan. Like so many other students, I saw in her a spark of enthusiasm which has now burst into a blazing inferno."

"Thank you, Clay, and you, my friends and neighbors. You've made me feel very special, but really, I'm still Julie Morgan Weston. The glass slipper I've put on has changed me only when I'm on stage. Off stage, I don't feel like a star. I only hope I will never become aloof or unattainable to my friends."

Behind her she heard a commotion and turned to see Hunter and Greg enter the gym, amid the applause of those gathered.

Before she could say anything, Hunter took her hand in his. "I knew Minter was a small town, I've heard you say it often enough, but really, Jewel, being escorted by two police cars and a fire engine? Don't you think it's a bit much?"

"It's all part of living in a small town, guys," Julie said, falling into an easy banter with her friends. "Besides, this is all Frank's fault."

"I suppose you have to blame it on someone." Hunter paused for the laughter his statement prompted. "Now, why don't you explain this fire engine and police car thing?"

"Let me explain, Julie," Clay insisted. "You see, gentlemen, small towns do things like this to honor their outstanding citizens."

"Like football, basketball, and baseball teams," Julie interrupted, trying to sound sarcastic.

"Times are changing, Julie. Now scholastics and even the FFA are included."

"Let me get this straight," Greg commented. "This is an honor and who better to receive it than Jewel West? As Jewel's agent, I've brought a gift to the people who know her best, for the town that dominates her monologues. Since not everyone could be at last evening's performance, we've brought the show to you. I have here the uncut tape of last night's gala."

Greg held up the videocassette and Julie shuddered, inwardly. "This could have waited until they showed the edited version on cable," she protested.

A loud '*No!*' sounded from the people seated on the bleachers.

"I agree with your friends, Jewel," Hunter said. "They deserve to see the whole thing, live and uncut. We have some folks bringing in a big screen TV and a VCR. Now, I see a space, right down front, for you to sit and enjoy the show, for a change."

Julie recognized the manager of the appliance store, along with two of his deliverymen, enter the gym with the TV and VCR.

The tape began with the interview done in her dressing room. She experienced the same apprehension as when she had watched the tape of her Texas performance, in the Rockford hotel room. Would her neighbors accept her, once they knew exactly what she did for a living?

Around her, laughter and applause put her at ease, allowed her to enjoy the good-natured teasing of her friends captured forever. The hour and a half tape gave her time to reflect on the events of the previous evening.

The tape ended and Hunter got to his feet, extending his hand to her. "And now, Miss West, I've been informed there will be a pot luck, in your honor, in the cafeteria. It's another small town custom, I'm told. Even though Greg and I came empty-handed, we've been told we can join you. Next time, we'll be better prepared."

~ * ~

"Let me get you something to eat," Greg said, once Julie finished greeting friends who came through the reception line.

"What?" she asked.

"Something to eat," Greg repeated.

They filled their plates and made their way to a table. "Now just how did you get here ahead of me when your flight for Chicago left twenty minutes after mine."

"I took my own plane to Philadelphia," Greg commented. "We flew directly into the county airport here. This has been planned for weeks. We have reservations for tonight and tomorrow and we want you to show us Minter. I think it's time we saw the place we've heard so much about."

Julie nodded. She would enjoy showing off her town, but deep down, she wished she were going to be spending the next two days with Devan. She thought about the business card he gave her before she boarded the plane for home, and wished she had the courage to call him.

Twenty-eight

A cool breeze blew in through the patio doors, and Julie got up to close them in order to avoid a draft in the house. She stood for a moment and allowed the breeze to kiss her cheek.

As she stared out at the dusk of evening, she thought about the turns her life had taken. She no longer led a private life. Over the past two weeks, she had been called to give interviews as well as to speak at various functions. Tonight, she enjoyed playing Grandma. Being with her kids had made the transition from Julie Weston to Jewel West a bit easier to handle.

From the den, JJ made baby noises in her sleep. Julie wondered if babies dreamed and if their soft moanings denoted pleasurable subconscious thoughts.

She closed the patio doors and went out to the kitchen to brew a cup of tea. Before sitting down, she switched on the stereo and engaged the cassette that sat in the holder. She didn't care what music she heard, she only needed some background noise to erase the silence of the house.

The soundtrack of *Evita* began before she settled into the recliner. She leaned back, closed her eyes and allowed herself to be transported to the weekend with Devan, in Milwaukee. With no prompting, she remembered the way he touched her shoulders, held her, and kissed her. She also remembered the look on his face, two weeks ago, when he gave her the card with his phone number on it. *We may never be lovers, Julie, but I refuse to lose you as a friend.* His words echoed in her ears.

In a week and a half, she would see him. How would she handle it? Maybe they could talk, try to overcome the invisible barrier between them, but with her moving to Los Angeles and him staying in Philadelphia, she doubted they could ever become close.

Good Night And Thank You, the words of the song prompted tears. Had she become like the main character in the musical, using men, like a revolving door, to gain success? *Good Night And Thank You— Don't Forget To Zip Up Your Fly.* The song continued and she thought of the men she'd been with in her life. Three, she'd only allowed three men to get close, and each of them had hurt her.

Had she hurt others? Frank would have easily slipped into my bed, become my lover, but I held him at arm's length.

"I love you, Jewel West," she heard Hunter say in her mind. *Does he love me? Should I give him a chance?*

Before she could answer her own questions, the phone rang. She picked it up, half expecting to find Devan on the other end.

"Hi Jewel," Hunter's voice surprised her.

"Hunter, it's good to hear from you."

"I wanted to check on next week. Are we still on, or should I make other plans?"

"Of course we're still on. I'm looking forward to spending the Fourth with you. Everyone is anxious to get to know you."

"Everyone?"

"All the neighbors. We're invited to a picnic and pool party at George and Shirley's after the parade."

"Picnic? What can I bring?"

"Yourself. We have the menu under control. George is doing a turkey on the grill and everyone else is bringing their specialties."

"Is someone bringing beans?"

"Yes, Jill."

"Good. Tell her to concentrate on JJ and I'll make them. I came to one pot luck empty handed and I don't plan to do it again."

Julie laughed. "I didn't know you could cook."

"I started out to be a chef, then worked my way through college cooking at a country club just outside Chicago. Once I got my degree, I went off to Hollywood to be a great producer. Instead I went back to the kitchen. Until someone decided I might be funny, that is. The rest, as they say, is history, a bit like you."

"Touché. When can I expect you?"

"Late afternoon on the third. Don't make plans. I'll take you out to dinner."

A wall went up in Julie's mind. The years of Steve's put downs about her weight and making a spectacle of herself in public returned, unbidden. "It's not necessary," she said, defensively. "I'll fix something here."

"I didn't say it was necessary. I said I'd like to take you to dinner."

"By the way," Julie began, anxious to change the subject. "I had a call from the Fourth of July committee this week. They want us to ride in the parade, to promote *Black And White*."

"I'd hoped to relax, but sure, why not? Vaureen will get a kick out of it."

"Good, because I already said we'd do it." Julie paused, unsure of what to say next.

"You sound a little strange, Jewel. Is something wrong?"

"No. I've just been sitting here, thinking. I shouldn't do that, shouldn't dwell on what can't be."

"You were thinking about Devan, weren't you?"

"How did you guess?"

"It's not hard. Don't forget, I know you pretty well. Maybe I shouldn't stay for the entire week."

"Don't be silly. There's no way you're backing out of the reunion. I still need an escort."

"Do you, or do you just think you need one?"

"I need one, end of discussion. Now, let's just drop the subject."

"For now," Hunter agreed. "Are you there alone?"

"Of course not. JJ and I are having a wonderful time. The kids took advantage of having a built in baby-sitter and went out for the evening."

"I see, and you're feeling a little sorry for yourself."

"Not really. I'm just putting my priorities in perspective."

"Okay, I won't push. Did Lance get to Los Angeles all right?"

"He arrived on Thursday. So far he's put the letter of credit on deposit, checked into a motel, and will start looking for an apartment next week."

"I should have said something before this. Tell him not to jump at the first place he sees. Have him stop at Cameron's office tomorrow and pick up the keys to my house."

"You have a house? Aren't you worried about it sitting empty for so long?"

Hunter laughed at Julie's question. "Of course, I worry. That's why I've been subletting it while I'm on the road. The tenants moved out today. It's completely furnished, so Lance can move right in and save those motel bills."

They continued their conversation for a few more minutes before hanging up.

The tape ended and Julie turned off the stereo. On an impulse, she picked up the video of her performance in Philadelphia and put it into the VCR. Using the remote, she fast-forwarded past the opening segment to the portion of the show where she met Devan.

She closely studied the exchange, rewinding and replaying the segment again and again. After several minutes she'd memorized every word of their exchange and every line on Devan's face had been etched into her memory.

The tape finished, and Julie picked up the phone. It would be late in Philadelphia, but Devan had insisted she call.

This is Todd and Devan's answering machine. We can't come to the phone right now, but please leave a message after the tone.

Julie waited for the message to end before hanging up. Devan had promised to return her call, but her own apprehensions kept her from speaking on the tape. She'd see him in a few days and addressing him face to face would be easier.

JJ's hungry cries gave Julie an excuse to get up and quit dwelling on Devan. Her granddaughter needed her, and that need came before any of her own.

~ * ~

Hunter held Julie's chair as she seated herself at the secluded table of the Cafe Parisian. He'd arrived an hour and a half earlier, carrying bags of groceries and a small cooler filled with meat.

"I didn't expect you to bring your dad's store," she'd greeted him.

"I didn't either. I only stopped to pick up a few things to make baked beans and the next thing I knew, Dad had the back of Mom's car looking like his delivery van. There's enough food here to feed an army. I hope Jill has room for all of it."

"We can always make room," Julie replied. She'd helped him carry in the food and put it away, before they left for the restaurant.

"This is quite a place," Hunter said, bringing thoughts of his arrival to an end.

"You know, it used to be a Burger Chef," she commented.

"You're kidding."

"No, it really did. I'd bring the kids here for hamburgers. Steve hated fast food, but the kids loved it, especially when they put in the works bar. The boys enjoyed being able to put anything they wanted on their burgers. I have to admit, I liked coming here, too. I used to adore a good hamburger and Steve wouldn't let me serve them at home. He called it 'junk food.' He said we were above eating things like hamburgers and hot dogs, although he'd scream when I went over the budget on food. It's nearly impossible to be a creative gourmet on a budget. Those days seem long ago."

"Good. Let's forget they ever happened. I've brought along something I want you to read." He reached into the pocket of his suit coat and produced a white business envelope.

Julie's heart pounded. She could only guess as to what the envelope contained. "Look, if that's what I think it is," she began.

Without giving her a chance to continue, Hunter held up his hand. "It's what you think it is and you are going to read it. The original plan was for you to read it while we were with you. I stopped at Greg's office on Friday and picked it up."

"Why in the world would he have kept such a thing?"

"Because, it's important."

Julie reached across the table and put her hand over Hunter's. "Before I read it, let me say something. In Philadelphia, you told me you loved me. If you meant what you said, don't make me do this. I've given the matter a lot of thought. Maybe we should become lovers off screen as well as on."

Hunter looked deep into her eyes, his gaze making her uncomfortable. "Don't think I haven't given the idea a lot of thought as well. It would be very easy to say yes. You have to know, it's not right."

Julie smiled, a warmth spreading through her body. "I didn't say it had to be right. I just want to know why we don't become lovers?"

"You're in love with someone else, Julie—"

His use of her real name came as a surprise. "You called me Julie. You've never called me anything but Jewel before. Why?"

"Because here you are Julie, and it's Julie who is in love with Devan Yates. As far as this being right is concerned, you said it yourself, when Vaureen offered you the part of Sylvie, you aren't black. Do you realize the amount of scandal we'd create?"

"But I'm not black on the show and I'm your lover. Why is this different?"

"The show is make-believe. The fans like their stars lily white. Unless you've made it big, they don't approve of black and white dating. Feelings don't matter. Your fans will make or break you in the next few months. I can't, I won't, jeopardize your future and neither will you."

"It doesn't seem fair," Julie said, a bit sadly.

"Life isn't fair. It won't ever be fair. There's a line between black and white, and people like us don't cross it."

The waitress arrived and took their order, ending the conversation. Julie knew the things Hunter said were true. Black and white didn't mix, never would for people like them. The thought of becoming Hunter's lover had been a spur of the moment idea, an exciting adventure. She'd thought it would make her happy, but would it be fair to Hunter? She didn't love him, not the way she should love a man whose bed she would willingly share.

"I had a call from Lance this morning," Hunter said, breaking the silence between them. "He's all settled in at the house. You know, I'm relieved not having it sit empty, even for such a short time."

"It still seems like a terrible imposition to me."

"Nonsense. Wait until you get to Los Angeles, you'll see. The house is huge, too big really. I think I bought it to say, look what the little black boy can do. I've been considering putting it on the market, getting something smaller, something more suited to my needs. Besides, the time you and Lance spend with me will give you the opportunity to find the right place. He's already talking about buying a house or a condo, but I've tried to discourage him. He needs to know where he wants to settle down and not get into a neighborhood not suited for him. For now, you'll both be better off with me."

"So, you're looking out for my interests as well as those of my son." Julie hoped her voice sounded light.

"Yes, I am, Julie. Now, I want you to read this letter."

Obediently, she opened the envelope she'd been nervously fingering throughout their conversation. The words on the taped together page had the same impact they'd had two months earlier.

Devan's confession to being her secret admirer left her hurt and angry. She automatically skipped the first two paragraphs, the words, which had haunted her ever since the afternoon in Greg's office. When she finished reading, she wiped away a tear with her napkin. "He cares," she whispered.

"We've been trying to tell you he did. I knew he cared as soon as I read the letter and I envied him, because it's obvious you care for him as well. Have you called him?"

"I tried, the other night, after I talked to you."

"And?"

"I didn't get an answer. I hung up as soon as the message ended."

"Then you didn't leave a message for him to call you back?"

"No. I'm not good on those things. I'm better face-to-face. I'll see him next Saturday night. We'll talk then."

"Are you certain you still want me—"

Julie cut Hunter's words short. "You're not leaving. I need you here for moral support. If I've misread this letter or worse yet, if I've killed my chances with Devan, I need you beside me to pick up the pieces."

The waitress served their dinners and they fell silent while they tasted the food. "This is excellent," Hunter commented, "and so is the company. You see, it's not so bad allowing me to take you to dinner."

"I don't always feel comfortable in local restaurants. It has nothing to do with you."

"If I'm not the problem, what is?"

"Bad question."

"I should have known all of this had something to do with your husband. I wish you'd put him behind you."

"I'm working on it. It's still pretty recent, you know. He's only been gone for eighteen months and I've only known about his second life for the last six. Someday it will be only a memory, but not just yet. Now, I didn't come here to talk about the past. I came to have a good time."

The table talk turned to more general things, including the natural beauty of Wisconsin.

"You know," Hunter said, "I grew up in Chicago and we never got up here. Mom and Dad were tied to the store all the time."

"Then I'm glad I made plans for the rest of the week."

"Plans?"

"We're going to the Dells. I want you to see the area where Steve and I spent so much of our time. It will give you a chance to get to know me better."

Twenty-nine

Devan sat on the deck behind Jerry's house and enjoyed his morning coffee. Why had he allowed Jerry to talk him into coming to Minter for the Fourth? The day of the reunion would have given him plenty of time to see the people he wanted to see. It would be hard enough to avoid Julie for one evening, but an entire week could prove to be impossible. He studied his coffee for several minutes, as though by doing so he would magically receive the answers to life's questions.

The doorbell rang, but he paid little attention. Whoever the visitor turned out to be didn't concern him.

"Hey, Dev," Jerry said, coming out onto the deck, "look who's here."

Devan looked up and saw Jerry followed by Bonnie Stewart, a girl Devan and Jerry both dated in high school.

"Why, Devan Yates," Bonnie said, holding out her hands to him. "I didn't think you'd be here until Saturday."

Devan took her hands and pecked her on the cheek. "Somebody talked me into coming early and taking a much needed vacation," he said, glancing at Jerry.

"I came over to talk Jerry into riding on the class float."

"The class what?" Devan questioned.

"Oh, it's something new they're doing," Jerry replied. "If a class is having a reunion close to the Fourth, they put a float in the parade. You know, to let everyone see how old we're getting."

329

"Well," Bonnie began, "since I'm on the reunion committee with Jerry, I talked Les Evers into loaning us one of his trucks. He runs his own trucking company now, you know, and is bringing over one of his flat beds. We aren't doing anything extravagant, just having a good time. We're getting a tub of soda, of course, I'd rather have beer, but the parade rules say no alcohol."

"Will Julie be on the float?" Devan inquired.

"The Great One?" Bonnie sneered. "She's too good to ride with the rest of us. She has her own car, her and that Rob Hunter character. I never thought she'd take up with a black man."

"I don't think she's actually taken up with him," Jerry said.

"All I know is what I hear, and I hear plenty. Like he's spending the week with her and her family and she's bringing him to the reunion. I just can't imagine anyone from our class bringing a black man to the reunion."

For a moment, Devan stood, unable to comprehend the meaning behind Bonnie's statement. Could Julie and Hunter be lovers? They'd been traveling together for the past three months. The way he kissed her at the show in Philadelphia certainly hadn't been staged. Passion like his would have been impossible to fake. Could her feelings for Hunter be the reason Julie hadn't called him, even though she now had his home number?

"It's the twenty-first century, Bonnie." Jerry's voice shattered Devan's thoughts of self-doubt. "Just because people work together doesn't mean they're lovers. Besides, I know Hunter. He's Julie's friend, nothing more. You can believe me."

"Do I have any choice?" Bonnie asked. "Oh, well, who cares, anyway? Do you have a date for the reunion, Devan?"

Devan glanced up at Bonnie, noting the expression of mischief in her eyes. "No, I thought I'd go alone."

"Well, neither do I. My husband and I sort of parted company a few months back."

"Which husband are you talking about, Bonnie?" Jerry asked, winking slyly at Devan.

"Oh, Bob Radcliff. Do you remember him? No, I guess you wouldn't. I went to the last reunion with Don."

"How many husbands have you had?" Devan inquired.

"Oh, four—no five. It doesn't make much difference. Four or five, I still don't have a date for Saturday night. So will you take me?" Without waiting for Devan to answer, she continued. "Of course, you will. We'll decide what time you'll pick me up after the parade. I'd love to stay and talk but I've got a kajillion things to do today. You don't have to show me out, Jerry. I know the way. See you guys at the grade school at eleven-thirty."

Bonnie disappeared into the house and Devan turned to Jerry. "What just happened here?"

"I think you're taking Bonnie to the reunion."

"I don't seem to remember asking her out."

Jerry laughed. "You didn't, but I think you're stuck. Could be the best thing to happen, you know with Julie taking Hunter to the reunion. It might just ignite a spark of jealousy in her."

"I guess so. Do you think Bonnie's right about Julie and Hunter?"

"Do you?"

"No. At least I don't want to, but it's hard to get a handle on things anymore. He seemed like a nice guy when I met him in Philadelphia, but you never know."

"Well, the answer is no. I told you before, the only relationships Julie cultivates these days are friendships."

Devan nodded. "So you did. I want to believe it, but not hearing from her doesn't make it easy."

"I guess it doesn't, but you'd better face the fact they'll be there together. Julie's gone on with her life, but you've put yours on hold. This week may be your last chance to reestablish your relationship with her."

They continued talking until Karen came out to remind them of the time. "If you two are going to be down at the grade school by eleven-thirty, you'd better get going."

Devan looked at his watch. Ten forty-five, in less than an hour he would see Julie. With so little time left, he would have to decide what to say to her and how to say it.

~ * ~

The parking lot of the grade school had filled to overflowing with floats and cars, while marching bands, baton twirlers, and scout troops spilled over onto the playground. In the street, in front of the school, well-groomed horses pranced, anxious to begin the mile and a half parade route.

At last, Devan and Jerry located their float. Seeing several old friends, Devan greeted them with handshakes for the balding men with paunchy stomachs and hugs for the women who were overweight but still sounded like the girls he remembered from high school.

"I didn't know you were in town," Les greeted him.

"I've been planning on coming to the reunion, and Jerry persuaded me to take a vacation and come out early."

"We saw you on the tape," Les continued. "You know, the one of Julie's show in Philadelphia."

"Jerry told me about it. It sounds like you had quite a crowd."

"We gave Julie a nice homecoming. Speaking of Julie, have you seen her since you got in?"

Devan shook his head. "I didn't get here until late last night. There hasn't been time. Bonnie said she'd be here today. I'm sure I'll run into her sometime soon."

"Yeah," Les said, "one of the dealerships provided her with a convertible. Black with a white interior. *Black And White*, what do you think of all that crap?"

"I think it's great. Julie deserves it."

"Do you actually believe in what you say, or are you only saying it because you were one of The Musketeers? I mean he's black, for God's sake. Do you think she's making it with him?"

"No, Les, I don't. He's just a nice guy who happens to be a very important part of Julie's new life. I met him in Philadelphia. From what I hear, he's been a very good friend to her."

Bonnie joined the group. "He looked like a *real* good friend when he kissed her at the end of the show. If you ask me, he can't hold a candle to you. You and Jerry certainly made Julie and her group look shabby."

"What do you have against Julie?" Les asked, turning on Bonnie, before Devan could speak. "I don't approve of her bringing a black guy to the reunion, but I'm happy she's doing something she enjoys."

"I don't have anything against her, but we all know she's always had it all."

"Oh, come on, Bonnie," Les continued. "You heard all the rumors about Steve."

Devan ached as he watched Jerry turn away from the group.

"Sorry, Jerry, I forgot about Steve and Karen," Les said, putting his hand on Jerry's shoulder.

"It's all right. I'm not proud of Karen's affair, anymore than I am of being the one who told Julie about it. It's ancient history. Something we'll never be able to change. Thank God, Julie is adult enough to let it remain in the past where it belongs."

"So what are you doing up here anyway?" Devan asked, purposely changing the subject.

Les appeared relieved to put the topic of Julie behind them. "Bob will be coming over with the soda and lawn chairs. I brought my kid's boom box and found some good CDs from our era. There won't be many chairs, but there's plenty of room around the edge. We'll just throw ourselves a private party."

Devan thought about the private parties they'd had as kids, the ones without soda and lawn chairs. At those parties, usually held in the woods behind the Evers farm, someone brought beer and those in attendance planned on getting drunk. At one of those parties, during their junior year, Devan lost his virginity. He'd been dating Bonnie, at the time, but she hadn't been able to attend the party. Who had he awkwardly made love to that evening? For a moment he tried to remember, but the only face he could see, the only body he could feel, belonged to Julie.

"Devan," he jumped at the sound of Julie's voice and turned abruptly to face her.

"Julie, it's good to see you again. You too, Hunter," Devan said, deliberately pulling Hunter into the group.

"I've been looking forward to seeing you," Julie began. "I just didn't think you'd be here today."

"Jerry talked me into coming. You know the good old Fourth of July in Minter. It beats sitting alone in Philadelphia."

"Alone?" Julie questioned.

"Todd and Andy flew out to Seattle to spend the holiday with Missy."

"How is Todd doing?"

Devan hated this polite conversation. Why didn't she just come out with it and say what was on her mind? "Very well. He's gotten to the point where he only needs a cane."

"I noticed the night of the show. I'm sorry I didn't get to meet him. It turned out to be a crazy night."

"I know. I didn't get to tell you, but you were wonderful."

"Thank you. You weren't bad yourself."

"Julie, I—" Devan's words were cut short by Bonnie's shrill voice.

"Why Julie, I just knew I'd get to see you today. This must be your friend, Mr. Hunter. I'm Bonnie, Bonnie Radcliff."

"It's a pleasure, Mrs. Radcliff," Hunter said.

"Oh, it's Ms., my current husband and I parted company, so to speak. I haven't been lucky in love. I just can't seem to find someone as good as Devan was in high school." Devan held his breath as he listened to Bonnie make a fool of herself.

"Oh, Julie, did you know Devan's taking me to the reunion?"

"No, I didn't. It's nice, neither of you will have to go alone. Hunter's coming with me."

"Isn't it lovely, Julie and her friend are coming to the reunion."

Devan nodded, embarrassed by Bonnie's words. Before he could silence her, she continued. "I think it's so exciting about your show. I've never heard of anything so exciting happening to someone from Minter before. I can just hardly wait to see it for myself. Well, I guess I'll be seeing you at the reunion Saturday night. Devan and I have to get on the float."

Bonnie grabbed Devan's hand and pulled him toward the truck. He jerked his hand from hers and turned back toward Julie. "I'd like to talk to you," he said.

"I don't think there is anything to say. Bonnie just said it all. I hope you're as good after the reunion as Bonnie remembers from high school. It would be a shame to disappoint her."

Julie's words hurt, but he couldn't blame her. He wanted to slap Bonnie, but his morals stopped him. He watched Julie turn away and longed to follow her.

"Devan," Jerry said, "are you okay?"

"I don't think so. Damn it, Jerry, I've got to talk to her. I can't let it go on like this."

~ * ~

Julie turned from Devan, just before tears sprang to her eyes.

"She's a cat," Hunter said, putting his arm around her shoulders.

"She's always been a cat. I don't know why I thought she'd be any different now," Julie sniffed.

"Are you going to give in to her?"

"It doesn't look like I have much choice, does it? You don't need to answer such a ridiculous question. You heard her, Devan asked her to go to the reunion with him."

"Did he? I didn't hear her say he asked. I heard her say they were going together. Didn't you hear it in Devan's voice, see it in his eyes?"

"I didn't listen, or notice for that matter. I need you now, more than ever. You might find yourself picking up the pieces sooner than you thought."

"Go back and tell him, Julie. Tell him how you feel. Don't let it end like this."

"Drop it, Hunter," she said, angrily shrugging away his arm from her shoulders. In front of her she saw the black and white convertible. "There's the car we're supposed to ride in. We'd better get ready, the parade is about to start."

Hunter took her hand in his. "Maybe you aren't up to this."

"Of course, I am. All I need to do is put on my Jewel West face. It's like being on stage. I'll take a deep breath, then smile and wave."

She turned away, unwilling to allow Hunter to see the pain she knew her eyes reflected. The car had a white poster board sign with black lettering affixed to the side. Julie squatted beside it and traced the lettering with her finger.

JEWEL WEST

MINTER'S OWN JULIE WESTON

AND

ROB HUNTER

STARS OF

BLACK AND WHITE

"What's all this candy for?" She heard Hunter ask.

She looked up and saw he had opened the door on the other side of the car. Standing up, she looked into the back seat.

"It's to throw to the kids," she said, as she opened the door on her side of the car.

"Isn't that dangerous?"

Julie slipped off her heels and dropped them on the floor of the back seat before she answered his question. "I never thought about it. Everyone throws candy to the kids during the Fourth of July parade, they all wait for it."

"You do have some strange traditions in small towns. Did you actually let your kids run out into the street after candy?"

"Of course, I did. There's nothing wrong with it. I chased candy when I was a kid, just like everybody else. Look, when you see a bunch of kids, you throw a handful of candy in their direction. Lighten up, Hunter, it will be fun."

"I'm sure it will," Hunter said, a hint of laughter in his voice.

Julie climbed up and seated herself on the back deck of the car. Just ahead of them sat the class float. She watched as Bonnie fawned over Devan. If she hadn't become Jewel West, she'd be the one on the float, the one at Devan's side, or would she?

"Oh, Hunter, I hope I'm doing the right thing," she sighed.

"What? Being a fool where Devan is concerned? I know you're not doing the right thing there."

"I didn't mean that. I was talking about the show."

"Of course, you're doing the right thing. Vaureen wouldn't have offered you the part if you weren't right for it. Now come on, tell me what's really bothering you."

"I don't know. Maybe it's just me. Being Julie Weston these past two weeks has made me wonder if Jewel West ever existed."

"Believe me, Julie, she does. Give it another couple of months and you'll be asking the same question about Julie Weston."

She nodded. Hunter knew her well, maybe too well. No matter what kind of face she put on for everyone else, Hunter knew her innermost thoughts. He had become as close a confidant to Jewel West as Jerry had always been to Julie Morgan Weston.

The parade ended and Julie thanked their driver before she joined Hunter. "You looked very happy during the parade," he said.

"I am happy, Hunter. Jewel West makes me happy and tomorrow will make me even happier."

"Do you mean the trip to the Dells?"

"I mean the trip to the Dells."

"Did you plan it to get out of Minter for the week?"

"I can't fool you, can I? At first I only wanted to show you the place where I spent so much time, but yes, it is a good excuse to get away from here and Devan."

"I thought you were a levelheaded person, but I'm beginning to wonder. On the subject of Devan Yates, you become bullheaded."

"Then we'll just have to avoid that subject," she said, before she started to leave the park.

"Aren't you going to put on your shoes?" Hunter asked, when he caught up with her.

"And ruin my feet? No way. I love going barefoot."

"Are you certain you want to walk all the way back to the house? Look at that hill."

"Oh, Hunter, you sound like a spoiled superstar. Walking is excellent exercise. As for the hill, it's nothing compared with the bluffs around the Dells."

They arrived at George and Shirley's just before three. Julie began bustling around Shirley's buffet table, while Hunter joined the men.

"I hope Julie told you to bring your suit and enjoy the pool," George greeted him.

"We stopped at her place and changed before we came over."

"What do you mean 'we'?" George asked. "Julie doesn't ever swim."

"She'll be swimming today," Hunter replied.

Julie smiled at the conversation she'd just overheard and joined the men at the pool area.

"I thought you listened to the show the other night, George. Didn't you hear what Devan said about how I swam anchor on the girls relay team?"

"I guess I did, but never seeing you do it before, I dismissed it."

"I never dismiss anything about Julie," Hunter said. "When we were on the road, we swam every day and I must say, I'm hard put to keep up with her."

Thirty

The festivities of the afternoon wound down and Jerry worked in the kitchen putting away the remainder of the ham from lunch. In the backyard all seemed quiet. Karen dozed in a lawn chair, catching the last rays of the sun, the kids went to the lake with their friends, and Devan retired to the basement guestroom.

Feeling uneasy, rather than tired, Jerry found pen and paper, and jotted a quick note.

Went for a walk—won't be gone long.

J.

As he formed his one letter signature, he thought of what things had been like less than two years earlier, when Karen and Steve were an item. Back then there were no notes, no acts of consideration for each other. Thanks to Julie, things were different now. He desperately wanted to make her life as complete as she had made his.

He walked without purpose, lost in his own thoughts, his own plans, until he saw Hunter approaching from the opposite direction.

"Are they all crashed out at Julie's place?" Jerry asked.

Hunter nodded. "Julie's exhausted."

"I've never heard you call her that before."

"On the road, in Greg's office, on stage, she's Jewel. This is the one place on earth where she's Julie."

"How true. The meeting she had with Devan this morning certainly turned out to be a fiasco."

"It did look like your friend, Bonnie, had her claws sunk pretty deep. It certainly didn't look like Devan's as happy about Saturday night as she is."

"She's always been able to put out her claws when she's the one to benefit. I think she loves Devan, in her own twisted way, only this time it's something to use to hurt Julie."

"I take it they don't get along."

"You don't have to be a genius to see it. Bonnie has been jealous of Julie for years. It started in high school, when Bonnie dated Devan. More than anything else she wanted to be one of The Musketeers. She never understood the bond the four of us shared, living in the same neighborhood."

"You know how it is," Hunter said. "Kids do foolish things, subject themselves to petty jealousies. Maybe The Musketeers ought to do something foolish about this situation. It might get our bullheaded friends back together."

Jerry looked at Hunter, surprised. "I never thought I'd hear you say something like that. Somehow I got the impression Julie's—ah, well, you know."

"The word you're looking for is special, and yes, Julie is very special to me, to a lot of people. If I weren't black, I wouldn't be pushing this."

"What difference does race make? It's not the seventies, nobody cares anymore."

Jerry noticed the seriousness of Hunter's expression and the determination in his voice. "The difference is what it would do to her professional life. It's one thing for her to be my lover on the sitcom and quite another for her to be my lover in real life."

"You amaze me, Hunter. I don't know if I'd restrain myself if I were in your position."

"I think you would, especially if you knew how deeply she cares for Devan. I know she loves him, so does she, but she's scared. She's worried about how he'll react to her."

"Funny, Devan tells me the same story. You're right. They are bullheaded fools. Maybe it's time The Musketeers did something to shake them up."

"So, do you have any ideas?"

"A head full of them. I've been trying to formulate a plan ever since I left the house. It isn't easy. Julie and Sandy always did the planning, but I think I've come up with an idea. How would you like to become the fourth member of The Musketeers?"

Hunter laughed. "If I don't have to chop down trees or run some poor lady's panties up a flag pole, it might be fun."

~ * ~

Devan came up from the basement and saw Jerry's note. He wondered if Jerry's walk took him to Julie's house. More than anything, he wanted to dial Julie's number, but the hurt he'd seen on her face stopped him. He wished he hadn't planned to go to Milwaukee to spend the rest of the week with his older brother. If he were staying in town, he might be able to talk to her alone, but his plans were already made.

He heard voices from the deck and went out to join Jerry and Karen. "Would you like a lemonade?" Karen asked, getting up from the deck chair.

"Sit still. I'll pour it myself," Devan said, before pulling another chair over to the table.

"You look rested," Jerry commented.

"Surprisingly, I've slept better here than I have in months. I'd forgotten how good it feels to rest peacefully. Even with Todd's improvement, I worry about him all the time. He's right there in the apartment. He's my responsibility. With him in Seattle for the holiday, I'm relieved."

"I'm going to make us some sandwiches," Karen said. "If you two are going to be at the park at seven you'd better have something to eat now."

"What's going on at seven?" Devan asked, once Karen went into the house.

"We're going to see Julie and The Musketeers will do something people are going to talk about for years."

"How does Julie feel about this?" Devan asked.

"She doesn't know. Hunter will be joining us and we're going to climb the water tower."

"The water tower!" Devan echoed. "We did some crazy things thirty years ago, but we never considered anything like that."

"Didn't we? How many times did Julie and Sandy suggest it? Look, the only thing they ever suggested that we didn't do was climbing the tower."

Devan nodded. They hadn't agreed to do it, but that didn't stop the girls from suggesting it every time they planned another prank. "As I remember we always nixed the idea because it was dangerous. What makes it any less dangerous now?"

"I walked over there today. They've raised the ladder and enclosed it in a metal frame. I know we can do it, you can do it."

"Whoa! How did we change to me all of a sudden?"

"You want to talk to Julie alone, don't you?"

"Of course, I do, but—"

"But what? Julie made us famous with her monologue. She won't back out, I promise. Once the two of you are up there, you'll be alone with her. No one will be around to interrupt you."

~ * ~

The park bustled with activity. Devan marveled at the amount of people who were packed into such a small area. From the beer tent on the top of the hill, to a fifties band which competed for attention with the din of the carnival.

He put his hand into his pocket to assure himself that the two items he had put there earlier were still with him. When he had seen the small packet of restaurant jelly on Jerry's counter, he had thought of the symbolism. Luckily, Karen had a package of Kool-Aid in the cupboard. He certainly couldn't bring Julie champagne and strawberries, but strawberry jelly and grape Kool-Aid would be the next best things.

"How do you expect to find Julie in this crowd?" he asked Jerry.

"Easy. Hunter said he'd meet us at the Tilt-A-Whirl."

Devan scanned the sea of faces, looking for Julie, as the ride in front of him spun furiously. The spinning stopped and he saw Hunter emerge from one of the metal and mesh cars. He held out his hand to his companion, and Julie joined him a bit unsteadily.

Devan saw her smile, then begin to laugh. Although he couldn't actually hear her, he remembered her laugh and how infectious he always found it.

She passed within feet of where they stood, but didn't look in his direction. "Julie," he said, hoping to catch her attention.

She turned abruptly, her smile fading when she saw him. "Does Bonnie know you're here?" she greeted him.

"You know she staged the scene this morning for your benefit. She hasn't changed much from high school. She's still jealous of you. This time she's found a way to get to you."

"Maybe she did, but you are taking her to the reunion, aren't you?"

"No. I'll see her at the Minitree, the same as I'll see everyone else."

Julie nodded, but said nothing.

"I told you this morning I wanted to talk to you, but not here." He took her hand in his and started to leave the park.

~ * ~

Julie looked down as Devan encircled her hand with his. Her emotions churned and she could feel warmth starting to spread through her body from his touch. He guided her away from the carnival, out of the park. She looked over her shoulder and saw Jerry and Hunter following them. They each wore a silly smile and she wondered what it meant. It didn't take much thought to realize she'd become the victim of their conspiracy.

"Where are we going?" she asked, as they walked down the dusty gravel road leading out of the park.

"You'll see," Devan assured her.

"No, tell me now, or I won't take another step," she demanded, refusing to move.

"Then we'll have to carry you," Jerry said, as he and Hunter caught up with them.

"I guess I don't have any choice but to go along with the three of you. Since I can only surmise you've all gone crazy, it's better not to provoke any weird behavior."

"We're not crazy, Julie," Hunter said. "Your friends have graciously allowed me to become one of The Musketeers."

"One of The Musketeers? What are you guys planning? We haven't done anything in thirty years. Aren't we a little too old to—"

"To be ourselves?" Jerry finished her statement with a question. "Until a few weeks ago, no one knew about the things we did when we were kids. Now everyone knows, and truthfully, they're all expecting us to do something again."

Julie tried to sound annoyed, but inside the thought of pulling one more prank excited her. "Something like what?"

"You'll see," Devan said again, as though he could think of nothing more original to say. He started walking and since he held her hand tightly, she had no recourse but to follow him.

She quit trying to get answers from her companions. Who could have masterminded this? As teenagers, it had always been herself and Sandy who thought up the mischief, Jerry and Devan who went along with whatever they devised.

She became so lost in her own thoughts that stopping at Water Tower Park surprised her.

"We're here," Jerry announced, interrupting her rambling thoughts.

Julie didn't even try to mask her shock. "Here?" she echoed. "The water tower? Now I know you've all lost your minds."

"Don't tell me the great Julie Morgan is chicken?" Devan teased.

"Chicken? Not me. You and Jerry are the ones who wouldn't ever climb the tower." Julie pulled her hand free of Devan's grip, walked over to the tower, and placed her hand on one of the legs. Instantly, she found herself transported back thirty years. She and Sandy had begged the guys to climb the tower repeatedly during their senior year. Finally it came down to the two of them. On the Wednesday night before graduation, they'd come to this park and climbed to the top of the tower. Back then, the ladder touched the ground and the sheer height of the tower excited her.

Now she looked up at the ladder that had been raised ten feet off the ground. *::You can do this,::* Sandy's voice whispered in her ear.

::We conquered it thirty years ago. Show these guys what we're made of. If I were there, I'd go with you.::

"This one's for you, San," Julie whispered.

"Did you say something?" Jerry asked.

Julie shook her head and wiped her eyes with her sleeve.

"Are you crying?"

"Just thinking about Sandy. I wish she were here tonight. Damn, I miss her."

"I think she is here," Jerry said. "Whenever I think about the old days, she's here. The only difference is she never ages."

Julie laughed. "I guess she doesn't. Something tells me we didn't come here to talk about Sandy. Are we going to climb this sucker or what?"

"We're going to climb it," Devan said.

Julie again looked up at the ladder. "It's a great idea, guys, but how do you intend to get the ladder within reach?"

"Just watch," Jerry said. "Give me a hand guys."

Devan and Hunter cupped their hands and boosted Jerry up until he caught hold of the bottom rung. Julie held her breath as Jerry hung suspended until he managed to pull the ladder to within two feet of the ground. Metal clinked against metal and she breathed a sigh of relief.

"How did you do that?" she asked.

"Magic," Jerry said, winking broadly.

To Julie's surprise, someone grabbed her around the waist and lifted her until her feet touched the first rung of the ladder. She looked back into Hunter's face. "Hey guys, what if we get caught?"

"It will be worth it," Hunter said.

"Have we ever got caught before?" Jerry asked.

"No, but there's always a first time for everything."

"Not tonight," Devan assured her. "Everyone in town is at the park. We're home free."

"When you get to the top, stick this to the railing," Hunter said, as he slipped something heavy into the pocket of her sweatshirt.

She started climbing, one rung at a time, looking upward as she had thirty years earlier. Ten feet up she entered the enclosure, which had been installed for safety purposes. Below her, a tug on the ladder alerted her to the fact someone else had begun the ascent. She didn't look down, but continued to climb.

Ahead of her a square hole signaled the end of the quest. The ladder continued up and over the top of the reservoir, but Julie sidestepped onto the catwalk rather than continue to climb.

Dusk had begun to fall and she stood for a moment, awed by the view from this height. For the first time, she reached into her pocket and produced a blinking light, the kind used on road barricades. She smiled and affixed the self-contained unit to the railing.

"I know why we never did this when we were kids," Devan said, when he joined her on the catwalk. "This is one hell of a climb, but it's worth it, if for no other reason than to get you alone."

"Alone? What about Jerry and Hunter?"

Devan pointed toward the ground. "We planned this, Julie. I want you to hear what I have to say."

"Why here? Why something like this? Why not just stop over at the house?"

Without answering, Devan took her in his arms. "Why here? Because you tear up my letters, you haven't called, even though I gave you my number, we can't ever seem to be alone, and I've hurt you. Pretty rotten excuses for something like this, but they're the only ones I have. I love you, Julie, but I'm not going to make the same mistake I made six months ago. I refuse to jump into things the way we did then. You aren't Julie Morgan any longer and I'm not eighteen. We're different people and we need to become reacquainted."

Tears washed Julie's cheeks. "I'm sorry about the letter. I did read it. Hunter brought it with him and made me read it last night. It seems that Greg taped it back together. They know me too well. Hunter said they both knew I love you. I agree, we do need to get to know each other better."

"Good, then this is a promise of things to come."

She watched as he reached in his pocket and retrieved a packet of grape Kool-Aid and a container of strawberry jelly.

"Until I have the chance to get you the real thing, this will have to do. Considering strawberries are out of season, and a bottle of champagne would be too hard to carry, this was the best I could come up with."

Tears of happiness washed her cheeks as she laughed at the symbols Devan held in his hand of their two weekends together.

Before she could think of anything to say, he drew her close and kissed her, as the first skyrockets soared into the darkening sky.

Minutes later, Julie and Devan sat beneath the water tower with Jerry and Hunter. The ladder had been returned to its original position and between bursts of light from the skyrockets the little yellow light blinked brightly.

"Are you sorry you came with us?" Devan asked.

"Sorry? Are you kidding? How would we have ever cleared the air at the reunion with everyone around? Getting to know each other long distance is going to be a challenge, though."

"I don't think it will be too hard," Devan replied. "Just before I left Philadelphia, my boss called and offered me a big promotion. It does mean relocating, so I asked to consider it over the holiday. I've decided to take it. Starting August first, I'll be the Vice President in charge of Personnel in our Los Angeles office."

Julie squealed with delight, and allowed Devan to again take her into his arms and kiss her tenderly.

"Mushy stuff," she heard Jerry say to Hunter. She didn't care, not even when they began to laugh.

The last of the skyrockets shot into the air in a burst of brilliant lights and loud bangs. In the afterglow, Julie nestled into Devan's arms until a bright blinding light, from the street twenty yards away, broke them apart.

"What's going on?" Jerry asked.

"Oh, it's you, Mr. Gaines," the young officer said. "Someone reported some vandalism to the water tower."

"You must mean the light up there," Julie replied innocently. "We've been trying to figure out how it got up there, too."

"Mrs. Weston, what are you doing out here? I'd have thought you'd be at the park."

"You must realize, Officer," Hunter began, "it isn't easy being a celebrity, even in your hometown. Julie's friends and I decided it would be better to watch the fireworks from afar rather than take a chance of something unfortunate happening."

When the squad car pulled away from the curb, Julie convulsed in laughter. "We did it! We actually pulled it off and no one will ever guess it was us."

"Won't they?" Hunter asked. "I expect to hear about this in your monologue."

"You know I'm through with the road," Julie replied, surprised by his statement.

"Are you? I doubt it. You're like me. It's in your blood. Once the filming of *Black And White* is done for the year, I expect you'll be knocking on Greg's door, the way I do every year. Even if you don't go on the road, you'll find yourself doing some of the clubs in Los Angeles."

Devan squeezed her hand. "Don't think I'd try to stop you, either. I kind of enjoy being the main topic of Jewel West's monologues. As a matter of fact, I may have to do a little traveling in my new position. Maybe we can combine business with pleasure and do it together."

"The Musketeers, together again, forever!" Jerry shouted, before they all began to laugh at themselves.

Julie thought about all the crazy things they'd done together, all the crazy things they would do in the future. Suddenly, none of it mattered. Tonight she had found her destiny.

Meet Sherry Derr-Wille

When her sophomore English teacher assigned a handful of students to write for an entire year, Sherry Derr-Wille fell in love. Since then, writing has been more than a hobby. With over twenty books to her credit, she has seventeen contracts for release dates in 2003-2005.

Married for almost forty years to her high school sweetheart, she describes her husband, Bob, as a saint saying, "I doubt of a mortal man would put up the eccentricities of a writer."

Along with her writing, she claims three children and eight grandchildren ranging from infants to adults.

Now that her children are grown, she and Bob enjoy their empty nest and the success of her writing career.

"If nothing else," Sherry often says, "I'm an overnight success after forty years."